The Dark Forest by Hugh Walpole

Sir Hugh Seymour Walpole, CBE was born in Auckland, New Zealand, on March 13th, 1884.

His parents had moved to New Zealand in 1877, but his mother, Mildred, unable to settle there, eventually persuaded her husband, Somerset, an Anglican clergyman, to accept another post, this time in New York in 1889. Walpole's early years involved being educated by a Governess until, in 1893, his parents decided he needed an English education and the young Walpole was sent to England.

He first attended a preparatory school in Truro. He naturally missed his family but was reasonably happy. A move to Sir William Borlase's Grammar School in Marlow in 1895, found him bullied, frightened and miserable.

The following year, 1897, the Walpole's returned to England and Walpole was moved to be a day boy at Durham School. His sense of isolation increased. His refuge was the local library and reading.

From 1903 to 1906 Walpole studied history at Emmanuel College, Cambridge and there, in 1905, had his first work published, the critical essay "Two Meredithian Heroes".

Walpole was also attempting to cope with and come to terms with his homosexual feelings and to find "that perfect friend".

After a short spell tutoring in Germany and then teaching French at Epsom in 1908 he found the desire to fully immerse himself in the literary world. He moved to London to become a book reviewer for The Standard and to write fiction in his spare time. In 1909, he published his first novel, The Wooden Horse. The book received good reviews but sold little.

Better was to come in 1911 when he published Mr Perrin and Mr Traill. In early 1914 Henry James wrote an article for The Times Literary Supplement surveying the younger generation of British novelists. Walpole was greatly encouraged that one of the greatest living authors had publicly ranked him among the finest young British novelists.

As war approached, Walpole realised that his poor eyesight would disqualify him from service and accepted an appointment, based in Moscow, reporting for The Saturday Review and The Daily Mail. Although allowed to visit the front in Poland, these dispatches were not enough to stop hostile comments at home that he was not 'doing his bit' for the war effort.

Walpole was ready with a counter; an appointment as a Russian officer, in the Sanitar. He explained they were "part of the Red Cross that does the rough work at the front, carrying men out of the trenches, helping at the base hospitals in every sort of way, doing every kind of rough job".

During a skirmish in June 1915 Walpole rescued a wounded soldier; his Russian comrades refused to help and this meant Walpole had to carry one end of a stretcher, dragging the man to safety. He was awarded the Cross of Saint George. By late 1917 it was clear to Walpole, and the authorities, that his work was at an end. In London Walpole joined the Foreign Office and remained there until resigning in February 1919. For his wartime work he was awarded the CBE in 1918.

Walpole continued to write and publish and now also began a career on the highly lucrative lecture tour in the United States.

In 1924 Walpole moved to a house, Brackenburn, near Keswick in the Lake District. Although he maintained a flat in Piccadilly, Brackenburn was to be his main home for the rest of his life.

At the end of 1924 Walpole met Harold Cheevers, who soon became his friend and constant companion and remained so for the rest of his life; "that perfect friend".

Hollywood, in the shape of MGM, invited him in 1934 to write the script for a film of David Copperfield. He also had a small acting role in the film.

In 1937 Walpole was offered a knighthood. He accepted although Kipling, Hardy, Galsworthy had all refused. "I'm not of their class... Besides I shall like being a knight," he said.

Unfortunately his health was undermined by diabetes made worse by the frenetic pace of his life. Sir Hugh Seymour Walpole, CBE died of a heart attack at Brackenburn, aged 57 on June 1st, 1941. He was buried in St John's churchyard in Keswick.

Index of Contents

PART ONE

CHAPTER I

SPRING IN THE TRAIN

His was the first figure to catch my eye that evening in Petrograd; he stood under the dusky lamp in the vast gloomy Warsaw station, with exactly the expression that I was afterwards to know so well, impressed not only upon his face but also upon the awkwardness of his arms that hung stiffly at his side, upon the baggy looseness of his trousers at the knees, the unfastened straps of his long black military boots. His face, with its mild blue eyes, straggly fair moustache, expressed anxiety and pride, timidity and happiness, apprehension and confidence. He was in that first moment of my sight of him as helpless, as unpractical, and as anxious to please as any lost dog in the world—and he was also as proud as Lucifer. I knew him at once for an Englishman; his Russian uniform only accented the cathedral-town, small public-school atmosphere of his appearance. He was exactly what I had expected. He was not, however, alone, and that surprised me. By his side stood a girl, obviously Russian, wearing her Sister's uniform with excitement and eager anticipation, her eyes turning restlessly from one part of the platform to another, listening with an impatient smile to the remarks of her companion.

From where I stood I could hear his clumsy, hesitating Russian and her swift, preoccupied replies. I came up to them.

"Mr. Trenchard?" I asked.

He blushed, stammered, held out his hand, missed mine, blushed the more, laughed nervously.

"I'm glad ... I knew ... I hope...."

I could feel that the girl's eyes were upon me with all the excited interest of one who is expecting that every moment of her new wonderful experience will be of a stupendous, even immortal quality.

"I am Sister Marie Ivanovna, and you are, of course, Mr. Durward," she said. "They are all waiting for you—expecting you—you're late, you know!" She laughed and moved forward as though she would accompany me to the group by the train. We went to the train together.

"I should tell you," she said quickly and suddenly with nervousness, "that we are engaged, Mr. Trenchard and I—only last night. We have been working at the same hospital.... I don't know any one," she continued in the same intimate, confiding whisper. "I would be frightened terribly if I were not so excited. Ah! there's Anna Mihailovna.... I know her, of course. It was through, her aunt—the one who's on Princess Soboleff's train—that I had the chance of going with you. Oh! I'm so happy that I had the chance—if I hadn't had it...."

We were soon engulfed now. I drew a deep breath and surrendered myself. The tall, energetic figure of Anna Mihailovna, the lady to whose practical business gifts and unlimited capacity for compelling her friends to surrender their last bow and button in her service we owed the existence of our Red Cross unit, was to be seen like a splendid flag waving its followers on to glory and devotion. We were devoted, all of us. Even I, whose second departure to the war this was, had after the feeblest resistance surrendered myself to the drama of the occasion. I should have been no gentleman had I done otherwise.

After the waters had closed above my head for, perhaps, five minutes of strangled, half-protesting, half-willing surrender I was suddenly compelled, by what agency I know not, to struggle to the surface, to look around me, and then quite instantly to forget my immersion. The figure of Trenchard, standing exactly as I had left him, his hands uneasily at his sides, a half-anxious, half-confident smile on his lips, his eyes staring straight in front of him, absolutely compelled my attention. I had forgotten him, we had all forgotten him, his own lady had forgotten him. I withdrew from the struggling, noisy group and stepped back to his side. It was then that, as I now most clearly remember, I was conscious of something else, was aware that there was a strange faint blue light in the dark clumsy station, a faint throbbing glow, that, like the reflection of blue water on a sunlit ceiling, hovered and hung above the ugly shabbiness of the engines and trucks, the rails with scattered pieces of paper here and there, the iron arms that supported the vast glass roof, the hideous funnel that hung with its gaping mouth above the water-tank. The faint blue light was the spring evening—the spring evening that, encouraged by God knows what brave illusion, had penetrated even these desperate fastnesses. A little breeze accompanied it and the dirty pieces of paper blew to and fro; then suddenly a shaft of light quivered upon the blackness, quivered and spread like a golden fan, then flooded the huge cave with trembling ripples of light. There was even, I dare swear, at this safe distance, a smell of flowers in the air.

"It's a most lovely ..." Trenchard said, smiling at me, "spring here ... I find...."

I was compelled by some unexpected sense of fatherly duty to be practical.

"You've got your things?" I said. "You've found your seat?"

"Well, I didn't know ..." he stammered.

"Where are they?" I asked him.

He was not quite sure where they were. He stood, waving his hands, whilst the golden sunlight rippled over his face. I was suddenly irritated.

"But please," I said, "there isn't much time. Four of us men have a compartment together. Just show me where your things are and then I'll introduce you." He seemed reluctant to move, as though the spot that he had chosen was the only safe one in the whole station; but I forced him forward, found his bags, had them placed in their carriage, then turned to introduce him to his companions.

Anna Mihailovna had said to me: "This detachment will be older than the last. Doctor Nikitin—he'll take that other doctor's place, the one who had typhus—and Andrey Vassilievitch—you've known him for years. He talks a great deal but he's sympathetic and such a good business man. He'll be useful. Then there's an Englishman; I don't know much about him, except that he's been working for three months at the English Hospital. He's not a correspondent, never written a line in his life. I only saw him for a moment, but he seemed sympathetic...."

Anna Mihailovna, as is well known to all of us, finds every one sympathetic simply because she has so much to do and so many people to see that she has no time to go deeply into things. If you have no time for judging character you must have some good common rule to go by. I had known little Andrey Vassilievitch for some years and had found him tiresome. Finally, I did not care about the possibility of an Englishman. Perhaps I had wished (through pride) to remain the only Englishman in our "Otriad." I had made friends with them all, I was at home with them. Another Englishman might transplant me in their affections. Russians transfer, with the greatest ease, their emotions from one place to another; or he might be a failure and so damage my country's reputation. Some such vain and stupid prejudice I had. I know that I looked upon our new additions with disfavour.

There, at any rate, Dr. Nikitin and little Andrey Vassilievitch were, and a strange contrast they made. Nikitin's size would have compelled attention anywhere, even in Russia, which is, of course, a country of big men. It was not only that he was tall and broad; the carriage of his head, the deep blackness of his beard, his eyebrows, his eyes, the sure independence with which he held himself, as though he were indifferent to the whole world (and that I know that he was), must anywhere have made him remarked and remembered. He looked now immensely fine in his uniform, which admirably suited him. He stood, without his greatcoat, his hand on his sword, his eyes half-closed as though he were almost asleep, and a faint half-smile on his face as though he were amused at his thoughts. I remember that my first impression of him was that he was so completely beneath the domination of some idea or remembrance that, at that moment, no human being could touch him. When I took Trenchard up to him I was so conscious of his remoteness that I was embarrassed and apologetic.

And if I was aware of Nikitin's remoteness I was equally conscious of Andrey Vassilievitch's proximity. He was a little man of a round plump figure; he wore a little imperial and sharp, inquisitive moustaches; his hair was light brown and he was immensely proud of it. In Petrograd he was always very smartly dressed. He bought his clothes in London and his plump hands had a movement familiar to all his friends, a flicker of his hands to his coat, his waistcoat, his trousers, to brush off some imaginary speck of dust. It was obvious now that he had given very much thought to his uniform. It fitted him perfectly, his epaulettes glittered, his boots shone, his sword was magnificent, but he looked, in spite of all his efforts, exactly what he was, a rich successful merchant; never was there any one less military. He had dressed up, one might suppose, for some fancy-dress ball.

I could see at once that he was ill at ease, anxious as ever to please every one, to like every one, to be liked in return, but unable, because of some thought that troubled him, to give his whole attention to this business of pleasing.

He greeted me with a warmth that was really genuine although he bestowed it upon his merest acquaintances. His great dream in life was a universal popularity—that every one should love him. At any rate at that time I thought that to be his dream—I know now that there was something else.

"But Ivan Petrovitch!... This is delightful! Here we all are! What pleasure! Thank God, we're all here, no delays, nothing unfortunate. An Englishman?... Indeed, I am very glad! Your friend speaks Russian? Not very much, but enough?... You know Vladimir Stepanovitch? Dr. Nikitin ... my friend Meester Durward. Also Meester?... ah, I beg your pardon, Tronsart. Two Englishmen in our Otriad ... the alliance, yes, delightful!"

Nikitin slowly opened his eyes, shook hands with me and with Trenchard, said that he was glad to see us and was silent again. Trenchard stammered and blushed, said something in very bad Russian, then glanced anxiously, with an eager light in his mild blue eyes, in the direction of the excited crowd that chattered and stirred about the train. There was something, in that look of his, that both touched and irritated me. "What does he come for?" I thought to myself. "With his bad Russian and his English prejudices. Of course he'll be lonely and then he'll be in every one's way."

I could remember, readily enough, some of the loneliness of those first months of my own, when both war and the Russians had differed so from my expectations. This fellow looked just the figure for high romantic pictures. He had, doubtless, seen Russia in the colours of the pleasant superficial books of travel that have of late, in England, been so popular, books that see in the Russian a blessed sort of Idiot unable to read or write but vitally conscious of God, and in Russia a land of snow, ikons, mushrooms and pilgrims. Yes, he would be disappointed, unhappy, and tiresome. Upon myself would fall the chief burden of his trouble—I should have enough upon my shoulders without him.

The golden fan had vanished from the station walls. A dim pale glow, with sparkles as of gold dust shining here and there upon that grimy world, faltered and trembled before the rattle and roar that threatened it. Nevertheless, Spring was with us at our departure. As the bells rang, as the ladies of our Committee screamed and laughed, as Anna Mihailovna showered directions and advice upon us, as we crowded backwards into our compartment before the first jolt of the departing train, Spring was with us … but of course we were all of us too busy to be aware of it.

Nikitin, I remember, reduced us very quickly, for all practical purposes, to a company of three. He lowered one of the upper beds, climbed into it, stretched himself out and lay in silence staring at the carriage-roof. His body was a shadow in the half-light, touched once and again by the gesture of the swinging lamp, that swept him out of darkness and back into it again. The remaining three of us did not during either that evening or the next day make much progress. At times there would of course be tea, and then the two Sisters who were in a compartment close at hand joined us.

Marie Ivanovna, Trenchard's lady, was quieter than she had been before. Her face, which now seemed younger than ever, wore a look of important seriousness as though she were conscious of the indecency of her earlier excitement. She spoke very little, but no one could be in her presence without feeling the force of her vitality like some hammer, silent but of immense power, beating relentlessly upon the atmosphere. Its effect was the stronger in that one realised how utterly at present she was unable to deal with it. Her very helplessness was half of her power—half of her danger too. She was most certainly not beautiful; her nose was too short, her mouth too large, her forehead, from which her black hair was brushed straight back, too high. Her complexion was pale and when she was confused, excited, or pleased, the colour came into her face in a faint flush that ebbed and flowed but never reached its full glow. Her hands were thin and pale. It was her eyes that made her so young; they were so large and round and credulous, scornful sometimes with the scorn of the very young for all the things in the world that they have not experienced—but young especially in all their urgent capacity for life, in their confidence of carrying through all the demands that the High Gods might make upon them. I knew as I looked at her that at present her eagerness for experience was stronger, by far, than her eagerness for any single human being. I wondered whether Trenchard knew that. He was, beyond discussion, most desperately in love; the love of a shy man who has for so many years wondered and dreamed and finds, when the reality comes to him, that it is more, far more, than he had expected. When she came in to us he sat very quietly by her side and talked, if he talked at all, to the other Sister, a stout comfortable woman with no illusions, no expectations, immense capacity and an intensely serious attitude to food and drink.

Trenchard let his eyes rest upon his lady's face whenever she was unaware, but I could see that he was desperately anxious not to offend her. His attitude to all women, even to Anna Petrovna, the motherly Sister, was that of a man who has always blundered in their company, who has been mocked, perhaps, for his mistakes. I could see, however, that his pride in his new possession, his pride and his happiness, carried with it an absolute assurance of his security. He had no doubts at all. He seemed, in this, even younger than she.

Through all that long Spring day we wandered on—wandering it seemed as the train picked its way through the fields under a sky of blue thin and fine like glass; through a world so quiet and still that birds and children sang and called as though to reassure themselves that they were not alone. Nothing of the war in all this. At the stations there were officers eating "Ztchee" soup and veal and drinking glasses of weak tea, there were endless mountains of hot meat pies; the ikons in the restaurants looked down with benignancy and indifference upon the food and the soldiers and beyond the station the light green trees blowing in the little wind; the choruses of the soldiers came from their trains as though it were the very voice of Spring itself. It sounded in the distance like—

Barinisha Barinisha—Pop. Barinisha—Pop.   So—la, la—la ... Bar ... inisha la.

The bell rang, officers with meat pies in their hands came running across the platform. We swung on again through the green golden day.

Andrey Vassilievitch of course chattered to us all. It was his way, and after a very brief experience of it one trained oneself to regard it as an inevitable background, like the jerking and smoke of the train, the dust, the shrill Russian voices in the next compartment, the blowing of paper to and fro in the corridor. I very quickly discovered that he was intensely conscious of Nikitin, who scarcely throughout the day moved from his upper bunk. Andrey Vassilievitch handed him his tea, brought his meat pies and sandwiches from the station, and offered him newspapers. He did not, however, speak to him and I was aware that throughout that long day he was never once unconscious of him. His chatter, which was always the most irrepressible thing in the world, had, perhaps, to-day some direction behind it. For the first time in my long acquaintance with Andrey Vassilievitch he interested me. The little man was distressed by the heat and dirt; his fingers were always flickering about his clothes. He was intensely polite to every one, especially to Trenchard, paying him many compliments about England and the English. The English were the only "sportsmen" in the world. He had been once in London for a week; it had rained very much, but one afternoon it had been fine, and then what clothes he had seen! But the City! He had been down into the City and was lost in admiration; he had also been lost in practical earnest and had appealed to one of the splendid policemen as to the way to Holborn Viaduct, a name that he was quite unable to pronounce. This incident he told us several times. Meanwhile ... he hoped he might ask without offence ... what was our Navy doing? Why weren't our submarines as active as the German submarines? And in France ... how many soldiers had we now? He did hope that he was not offending.... He spoke rapidly and indistinctly and much of his conversation Trenchard did not understand; he made some rather stupid replies and Marie Ivanovna laughed.

She spoke English very well, with an accent that was charming. She had had, she said, an English nurse, and then an English governess.

Of course they asked me many questions about the future. Would we be close to the Front? How many versts? Would there be plenty of work, and would we really see things? We wanted to be useful, no use going if we were not to be useful. How many Sisters were there then already? Were they "sympathetic"? Was Molozov, the head of the Otriad, an agreeable man? Was he kind, or would he be angry about simply nothing? Who would bandage and who would feed the villagers and who would bathe the soldiers? Were the officers of the Ninth Army pleasant to us? Where? Who? When? The day slipped away, the colours were drawn from the sky, the fields, the hills, the stars came out in their myriads, thickly clustered in ropes, and lakes and coils of light; the air was scented with flowers. The second night passed.

The greater part of the next day was spent in H—, a snug town with a little park like a clean handkerchief, streets with coloured shops, neat and fresh-painted like toys from a toy-shop, little blue trains, statues of bewigged eighteenth-century kings and dukes, and a restaurant, painted Watteau-fashion with bright green groves, ladies in hoops and powder, and long-legged sheep. Here we wandered, five of us. Nikitin told us that he would meet us at the station that evening. He had his own business in the place. The little town was delivered over to the Russian army but seemed happy enough in its deliverance. I have never realised in any place more completely the spirit of bright cheerfulness, and the soldiers who thronged the little streets were as far from alarm and thunder as the painted sheep in the restaurant. Marie Ivanovna was as excited as though she had never been in a town before. She bought a number of things in the little expensive shops—eau-de-Cologne, sweets, an electric lamp, a wrist-watch, and some preserved fruit. Trenchard made her presents; she thanked him with a gratitude that made him so happy that he stumbled over his sword more than ever, blushing and pushing his cap back from his head. There are some who might have laughed at him, carrying her parcels, his face flushed, his legs knocking against one another, but it was here, at H—, that, for the first time, I positively began to like him. By the evening when we were assembled in the station again as I looked at him standing, waiting for directions, smiling, hot, untidy and awkward, I knew that I liked him very much indeed....

Our new train overflowed: with the greatest difficulty we secured a small wooden compartment with seats sharp and narrow and a smell of cabbage, bad tobacco, and dirty clothes. The floor was littered with sunflower seeds and the paper wrappings of cheap sweets. The air came in hot stale gusts down the corridor, met the yet closer air of our carriage, battled with it and retired defeated. We flung open the windows and a cloud of dust rose gaily to meet us. The whole of the Russian army seemed to be surging upon the platform; orderlies were searching for their masters, officers shouting for their orderlies, soldiers staggering along under bundles of clothes and rugs and pillows; here a group standing patiently, each man with his blue-painted kettle and on his face that expression of happy, half-amused, half-inquisitive, wholly amiable tolerance which reveals the Russian soldier's favourite attitude to the world. Two priests with wide dirty black hats, long hair, and soiled grey gowns slowly found their way through the crowd. A bunch of Austrian prisoners in their blue-grey uniform made a strange splash of colour in a corner of the platform, where, very contentedly, they were drinking their tea; some one in the invisible distance was playing the balalaïka and every now and then some church bell in the town rang clearly and sharply above the tumult. The thin films of dust, yellow in the evening sun, hovered like golden smoke under the station roof. At last with a reluctant jerk and shiver the train was slowly persuaded to totter into the evening air; the evening scents were again around us, the balalaïka, now upon the train, hummed behind us, as we pushed out upon her last night's journey.

The two Sisters had the seats by the windows; Nikitin curled up his great length in another corner and Andrey Vassilievitch settled himself with much grunting and many exclamations beside him. I and Trenchard sat stiffly on the other side.

I had, long ago, accustomed myself to sleep in any position on any occasion, however sudden it might be, and I fancied that I should now, in a moment, be asleep, although I had never, in my long travelling experience, known greater discomfort. I looked at the dim lamp, at the square patch beyond the windows, at Nikitin's long body, which seemed nevertheless so perfectly comfortable, and at Andrey Vassilievitch's short fat one, which was so obviously miserably uncomfortable; I smelt the cabbage, the dust, the sunflower seeds; first one bone then another ached, in the centre of my back there was an intolerable irritation; above all, there was in my brain some strange insistent compulsion, as though some one were forcing me to remember something that I had forgotten, or as though again some one were fore-warning me of some peril or complication. I had, very distinctly, that impression, so familiar to all of us, of passing through some experience already known: I had seen already the dim lamp, the square patch of evening sky, Nikitin, Andrey Vassilievitch.... I knew that in a moment Trenchard.... He did.... He touched my arm.

"Can you sleep?" he whispered.

"No," I answered.

"It's terribly hot, close—smell.... Are you going to sleep?"

"No," I whispered back again.

"Let us move into the corridor. It will be cooler there."

There seemed to me quite a new sound of determination and resolve in his voice. His nervousness had left him with the daylight. He led the way out of the carriage, turned down the little seats in the corridor, provided cigarettes.

"It isn't much better here, but we'll have the window open. It'll get better. This is really war, isn't it, being so uncomfortable as this? I feel as though things were really beginning."

"Well, we shall be there to-morrow night," I answered him. "I hope you're not going to be disappointed."

"Disappointed in what?" His voice was quite sharp as he spoke to me, "You don't know what I want."

"I suppose you're like the rest of us. You want to see what war really is. You want to do some good if you can. You want to be seriously occupied in it to prevent your thinking too much about it. Then, because you're English, you want to see what the Russians are really like. You're curious and sympathetic, inquisitive and, perhaps, a little sentimental about it.... Am I right?"

"No, not quite—there are other things. I'd like to tell you. Do you mind," he said suddenly looking up straight into my face with a confiding smile that was especially his own, "if I talk, if I tell you why I've come? I've no right, I don't know you—but I'm so happy to-night that I must talk—I'm so happy that I feel as though I shall never get through the night alive."

Of our conversation after this, or rather of his talk, excited, eager, intimate and shy, old and wise and very, very young, I remember now, I think, every word with especial vividness. After events were to fix it all in my brain with peculiar accuracy, but his narration had that night of itself its own individual quality. His was no ordinary personality, or, at any rate, the especial circumstances of the time drove it into no ordinary shape, and I believe that never before in all his days had he spoken freely and eagerly to any one. It was simply to-night his exultation and happiness that impelled him, perhaps also some sense of high adventure that his romantic character would, most inevitably, extract from our expedition and its purposes.

At any rate, I listened, saying a word now and then, whilst the hour grew dark, lit only by the stars, then trembled into a pale dawn overladen with grey dense clouds, which again broke, rolled away, before another shining, glittering morning. I remember that it was broad daylight when we, at last, left the corridor.

"I'm thirty-three," he said. "I don't feel it, of course; I seem to be now only just beginning life. I'm a very unpractical person and in that way, perhaps, I'm younger than my age."

I remember that I said something to him about his, most certainly, appearing younger.

"Most certainly I do. I'm just the same as when I went up to Cambridge and I was then as when I first went to Rugby. Nothing seems to have had any effect upon me—except, perhaps, these last two days. Do you know Glebeshire?" he asked me abruptly.

I said that I had spent one summer there with a reading party.

"Ah," he answered, smiling, "I can tell, by the way you say that, that you don't really know it at all. To us Glebeshire people it's impossible to speak of it so easily. There are Trenchards all over Glebeshire, you know, lots of them. In Polchester, our cathedral town, where I was born, there are at least four Trenchard families. Then in Truxe, at Garth, at Rasselas, at Clinton—but why should I bother you with all this? It's only to tell you that the Trenchards are simply Glebeshire for ever and ever. To a Trenchard, anywhere in the world, Glebeshire is hearth and home."

"I believe I've met," I said, "your Trenchards of Garth. George Trenchard.... She was a Faunder. They have a house in Westminster. There's a charming Miss Trenchard with whom I danced."

"Yes, those are the George Trenchards," he answered with eagerness and delight, as though I had formed a new link with him. "Fancy your knowing them! How small the world is! My father was a cousin, a first cousin, of George Trenchard's. The girl—you must mean Millie—is delightful. Katherine, the elder sister, is married now. She too is charming, but in a different, graver way."

He spoke of them all with a serious lingering pleasure, as though he were summoning them all into the dusty, stuffy corridor, carrying them with him into these strange countries and perilous adventures.

"They always laughed at me—Millie especially; I've stayed sometimes with them at Garth. But I didn't mean really to talk about them—I only wanted to show you how deeply Glebeshire matters to the Trenchards, and whatever happens, wherever a Trenchard goes, he always really takes Glebeshire with him. I was born in Polchester, as I said. My father had a little property there, but we always lived in a little round bow-windowed house in the Cathedral Close. I was simply brought up on the Cathedral. From my bedroom windows I looked on the whole of it. In our drawing-room you could hear the booming of the organ. I was always watching the canons crossing the cathedral green, counting the strokes of the cathedral bell, listening to the cawing of the cathedral rooks, smelling the cathedral smell of cold stone, wet umbrellas and dusty hassocks, looking up at the high tower and wondering whether anywhere in the world there was anything so grand and fine. My moral world, too, was built on the cathedral—on the cathedral 'don'ts' and 'musts,' on the cathedral hours and the cathedral prayers, and the cathedral ambitions and disappointments. My father's great passion was golf. He was not a religious man. But my mother believed in the cathedral with a passion that was almost a disease. She died looking at it. Her spirit is somewhere round it now, I do believe."

He paused, then went on:

"It was the cathedral that made me so unpractical, I suppose. I who am an only child—I believed implicitly in what I was told and it always was my mother who told me everything."

He was, I thought, the very simplest person to whom I had ever listened. The irritation that I had already felt on several occasions in his company again returned. "My father's great passion was golf" would surely in the mouth of another have had some tinge of irony.

In Trenchard's mild blue eyes irony was an incredible element. I could fancy what he would have to say to the very gentlest of cynics; some of the sympathy I had felt for him during the afternoon had left me.

"He's very little short of an idiot," I thought. "He's going to be dreadfully in the way."

"I was the only child, you see," he continued. "Of course I was a great deal to my mother and she to me. We were always together. I don't think that even when I was very young I believed all that she told me. She seemed to me always to take everything for granted. Heaven to me was so mysterious and she had such definite knowledge. I always liked things to be indefinite ... I do still." He laughed, paused for a moment, but was plainly now off on his fine white horse, charging the air, to be stopped by no mortal challenge. I had for a moment the thought that I would slip from my seat and leave him; I didn't believe that he would have noticed my absence; but the thought of that small stuffy carriage held me.

But he was conscious of me; like the Ancient Mariner he fixed upon my arm his hand and stared into my eyes:

"There were other things that puzzled me. There was, for instance, the chief doctor in our town. He was a large, fat, jolly red-faced man, clean-shaven, with white hair. He was considered the best doctor in the place—all the old maids went to him. He was immensely jolly, you could hear his laugh from one end of the street to the other. He was married, had a delightful little house, where his wife gave charming dinners. He was stupid and self-satisfied. Even at his own work he was stupid, reading nothing, careless and forgetful, thinking about golf and food only all his days. He was a snob too and would give up any one for the people at the Castle. Even when I was a small boy I somehow knew all this about him. My father thought the world of him and loved to play golf with him.... He was completely happy and successful and popular. Then there was another man, an old canon who taught me Latin before I went to Rugby, an old, untidy, dirty man, whose sermons were dull and his manners bad. He was a failure in life—and he was a failure to himself; dissatisfied with what he used to call his 'bundle of rotten twigs,' his life and habits and thoughts. But he thought that somewhere there was something he would find that would save him—somewhere, sometime ... not God merely—'like a key that will open all the doors in the house.' To me he was fascinating. He knew so much, he was so humble, so kind, so amusing. Nobody liked him, of course. They tried to turn him out of the place, gave him a little living at last, and he married his cook. Was she his key? She may have been ... I never saw him again. But I used to wonder. Why was the doctor so happy and the little canon so unhappy, the doctor so successful, the canon so unsuccessful? I decided that the great thing was to be satisfied with oneself. I determined that I would be satisfied with myself. Well, of course I never was—never have been. Something wouldn't let me alone. The key to the door, perhaps ... everything was shut up inside me, and at last I began to wonder whether there was anything there at all. When at nineteen I went to Cambridge I was very unhappy. Whilst I was there my mother died. I came back to the little bow-windowed house and lived with my father. I was quite alone in the world."

In spite of myself I had a little movement of impatience.

"How self-centred the man is! As though his case were at all peculiar! Wants shaking up and knocking about."

He seemed to know my thought.

"You must think me self-centred! I was. For thirteen whole years I thought of nothing but myself, my miserable self, all shut up in that little town. I talked to no one. I did not even read—I used to sit in the dark of the cathedral nave and listen to the organ. I'd walk in the orchards and the woods. I would wonder, wonder, wonder about people and I grew more and more frightened of talking, of meeting people, of little local dinner-parties. It was as though I were on one side of the river and they were all on the other. I would think sometimes how splendid it would be if I could cross—but I couldn't cross. Every year it became more impossible!"

"You wanted some one to take you out of yourself," I said, and then shuddered at my own banality. But he took me very seriously.

"I did. Of course," he answered. "But who would bother? They all thought me impossible. The girls all laughed at me—my own cousins. Sometimes people tried to help me. They never went far enough. They gave me up too soon."

"He evidently thinks he was worth a lot of trouble," I thought irritably. But suddenly he laughed.

"That same doctor one day spoke of me, not knowing that I was near him; or perhaps he knew and thought it would be good for me. 'Oh, Trenchard,' he said. 'He ought to be in a nunnery ... and he'd be quite safe, too. He'd never cause a scandal!' They thought of me as something not quite human. My father was very old now. Just before he died, he said: 'I'd like to have had a son!' He never noticed me at his bedside when he died. I was a great disappointment to him."

"Well," I said at last to break a long pause that followed his last words, "what did you think about all that time you were alone?"

"I used to think always about two things," he said very solemnly. "One was love. I used to think how splendid it would be if only there would be some one to whom I could dedicate my devotion. I didn't care if I got much in return or no, but they must be willing to have it ready for me to devote myself altogether. I used to watch the ladies in our town and select them, one after another. Of course they never knew and they would only have laughed had they known. But I felt quite desperate sometimes. I had so much in me to give to some one and the years were all slipping by and it became, every day, more difficult. There was a girl ... something seemed to begin between us. She was the daughter of one of the canons, dark-haired, and she used to wear a lilac-coloured dress. She was very kind; once when we were walking through the town I began to talk to her. I believe she understood, because she was very, very young—only about eighteen—and hadn't begun to laugh at me yet. She had a dimple in one cheek, very charming—but some man from London came to stay at the Castle and she was engaged to him. Then there were Katherine and Millie Trenchard, of whom we were talking. Katherine never laughed at me; she was serious and helped her mother about all the household things and the village where they lived. Afterwards she ran away with a young man and was married in London—very strange because she was so serious. There was a great deal of talk about it at the time. Millie too was charming.

She laughed at me, of course, but she laughed at every one. At any rate she was only cousinly to me; she would not have cared for my devotion."

As he spoke I had a picture in my mind of poor Trenchard searching the countryside for some one to whom he might be devoted, tongue-tied, clumsy, stumbling and stuttering, a village Don Quixote with a stammer and without a Dulcinea.

"They must have been difficult years," I said, and again cursed myself for my banality.

"They were," he answered very gravely, "Very difficult."

"And your other thoughts?" I asked him.

"They were about death," he replied. "I had, from my very earliest years, a great terror of death. You might think that my life was not so pleasant that I should mind, very greatly, leaving it. But I was always thinking—hoping that I should live to be very old, even though I lost all my limbs and faculties. I believed that there was life of some sort after death, but just as I would hesitate outside a house a quarter of an hour from terror of meeting new faces so I felt about another life—I couldn't bear all the introductions and the clumsy mistakes that I should be sure to make. But it was more personal than that. I had a horrible old uncle who died when I was a boy. He was a very ugly old man, bent and whitened and gnarled, a face and hands twisted with rheumatism. I used to call him Quilp to myself. He always wore, I remember, an old-fashioned dress. Velvet knee-breeches, a white stock, black shoes with buckles. I remember that his hands were damp and hair grew in bushes out of his ears. Well, I saw him once or twice and he filled me with terror like a figure out of the tapestry up at the Castle. Then he died.

"Our house was small and badly shaped, full of dark corners, and after his death he seemed to me to haunt the place. He figured Death to me and until I was quite old, until I went to Rugby, I fancied that he was sitting in a dark corner, on a chair, waiting, with his hands on his lap, until the time came for him to take me. Sometimes I would fancy that I heard him moving from one room to another, bringing his chair with him. Then I began to have a dream, a dream that frequently recurred all the time that I was growing up. It was a dream about a huge dark house in a huge dark forest. It was early morning, the light just glimmering between the thick damp trees. A large party of people gathered together in a high empty room prepared for an expedition. I was one of them and I was filled with sharp agonising terror. Sometimes in my dream I drank to give myself courage and the glass clattered against my lips. Sometimes I talked with one of the company; the room was very dark and I could see no faces. Then we would start trooping out into the bitterly cold morning air. There would be many horses and dogs. We would lead off into the forest and soon (it always happened) I would find myself alone—alone with the dripping trees high around me and the light that seemed to grow no lighter and the intense cold. Then suddenly it would be that I was the hunted, not the hunter. It was Death whom we were hunting— Death, for me my uncle—and I would fancy him waiting in the darkness, watching me, smiling, hearing his hunters draw off the scent, knowing that they would not find him, but that he had found me. Then my knees would fail me, I would sink down in a sweat of terror, and—wake!... Brrr!... I can see it now!"

He shook himself, turning round to me as though he were suddenly ashamed of himself, with a laugh half-shy, half-retrospective.

"We all have our dreams," he continued. "But this came too often—again and again. The question of death became my constant preoccupation as I grew to think I would never see it, nor hear men speak of it, nor—"

"And you have come," I could not but interrupt him, "here, to the very fortress—Why, man!—"

"I know," he answered, smiling at me. "It must seem to you ridiculous. But I am a different person now—very different. Now I am ready, eager for anything. Death can be nothing to me now, or if that is too bold, at least I may say that I am prepared to meet him—anywhere—at any time. I want to meet him—I want to show—"

"We have all," I said, "in our hearts, perhaps, come like that—come to prove that our secret picture of ourselves, that picture so different from our friends' opinion of us, is really the true one. We can fancy them saying afterwards: 'Well, I never knew that so-and-so had so much in him!' We always knew."

"No, you see," Trenchard said eagerly, "there can be only one person now about whose opinion I care. If she thinks well of me—"

"You are very much in love," I said, and loosed, as I had expected, the torrents of his happiness upon me.

"I was in Polchester when the war broke out. The town received it rather as though a first-class company had come from London to act in the Assembly Rooms for a fortnight. It was dramatic and picturesque and pleasantly patriotic. They see it otherwise now, I fancy. I seemed at once to think of Russia. For one thing I wanted desperately to help, and I thought that in England they would only laugh at me as they had always done. I am short-sighted. I knew that I should never be a soldier. I fancied that in Russia they would not say: 'Oh, John Trenchard of Polchester.... He's no good!' before they'd seen whether I could do anything. Then of course I had read about the country—Tolstoi and Turgeniev, and a little Dostoevsky and even Gorki and Tchekov. I went quite suddenly, making up my mind one evening. I seemed to begin to be a new man out of England. The journey delighted me.... I was in Moscow before I knew. I was there three months trying to learn Russian. Then I came to Petrograd and through the English Embassy found a place in one of the hospitals, where I worked as a sanitar for three months. I did not leave England until November, so that I have been in Russia now just six months. It was in this hospital that I met Miss Krassovsky—Marie Ivanovna. From the first moment I loved her, of course. And she liked me. She was the first woman, since my mother, who had really liked me. She quickly saw my devotion and she laughed a little, but she was always kind. I could talk to her and she liked to listen. She had—she has, great ideals, great hopes and ambitions. We worked together there and then, afterwards, in those beautiful spring evenings in Petrograd when the canals shone all night and the houses were purple, we walked.... The night before last night I begged her to marry me ... and she accepted. She said that we would go together to the war, that I should be her knight and she my lady and that we would care for the wounds of the whole world. Ah! what a night that was—shall I ever forget it? After she had left me, I walked all night and sang.... I was mad.... I am mad now. That she should love me! She, so beautiful, so pure, so wonderful. I at whom women have always laughed. Ah! God forgive me, my heart will break—"

As he spoke the heavy grey clouds of the first dawn were parting and a faint very liquid blue, almost white and very cold, hovered above dim shapeless trees and fields. I flung open the corridor window and a sound of running water and the first notes of some sleepy bird met me.

"And her family?" I said. "Who are they, and will they not mind her marrying an Englishman?"

"She has only a mother," he answered. "I fancy that Marie has always had her own way."

"Yes," I thought to myself. "I also fancy that that is so." A sense of almost fatherly protection had developed in myself towards him. How could he, who knew nothing at all of women, hope to manage that self-willed, eager, independent girl? Why, why, why had she engaged herself to him? I fancied that very possibly there were qualities in him—his very childishness and helplessness—which, if they only irritated an Englishman, would attract a Russian. Lame dogs find a warm home in Russia. But did she know anything about him? Would she not, in a week, be irritated by his incapacity? And he—he—bless his innocence!—was so confident as though he had been married to her for years!

"Look here!" I said, moved by a sudden impulse. "Will you mind if, sometimes, I tell you things? I've been to the war before. It's a strange life, unlike anything you've ever known—and Russians too are strange—especially at first. You won't take it badly, if—"

He touched my arm with his hand while his whole face was lighted with his smile. "Why, my dear fellow, I shall be proud. No one has ever thought me worth the bother. I want to be—to be—at my best here. Practical, you know—like others. I don't want her to think me—"

"No, exactly," I said hurriedly, "I understand." Gold was creeping into the sky. A lark rose, triumphant. A pool amongst the reeds blazed like a brazen shield. The Spring day had flung back her doors. I saw that suddenly fatigue had leapt upon my friend. He tottered on his little seat, then his face, grey in the light, fell forward. I caught him in my arms, half carried, half led him into our little carriage, arranged him in the empty corner, and left him, fast, utterly fast, asleep.

CHAPTER II

THE SCHOOL-HOUSE

The greater part of the next day was spent by us in the little town of S—, a comfortable place very slightly disturbed by the fact that it had been already the scene of four battles; there was just this effect, as it seemed to me, that the affairs of the day were carried on with a kind of somnolent indifference.... "You may order your veal," the waiter seemed to say, "but whether you will get it or no is entirely in the hands of God. It is, therefore, of no avail that I should hurry or that you should show temper should the veal not appear. At any moment your desire for veal and my ability to bring it you may have ceased for ever."

For the rest the town billowed with trees of the youngest green; also birds of the tenderest age, if one may judge by their happiness at the spring weather. There were many old men in white smocks and white trousers and women in brightly-coloured kerchiefs. But, except for the young birds, it was a silent place.

I had much business to carry through and saw the rest of our company only at luncheon time; it was after luncheon that I had a little conversation with Marie Ivanovna. She chose me quite deliberately from the others, moved our chairs to the quieter end of the little balcony where we were, planted her elbows on the table and stared into my face with her large round credulous eyes. (I find on looking back, that I have already used exactly those adjectives. That may stand: I mean that, emphatically, and beyond every other impression she made, her gaze declared that she was ready to believe anything that she were told, and the more in the telling the better.)

She spoke, as always, with that sense of restrained, sharply disciplined excitement, as though her eager vitality were some splendid if ferocious animal struggling at its chain.

"You talked to John—Mr. Trenchard—last night," she said.

"Yes," I said, smiling into her eyes.

"I know—all night—he told me. He's splendid, isn't he? Splendid!"

"I like him very much," I answered.

"Ah! you must! you must! You must all like him! You don't know—his thoughts, his ideals—they are wonderful. He's like some knight of the Middle Ages.... Ah, but you'll think that silly, Mr. Durward. You're a practical Englishman. I hate practical Englishmen."

"Thank you," I said, laughing.

"No, but I do. You sneer at everything beautiful. Here in Russia we're more simple. And John's very like a Russian in many ways. Don't you think he is?"

"I haven't known him long enough—" I began.

"Ah, you don't like him! I see you don't.... No, it's no use your saying anything. He isn't English enough for you, that's what it is. You think him unpractical, unworldly. Well, so he is. Do you think I'd ever be engaged to an ordinary Englishman? I'd die of ennui in a week. Oh! yes, I would. But you like John, really, don't you?"

"I tell you that I do," I answered, "but really, after only two days—"

"Ah! that's so English! So cautious! How I hate your caution! Why can't you say at once that you haven't made up your mind about him—because that's the truth, isn't it? I wish he would not sit there, looking at me, and not talking to the others. He ought to talk to them, but he's afraid that they'll laugh at his Russian. It's not very good, his Russian, is it? I can't help laughing myself sometimes!"

Her English was extremely good. Sometimes she used a word in its wrong sense; she had one or two charming little phrases of her own: "What a purpose to?" instead of: "Why?" and sometimes a double negative. She rolled her r's more than is our habit.

I said, looking straight into her eyes:

"It's a tremendous thing to him, his having you. I can see that although I've known him so short a time. He's a very lucky man and—and—if his luck were to go, I think that he'd simply die. There! That isn't a very English thing to have said, is it?"

"Why did you say it?" she cried sharply. "You don't trust me. You think—"

"I think nothing," I answered. "Only he's not like ordinary men. He's so much younger than his age."

She gave me then the strangest look. The light seemed suddenly to die out of her face; her eyes sought mine as though for help. There were tears in them.

"Oh! I do want to be good to him!" she whispered. Then got up abruptly and joined the others.

Late in the afternoon an automobile arrived and carried off most of our party. I was compelled to remain for several hours, and intended to drive, looking forward indeed to the long quiet silence of the spring evening. Moved by some sudden impulse I suggested to Trenchard that he should wait and drive with me: "The car will be very crowded," I said, "and I think too that you'd like to see some of the country properly. It's a lovely evening—only thirty versts.... Will you wait and come with me?"

He agreed at once; he had been, all day, very quiet, watching, with that rather clumsy expression of his, the expression of a dog who had been taught by his master some tricks which he had half-forgotten and would presently be expected to remember.

When I made my suggestion he flung one look at Marie Ivanovna. She was busied over some piece of luggage, and half-turned her head, smiling at him:

"Ah, do go, John—yes? We will be so cr-rowded.... It will be very nice for you driving."

I fancied that I heard him sigh. He tried to help the ladies with their luggage, handed them the wrong parcels, dropped delicate packages, apologised, blushed, was very hot, collected dust from I know not where.... Once I heard a sharp, angry voice: "John! Oh!..." I could not believe that it was Marie Ivanovna. Of course she was hot and tired and had slept, last night, but little. The car, watched by an inquisitive but strangely apathetic crowd of peasants, snorted its way down the little streets, the green trees blowing and the starlings chattering. In a moment the starlings and our two selves seemed to have the whole dead little town to ourselves.

I saw quite clearly that he was unhappy; he could never disguise his feelings; as he waited for the trap to appear he had the same lost and abandoned appearance that he had on my first vision of him at the Petrograd station. The soldier who was to drive us smiled as he saw me.

"Only thirty versts, your honour ... or, thank God, even less. It will take us no time." He was a large clumsy creature, like an eager overgrown puppy; he was one of the four or five Nikolais in our Otriad, and he is to be noticed in this history because he attached himself from the very beginning to Trenchard with that faithful and utterly unquestioning devotion of which the Russian soldier is so frequently capable. He must, I think, have seen something helpless and unhappy in Trenchard's appearance on this evening. Sancho to our Don Quixote he was from that first moment.

"Yes, he's an English gentleman," I said when he had listened for a moment to Trenchard's Russian.

"Like yourself," said Nikolai.

"Yes, Nikolai. You must look after him. He'll be strange here at first."

"Slushaiu (I hear)."

That was all he said. He got up on to his seat, his broad back was bent over his horses.

"Well, and how have things been, Nikolai, busy?"

"Nikak nyet—not at all. Very quiet."

"No wounded?"

"Nothing at all, Barin, for two weeks now."

"Have you liked that?"

"Tak totchno. Certainly yes."

"No, but have you?"

"Tak totchno, Barin."

Then he turned and gave, for one swift instant, a glance at Trenchard, who was, very clumsily, climbing into the carriage. Nikolai looked at him gravely. His round, red face was quite expressionless as he turned back and began to abjure his horses in that half-affectionate, half-abusive and wholly human whispering exclamation that Russians use to their animals. We started.

I have mentioned in these pages that I had already spent three months with our Otriad at the Front. I cannot now define exactly what it was that made this drive on this first evening something utterly distinct and apart from all that I had experienced during that earlier period. It is true that, before, I had been for almost two months in one place and had seen nothing at all of actual warfare, except the feeding and bandaging of the wounded. But I had imagined then, nevertheless, that I was truly "in the thick of things," as indeed, in comparison with my Moscow or Petrograd life, I was. We had not now driven through the quiet evening air for ten minutes before I knew, with assured certainty, that a new phase of life was, on this day, opening before me; the dark hedges, the thin fine dust on the roads, the deep purple colour of the air, beat at my heart, as though they themselves were helping with quiet insistency to draw me into the drama. And yet nothing could have been more peaceful than was that lovely evening. The dark plum-colour in the evening sky soaked like wine into the hills, the fields, the thatched cottages, the streams and the little woods.

The faint saffron that lingered below the crests and peaks of rosy cloud showed between the stems of the silver birches like the friendly smile of a happy day. The only human beings to be seen were the peasants driving home their cows; far on the horizon the Carpathian mountains were purple in the dusk, the snow on their highest ridges faintly silver. There was not a sound in the world except the ring of our horses' hoofs upon the road. And yet this sinister excitement hammered, from somewhere, at me as I had never felt it before. It was as though the lovely evening were a painted scene lowered to hide some atrocity.

"This is scarcely what you expected a conquered country to look like, is it?" I said to Trenchard.

He looked about him, then said, hesitating: "No ... that is ... I don't know what I expected."

A curved moon, dull gold like buried treasure, rose slowly above the hill; one white star flickered and the scents of the little gardens that lined the road grew thicker in the air as the day faded.

I was conscious of some restraint with Trenchard: "He's probably wishing," I thought, "that he'd not been so expansive last night. He doesn't trust me."

Once he said abruptly:

"They'll give me ... won't they ... work to do? It would be terrible if there wasn't work. I'm not so ... so stupid at bandaging. I learnt a lot in the hospital and although I'm clumsy with my hands generally I'm not so clumsy about that—"

"Why of course," I answered. "When there's work they'll be only too delighted. But there won't always be work. You must be prepared for that. Sometimes our Division is in reserve and then we're in reserve too. Sometimes for so much as a fortnight. When I was out here before I was in one place for more than two months. You must just take everything as it comes."

"I want to work," he said. "I must."

Once again only he spoke:

"That little fat man who travelled with us...."

"Andrey Vassilievitch," I said.

"Yes.... He interests me. You knew him before?"

"Yes. I've known him slightly for some years."

"What has he come for? He's frightened out of his life."

"Frightened?"

"Yes, he himself told me. He says that he's very nervous but that he must do everything that every one else does—for a certain reason. He got very excited when he talked to me and asked me whether I thought it would all be very terrible."

"He is a nervous fussy little man. Russians are not cowards, but Andrey Vassilievitch lost his wife last year. He was very devoted to her—very. He is miserable without her, they say. Perhaps he has come to the war to forget her."

I was surprised at Trenchard's interest; I had thought him so wrapt in his own especial affair that nothing outside it could occupy him. But he continued:

"He knew the tall doctor—Nikitin—before, didn't he?"

"Yes.... Nikitin knew his wife."

"Oh, I see.... Nikitin seems to despise him—I think he despises all of us."

"Oh no. That's only his manner. Many Russians look as though they were despising their neighbours when, as a matter of fact, they're really despising themselves. They're very fond of despising themselves: their contempt allows them to do what they want to."

"I don't think Nikitin despises himself. He looks too happy—at least, happy is not the word. Perhaps triumphant is what I mean."

"Ah, if you begin speculating about Russian expression you're lost. They express so much in their faces that you think you know all their deepest feelings. But they're not their deep feelings that you see. Only their quick transient emotions that change every moment." I fancied, just at that time, that I had studied the Russian character very intently and it was perhaps agreeable to me to air my knowledge before an Englishman who had come to Russia for the first time so recently.

But Trenchard did not seem to be greatly impressed by my cleverness. He spoke no more. We drove then in silence whilst the moon, rising high, caught colour into its dim outline, like a scimitar unsheathed; the trees and hedges grew, with every moment, darker. We left the valley through which we had been driving, slowly climbing the hill, and here, on the top of the rising ground, we had our first glimpse of the outposts of the war. A cottage had been posted on the highest point of the hill; now all that remained of it was a sheet of iron, crumpled like paper, propped in the centre by a black and solitary post, trailing thence on the ground amongst tumbled bricks and refuse. This sheet of iron was silver in the moonlight and stood out with its solitary black support against the night sky, which was now breaking into a million stars. Behind it stretched a flat plain that reached to the horizon.

"There," I said to Trenchard, "there's your first glimpse of actual warfare. What do you say to every house in your village at home like that? It's ghastly enough if you see it as I have done, still smoking, with the looking-glasses and flower-pots and pictures lying about."

But Trenchard said nothing.

We started across the plain and at once, as with "Childe Roland":

    For mark! no sooner was I fairly found   Pledged to the plain, after a pace or two,   Than, pausing to throw backward a last view   O'er the safe road, 'twas gone! grey plain all round: Nothing but plain to the horizon's bound.   I might go on; nought else remained to do.

Our "safe road" was a rough and stony track; far in front of us on the rising hill that bounded the horizon a red light watched us like an angry eye. There were cornfields that stirred and whispered, but no hedges, no trees, and not a house to be seen.

Nikolai turned and said: "A very strong battle here, Your Honour, only three weeks back."

By the side of the road stood a little cluster of wooden crosses and behind them were two large holes filled now with water upon which the moon was shining. In these holes the frogs were making a tremendous noise.

"That was shell," I said to Trenchard, pointing. The frogs drowned my voice; there was something of a melancholy triumph in their cry and their voices seemed to be caught up and echoed by thousands upon thousands of other frogs inhabiting the plain.

We came then upon a trench; the ridge of it stretched like a black cord straight across the cornfield and here for a moment the road seemed lost.

I got out. "Here, Trenchard. You must come and look at this. Your first Austrian trench. You may find treasure."

We walked along in single file for some time and then suddenly I lost him: the trench, just where we were, divided into two. I waited thinking that in a moment he would appear. There was nothing very thrilling about my trench; it was an old one and all that remained now of any life was the blackened ground where there had been cooking, the brown soiled cartridge-cases, and many empty tin cans. And then as I waited, leaning forward with my elbows on the earthwork, the frogs the only sound in the world, I was conscious that some one was watching me. In front of me I could see the red light flickering and turning a little as it seemed—behind me nothing but the starlight. I turned, looked back, and for my very life could not hold myself from calling out:

"Who's there?"

I waited, then called more loudly: "Trenchard! Trenchard!" I laughed at myself, leant again on the trench and puffed at my cigarette. Then once more I was absolutely assured that some one watched me.

I called again: "Who's there?"

Then quite suddenly and to my own absurd relief Trenchard appeared, stumbling forward over some roughness in the ground almost into my arms:

"I say, it's beastly here," he cried. "Let's go on—the frogs...."

He had caught my hand.

"Well," I said, "what did you find?"

"Nothing—only ... I don't know.... It's as though some one were watching me. It's getting late, isn't it? The frogs...." he said again—"I hate them. They seem to be triumphing."

We climbed into the trap and drove on in silence.

I was half asleep when at last we left the plain and dropped down into the valley beyond. I was surprised to discover on looking at my watch that it was only eleven o'clock; we had been, it seemed to me, hours crossing that plain. "It's a silly thing," I said to Trenchard, "but it would take quite a lot to get me to drive back over that again." He nodded his head. We drove over a bridge, up a little hill and were in the rough moonlit square of O—, our destination. Almost immediately we were climbing the dark rickety stairs of our dwelling. There were lights, shouts of welcome, Molozov our chief, sisters, doctors, students, the room almost filled with a table covered with food—cold meat, boiled eggs, sausage, jam, sweets, and of course a huge samovar. I can only say that never once, during my earlier experience with the Otriad, had I been so rejoiced to see lights and friendly faces. I looked round for Trenchard. He had already discovered Marie Ivanovna and was standing with her at the window.

I learned at breakfast the next morning that we were at once to move to a house outside the village. The fantastic illusions that my drive of the evening before had bred in me now in the clear light of morning entirely deserted me. Moreover fantasy had slender opportunity of encouragement in the presence of Molozov.

Molozov, I would wish to say once and for all, was the heart and soul of our enterprise. Without him the whole organisation so admirably supported by the energetic ladies and gentlemen in Petrograd, would have tumbled instantly into a thousand pieces. In Molozov they had discovered exactly the man for their purpose; a large land-owner, a member of one of the best Russian families, he had, since the beginning of the war, given himself up to the adventure with the whole of his energy, with the whole of that great capacity for organisation that the management of his estates had already taught him. He was in appearance, short, squarely built, inclined, although he was only thirty-two or three, to be stout; he wore a dark black moustache and his hair was already grey. He was a Russian of the purest blood and yet possessed all the qualities that the absolute Russian is supposed to lack. He was punctual to the moment, sharply accurate in all his affairs, a shrewd psychologist but never a great talker and, above all, a consummate diplomatist. As I watched him dealing with the widely opposed temperaments and dispositions of all our company, soothing one, scolding another, listening attentively, cutting complaints short, comforting, commanding, soliciting, I marvelled at the good fortune of that Petrograd committee. In spite of his kind heart—and he was one of the kindest-hearted men I have ever met—he could be quite ruthless in dismissal or rebuke when occasion arrived. He had a great gift of the Russian irony and he could be also, like all Russians, a child at an instant's call, if something pleased him or if he simply felt that the times were good and the sun was shining. I only once, in a moment that I shall have, later on, to describe, saw him depressed and out of heart. He was always a most courteous gentleman.

I drove now with him in a trap at the head of the Oboz, as our long train, with our tents, provisions, boxes and beds, was called. We were a fine company now and my heart was proud as I looked back up the shining road and saw the long winding procession of carts and "sanitars" and remembered how tiny an affair we had been in the beginning.

"Well," said Molozov, "and what of your Englishman?"

"Oh, I like him," I said rather hurriedly. "He'll do."

"I'm glad you think so—very glad. I was not sure last night.... He doesn't speak Russian very well, does he? He was tired last night. I'm very glad that he should come, of course, but it's unpleasant ... this engagement ... the Sister told me. It's a little difficult for all of us."

"They were engaged the evening before they left."

"I know ... nothing to do about it, but it would have been better otherwise. And Andrey Vassilievitch! Whatever put it into Anna Mihailovna's head to send him! He's a tiresome little man—I've known him earlier in Petrograd! He's on my nerves already with his chatter. No, it's too bad. What can he do with us?"

"He has a very good business head," I said. "And he's not really a bad little man. And he's very anxious to do everything."

"Ah, I know those people who are 'anxious to do everything.'... Don't I know? Don't you remember Sister Anna Maria? anxious to do everything, anything—and then, when it came to it, not even the simplest bandage.... Nikitin's a good man," he added, "one of the best doctors in Petrograd. We've no doctors of our own now, you know—except of course Alexei Petrovitch. The others are all from the Division—"

"Ah, Semyonov!" I said. "How is he?"

At that moment he rode up to us. Seen on horseback Alexei Petrovitch Semyonov appeared a large man; he was, in reality, of middle height but his back was broad, his whole figure thickly-set and muscular. He wore a thick square-cut beard of so fair a shade that it was almost white! His whole colour was pale and yet, in some way, expressive of immense health and vitality. His lips showed through his beard and moustache red and very thick. His every movement showed great self-possession and confidence. He had, indeed, far more personality than any other member of our Otriad.

Although he was an extremely capable doctor his main business in life seemed to be self-indulgence. He apparently did not know the meaning of the word "restraint." The serious questions in life to him were food, drink, women.

He believed in no woman's virtue and no man's sincerity. He hailed any one as a friend but if he considered some one a fool he said so immediately. He concealed his opinions from no one.

When he was at work his indulgence seemed for the moment to leave him. He was a surgeon of the first order and loved his profession. He was a man now of fifty, but had never married, preferring a long succession of mistresses—women who had loved him, at whom he had always laughed, to whom he had been kind in a careless fashion.... He always declared that no woman had ever touched his heart.

He had come to the war voluntarily, forsaking a very lucrative practice. This was always a puzzle to me. He had no romantic notions about the war, no altruistic compulsions, no high conceptions of his duty ... no one had worked more magnificently in the war than he. He could not be said to be popular amongst us; we were all of us perhaps a little afraid of him. He cared, so obviously, for none of us. But we admired his vitality, his courage, his independence. I myself was assured that he allowed us to see him only with the most casual superficiality.

As he rode up to me I wondered how he and Nikitin would fare. These were two personalities worthy of attention. Also, what would he think of Trenchard? His opinion of any one had great weight amongst us.

I had not seen him last night and he leant over his horse now and shook hands with me with a warm friendliness that surprised me. He laughed, joked, was evidently in excellent spirits. He rode on a little, then came back to us.

"I like your new Sister," he said. "She's charming."

"She's engaged," I answered, "to the new Englishman."

"Ah! the new Englishman!" He laughed. "Apologies, Ivan Andreievitch (myself), to your country ... but really ... what's he going to do with us?"

"He'll work," I said, surprised at the heat that I felt in Trenchard's defence. "He's a splendid fellow."

"I have no doubt"—again Semyonov laughed. "We all know your enthusiasms, Ivan Andreievitch, ... but an Englishman! Ye Bogu!..."

"Engaged to that girl!" I heard him repeat to himself as again he rode forward. Trenchard, little Andrey Vassilievitch, Semyonov, Nikitin ... yes, there was promise of much development here.

We had dropped down into the valley and, at a sudden turn, saw the school-house in front of us. It is before me now as I write with its long low whitewashed two-storied front, its dormer-windows, its roof faintly pink with a dark red bell-tower perched on the top. Behind it is a long green field stretching to where hills, faintly blue in the morning light, rose, with very gradual slopes against the sky. To the right I could see there was a garden hidden now by trees, on the left a fine old barn, its thatched roof deep brown, the props supporting it black with age. In front of the pillared porch there was a little square of white cobble-stones and in the middle of these an old grey sundial. The whole place was bathed in the absolute peace of the spring morning.

As we drove up a little old lady with two tiny children clinging to her skirts came to the porch. I could see, as we came up to her, that she was trembling with terror; she put up her hand to her white hair, clutched again desperately the two children, found at last her voice and hoped that we would be "indulgent."

Molozov assured her that she would suffer in no kind of way, that we must use her school for a week or so and that any loss or damage that she incurred would of course be made up to her. She was then, of a sudden, immensely fluent, explaining that her husband—"a most excellent husband to me in every way one might say"—had been dead fifteen years now, that her two sons were both fighting for the Austrians, that she looked after the school assisted by her daughter. These were her grandchildren.... Such a terrible year she, in all her long life, had never remembered. She....

The arrival of the rest of the Oboz silenced her. She remained, with wide-open staring eyes, her hand at her breast, watching, saying absent-mindedly to the children: "Now Katya.... Now Anna.... See what you're about!"

The school was spotlessly clean. In the schoolroom the rough benches were marked with names and crosses. On the whitewashed walls were coloured maps of Galicia and tables of the Austrian kings and queens; on the blackboard still an unfinished arithmetical sum and on the master's desk a pile of exercise books.

In a moment everything was changed; the sanitars had turned the schoolroom into a dormitory, another room was to be our dining-room, another a bedroom for the Sisters. In the high raftered kitchen our midday meal was already cooking; the little cobbled court was piled high with luggage. In the field beyond the house the sanitars had pitched their tents.

I walked out into the little garden—a charming place with yew hedges, a lichen-covered well and old thick apple-trees, and here I found an old man in a broad-brimmed straw hat tending the bees. The hives were open and he was working with a knife whilst the bees hung in a trembling hovering cloud about him. I spoke to him but he paid no attention to me at all. I watched him then spoke again; he straightened himself then looked at me for a moment with eyes full of scorn. Words of fury, of abuse perhaps, seemed to tremble on his lips, then shaking his head he turned his back upon me and continued his work. Behind us I could hear the soldiers breaking the garden-fence to make stakes for their tents.

Here we were for a fortnight and it was strange to me, in the days of stress and excitement that followed, to look back to that fortnight and remember that we had, so many of us, been restless and discontented at the quiet of it. Oddly enough, of all the many backgrounds that were, during the next months, to follow in procession behind me, there only remain to me with enduring vitality: this school-house at O—, the banks of the River Nestor which I had indeed good reason to remember, and finally the forest of S—. How strange a contrast, that school-house with its little garden and white cobbles and that forest which will, to the end of my life, ever haunt my dreams.

And yet, by its very contrast, how fitting a background to our Prologue this school-house made! I wonder whether Nikitin sees it still in his visions? Trenchard and Semyonov ... does it mean anything to them, where they now are? First of them all, Marie Ivanovna.... I see her still, bending over the well looking down, then suddenly flinging her head back, laughing as we stood behind her, the sunlight through the apple-trees flashing in her eyes.... That fortnight must be to many of us of how ironic, of how tragic a tranquillity!

So we settled down and did our best to become happily accustomed to one another. Our own immediate company numbered twenty or so—Molozov, two doctors, myself, Trenchard and Andrey Vassilievitch, the two new Sisters and the three former ones, five or six young Russians, gentlemen of ease and leisure who had had some "bandaging" practice at the Petrograd hospitals, and three very young medical students, directly attached to our two doctors. In addition to these there were the doctors, Sisters and students belonging to the army itself—the Sixty-Fifth Division of the Ninth Army. These sometimes lived with us and sometimes by themselves; they had at their head Colonel Oblonsky, a military doctor of much experience and wide knowledge. There were also the regular sanitars, some thirty or forty, men who were often by profession schoolmasters or small merchants, of a better class for the most part than the ordinary soldier.

It is not, of course, my intention to describe with any detail the individuals of this company. I have chosen already those of us who are especially concerned with my present history, but these others made a continually fluctuating and variable background, at first confusing and, to a stranger, almost terrifying. When the army doctors and Sisters dined with us we numbered from thirty to forty persons: sometimes also the officers of the Staff of the Sixty-Fifth came to our table. There were other occasions when every one was engaged on one business or another and only three or four of us were left at the central station or "Punkt," as it was called.

And, of all these persons, who now stands out? I can remember a Sister, short, plain, with red hair, who felt that she was treated with insufficient dignity, whose voice rising in complaint is with me now; I can see her small red-rimmed eyes watching for some insult and then the curl of her lip as she snatched her opportunity.... Or there was the jolly, fat Sister who had travelled with us, an admirable worker, but a woman, apparently, with no personal life at all, no excitements, dreads, angers, dejections. Upon her the war made no impression at all. She spoke sometimes to us of her husband and her children. She was not greedy, nor patriotic, neither vain nor humble, neither egoistic nor unselfish. She was simply reliable.

Or there was the tall gaunt Sister, intensely religious and serious. She was regarded by all of us as an excellent woman, but of course we did not like her.

One would say to another: "Sister K—, what an excellent worker!"

"Yes. How she works!"

"Splendid! Splendid!"

When owing to the illness of her old mother she was compelled to return to Petrograd what relief we all felt! How gay was our supper the night of her departure! There was something very childish at the heart of all of us.

Of the young gentlemen from Petrograd I remember only three. The family name of one was Ivanoff, but he was always known to the Otriad as Goga, a pet diminutive of George. He was perhaps the youngest person whom I have ever known. He must have been eighteen years of age; he looked about eleven, with a round red face and wide-open eyes that expressed eternal astonishment. Like Mr. Toots', his mind was continually occupied with his tailor and he told me on several occasions that he hoped I should visit him in Petrograd because there in the house of his mother he had many splendid suits, shirts, ties, that it would give him pleasure to show me. In spite of this little weakness, he showed a most energetic character, willing to do anything for anybody, eager to please the whole world. I can hear his voice now:

"Yeh Bogu! Ivan Andreievitch!... Imagine my position! There was General Polinoff and the whole Staff.... What to do? Only three versts from the position too and already six o'clock...."

Or there was another serious gentleman, whose mind was continually occupied with Russia: "It may be difficult for you, Ivan Andreievitch, to see with our eyes, but for those of us who have Russia in our hearts ... what rest or peace can there be? I can assure you...."

He wore pince-nez and with his long pear-shaped head, shaven to the skin, his white cheeks, protruding chin and long heavy white hands he resembled nothing so much as a large fish hanging on a nail at a fishmonger's. He worked always in a kind of cold desperate despair, his pince-nez slipping off his shiny nose, his mouth set grimly. "What is the use?" he seemed to say, "of helping these poor wounded soldiers when Russia is in such a desperate condition? Tell me that!"

Or there was a wild rough fellow from some town in Little Russia, a boy of the most primitive character, no manners at all and a heart of shining gold. Of life he had the very wildest notions. He loved women and would sing Southern Russian songs about them. He had a strain of fantasy that continually surprised one. He liked fairy tales. He would say to me: "There's a tale? Ivan Andreievitch, about a princess who lived on a lake of glass. There was a forest, you know, round the lake and all the trees were of gold. The pond was guarded by three dwarfs. I myself, Ivan Andreievitch, have seen a dwarf in Kiev no higher than your leg, and in our town they say there was once a whole family of dwarfs who lived in a house in the chief street in our town and sold potatoes.... I don't know.... People tell one such things. But for the rest of that tale, do you remember how it goes?"

He could ride any horse, carry any man, was never tired nor out of heart. He had the vaguest ideas about the war. "I knew a German once in our town," he told me. "I always hated him.... He was going to Petrograd to make his fortune. I hope he's dead." This fellow was called Petrov.

My chief interest during this fortnight was to watch the fortunes of Marie Ivanovna and Trenchard with their new companions. It was instantly apparent that Marie Ivanovna was a success. On the second day after our arrival at the school-house there were continual exclamations: "But how charming the new Sister! How sympathetic!... Have you talked to the new Sister?"

Even Sister K—, so serious and religious, approved. It was evident at once that Marie Ivanovna was, on her side, delighted with every one. I could see that at present she was assured that what she wanted from life would be granted to her. She gave herself, with complete confidence, to any one and every one, and, with that triumphing vitality that one felt in her from the first moment of meeting her, she carried all before her. In the hospital at Petrograd they had been, I gathered, "all serious and old," had treated her I fancy with some sternness. Here, at any rate, "serious and old" she would not find us. We welcomed, with joy, her youth, her enthusiasm, her happiness.

Semyonov, who never disguised nor restrained his feelings, was, from the first instant, strangely attracted to her. She, I could see, liked him very much, felt in him his strength and capacity and scorn of others. Molozov also yielded her his instant admiration. He always avoided any close personal relationship with any of us but I could see that he was delighted with her vitality and energy. She pleased the older Sisters by her frank and quite honest desire to be told things and the younger Sisters by her equally honest admiration of their gifts and qualities. She was honest and sincere, I do believe, in every word and thought and action. She had, in many ways, the naive purity, the unconsidered faith and confidence of a child still in the nursery. She amazed me sometimes by her ignorance; she delighted me frequently by her refreshing truth and straightforwardness. She felt a little, I think, that I did not yield her quite the extravagant admiration of the others. I was Trenchard's friend....

Yes, I was now Trenchard's friend. What had occurred since that night in the train, when I had felt, during the greater part of the time, nothing but irritation? Frankly, I do not know. It may be, partly, that he was given to me by the rest of the Otriad. He was spoken of now as "my" Englishman. And then, poor Trenchard!... How, during this fortnight, he was unhappy! It had begun with him as I had foreseen. In the first place he had been dismayed and silenced by the garrulity of his new companions. It had seemed to him that he had understood nothing of their conversation, that he was in the way, that finally he was more lonely than he had ever been in his life before. Then, however strongly he might to himself deny it, he had arrived in Russia with what Nikitin called "his romantic notions." He had read his Dostoevski and Turgenev; he had looked at those books of Russian impressions that deal in nothing but snow, ikons, and the sublime simplicity of the Russian peasant. He was a man whose circumstances had led him to believe profoundly in his own incapacity, unpopularity, ignorance. For a moment his love had given him a new confidence but now how was that same love deserting him? He had foreseen a glorious campaign, his lady and himself side by side, death and terror flying before him. He found himself leading a country life of perfect quiet and comfort, even as he might have led it in England, with a crowd of people, strangely unfamiliar to him, driving him, as he had been driven in the old days, into a host of awkwardnesses, confusions and foolishnesses. I could not forgive Marie Ivanovna for her disappointment in him, and yet I could understand how different he must have appeared to her during those last days in Petrograd, when alone with her and on fire with love, he had shown his true and bravest self to her. She was impatient, she had hoped that the others would see him as she had seen him. She watched them as they expressed their surprise that he was not the practical, fearless and unimaginative Englishman who was their typical figure. Whilst he found them far from the Karamazovs, the Raskolnikoffs, of his imagination, they in their turn could not create the "sportsman" and "man of affairs" whom they had expected.

To all of this Semyonov added, beyond question, his personal weight. He had from the first declared Trenchard "a ridiculous figure." Whilst the others were unfailingly kind, hospitable and even indulgent to Trenchard, Semyonov was openly satirical, making no attempt to hide his sarcastic irony. I do not know how much Trenchard's engagement to Marie Ivanovna had to do with this, but I know that "my Englishman" could not to his misfortune have had a more practical, more efficient figure against whom to be contrasted than Semyonov.

During these weeks I think that I hated Semyonov. There was, however, one silent observer of all this business upon whose personal interference I had not reckoned. This was Nikitin, who, at the end of our first week at the school-house, broke his silence in a conversation with me.

Nikitin, although he spoke as little as possible to any one, had already had his effect upon the Otriad. They felt behind his silence a personality that might indeed be equal to Semyonov's own. By little Andrey Vassilievitch they were always being assured: "Nikitin! A most remarkable man! You may believe me. I have known him for many years. A great friend of my poor wife's and mine...."

They did not appear to be great friends. Nikitin quite obviously avoided the little man whenever it was possible. But then he avoided us all.

Upon a lovely afternoon Nikitin and I were alone in the wild little garden, he lying full length on the grass, I reading a very ancient English newspaper, with my back against a tree.

He looked up at me with a swift penetrating glance, as though he were seeing me for the first time and would wish at once to weigh my character and abilities.

"Your Englishman," he said. "He's not happy, I'm afraid."

"No," I said, feeling the surprise of his question—it had become almost a tradition with me that he never spoke unless he were first spoken to. "He feels strange and a little lonely, perhaps ... it's natural enough!"

"Yes," repeated Nikitin, "it's natural enough. What did he come for?"

"Oh, he'll be all right," I said hastily, "in a day or two."

Nikitin lay on his back looking at the green, layer upon layer, light and dark, with golden fragments of broken light leaping in the breeze from branch to branch. "Why did he come? What did he expect to see? I know what he expected to see—romantic Russia, romantic war. He expected to find us, our hearts exploding with love, God's smile on our simple faces, God's simple faith in our souls.... He has been told by his cleverest writers that Russia is the last stronghold of God. And war? He thought that he would be plunged into a scene of smoke and flame, shrapnel, horror upon horror, danger upon danger. He finds instead a country house, meals long and large, no sounds of cannon, not even an aeroplane. Are we kind to him? Not at all.... We are not unkind but we simply have other things to think about, and because we are primitive people we do what we want to do, feel what we want to feel, and show quite frankly our feelings. He is not what we expected, so that we prefer to fill our minds with things that do not give us trouble. Later, like all Englishmen, he will dismiss us as savages, or, if he is of the intellectual kind, he will talk about our confusing subtleties and contradictions. But we are neither savages nor confusing. We have simply a skin less than you.... We are a very young people, a real and genuine Democracy, and we care for quite simple things, women, food, sleep, money, quite simply and without restraint. We show our eagerness, our disgust, our disappointment, our amusement simply as the mood moves us. In Moscow they eat all day and are not ashamed. Why should they be? In Kiev they think always about women and do not pretend otherwise ... and so on. We have, of course, no sense of time, nor method, nor system. If we were to think of these things we would be compelled to use restraint and that would bother us. We may lose the most important treasure in the world by not keeping an appointment ... on the other hand we have kept our freedom. We care for ideas for which you care nothing in England but we have a sure suspicion of all conclusions. We are pessimists, one and all. Life cannot be good. We ironically survey those who think that it can.... We give way always to life but when things are at their worst then we are relieved and even happy. Here at any rate we are on safe ground. We have much sentiment, but it may, at any moment, give way to some other emotion. We are therefore never to be relied upon, as friends, as enemies, as anything you please. Except this—that in the heart of every Russian there is a passionate love of goodness. We are tolerant to all evil, to all weakness because we ourselves are weak. We confess our weakness to any one because that permits us to indulge in it—but when we see in another goodness, strength, virtue, we worship it. You may bind us to you with bands of iron by your virtues—never, as all foreigners think, by your vices. In this, too, we are sentimentalists. We may not believe in God but we have an intense curiosity about Him—a curiosity that with many of us never leaves us alone, compels us to fill our lives, to fill our lives.... We love Russia.... But that is another thing.... Never forget too that behind every Russian's simplicity there is always his Ideal—his secret Ideal, perhaps, that he keeps like an ikon sacred in his heart. Yes, of every Russian, even of the worst of us, that is true. And it complicates our lives, delivers us to our enemies, defeats all our worldly aims, renders us helpless at the moment when we should be most strong. But it is good, before God, that it should be so...."

He suddenly sprang up and stood before me. "To-morrow I shall think otherwise—and yet this is part of the truth that I have told you.... And your Englishman? I like him ... I like him. That girl will treat him badly, of course. How can she do otherwise? He sees her like Turgenev's Liza. Well, she is not that. No girl in Russia to-day is like Turgenev's Liza. And it's a good thing." He smiled—that strange, happy, confident mysterious smile that I had seen first on the Petrograd platform. Then he turned and walked slowly towards the house.

What Nikitin had said about Trenchard's expectation of "romantic war" was perhaps true, in different degrees, of all of us. Even I, in spite of my earlier experience, felt some irritation at this delay, and to those of us who had arrived flaming with energy, bravery, resolution to make their name before Europe, this feasting in a country garden seemed a deliberate insult. Was this "romantic war?" These long meals under the trees, deep sleeps in the afternoon when the pigeons cooed round the little red bell-tower and the pump creaked in the cobbled courtyard and the bees hummed in the garden? Bees, cold water shining deep in the well, and the samovar chuckling behind the flower-beds, and fifteen versts away the Austrians challenging the Russian nation!... "You know," Andrey Vassilievitch said to me, "it's very disheartening."

Marie Ivanovna at the end of the first week spoke her mind. I found her one evening before supper leaning over the fence, gazing across the long flat field, pale gold in the dusk with the hills like grey clouds beyond it.

"They tell me," she said, turning to me, "that we may be another fortnight like this."

"Yes," I said, "it's quite possible, or even longer. We can't provide wounded and battles for you if there aren't any."

"But there are!" she cried. "Isn't the whole of Europe fighting and isn't it simply disgusting of us to be sitting down here, eating and sleeping, just as though we were in a dacha in the country? At least in the hospital in Petrograd I was working ... here...."

"We've got to stick to our Division," I answered. "They can't have it in reserve very long. When it goes, we'll go. The whole secret of leading this life out here is taking exactly what comes as completely as you can take it. If it's a time for sleeping and eating, sleep and eat—there'll be days enough when you'll get nothing of either."

She laughed then, swinging round to me, with the dusk round her white nurse's cap and her eyes dark with her desires and hopes and disappointments.

"Oh, I've no right to be discontented.... Every one is so good to me. I love them all—even you, Mr. Durward. But I want to begin, to begin, to begin! I want to see what it's like, to find what there is there that frightens them, or makes them happy. We had a young officer in our hospital who died. He was too ill ... he could tell us nothing, but he was so excited by something ... something he was in the middle of.... Who was it? What was it? I must be there, hunt it out, find that I'm strong enough not to be afraid of anything." She suddenly dropped her voice, changing with sharp abruptness. "And John? He's not happy here, is he?"

"You should know," I answered, "better than any of us."

"Why should I know?" she replied, flaming out at me. "You always blame me about him, but you are unfair. I want him to be happy—I would make him so if I could. But he's so strange, so different from his time at the hospital. He will scarcely speak to me or to any one. Why can't he be agreeable to every one? I want them to like him but how can they when he won't talk to them and runs away if they come near him? He's disappointed perhaps at its being so quiet here. It isn't what he expected to find it, but then isn't that the same for all of us? And we don't sulk all day. He's disappointed with me perhaps but he won't tell me what he wants. If I ask him he only says 'Oh, it's all r-right—it's all r-right'—I hate that 'all r-right' of your language—so stupid! What a purpose not to say if he wants something?"

I said nothing. My silence urged her to a warmer defence.

"And then he makes such mistakes—always everything wrong that he's asked to do. Doctor Semyonov laughs at him—but of course! He's like a little boy, a man as old as he is. And Englishmen are always so practical, capable. Oh! speak to him, Mr. Durward; you can, please. If I say anything he's at once so miserable.... I don't understand, I don't understand!" she cried, raising her hands with a little despairing gesture. "How can he have been like that in Petrograd, and now like this!"

"Give him time, Marie Ivanovna," I answered her. "This is all new to him, confusing, alarming. He's led a very quiet life. He's very sensitive. He cares for you so deeply that the slightest thing wounds him. He would hide that if he could—it's his tragedy that he can't."

She would have answered had not supper arrived and with it our whole company. Shall I ever know a more beautiful night? As we sat there the moon came up, red-gold and full; the stars were clustered so thickly between the trees that their light lay heavy like smoke upon the air. The little garden seemed to be never still as our candlelight blew in the breeze; so it hovered and trembled about us, the trees bending beneath their precious load of stars, shuddering in their happiness at so good an evening.

We sat there as though we had known that it was to be our last night of peace.... Many times the glasses of tea were filled, many times the little blue tin boxes of sweets were pushed up and down the table, many times the china teapot on the top of the samovar was fed with fresh tea, many times spoons were dipped into the strawberry jam and then plunged into the glasses of tea, such being the Russian pleasure.

There occurred then an unfortunate incident. Some one had said something about England: there had been a joke then about "sportsmen," some allusion was made to some old story connected with myself, and I had laughingly taken up the challenge. Suddenly Semyonov leaned across the table and spoke to Trenchard. Trenchard, who had been silent throughout the meal, misunderstood the Russian, thought that Semyonov was trying to insult him, and sat there colouring, flaming at last, silent. We all of us felt the awkwardness of it. There was a general pause—Semyonov himself drew back with a little laugh.

Suddenly Marie Ivanovna, across the table, in English said softly but with a strange eager hostility:

"How absurd!... To let them all see ... to let them know...." Perhaps I, who was sitting next to her, alone heard her words.

The colour left Trenchard's face; he looked at her once, then got up and left the table. I could see then that she was distressed, but she talked, laughed more eagerly, more enthusiastically than before. Sometimes I saw her look towards the school-house.

When there came an opportunity I rose and went to find him. He was standing near his bed, his back to the door, his hands clenched.

"I say, come out again—just as though nothing had happened. No one noticed anything, only I...."

He turned to me, his face working and with a passionate gesture, in a voice that choked over the words, he cried: "She should not have said it. She should not ... every one there.... She knew how it would wound me.... Semyonov...."

He positively was silent over that name. The mild expression of his eyes, the clumsy kindness of his mouth gave a ludicrous expression to his rage.

"Wait! Wait!" I cried. "Be patient!"

As I spoke I could hear him in the railway carriage:

"I am mad with happiness.... God forgive me, my heart will break."

Breaking from me, despair in his voice, he whispered to the empty room, the desolate row of white beds watching him: "I always knew that I was hopeless ... hopeless ... hopeless."

"Look here," I said. "You mustn't take things so hard. You go up and down.... Your emotions...."

But he only shook his head:

"She shouldn't have said it—like that—before every one," he repeated.

I left him. Afterwards as I stood in the passage, white and ghostly in the moonlight, something suddenly told me that this night the prologue of our drama was concluded.

I waited on the steps of the house, heard the laughing voices in the distance, while over the rest of the world there was absolute silence; then abruptly, quite sharply, across the long low fields there came the rumble of cannon. Three times it sounded. Then hearing no more I returned into the house.

CHAPTER III

THE INVISIBLE BATTLE

On the evening of the following day Trenchard, Andrey Vassilievitch and I were sent with sanitars and wagons to the little hamlet of M—, five versts only from the Position. It was night when we arrived there; no sound of cannon, only on the high hills (the first lines of the Carpathians) that faced us the scattered watchfires of our own Sixty-Fifth Division, and in the little village street a line of cavalry moving silently, without a spoken word, on to the high-road beyond. After much difficulty (the village was filled with the officers of the Sixty-Fifth) we found a kitchen in which we might sleep. Upon the rough earth floor our mattresses were spread, my feet under the huge black oven, my head beneath a gilt picture of the Virgin and Child that in the candlelight bowed and smiled, in company with eight other pictures of Virgins and Children, to give us confidence and encouragement.

It was a terrible night. On a high pillared bed set into the farther wall, an old Galician woman, her head bound up in a red handkerchief, knelt all night and prayed aloud. Her daughter crouched against the wall, sleeping, perhaps, but nevertheless rocking ceaselessly a wooden cradle that hung from a black bar in the ceiling. In this cradle lay her son, aged one or two, and once and again he cried for half an hour or so, protesting, I suppose, against our invasion. There was a smell in the kitchen of sour bread, mice, and bad water. The heat was terrible but the old lady told us that the grandchild was ill and would certainly die were the window opened. The candle we blew out but there remained a little burning lamp under the picture of the Virgin immediately over the old lady's bed. I slept, but for how long I do not know. I was only aware that suddenly I was awake, staring through the tiny diamond-paned window, at the faint white light now breaking in the sky. I could see from my mattress only a thin strip of this light above the heavy mass of dark forest on the mountain-side.

I must have been still only half-awake because I could not clearly divide, before my eyes, the true from the false. I could see quite plainly in the dim white shadow the face of Trenchard; he was not asleep, but was leaning on his elbow staring in front of him. I could see the old woman with her red handkerchief kneeling in front of her lamp and her prayer came like the turning of a wheel, harsh and incessant. The cradle creaked, in the air was the heavy smell, and suddenly, beyond the window, a cock crowed. These things were real. But also I seemed to be in some place much vaster than the stuffy kitchen of the night before. Under the light that was with every minute growing stronger, I could fancy that many figures were moving in the shadows; it seemed to me as though I were in some place where great preparations were being made. I fancied then that I could discern Marie Ivanovna's figure, then Nikitin, then Semyonov, then Molozov.... There was a great silence but I felt that every one was busily occupied in making ready for some affair. This was with half my consciousness—with the other half I was perfectly aware of the actual room, of Trenchard, the creaking cradle and the rest.

Then the forest that had been on the hills seemed to draw closer to the house. I felt that it had invaded the garden and that its very branches were rubbing against the windows. With all of this I was aware that I was imagining some occurrence that I had already seen, that was not, in any way, new to me, I was assured of the next event. When we, all of us, Marie Ivanovna, Semyonov, Nikitin and the rest, were ready we should move out into the forest, would stand, a vast company, with our dogs and horses....

Why, it was Trenchard's dream that I was seeing! I was merely repeating to myself his own imaginations—and with that I had suddenly, as though some one had hypnotised me, fallen back into a heavy dreamless sleep. It was already midday when I was wakened by little Andrey Vassilievitch, who, sitting on my bed and evidently in a state of the very greatest excitement, informed me that Dr. Semyonov and the Sisters Marie Ivanovna and Anna Petrovna had arrived from —, and that we might be off at any moment. I was aware, as he spoke, of a great stir beyond the window and saw, passing up through the valley, a flood of soldiers, infantry, cavalry, kitchens with clumsy black funnels bobbing on their unsteady wheels, cannon, hundreds of carts; the soldiers came up through our own garden treading down the cabbages, stopping at the well near our door and filling their tin kettles, tramping up the road, spreading, like smoke, in the far distance, up the high road that led into the furthest forest.

"They say—to-night—for certain," said Andrey Vassilievitch, his fat hand trembling on my bed. He began to talk, his voice shaking with excitement. "Do you know, Ivan Andreievitch, I am continually surprised at myself: 'Here you are, Andrey Vassilievitch, here, at the war. What do you make of it?? I say to myself. Just consider.... No, but seriously, Ivan Andreievitch, of course I must seem to all of you something of a comic figure. When my wife was alive—how I wish that you could have known her! Such a remarkable woman; every one who met her was struck by her fine character—when my wife was alive I had my position to support. That I should have been a comic figure would have distressed her. But now, who cares? Nobody, you may very truly say.... Well, well. But the point is that this evening we shall really be in the thick of it. And—may I tell you something, Ivan Andreievitch? Only for yourself, because you are an Englishman and can be trusted: to speak quite truthfully I'm frightened. I say to myself that one is at the war and that one must be frightened at nothing, and still I remain frightened.... Frightened of what?... I really cannot tell you. Death, perhaps? But no, I should not be sorry to die—there are reasons....

"And yet although I should not be sorry to die, I remain frightened—all night I was awake—I do my utmost to control it, but there is something stronger than I—something. I feel as though if I once discovered what that something was I should not be frightened any longer. Something definite that you could meet and say to yourself: 'There, Andrey Vassilievitch, you're not frightened of that, are you? What is there to be frightened of?... Why then, you know, I don't believe I should be frightened any more!'"

I remember that he then explained to me that he wished Nikitin had been sent instead of Semyonov. Nikitin was much more sympathetic.

"You seem very fond of Nikitin," I said.

"We are friends ... we have been friends for many years. My wife was very fond of him. I am a lonely man, Ivan Andreievitch, since the death of my wife, and to be with any one who knew her is a great happiness ... yes, a great happiness."

"And Semyonov?" I asked.

"I have nothing to say against Alexei Petrovitch," he answered stiffly.

When later I joined the others at the cottage higher up the road taken by the doctors of the Division, I discovered Trenchard in an ecstasy of happiness. He did not speak to me but his shining eyes, the eagerness with which standing back from the group he watched us all, told me everything. Marie Ivanovna had been kind to him, and when I found her in the centre of them, her whole body alert with excitement, I forgot my anger at her earlier unkindness or, if I remembered it, laid it to the charge of my own imagination or Trenchard's sensitiveness.

Indeed we were all excited. How could we fail to be! There was some big business toward, and in it we were to have our share. We were, perhaps this very day, to penetrate into the reality of the thing that for nine months now we had been watching. All of us, with our little private histories like bundles on our backs, are venturing out to try our fortune.... What are we going to find?

I remember indeed that early on that afternoon I felt the drama of the whole affair so heavily that I saw in every soldier who passed me a messenger of fate. They called me to a meal. Eat! Now! How absurd it seemed! Semyonov watched me cynically:

"Eat and then sleep," he said, "or you'll be no use to any one."

Afterwards I went back to the kitchen and slept. That sleep was the end of my melodrama. I was awakened by a rough hand on my shoulder to find it dark beyond the windows and Semyonov watching me impatiently:

"Come, get up! It's time for us to start," and then moved out. I was conscious that I was cold and irritable. I looked back with surprised contempt to my earlier dramatic emotions. I was hungry; I put on my overcoat, shivered, came out into the evening, saw the line of wagons silhouetted against the sky, listened to the perfect quiet on every side of me, yawned and was vexed to find Trenchard at my side.

"Why this is actually dull!" I thought to myself. "It is as though I were going to some dinner that I know beforehand will be exceedingly tiresome—only then I should get some food."

I was disappointed at the lack of drama in the affair. I looked at my watch—it was ten o'clock. Semyonov was arranging everything with a masterly disregard of personal feelings. He swore fine Russian oaths, abused the sanitars, always in his cold rather satirical voice, his heavy figure moving up and down the road with a practical vivid alertness that stirred my envy and also my annoyance. I felt utterly useless.

He ordered me on to my wagon in a manner that, in my present half-sleepy, half-surly mood seemed to me abominably abrupt. Trenchard climbed up, very clumsily, after me.

I leaned back on the straw, let my arms fall and lay there, flat on my back, staring straight into the sky.... With that my mood suddenly changed. I was at peace with the whole world. To-night was again thick with a heavy burden of stars that seemed to weigh like the silver lid of some mighty box heavily down, down upon us, until trees and hills and the dim Carpathians were bent flat beneath the pressure. I lying upon my back, seeing only that sheet of stars, in my nostrils the smell of the straw, rocked by the slow dreamy motion of the wagon, was filled with an exquisite ease and lethargy. I was going into battle, was I? I was to have to-night the supreme experience of my life? It might be that to-night I should die—only last week two members of the Red Cross—a nurse and a doctor—had been killed. It might be that these stars, this straw, this quiet night were round me for the last time. It did not matter to me—nothing could touch me. My soul was somewhere far away, upon some business of its own, and how happy was my body without the soul, how contented, how undisturbed! I could fancy that I should go, thus rocking, into battle and there die before my soul had time to return to me. What would my soul do then? Find some other body, or go wandering, searching for me? A star, a flash of light like a cry of happiness or of glad surprise, fell through heaven and the other stars trembled at the sight.

My wagon stopped with a jerk. Some voice asked: what the devil were we doing filling the road with our carts at the exact moment that such-and-such a Division wished to move.

I heard Semyonov's voice, very cold, official and polite. Then again: "Well, in God's name, hurry then! ... taking up the road! ... hurry, I tell you!"

On we jogged again. Trenchard's voice came to me: he had been, it might be, talking for some time.

"And so I'm not surprised, Durward, that you thought me a terrible fool to show my feelings as I've done this last fortnight. But you don't know what it is to me—to have something at last in your hands that you've dreamed of all your life and never dared to hope for: to have it and feel that at any moment it may slip away and leave you in a worse state than you were before. I'd been wishing, these last weeks, that I'd never met her, that I'd simply come to the war by myself. But now—to-day—when she spoke to me as she did, asked me to forgive her for what happened last night, my God, Durward! I to forgive her!... But I'll show her this very night what I can do—this very night! They'll give me a chance, won't they? It would be terrible if they didn't. Semyonov won't give me a chance if he can help it. What have I done to Semyonov that he should hate me? What have...."

But I didn't answer Trenchard. That part of me that had any concern with him and his affairs was far away. But his voice had stirred some more active life in me. I thought to myself now: Will there be some concrete definite moment in this affair when I shall say to myself: "Ah, there it is! There's the heart of this whole business! There's the enemy! Slay him and you have settled the matter!" or, perhaps, "Ah, now I've seen the secret. Now I've hunted the animal to his lair. This is war, this thing here. Now all my days I remain quiet. There is nothing more to fear"—or would it be perhaps that I should face something and be filled, then, with ungovernable terror so that I should run for my life, run, hide me in the hills, cover up my days so that no one shall ever find me again?...

I raised myself on my elbow and looked at the country. We jolted over a little brook, brushed through a thicket of trees, came on to a path running at the forest's foot, and saw on our left a little wooden house, a high wood fire burning in front of it. I looked at my watch. It was one o'clock. Already a very faint glow throbbed in the sky. Out of the forest, at long intervals, came a dull booming sound like the shutting of a heavy iron door.

The wagons drew up. We had arrived at our destination.

"We shall be here," I heard Semyonov say, "some five hours or so. You'd better sleep if you can."

A group of soldiers round the wood fire were motionless, their faces glowing, their bodies dark. Our wagons, drawn up together, resembled in the twilight strange beasts; the two Sisters lay down on one wagon, Semyonov, Andrey Vassilievitch, Trenchard and I on another. My irritated mood had returned. I had been the last to climb on to the straw and the others had so settled themselves that I had no room to lie flat. Semyonov's big body occupied half the wagon, Andrey Vassilievitch's boots touched my head and at intervals his whole body gave nervous jerks. It was also quite bitterly cold, which was curious enough after the warmth of the earlier nights. And always, at what seemed to be regular intervals, there came, from the forest, the banging of the iron door.

I felt a passionate irritation against Andrey Vassilievitch. Why could he not keep quiet? What, after all, was he doing here? I could hear that he was dreaming. He muttered some woman's name:

"Sasha ... Sasha ... Sasha...."

"Can't you keep still?" I whispered to him, but in the cold I myself was trembling. The dawn came at last with reluctance, flushing the air with colour, then withdrawing into cold grey clouds, then stealing out once more behind the forest in scattered strips of pale green gold, then suddenly sending up into the heaven a flock of pink clouds like a flight of birds, that spread in extending lines to the horizon, covering at last a sky now faintly blue, with rosy bars. The flame of the soldiers' fire grew faint, white mists rose in the fields, the cannon in the forest ceased and the birds began.

I sat up on the cart, looked at my sleeping companions, and thought how unpleasant they looked. Semyonov like a dead man, Andrey Vassilievitch like a happy pig, Trenchard like a child who slept after a scolding. I felt intense loneliness. I wanted some one to comfort me, to reassure me against life which seemed to me suddenly now perilous and remorseless; moreover some one seemed to be reviewing my life for me and displaying it to me, laying bare all its uselessness and insignificance.

"But I'm in no way a fine fellow," I could fancy myself crying. "I'm sleepy and cold and hungry. If you'll remove Andrey Vassilievitch's boots for me I'll lie flat on this wagon and you can let loose every shrapnel in the world over my head and I'll never stir. I thought I was interested in your war, and I'm not.... I thought no discomfort mattered to me, but I find that I dislike so much being cold and hungry that it outweighs all heroism, all sense of danger ... let me alone!"

Then something occurred. Looking down over the side of the cart I saw, to my great surprise, Marie Ivanovna.

"You!" I whispered.

"Hush!" she answered. "Come down."

I let myself down and at once she put her hand into mine.

"Walk with me just a little way," she whispered, "to those trees and back." I had noticed at once that her voice trembled; now I perceived that her whole body was shaking; her hand gave little startled quivers under mine.

"You're cold," I said.

"No, I'm not cold," she answered still in a whisper, although we were now some way from the wagons. "I'm frightened, Mr. Durward, that's what's the matter—desperately frightened."

"Nonsense," I answered her. "You! Frightened! Never!"

"But I am. I've been terribly fr-frightened all night; and that Sister Anna Petrovna, he (she sometimes confused her pronouns) sleeps like a log. How can he? I've never slept, not for a moment, and I've been so cold and every time the cannon sounded I wanted to run away.... Oh, Mr. Durward, I'm so ashamed!"

Then, suddenly, desperately clutching my hand:

"Mr. Durward, you'll never tell any one, any one never.... Promise!"

"Never a soul," I answered. "It's only because you're cold and hungry and sleepy that you think you're frightened. You're not frightened really. But wouldn't you like me to wake Trenchard and get him to come to you.... He'd be so happy?..."

She started fiercely from me. "Never! Never! Why, what can you think! You must never tell, most of all you must never tell him.... He must never know—nothing—"

The cannon began again. She caught my arm and stood with her body trembling, pressed against mine. I could feel her draw a deep breath. As I looked at her, her face white in the dawn, her large eyes staring like a child's, her body so young and slender, she seemed another creature, utterly, absolutely apart from the woman of this last fortnight.

"Look here!" I said to her sternly. "You mustn't go on like this. You've got work to do to-day. You've simply got to hold yourself in, to tell yourself that nothing can touch you. Why to-night you'll laugh at me if I remind you of this. You'll...."

But there was better tonic than my words, Semyonov's voice came to us—"Hullo, you there! It's five o'clock—we're moving."

She drew herself sharply away from me. She raised her head, smiled at me, then said:

"Thank you, Mr. Durward. It's all well now. There's Dr. Semyonov—let us go back."

She greeted him with a voice that had in it not the slightest tremor.

There comes now a difficult matter. During the later months when I was to reflect on the whole affair I saw quite clearly that that hour between our leaving the wooden house and arriving in the trenches bridged quite clearly for me the division in this business between imagination and reality: that is, I was never after this to speak of war as I would have spoken of it an hour before. I was never again to regard the paraphernalia of it with the curiosity of a stranger—I had become part of it. This hour then may be regarded as in some ways the most important of all my experiences. It is certainly the occasion to which if I were using my invention I should make the most. Here then is my difficulty.

I have nothing to say about it. There's nothing at all to be made of it....

I may say at once that there was no atom of drama in it. At one moment I was standing with Marie Ivanovna under the sunrise, at another I was standing behind a trench in the heart of the forest with a battery to my left and a battery to my right, a cuckoo somewhere not very far away, and a dead man with his feet sticking out from under the cloth that covered him peacefully beneath a tree at my side. There had, of course, been that drive in the wagons, bumping over the uneven road whilst the sun rose gallantly in the heavens and the clanging of the iron door grew, with every roll of our wheels, louder and louder. But it was rather as though I had been lifted in a sheet from one life—a life of speculation, of viewing war from a superior and safe distance, of viewing indeed all catastrophe and reality from that same distance—into the other. I had been caught up, had hung for a moment in midair, had been "planted" in this new experience. For us all there must have been at this moment something of this passing from an old life into a new one, and yet I dare swear that not for any one of us was there any drama, any thrill, any excitement. We stood, a rather lonely little group, in the forest clearing whilst the soldiers in the trench flung us a careless glance, then turned back to their business of the day with an indifference that showed how ordinary and drab a thing custom had made it.

Yes, we made a desolate little group. Semyonov had gone to a house on the farther side of the road up which we had come, a house that flew the Red Cross flag. We had only the right to care for the wounded of certain Divisions and our presence had to be reported. We were left then, Marie Ivanovna, Anna Petrovna, Andrey Vassilievitch, Trenchard and I, all rather close together, uncomfortable, desolate and shy, as boys feel on their first day at school. The battery on our left was very near to us and we could see the sharp flash of its flame behind the trees. The noise that it made was terrific, a sharp, angry, clumsy noise, as though some huge giant clad in mail armour was flinging his body, in a violent rage, against an iron door that echoed through an empty house—my same iron door that I had heard all night. The rage of the giant spread beyond his immediate little circle of trees and one wondered at the men in the trenches because they were indifferent to his temper.

The noise of the more distant batteries was still, as it had been before, like the clanging of many iron doors very mild and gentle against the clamour of our own enraged fury. The Austrian reply seemed like the sleepy echo of this confusion, so sleepy and pleasant that one felt almost friendly to the enemy.

Our own battery was inconsistent in his raging. Had he only chosen to fling himself at his door every three minutes, say, or even every minute, we could have prepared ourselves, but he was moved by nothing, apparently, but his own irrational impulse. There would be a pause of two minutes, then three furious explosions, then a pause of five minutes, then another explosion.... I mastered quickly my impulse to leap into the air at every report, by a kind of prolonged extension in my mind of one report into another. Little Andrey Vassilievitch was not so successful. At each explosion his body jerked as though it had been worked by wires; then he glanced round to see whether any one had noticed his agitation, then drew himself up, brushed off imaginary dust from his uniform, coughed and frowned. Trenchard stood close to Marie Ivanovna and looked at her anxiously once or twice as though he would like to speak to her, but she, holding herself very stiffly, watched with sternness the whole world as though she personally had arranged the spectacle and was responsible for its success.

Soon Semyonov came back and said that he must go on to some further trenches to discover the best position for us. To my intense surprise Andrey Vassilievitch asked whether he might accompany him. I fancy that he felt that he would venture anything to escape our adjacency to the battery.

So they departed, leaving us more forlorn than before We sat down on the stretchers: Anna Petrovna, fat, heavy, phlegmatic, silent; Marie Ivanovna silent too but with a look now of expectation in her eyes as though she knew that something was coming for her very shortly; Trenchard near her, trying to be cheerful, but conscious of the dead soldier under the tree from whom he seemed unable to remove his eyes. There was, in the open space near us, a kipiatilnik, that is, a large boiler on wheels in which tea is made. To this the soldiers were crowding with their tin cans; the cuckoo, far away now, continued his cry....

At long intervals, out of the forest, a wounded soldier would appear. He seemed to be always the same figure, sometimes wounded in the head, sometimes in the leg, sometimes in the stomach, sometimes in the hand—but always the same, with a look in his eyes of mild protest because this had happened to him, also a look of dumb confidence that some one somewhere would make things right for him. He came either to us or to the Red Cross building across the road, according to his company. One soldier with a torn thumb cried bitterly, looking at his thumb and shaking his head at it, but he alone showed any emotion. The others suffered the sting of the iodine without a word, walking off when they were bandaged, or carried by our sanitars on the stretchers, still with that look of wonder and trust in their eyes.

And how glad we were when there was any work to do! The sun rose high in the sky, the morning advanced, Semyonov and Andrey Vassilievitch did not return. For the greater part of the time we did not speak, nor move. I was conscious of an increasing rage against the battery. I felt that if it was to cease I might observe, be interested, feel excitement—as it was, it kept everything from me. It kept everything from me because it insistently demanded my attention, like a vulgar garrulous neighbour who persists in his tiresome story. Its perpetual hammering had soon its physical effect. A sick headache crept upon me, seized me, held me. I might look at the soldiers, sleeping now like dead men in the trench, I might look at the Red Cross flag lazily flapping in the breeze across the road, I might look at the corpse with the soiled marble feet under the tree, I might look at Trenchard and Marie Ivanovna silent and unhappy on the stretchers, on Anna Petrovna comfortably slumbering with an open mouth, I might listen to the distant batteries, to the sudden quick impatient chatter of the machine guns, to the rattling give-and-take of the musketry somewhere far away where the river was, I might watch the cool green hollows of the forest glades, the dark sleepy shadows, the bright patches of burning sky between the branches, I might say to myself that all these things together made the impression of my first battle ... and then would know, in my heart, that there was no impression at all, no thrill, no drama, no personality—only a sick throb in my head and a cold hand upon my chest and a desire to fling myself into any horror, any danger, if I could but escape this indigestible monotony....

Once Trenchard, treading very softly as though every one around him were asleep, came across and talked to me.

"You know," he said in a whisper, "this isn't at all what I expected."

"You needn't whisper," I answered irritably, "that battery's making such a noise that I can't hear anything you say."

"Yes, isn't it!" he said with a little sigh. "It's very unpleasant indeed. Do you think Semyonov's forgotten us? We've been here a good many hours and we aren't doing very much."

"No," I answered. "We're doing nothing except get sick headaches."

There was a pause, then he said:

"Where is everything?"

"Everything?—What?"

"Well, the battle, for instance!"

"Oh, that's down the hill, I suppose. We're trying to cross the river and they're trying to prevent us."

"Yes," he answered. "But that isn't exactly what I mean.... It's hard to explain, but even if we were to see our soldiers trying to cross the river and the Austrians trying to prevent them that wouldn't be—well, wouldn't be exactly the real thing, would it? It would only be a kind of side-show, rather unimportant like that dead man there!"

But my headache prevented my interest in his speculations. I said nothing.

He added as though to himself:

"Perhaps each individual soldier sees the real thing for himself but can't express what he sees...."

As I still made no answer, with another little sigh he got up and walked back, on tip-toe, to the side of Marie Ivanovna.

Then suddenly, in the early hours of the afternoon, to our intense relief, Semyonov and Andrey Vassilievitch appeared. Semyonov was, as ever, short, practical, and unemotional.

"Been a long time, I'm afraid. We found it difficult to see exactly where would be the best place. And, after all, we've got to separate.... One Sister's wanted at the Red Cross over there. They've asked for our help. The other will come with me on to the Position until this evening. You three gentlemen, if you'll be so good, will wait here until a wagon comes. Then it will take you down to the trenches at the bottom of the hill. Then, if you don't mind, I would like you to wait until dusk when we shall go out to fetch the wounded.... Is that clear?"

We answered yes.

"Now which Sister will come with me? Marie Ivanovna, I think it would interest you. No danger, except a stray shrapnel or two. Will you come?"

There leapt upon us then, with an agitation that seemed to silence the very battery itself, Trenchard's voice:

"No.... No ... Marie. No, it's dangerous. Semyonov says so. Your first day...."

He spoke in English, his voice trembling. I turned to see his face white, his eyes wide open and at the same time blind; he passionately addressed himself to Marie Ivanovna and to her alone.

But she turned impatiently.

"Why, of course, Doctor. I'm ready at once."

Trenchard put his hand on her arm.

"You are not to go—Marie, do you hear? I have a right ... I tell you, you are not to go!"

"Don't be so stupid, John," she shook off his arm. "Please, Doctor, I'm ready."

Semyonov turned to Trenchard with a smile: "Mr. (they all called him Mr. now), it will be quite well ... I will look after her."

"You ... you" (Trenchard could not control his voice), "you can't prevent shrapnel—bullets. You don't care, you...."

Semyonov's voice was sharp: "I think it better that Sister Marie Ivanovna should come with me. You understand, the rest of you.... We shall meet at dusk."

Trenchard only said "Marie ..." then turned away from us. Anna Petrovna, who had said nothing during this scene and had, indeed, seemed to be oblivious of it, plunged with her heavy clumsy walk across the road to the Red Cross house. The Doctor and Marie Ivanovna disappeared behind the trench. I was, as was always my case with Trenchard, both sympathetic and irritated. It was difficult for him, of course, but what did he expect the girl to do? Could he have supposed for a single moment that she would remain? Could it be possible that she knew him so little as that? And why make a scene now before Semyonov when he obviously could do nothing? I knew, moreover, with a certainty that was almost ironic in its clarity, that Marie Ivanovna did not love, did not, perhaps, even care for him. By what moment in Petrograd, a moment flaming with their high purposes and the purple shadows of a Russian "white night," had she been entranced into some glorious vision of him? On the very day that followed, she had known, I was convinced, her mistake. At the station she had known it, and instead of the fine Sir Galahad "without reproach" of the previous night she saw some figure that, had she been English born, would have appeared to her as Alice's White Knight perchance, or at best the warm-hearted Uncle Toby, or that most Christian of English heroes—Parson Adams. I could imagine that life had been so impulsive, so straightforward, so simple a thing to her that this sudden implication in an affair complicated and even dishonest caused her bitter disquiet. Looking back now I could trace again and again the sudden flashes, through her happiness, of this distress.

He perhaps should have perceived it, but I could understand that he could not believe that his treasure had at last after all these years been given to him for so brief a moment. He could not, he would not, believe it. Well, I knew that his eyes must very soon be opened to the truth....

As I turned to see him sitting on the stretcher with his back to me, his head hanging a little as though it were too heavy for his neck, his back bent, his long arms fallen loose at his sides, I thought that Alice's White Knight he, in solemn truth, presented.

He had a talent for doing things to his uniform. His cap, instead of being raised in front, was flat, his jacket bulged out above his belt, and the straps on his boot had broken from their holdings. He filled the pockets of his trousers, in moments of absent-minded absorption, with articles that he fancied that he would need—sometimes food, black bread and sausage, sometimes a large pocket-knife, a folding drinking glass, a ball of string, a notebook. These things protruded, or gave his clothes a strange bulky look, fat in some places, thin in others. As I saw him his shoulder-blades seemed to pierce his coat: I could fancy with what agitation his hands were clenched.

We sat down, the three of us together, and again the battery leapt upon us. Now the sun was hot above the trees and the effect of the noise behind us was that we ourselves, every two or three minutes, were caught up, flung to the ground, recovered, breathless, exhausted, only to be hurled again!

How miserable we were, how lost, how desolate, Trenchard hearing in every sound the death of his lady, Andrey Vassilievitch dreaming, I fancy, that he had been caught in some cage out of which he would never again escape. I, sick, almost blind with headache, and yet exasperated, irritated by the emptiness of it all. If only we might run down that hill! There surely we should find....

At the very moment when the battery had finished as it seemed to me its work of smashing my head into pulp the wagon arrived.

"Now," I thought to myself as I climbed on to the straw, "I shall begin to be excited!" We, all three of us, kneeling on the cart, peered forward into the dim blue afternoon. We were very silent—only once Trenchard said to me, "Perhaps we shall find her down here: where we're going. What do you think, Durward?"

"I'm afraid not!" I answered. "But still she'll be all right. Semyonov will look after her!"

"Oh! Semyonov!" he answered.

How joyful we were to leave our battery behind us. As the trees closed around it we could fancy its baffled rage. Other batteries now seemed to draw nearer to us and the whole forest was filled with childish quarrelling giants; but as we began to bump down the hill out of the forest stranger sounds attacked us. On either side of us were cornfields and out of the heart of those from under our very feet as it seemed there were explosions of a strange stinging metallic kind—not angry and human as the battery had been, but rather like some huge bottle cracking in the sun. These huge bottles—one could fancy them green and shining somewhere in the corn—cracked one after another; positively the sound intensified the heat of the sun upon one's head. There were too now, for the first time in our experience, shrapnel. They were not over us, but ran somewhere on our right across the valley. Their sound was "fireworks" and nothing more—so that alarm at their gentle holiday temper was impossible. Brock's Fireworks on a Thursday evening at the Crystal Palace, oneself a small boy sitting with both hands between one's knees, one's mouth open, a damp box of chocolates on one's lap, the murmured "Ah ..." of the happy crowd as the little gentle "Pop!" showed green and red against the blue night sky. Ah! there was the little "Pop!" and after it a tiny curling cloud of smoke in the air, the whole affair so gentle, so kind even. There! sighing overhead they go! Five, six little curls of smoke, and then beneath our very horses' feet again a huge green bottle cracking in the sun!

And with all this noise not a living soul to be seen! We had before us as we slowly bumped down the hill a fair view. The river was hidden from us, but there was a little hamlet guarded happily by a green wood; there was a line of fair hills, fields of corn, and the long dusty white road. Not a soul to be seen, only our bumping cart and, now and then, against the burning sky those little curling circles of smoke. The world slumbered....

Suddenly from the ditch at the side of the road a soldier appeared, spoke to our driver and disappeared again.

"What did he say?" I asked.

"He says, your Honour, that we must hasten. We may be hit."

"Hit here—on this road?"

"Tak totchno."

"Well, hurry then."

I caught a little frightened sigh behind me from Andrey Vassilievitch, whom the events of the day had frozen into horror-stricken silence. We hurried, bumping along; at the bottom of the hill there was a farmhouse. From behind it an officer appeared.

"What are you doing there? You're under fire.... Red Cross? Ah yes, we had a message about you. Dr. Semyonov?... Yes. Please come this way. Hurry, please!"

We were led across the farmyard and almost tumbled into a trench at the farther end of it.

It wasn't until I felt some one touch my shoulder that I realised my position. We were sitting, the three of us, in a slanting fashion with our backs to the earthworks of the trench. To our right, under an improvised round roof, a little dried-up man like a bee, with his tunic open at the neck and a beard of some days on his chin, was calling down a telephone.

Next to me on the left a smart young officer, of a perfect neatness and even dandiness, was eating his supper, which his servant, crouching in front of him, ladled with a spoon out of a tin can. Beyond him again the soldiers in a long line under the farm wall were sewing their clothes, eating, talking in whispers, and one of them reading a newspaper aloud to himself.

A barn opposite us in ruins showed between its bare posts the green fields beyond. Now and then a soldier would move across the yard to the door of the farm, and he seemed to slide with something between walking and running, his shoulders bent, his head down. The sun, low now, showed just above the end of the farm roof and the lines of light were orange between the shadows of the barn. All the batteries seemed now very far away; the only sound in the world was the occasional sigh of the shrapnel. The farmyard was bathed in the peace of the summer evening.

The Colonel, when he had finished his conversation with some humorous sally that gave him great pleasure, greeted us.

"Very glad to see you, gentlemen.... Two Englishmen! Well, that's the Alliance in very truth ... yes.... How's London, gentlemen? Yes, golubchik, that small tin—the grey one. No, durak, the small one. Dr. Semyonov sent a message. Pray make yourselves comfortable, but don't raise your heads. They may turn their minds in this direction at any moment again. We've had them once already this afternoon. Eh, Piotr Ivanovitch (this to the smart young officer), that would have made your Ekaterina Petrovna jump in her sleep—ha, ha, ha—oh, yes, but I can see her jumping.... Hullo, telephone—Give it here! That you, Ivan Leontievitch? No ... very well for the moment.... Two Englishmen here sitting in my trench—truth itself! Well, what about the Second 'Rota'? Are they coming down?... Yeh Bogu, I don't know! What do you say?..."

The young officer, in a very gentle and melodious voice, offered Trenchard, who was sitting next to him, some supper.

"One of these cutlets?"

Trenchard, blushing and stammering, refused.

"A cigarette, then?"

Trenchard again refused and Piotr Ivanovitch, having done his duty, relapsed into his muffled elegance. We sat very quietly there; Trenchard staring with distressed eyes in front of him. Andrey Vassilievitch, very uncomfortable, his fat body sliding forward on the slant, pulling itself up, then sliding again— always he maintained his air of importance, giving his cough, twisting the ends of his moustache, staring, fiercely, at some one suddenly that he might disconcert him, patting, with his plump little hands, his clothes.

The shadows lengthened and a great green oak that hung over the barn seemed, as the evening advanced, to grow larger and larger and to absorb into its heart all the flaming colours of the day, to press them into its dark shadow and to hide them, safe and contented, until another morning.

I sat there and gradually, caught, as it seemed to me, into a world of whispers and half-lights, I slipped forward a little down into the dark walls of the trench and half-slumbered, half clung still to the buzzing voice of the Colonel, the languid replies of the young officer. I felt then that some one was whispering to me that my real adventure was about to begin. I could see quite plainly, like a road up which I had gone, the events of the day behind me. I saw the ride under the stars, the cold red dawn. Marie Ivanovna standing beneath my cart, the sudden battery and the desolate hours of waiting, the wounded men stumbling out of the forest, the ride down the hill and the green bottles bursting in the sun, the sudden silences and the sudden sounds, my own weariness and discomfort and loneliness and now Something— was it the dark green oak that bent down and hid the world for me?—whispered, "You're drawing near—you're close—you're almost there.... In a moment you will see ... you will see ... you will see...."

Somewhere the soldiers were singing, and then all sounds ceased. We were standing, many of us, in the dark, the great oak and many other giant trees were about us and the utter silence was like a sudden plunge into deep water on a hot day. We were waiting, ready for the Creature, breathless with suspense.

"Now!" some one cried, and instantly there was such a roar that I seemed to be lifted by it far into the sky, held, rocked, then dropped gently. I woke to find myself standing up in the trench, my hands to my ears. I was aware first that the sky had changed from blue into a muddy grey, then that dust and an ugly smell were in my eyes, my mouth, my nose. I remembered that I repeated stupidly, again and again: "What? what? what?" Then the grey sky slowly fell away as though it were pushed by some hand and I saw the faint evening blue, with (so strange and unreal they seemed) silver-pointed stars. I caught my breath and realised that now the whole right corner of the barn was gone. The field stretched, a dark shadow, to the edge of the yard. In the ground where the stakes of the barn had been there was a deep pit; scattered helter-skelter were bricks, pieces of wood, and over it all a cloud of thin fine dust that hovered and swung a little like grey silk. The line of soldiers was crouched back into the trench as though it had been driven by some force. From, as it appeared, a great distance, I heard the Colonel's voice: "Slava Bogu, another step to the right and we'd not have had time to say 'good-bye.'... Get in there, you ... with your head out like that, do you want another?" I was conscious then of Andrey Vassilievitch sitting huddled on the ground of the trench, his head tucked into his chest.

"You're not hurt, are you?" I said, bending down to him,

He got up and to my surprise seemed quite composed. He was rubbing his eyes as though he had waked from sleep.

"Not at all," he answered in his shrill little voice. "No.... What a noise! Did you hear it, Ivan Andreievitch?"

Did I hear it? A ridiculous question!

"But I assure you I was not alarmed," he said eagerly, turning round to the young officer, who was rather red in the face but otherwise unruffled. "The first time that one has been so close to me. What a noise!"

Trenchard searched in his pockets for something.

"What is it?" I asked.

"My handkerchief!" he answered. "So dusty after that. It's in my eyes!"

He tumbled on to the ground a large clasp pocket-knife, a hunk of black bread, a cigarette-case and some old letters. "I had one," he muttered anxiously. "Somewhere, I know...."

I heard the Colonel's voice again. "No one touched! There's some more of their precious ammunition wasted.... What about your Ekaterina, Piotr Ivanovitch—Ho, ho, ho!... Here, golubchik, the telephone!... Hullo! Hullo!"

For myself I had the irritation that one might feel had a boy thrown a stone over the wall, broken a window and run away. Moreover, I felt that again I had missed—IT. Always round the corner, always just out of sight, always mocking one's clumsy pursuit. And still, even now, I felt no excitement, no curiosity. My feet had not yet touched the enchanted ground....

The trench had at once slipped back into its earlier composure. The dusk was now creeping down the hill; with every stir of the breeze more stars were blown into the sky; the oak was all black now like a friendly shadow protecting me.

"There'll be no more for a while," said the Colonel. He was right. There was stillness; no battery, however distant, no pitter-patter of rifle fire, no chattering report of the machine guns.

Men began to cross the yard, slowly, without caution. The dusk caught us so that I could not see the Colonel's face; a stream that cut the field, hidden in the day, was now suddenly revealed by a grinning careless moon.

Then a soldier crossed the yard to us, told us that Dr. Semyonov wished us to start and had sent us a guide; the wagons were ready.

At that instant, whence I know not, for the first time that day, excitement leapt upon me.

Events had hitherto passed before me like the shadowed film of a cinematograph; it had been as though some one had given me glimpses of a life, an adventure, a country with which I should later have some concern but whose boundaries I was not yet to cross. Now, suddenly, whether it was because of the dark and the silence I cannot say, I had become, myself, an actor in the affair. It was not simply that we were given something definite to do—we had had wounded during the morning—it was rather that, as in the children's game we were "hot," we had drawn in a moment close to some one or something of whose presence we were quite distinctly aware. As we walked across the yard into the long low field, speaking in whispers, watching a shaft of light, perhaps some distant projector that trembled in pale white shadows on the horizon, we seemed to me to be, in actual truth, the hunters of Trenchard's dream.

Never, surely, before, had I known the world so silent. Under the hedges that lined the field there were soldiers like ghosts; our own wagons, with the sanitars walking beside them, moved across the ground without even the creak of a wheel. Semyonov was to meet us in an hour's time at a certain crossroad. I was given the command of the party. I was now, in literal truth, breathlessly excited. My heart was beating in my breast like some creature who makes running leaps at escape. My tongue was dry and my brain hot. But I was happy ... happy with a strange exaltation that was unlike any emotion that I had known before. It was in part the happiness that I had known sometimes in Rugby football or in tennis when the players were evenly matched and the game hard, but it was more than that. It had in it something of the happiness that I have known, after many days at sea, on the first view of land—but it was more than that. Something of the happiness of possessing, at last, some object which one has many days desired and never hoped to attain—but more, too, than that. Something of the happiness of danger or pain that one has dreaded and finds, in actual truth, give way before one's resolution—but more, again, than that. This happiness, this exultation that I felt now but dimly, and was to know more fully afterwards (but never, alas, as my companions were to know it) is the subject of this book. The scent of it, the full revelation of it, has not, until now, been my reward; I can only, as a spectator, watch that revelation as it came afterwards to others more fortunate than I. But what I write is the truth as far as I, from the outside, have seen it. If it is not true, this book has no value whatever.

We were warned by the soldier who guarded us not to walk in a group and we stole now, beneath a garden-wall, white under the moon, in a long line. I could hear Trenchard behind me stumbling over the stones and ruts, walking as he always did with little jerks, as though his legs were beyond his control. We came then on to the high road, which was so white and clear in the moonlight that it seemed as though the whole Austrian army must instantly whisper to themselves: "Ah, there they are!" and fire. The ditch to our right, as far as I could see, was lined with soldiers, hidden by the hedge behind them, their rifles just pointing on to the white surface of the land. Our guide asked them their division and was answered in a whisper. The soldiers were ghosts: there was no one, save ourselves, alive in the whole world....

Then a little incident occurred. I was walking in the rear of our wagons that I might see that all were there. I felt a touch on my arm and found Andrey Vassilievitch standing in the middle of the road. His face, staring at me as though I were a stranger, expressed desperate determination.

"Come on," I said. "We've no time to waste."

"I'm not coming," he whispered back. His voice was breathless as though he had been running.

"Nonsense," I answered roughly, and I put my hand on his arm. His body trembled in jerks and starts.

"It's madness ... this road ... the moon.... Of course they'll fire.... We'll all be killed. But it isn't ... it isn't ... I can't move...."

"You must move.... Come, Andrey Vassilievitch, you've been brave enough all day. There's no danger, I tell you. See how quiet everything is. You must...."

"I can't.... It's nothing ... nothing to do with me.... It's awful all day—and now this!"

I thought of Marie Ivanovna early in the morning. I looked down the road and saw that the wagons were slowly moving into the distant shadows.

"You must come," I repeated. "We can't leave you here. Don't think of yourself. And nothing can touch you—nothing, I tell you."

"I'll go back, I must. I can't go on."

"Go back? How can you? Where to? You can't go back to the trench. We shan't know where to find you." A furious anger seized me; I caught his arm. "I'll leave you, if you like. There are other things more important."

I move away from him. He looked down the long road, looked back.

"Oh, I can't ... I can't," he repeated.

"What did you come for?" I whispered furiously. "What did you think war was?... Well, good-bye, do as you please!"

As I drew away I saw a look of desperate determination in his eyes. He looked at me like a dog who expects to be beaten. Then what must have been one of the supreme moments of his life came to him. I saw him struggle to command, with the effort of his whole soul, his terror. For a moment he wavered. He made a hopeless gesture with his hand, took two little steps as though he would run into the hedge amongst the soldiers and hide there, then suddenly walked past me, quickly, towards the wagons, with his own absurd little strut, with his head up, giving his cough, looking, after that, neither to the right, nor to the left.

In silence we caught up the wagons. Soon, at some cross-roads, they came to a pause. The guide was waiting for me. "It would be better, your Honour," he whispered, "for the wagons to stay here. We shall go now simply with the stretchers...."

We left the wagons and, some fifteen of us, turned off down a lane to the left. Sometimes there were soldiers in the hedges, sometimes they met us, slipping from shadow to shadow. Always we asked whether they knew of any wounded. We found a wounded soldier groaning under the hedge. One leg was soaked in blood and he gave little shrill desperate cries as we lifted him on to the stretcher. Another soldier, lying on the road in the moonlight, murmured incessantly: "Bojé moi! Bojé moi! Bojé moi!" But they were all ghosts. We alone, in that familiar and yet so unreal world, were alive. When a stretcher was filled, four sanitars turned back with it to the wagons, and we were soon a very small party. We arrived at a church—a large fantastic white church with a green turret that I had seen from the opposite hill in the morning. Then it had seemed small and very remote. I had been told that much firing had been centring round it, and it seemed now for me very strange that we should be standing under its very shadow, its outline so quiet and grave under the moon, with its churchyard, a little orchard behind it, and a garden, scenting the night air, close at hand. Here in the graveyard there was a group of wounded soldiers, in their eyes that look of faithful expectation of certain relief. Our stretchers were soon full.

We were about to turn back when suddenly the road behind us was filled with shadows. As we came out of the churchyard an officer stepped forward to meet us. We saluted and shook hands. He seemed a boy, but stood in front of his men with an air as though he commanded the whole of this world of ghosts.

"What are you doing here?" he asked.

We explained.

"Well, if you'll excuse me, you'd better make haste. An attack very shortly ... yes. I should advise you to be out of this. Petrogradsky Otriad? Yes ... very glad to have the pleasure...."

We left him, his men a grey cloud behind him, and when we had taken a few steps he seemed, with his young air of importance, his happy serious courtesy, to have been called out of the ground, then, with all his shadows behind him, to have been caught up into the air. These were not figures that had anything to do with the little curling wreaths of smoke, the bottles cracking in the sun, our furious giants of the morning.

"Ah, Bojé moi, Bojé moi!" sighed the wounded.... It was impossible, in such a world of dim shadow, that there should ever be any other sound again.

My excitement had never left me; I had had no doubt, during this last half-hour, that I was on the Enchanted Ground of the Enemy, so stray and figurative had been my impressions all day. Now they were all gathered into this half-hour and the whole affair received its climax. "Ah," I thought to myself, "if I might only stay here now I should draw closer and closer—I should make my discovery, hunt him down. But just when I am on the verge I must leave it all. Ah, if I could but stay!"

Nevertheless we hastened. The world, in spite of the ghosts, was real enough for us to be conscious of that attack looming behind us. We found our wagons, transferred our wounded, then hurried down the road. We found the cross-roads and there, waiting for us, Semyonov and Marie Ivanovna. Standing in the moonlight, commanding, as it seemed to me, all of us, even Semyonov, she was a very different figure from the frightened girl of the early morning. Now her life was in her eyes, her body inflamed with the fire of the things that had come to her. So young in experience was she, so ignorant of all earlier adventure, that she could well be seized, utterly and completely, by her new vision ... possessed by some vision she was.

And that vision was not Trenchard. Seeing her, he hurried towards her, with a glad cry:

"Ah, you are safe!"

But she did not notice him.

"Quick, this way!... Yes, the stretchers here.... No, I have everything.... At once. There is little time!"

The wounded were laid on the stretchers in the square of the cross-roads. Semyonov and Marie Ivanovna bandaged them under the moonlight and with the aid of electric-torches. On every side of me there were little dialogues: "No ... not there. More this way. Yes, that bandage will do. It's fresh. Hold up his leg. No, durak, under the knee there.... Where's the lint?... Turn him a little—there—like that. Horosho, golubchik. Seitchass! No, turn it back over the thigh. Now, once more ... that's it. What's that— bullet or shrapnel?... Take it back again, over the shoulder.... Yes, twice!"

Once I caught sight of Trenchard, hurrying to be useful with the little bottle of iodine, stumbling over one of the stretchers, causing the wounded man to cry out.

Then Semyonov's voice angrily:

"Tchort! Who's that?... Ah, Meester! of course!"

Then Marie Ivanovna's voice: "I've finished this, Alexei Petrovitch.... That's all, isn't it?"

These voices were all whispers, floating from one side of the road to the other. The wounded men were lifted back on to the wagons. We moved off again; Semyonov, Trenchard, Marie Ivanovna and I were now sitting together.

We left the flat fields where we had been so busy. Very slowly we began to climb the hill down which I had come this afternoon. Behind me was a great fan of country, black now under a hidden moon, dead as though our retreat from it, depriving it of the last proofs of life, had flung it back into non-existence. Before us was the black forest. Not a sound save the roll of our wheels and, sometimes, a cry from one of the wounded soldiers, not a stir of wind....

I looked back. Without an instant's warning that dead world, as a match is set to a waiting bonfire, broke into flame. A thousand rockets rose, soaring, in streams of light into the dark sky; the fields that had been vapour ran now with light. A huge projector, the eye, as it seemed to me, of that enemy for whom I had all day been searching, slowly wheeled across the world, cutting a great path across the plain, picking houses and trees and fields out of space, then dropping them back again. The rockets were gold and green, sometimes as it seemed ringed with fire, sometimes cold like dead moons, sometimes sparkling and quivering like great stars. And with this light the whole world crackled into sound as though the sky, a vast china plate, had been smashed by some angry god and been flung, in a million pieces, to earth. The rifle-fire rose from horizon to horizon like a living thing. Now the shrapnel rose, breaking on the dark sky in flashes of fire. Suddenly some house was burning! The flames rose in a column, breaking into tongues that advanced and retreated, climbed and fell again. In the farthest distance other houses had caught and their glow trembled in faint yellow light fading into shadow when the projector found them. With a roar at our back our own cannon began; the world bellowed and shook and trembled at our feet.

We reached the top of the hill. I caught one final vision, the picture seeming to sway with all its lights, its shadows, its giant eye that governed it, its colours and its mist, like a tapestry blown by wind. I saw in our wagon, their faces lighted by the fire, Semyonov and Marie Ivanovna. Semyonov knelt on the wooden barrier of the cart, his figure outlined square and strong. She was kneeling behind him, her hands on his shoulders. Her face was exultant, victorious. She seemed to me the inspirer of that scene, to have created it, to hold it now with the authority of her gaze.

Behind her Trenchard was in shadow.

We were on the hill-top, the cannon, as it seemed, on every side of us. We hung for a moment so, the sky flaming up to our feet. Then we had fallen down between the woods, every step muffling the sounds. Everything was dark as though a curtain had been dropped.

Semyonov turned round to me.

"Well," he said, "there's your battle.... You've been in the thick of it to-day!"

I saw his eyes turned to Marie Ivanovna as though already he possessed her.

I was suddenly tired, disappointed, exhausted.

"We've not been in the thick of it," I answered. "We have missed it—all day we have missed it!"

I tried to settle down in my wagon. "I beg your pardon," I said irritably to Trenchard, "but your boot is in my neck!"

CHAPTER IV

NIKITIN

But this is not my story. If I have hitherto taken the chief place it is because, in some degree, the impressions of Trenchard, Marie Ivanovna, Andrey Vassilievitch must, during those first days, have run with my own. We had all been brought to the same point—that last vision from the hill of the battle of S— and from that day we were no longer apprentices.

I now then retire. What happened to myself during the succeeding months is of no matter. But two warnings may be offered. The first is that it must not be supposed that the experiences of myself, of Trenchard, of Nikitin in this business found their parallel in any other single human being alive. It would be quite possible to select every individual member of our Otriad and to prove from their case that the effect of war upon the human soul—whether Russian or English—was thus and thus. A study, for example, might be made of Anna Petrovna to show that the effect of war is simply nothing at all, that any one who pretends to extract cases and contrasts from the contact of war with the soul is simply peddling in melodrama. Anna Petrovna herself would certainly have been of that opinion. Or one might select Sister K— and prove from her case that the effect of war was to display the earthly failings and wickedness of mankind, that it was a punishment hurled by an irate God upon an unrepentant people and that any one who saw beauty or courage in such a business was a sham sentimentalist. Sister K— would take a gloomy joy in such a denunciation. Or if one selected the boy Goga it would be simply to state that war was an immensely jolly business, in which one stood the chance of winning the Georgian medal and thus triumphing over one's schoolfellows, in which people were certainly killed but "it couldn't happen to oneself"; meals were plentiful, there were horses to ride, one was spoken to pleasantly by captains and even generals. Moreover one wore a uniform.

Or if Molozov, our chief, were questioned he would most certainly say that war, as he saw it, was mainly a business of diplomacy, a business of keeping the people around one in good temper, the soldiers in good order, the generals and their staffs in good appetite, the other Red Cross organisations in good self-conceit, and himself in good health. All these things he did most admirably and he had, moreover, a heart that felt as deeply for Russia as any heart in the world; but see the matter psychologically or even dramatically he would not. He had his own "nerves" and on occasion he displayed them, but war was for him, entirely, a thing of training opposed to training, strategy opposed to strategy, method and system opposed to method and system. For our doctors again, war was half an affair of blood and bones, half an affair of longing for home and children. The army doctors contemplated our voluntary efforts with a certain irony. What could we understand of war when we might, if we pleased, return home at any moment? Why, it was simply a picnic to us.... No, they saw in it no drama whatever.

Nevertheless how are we to be assured that these others, Anna Petrovna, Sister K—, Goga, the Doctors had not their own secret view? The subject here is simply the attitude of certain private persons with whom I was allowed some intimacy ... for the rest one has no right to speak.

There comes then the second difficulty, namely: that of Nikitin, Andrey Vassilievitch, Semyonov and Marie Ivanovna one can only present a foreign point of view. Of Nikitin and Andrey Vassilievitch, at least, I was the friend, but however deeply a Russian admits an Englishman into friendship he can, to the very last, puzzle, confuse, utterly surprise him. The Russian character seems, superficially, with its lack of restraint, its idealism, its impracticality, its mysticism, its material simplicities, to be so readily grasped that the surprise that finally remains is the more dumbfounding. Perhaps after all it is the very closeness of our resemblance the one to the other that confuses us. It is, perhaps, that in the Russians' soul the East can never be reconciled to the West. It is perhaps that the Russian never reveals his secret ideal even to himself; far distant is it then from his friend. It may be that towards other men the Russian is indifferent and towards women his relation is so completely sexual that his true character is hidden from her. Whatever it be that surprise remains. For to those whom Russia and her people draw back again and again, however sternly they may resist, this sure truth stands: that here there is a mystery, a mystery that may never be discovered. In the very soul of Russia the mystery is stirring; here the restlessness, the eagerness, the disappointment, the vision of the pursuit is working; and some who are outside her gates she has drawn into that same search.

I am not sure whether I may speak of Nikitin as my friend. I believe that no one in our Otriad save Trenchard could make, with truth, this claim. But for his own reasons or, perhaps, for no reason at all, he chose me on two occasions as his confidant, and of these two occasions I can recall every detail.

We returned that night from S— to find that the whole Otriad had settled in the village of M—, where I myself had been the night before. We were all living in an empty deserted farmhouse, with a yard, a big orchard, wide barns and a wild overrun garden. We were, I think, a little disappointed at the very languid interest that the history of our adventures roused, but the truth was that the wounded had begun to arrive in great numbers and there was no time for travellers' stories.

A dream, I know, yesterday's experiences seemed to me as I settled down to the business that had filled so much of my earlier period at the war. Here, with the wounded, I was at home—the bare little room, the table with the bottles and bandages and scissors, the basins and dishes, the air ever thicker and thicker with that smell of dried blood, unwashed bodies, and iodine that is like no other smell in the world. The room would be crowded, the sanitars supporting legs and arms and heads, nurses dashing to the table for bandages or iodine or scissors, three or four stretchers occupying the floor of the room with the soldiers who were too severely wounded to sit or stand, these soldiers often utterly quiet, dying perhaps, or watching with eyes that realised only dreams and shadows, the little window square, the strip of sky, the changing colours of the day; then the sitting soldiers, on ordinary of a marvellous and most simple patience, watching the bandaging of their arms and hands and legs, whispering sometimes "Bojé moi! Bojé moi!" dragging themselves up from their desperate struggle for endurance to answer the sanitars who asked their name, their regiments, the nature of their wounds. Sometimes they would talk, telling how the thing had happened to them:

"And there, your Honour, before I could move, she had come—such a noise—eh, eh, a terrible thing—I called out 'Zemliac. Here it is!' I said, and he...."

But as a rule they were very quiet, starting perhaps at the sting of the iodine, asking for a bandage to be tighter or not so tight, sometimes suddenly slipping in a faint to the ground, and then apologising afterwards. And in their eyes always that look as though, very shortly, they would hear some story so marvellous that it would compensate for all their present pain and distress. There would be the doctors, generally two at a time—Semyonov, unmoved, rough apparently in his handling of the men but always accomplishing his work with marvellous efficiency, abusing the nurses and sanitars without hesitation if they did not do as he wished, but never raising his soft ironic voice, his square body of a solidity and composure that nothing could ruffle, his fair beard, his blue eyes, his spotless linen all sharing in his self-assured superiority to us all; one of the Division doctors, Alexei Ivanovitch, a man from Little Russia, beloved of us all, whether in the Otriad or the army, a character possessing it seemed none of the Russian moods and sensibilities, of the kindest heart but no sentimentality, utterly free from self-praise, self-interest, self-assertion, humorous, loving passionately his country and, with all his Russian romance and even mysticism, packed with practical common sense; another Division doctor, a young man, carving for himself a practice out of Moscow merchants, crammed with all the latest inventions and discoveries, caring for nothing save his own career and frankly saying so, but a lively optimist whose belief in his own powers was quite refreshing in its sincerity.

In such a place and under such conditions Semyonov had at the earlier period been master of us all. The effect of his personality was such that we had, every one of us, believed him invincible. The very frankness of his estimate of the world and ourselves as the most worthless and incompetent bundle of rubbish, caused us to yield completely to him. We believed that he rated himself but little higher than the rest of us. He was superior but only because he saw so clearly with eyes purged of sentiment and credulity. We, poor creatures, had still our moments of faith and confidence. I had never liked him and during these last days had positively hated him. I did not doubt that he was making the frankest love to Marie Ivanovna and I thought he was influencing her.... Trenchard was my friend, and what an infant indeed he seemed against Semyonov's scornful challenge!

But now, behold, Semyonov had his rival! If Semyonov cared nothing for any of us, Nikitin, it was plain enough, cared nothing for Semyonov. From the very first the two men had been opponents. It seemed as though Nikitin's great stature and fine air, as of a king travelling in disguise from some foreign country, made him the only man in the world to put out Semyonov's sinister blaze. Nikitin was an idealist, a mystic, a dreamer—everything that Semyonov was not. It is true that if we mattered nothing at all to Semyonov, we also mattered nothing at all to Nikitin, but for Nikitin there were dreams, visions, memories and hopes. We were contented to be banished from his attention when we were aware that happier objects detained him. We might envy him, we could not dislike him.

Semyonov never sneered at Nikitin. From the first he left him absolutely alone. The two men simply avoided one another in so far as was possible in a company so closely confined as ours. From the first they treated one another with a high and almost extravagant politeness. As Nikitin spoke but seldom, there was little opportunity for the manifestation of what Semyonov must have considered "his childishly romantic mind," and Nikitin, on his side, made on no single occasion a reply to the challenge of Semyonov's caustic cynicism.

But if Nikitin was an idealist he was also, as was quite evident, a doctor of absolutely first-rate ability and efficiency. I was present at the first operation that he conducted with us—an easy amputation. Semyonov was assisting and I know that he watched eagerly for some slip or hesitation. It was an operation that any medical student might have conducted with success, but the first incision of the knife showed Nikitin a surgeon of genius. Semyonov recognised it.... I fancied that from that moment I could detect in his attitude to Nikitin a puzzled wonder that such an artist could be at the same time such a fool.

I began to feel in Nikitin a very lively interest. I had from the first been conscious of his presence, his distinction, his attitude of patient expectation and continuously happy reminiscence; but I felt now for the first time a closer, more personal interest. From the first, as I have said on an earlier page, his relationship to Andrey Vassilievitch had puzzled me. If Nikitin were not of the common race of men, most assuredly was Andrey Vassilievitch of the most ordinary in the world. He was a little man of a type in no way distinctively Russian—a type very common in England, in America, in France, in Germany. He was, one would have said, of the world worldly, a man who, with a sharp business brain, had acquired for himself houses, lands, food, servants, acquaintances. Upon these achievements he would pride himself, having worked with his own hand to his own advantage, having beaten other men who had started the race from the same mark as himself. He would be a man of a kindly disposition, hospitable, generous at times when needs were put plainly before him, but yet of little imagination, conventional in all his standards, readily influenced outside his business by any chance acquaintance, but nevertheless having his eye on worldly advantage and progress; he would be timid of soul, playing always for safety, taking the easiest way with all emotion, treading always the known road, accepting day by day the creed that was given to him; he would be, outside his brain, of a poor intelligence, accepting the things of art on the standard of popular applause, talking with a stupid garrulity about matters of which he had no first-hand knowledge—proud of his position as a man of the world, wise in the character and moods of men of which, in reality, he knew nothing. Had he been an Englishman or a German, this would have been all and yet, because he was a Russian, this was not even the beginning of the matter.

I had, as I have already said, in earlier days known him only slightly. I had once stayed for three days in his country-house and it was here that I had met his wife. Russian houses are open to all the world and, with such a man as Andrey Vassilievitch, through the doors crowds of men and women are always coming and going, treating their host like the platform of a railway station, eating his meals, sleeping on his beds, making rendezvous with their friends, and yet almost, on their departure, forgetting his very name.

My visit had been of a date now some five years old. I can only remember that his wife did not make any very definite impression upon me, a little quiet woman, of a short figure, with kind, rather sleepy eyes, a soft voice, and the air of one who knows her housewifely business to perfection and has joy in her knowledge. "Not interesting," I would have judged her, but I had during my stay no personal talk with her. It was only after my visit that I was told that this quiet woman was the passion of Andrey Vassilievitch's life. He had been over thirty when he had married her; she had been married before, had been treated, I was informed, with great brutality by her husband who had left her. She had then divorced him. Praise of her, I discovered, was universal. She was apparently a woman who created love in others, but this by no marked virtues or cleverness; no one said of her that she was "brilliant," "charming," "fascinating." People spoke of her as though here at least there was some one of whom they were sure, some one too who made them the characters they wished to be, some one finally who had not surrendered herself, who gave them her love but not her whole soul, keeping always mystery enough to maintain her independence. No scandal was connected with her name. I heard of Nikitin and others as her friends, and that was all. Then, quite suddenly, two months before the beginning of the war, she died. They said that Andrey Vassilievitch was like a lost dog, wished also at first to talk to all who had known her, wearying her friends with his reminiscences, his laments, his complaints—then suddenly silent, speaking to no one about her, at first burying himself in his business, then working on some committee in connexion with one of the hospitals, then, as it appeared on the impulse of a moment, departing to the war.

I had expected to find him a changed man and was, perhaps, disappointed that he should appear the same chattering feather-headed little character whom I had known of old. Nevertheless I knew well enough that there was more here than I could see, and that the root of the matter was to be found in his connexion with Nikitin. In our Otriad, friendships were continually springing up and dying down. Some one would confide to one that so-and-so was "wonderfully sympathetic." From the other side one would hear the same. For some days these friends would be undivided, would search out from the Otriad the others who were of their mind, would lose no opportunity of declaring their "sympathy," would sit together at table, work together over the bandaging, unite together in the public discussions that were frequent and to a stranger's eye horribly heated. Then very soon there would come a rift. How could that Russian passionate longing for justified idealism be realised? Once more there were faults, spots on the sun, selfishness, bad temper, narrowness, what you please. And at every fresh disappointment would my companions be as surprised as though the same thing had not happened to them only a fortnight ago.

"But only last week you liked him so much!"

"How could I know that he would hold such opinions? Never in my life have I been more surprised."

So upon these little billows sailed the stout bark of Russian idealism, rising, falling, never overwhelmed, always bravely confident, never seeking for calm waters, refusing them indeed for their very placidity.

But in the midst of these shifting fortunes there were certain alliances and relationships that never changed. Amongst these was the alliance of Nikitin and Andrey Vassilievitch. Friendship it could not be called. Nikitin, although apparently he was kindly to the little man, yielded him no intimacy. It seemed to us a very one-sided business, depending partly upon Andrey Vassilievitch's continual assertions that Nikitin was "his oldest friend and the closest friend of his wife," that "Nikitin was one of the most remarkable men in the world," that "only his intimate friends could know how remarkable he was"; partly too upon the dog-like capacity of Andrey Vassilievitch to fetch and carry for his friend, to put himself indeed to the greatest inconvenience. It was pathetic to see the flaming pleasure in the man's eyes when Nikitin permitted him to wait upon him, and how ironically, upon such an occasion, would Semyonov watch them both!

In spite of Nikitin's passivity he did, I fancied, more than merely suffer this unequal alliance. It seemed to me that there was behind his silence some active wish that the affair should continue. I should speak too strongly if I were to say that he took pleasure in the man's company, but he did, I believe, almost in spite of himself, secretly encourage it. And there was, in spite of the comedy that persistently hovered about his figure and habits, some fine spirit in Andrey Vassilievitch's championship of his hero. How he hated Semyonov! How he lost no single opportunity of trying to bring Nikitin forward in public, of proving to the world who was the greater of the two men! Something very single-hearted shone through the colour of his loyalty; nothing, I was convinced, could swerve him from his fidelity. That, at least, was until death.

There arose then in these days of the wounded at M—a strange relationship between myself and Nikitin. Friendship, I have said, I may not call it. Nikitin afterwards told me it was my interest in the study of human character that led to his frankness—as though he had said, "Here is a man who likes to play a certain game. I also enjoy it. We will play it together, but when the game is finished we separate." Although discussions as to the characters of one or another of us were continuous and, to an Englishman at any rate, most strangely public, I do not think that the Russians in our Otriad were really interested in human psychology. One criticised or praised in order to justify some personal disappointment or pleasure. There was nothing that gave our company greater pleasure than to declare in full voice that "So-and-so was a dear, most sympathetic, a fine man." Public praise was continuous and the most honest and spontaneous affair; if criticism sometimes followed with surprising quickness that was spontaneous too; all the emotions in our Otriad were spontaneous to the very extreme of spontaneity. But we were not real students of one another; we were content to call things by their names, to call silence silence, obstinacy obstinacy, good temper good temper, and leave it at that.

No one, I think, really considered Nikitin at all deeply. They admired him for his "quiet" but would have liked him better had he shared some of their frankness—and that was all.

It happened that for several days I worked in the bandaging room directly under Nikitin. The work had a peculiar and really unanalysable fascination for me. It was perhaps the directness of contact that pleased me. I suppose one felt that here at any rate one was doing immediate practical good, relieving distress and agony that must, by some one, be immediately relieved; and, at any rate, in the first days at M— when the press of wounded was terrific (we treated, in one day and night, nine hundred wounded soldiers) there could be no doubt of the real demand for incessant tireless work. But there was in my pleasure more than this. It was as though, through the bodies of the wounded soldiers, I was helping to drive home the attack upon our enemy. By our enemy I do not mean anything as concretely commonplace as the German nation. One scarcely considered Germany as a definite personality. One was resolved to cripple its power because one believed that power to be a menace to the helpless, the innocent, the lovers of truth and beauty; but that resolve, although it never altered, seemed (the nearer one approached the citadel) in some way to be farther and farther removed from the real question. Germany was of no importance, and the ruin that Germany was wreaking was of no importance compared with the histories of the individual souls that were now in the making. Here were we: Nikitin, Trenchard, Sister K—, Molozov, myself and the others—engaged upon our great adventure. Across the surface of the world, at this same instant, out upon the same hunt, seeking the same answer to their mystery, were millions of our fellows. Somewhere in the heart of the deep forest the enemy was hiding. We would defeat him? He would catch us unawares? He had some plot, some hidden surprise? What should we find when we met him?... We hated Germany, God knows, with a quiet, unresting, interminable hatred, but it was not Germany that we were fighting.

And these wounded knew something that we did not. In the first moments of their agony when we met them their souls had not recovered from the shock of their encounter. It was, with many of them, more than the mere physical pain. They were still held by some discovery at whose very doors they had been. The discovery itself had not been made by them, but they had been so near to it that many of them would never be the same man again. "No, your Honour," one soldier said to me. "It isn't my arm.... That is nothing, Slava Bogu ... but life isn't so real now. It is half gone." He would explain no more.

Since the battle of S—, I had been restless. I wanted to be back there again and this work was to me like talking to travellers who had come from some country that one knew and desired.

In the early morning, when the light was so cold and inhuman, when the candles stuck in bottles on the window-sills shivered and quavered in the little breeze, when the big basin on the floor seemed to swell ever larger and larger, with its burden of bloody rags and soiled bandages and filthy fragments of dirty clothes, when the air was weighted down with the smell of blood and human flesh, when the sighs and groans and cries kept up a perpetual undercurrent that one did not notice and yet faltered before, when again and again bodies, torn almost in half, faces mangled for life, hands battered into pulp, legs hanging almost by a thread, rose before one, passed and rose again in endless procession, then, in those early hours, some fantastic world was about one. The poplar trees beyond the window, the little beechwood on the hill, the pond across the road, a round grey sheet of ruffled water, these things in the half-light seemed to wait for our defeat. One instant on our part and it seemed that all the pain and torture would rise in a flood and overwhelm one ... in those early morning hours the enemy crept very close indeed. We could almost hear his hot breath behind the bars of our fastened doors.

There was a peculiar little headache that I have felt nowhere else, before or since, that attacked one on those early mornings. It was not a headache that afflicted one with definite physical pain. It was like a cold hand pressing upon the brow, a hand that touched the eyes, the nose, the mouth, then remained, a chill weight upon the head; the blood seemed to stop in its course, one's heart beat feebly, and things were dim before one's eyes. One was stupid and chose one's words slowly, looking at people closely to see whether one really knew them, even unsure about oneself, one's history, one's future; neither hungry, tired, nor thirsty, neither sad nor joyful, neither excited nor dull, only with the cold hand upon one's brow, catching (with troubled breath) the beating of one's heart.

In normal times the night-duty was of course taken in rotation, but during the pressure of these four days we had to snatch our rest when we might.

About midnight on the fifth day the procession of wounded suddenly slackened, and by two o'clock in the morning had ceased entirely. The two nurses went to bed leaving Nikitin, myself, and some sleepy sanitars alone. The little room was empty of all wounded, they having been removed to the tent on the farther side of the road. The candles had sunk deep into the bottles and were spluttering in a sea of grease. The room smelt abominably, the blood on the floor had trickled in thin red lines into the cracks between the boards, and the basins with the soiled bandages overflowed. There was absolute silence. One sanitar, asleep, had leaned, still standing, over a chair, and his shadow with his heavy hanging head high above the candle against the wall.

Nikitin, seeming gigantic in the failing candlelight, stood back against the window. He did not keep, as did Semyonov, perfect neatness. A night of work left him with his hair on end, his black beard rough and disordered; his shirtsleeves were turned up, his arms stained with blood, and in his white apron he looked like some kingly butcher. I was tired, the cold headache was upon me. I wished that I could go, but I knew that both he and I must stay until eight o'clock. While there was work to do nothing mattered, but now in the silence the whole world seemed as empty and foul as a drained and stinking tub.

Nikitin looked at me.

"You're tired," he said.

"No, I'm not tired," I answered. "I shouldn't sleep if I went to bed. But I've got a headache that is not a headache, I smell a smell that isn't a smell, I'm going to be sick—and yet I'm not going to be sick."

"Come outside," he said, "and get rid of this air." We went out and sat down on a wooden bench that bordered the yard. Before us was the high-road that ran from the town of S— into the very heart of the Carpathians. As the cold grey faded we could catch the thin outline of those mountains, faint, like pencil-lines upon the sky now washed with pink, covered in their nearer reaches by thick forests, insubstantial, although they were close at hand, like water or long clouds. We could see the road, white and clear at our feet, melting into shadow beyond us, and catching in the little misty pools the coloured reflection of the morning sky.

The air was very fresh; a cock behind me welcomed the sun; the cold band withdrew from my forehead.

Nikitin was silent and I, silent also, sat there, almost asleep, happy and tranquil. It seemed to me very natural to him that he should neither move nor speak, but after a time he began to talk. I had in that early morning a strange impression, as though deep in my dreams I was listening to some history. I know that I did not sleep and yet even now as I recover his quiet voice and, I believe, many of his very words, in reminiscence those hours are still dreaming hours. I know that every word that he told me then was true in actual fact. And yet it seems to me that we were all slumbering, the world at our feet, the sun in the sky, the wounded in their tent, and that through the mist of all that slumber Nikitin's voice, soft, measured, itself like an echo of some other voice miles away, penetrated—but to my heart rather than to my brain. Afterwards this was all strangely parallel in my mind with that earlier conversation that I had had with Trenchard in the train.... And now as I sit here, in so different a place, amongst men so different, those other two come back to me, happy ghosts. Yes, happy I know that one at least of them is!

Like water behind glass, like music behind a screen, Nikitin's voice comes back to me—dim but so close, mysterious but so intimate. Ah, the questions that I would ask him now if only I might have those morning hours over again!

"You're a solemn man altogether, Durward. Perhaps all Englishmen seem so to us, and it may be only your tranquillity, so unlike our moods and nerves by which we kill ourselves dead before we're half way through life.... I had an English tutor for a year when I was a boy. He didn't teach me much: 'all right' and 'Tank you' is the only English I've kept, but I think of him now as the very quietest man in all the universe. He never seemed to breathe, so still he was. And how I admired him for that! My father was a very excitable man, his moods and tempers killed him when he was just over forty.... We have a proverb, 'In the still marshes there are devils,' and we admire and fear quiet men because they have something that we have not. And I like the way that you watch us, Durward. Your friend Trenchard does not watch us at all and one could be his friend. For you one has quite another feeling. It is as though I had something to give you that you really want. Why should I not give it you? My giving it will do me no harm, it may even yield me pleasure. You will not throw it away. You are an Englishman and will not for a moment's temper or passion reveal secrets. And there are no secrets. What I tell you you may tell the world—but I warn you that it will neither interest them nor will they believe it.... There is, you see, no climax to my story. I have no story, indeed; like an old feldscher in my village who hates our village Pope. 'Why, Georg Georgevitch,' I say, 'do you hate him? He is a worthy man.' 'Your Honour,' he says, 'there is nothing there; a fat man, but God has the rest of him—I hate him for his emptiness.' I'm in a humour to talk. I have, in a way, fulfilled the purpose that my English tutor created in me. I've grown a sort of quiet skin, you know, but under that skin the heart pounds away, the veins swell to bursting. I'm a fool behind it all—just a fool as every Russian is a fool with more in hand than he knows how to deal with. You don't understand Russia, do you? No, and I don't and no one does. But we can all talk about her—and love her too, if you like, although our sentiment's a bad thing in us, some say. But for us not to talk—for one of us to be silent—do you know how hard that is?... And through it all how I despise myself for wishing to tell them! What business is it of theirs? Then this war. Can you conceive what it is doing to Russians? If you have loved Russia and dreamed for her and had your dreams flung again and again to the ground and trampled on—and now, once more, the bubbles are in the sky, glittering, gleaming ... do we not have to speak, do you think? Must it not be hard, when before we have not been able to be silent about women and vodka, to be silent now about the dearest wish of our heart? We have come out here, all of us, to see what we will find. I have come because I want to get nearer to something—I had brought something in my heart about which I had learnt to be silent. 'That is enough!' I thought, 'there can be nothing else about which I can wish to talk; but now, suddenly, like that crucifix on the hillock by the road that the sun has just touched, there is something more. And now here we are nothing ... two souls come together out of space for an hour ... and it doesn't matter what I say to you, except that it's true and the truth will be something for you. Here's what I've come to the war with ... my little bit of possession, if you like, that I've brought with me, as we've all brought something. Will you understand me? Perhaps not, and it really doesn't matter. I know what I have, what I want, but not what I am. So how should you know if I do not? And I love life, I believe in God. I wish to meet Death. One can be serious without being absurd at an early hour like this, when nothing is real except such things.... Andrey Vassilievitch and myself have puzzled you, have we not? I have seen you watching us very seriously, as though we were figures in a novel, and that has amazed me, because you must not be solemn about us. You'll understand nothing about Russian life unless you laugh at it during at least half the week.

"Almost five years ago I met Andrey Vassilievitch at a friend's house in Petrograd. He was an acquaintance of mine of some years' duration, but I had avoided him because he seemed to me the last kind of man whom I would ever care to know. I had been at this time five years in Petrograd and had now a good practice there as a surgeon. I was a successful man and I knew it, but I was also a disappointed man because my idealism, that was being for ever wounded by my own actions, would not die. How I wished for it to die! I thought of the day when I should be without it as the day of liberation, of freedom. That had become my idea, I must tell you, the dominating idea of my life: that I should kill my idealism, laugh at the belief in God, lose faith in every one and everything, and then simply enjoy myself—my work which I loved and my pleasure which I should love when my idealism had died.... Sometimes during those years I thought that it was dying. Women helped to kill it, I believed, and I knew many women, desperately persistently laughing at them, leaving them or being left by them; and then, in spite of myself, bitterly, deeply disappointed. Something always saying to me: 'I am God and you cannot hide from me.' 'I am God and I will not be hidden.'

"And on this night, about five years ago, at the house of a friend, I met Andrey Vassilievitch. We left the house together, and because it was a fine night, walked down the Nevski. There at the corner of the Morskaia, because he was a nervous man who wished to be well with every one in the world and because he had nothing especial to say, he asked me to dinner, and I, because it was a fine night and there had been good wine, said that I would go.

"The next day I cursed my folly. I do not know to this day why I did not break the engagement, it would have been sufficiently easy, but break it I did not and a week later, reluctantly, I went. Do you know how houses and streets of which you have observed nothing, afterwards, called out by some important event, leap into detail? That night I swear that I saw nothing of that little street behind the Mariinsky Theatre. It was a fine 'white night' at the end of May and the theatre was in a bustle of arrivals because it was nearly eight o'clock. Not at all the hour of Russian dinner, as you know, but Andrey Vassilievitch always liked to be as English as possible. I tell you that I saw nothing of the street and yet now I know that at the door of the little trakteer there were two men and a woman laughing, that an isvotchik was drawn up in front of a high white block of flats, asleep, his head fallen on his breast, that the wonderful light, faintly blue and misty like gauze hung down from the sky, down over the houses, but falling not quite on to the pavement which was hard and ugly and grey. The little street was very silent and quiet and had, like so many Petrograd streets, a decorous intimacy with the eighteenth century ghosts thronging its air....

"Afterwards, how I was to know that street, every stone and corner of it! It seems wonderful to me now that I trod its pavement that night so carelessly. My destination was a square little house at the corner on the right. Andrey Vassilievitch boasted a whole house to himself, a rare pride in our city, as you know. When I was inside the doors I knew at once that it was not Andrey Vassilievitch's house at all. Some stronger spirit than his was there. Knowing him, I had expected to find there many modern things, some imitation of English manners, some bad but expensive pictures, a gramophone, a pianolo, a library of Russian classics in our hideous modern bindings, a billiard-room—you know the character. How quiet this little house was. In the little square hall an old faded carpet, a grandfather's clock and two eighteenth century prints of Petrograd. All the rooms were square, so Russian with their placid family portraits, their old tables and chairs, not beautiful save for their fidelity, and old thumbed editions of Pushkin and Gogol and Lermontov in the bookshelves. Clocks, old slow clocks, all telling different time, all over the house. The house was very neat, but in odd corners there were all those odd family things that Russians collect, china of the worst period, brass trays, large candlesticks, musical boxes, anything you please. Only in the dining-room there was some attempt at modernity. Bad modern furniture, on the walls bad copies of such things as Somoff's 'Blue Lady,' Vrubel's 'Pan' and one of Benoit's 'Peter the Great' water-colours. Beyond this room the house was of eighty years ago, muffled in its old furniture, speaking with the voice of its old clocks, scented with the scent of its musk and lavender, watched by the contented gaze of the old family portraits.

"Alexandra Pavlovna, Andrey Vassilievitch's wife, was waiting for us. Has it happened to you yet that your life that has been such and such a life is in the moment of a heart-beat all another life? You have passed an examination, you are suddenly ill, you break your back by a fall, or more simply than all of these, you enter a town, see a picture, hear a bar of music.... The thing's done: all values changed: what you saw before you see no longer, what you needed before you need no longer, what you expected before you expect no longer.... Alexandra Pavlovna was not a beautiful woman. Not tall, with hair quite grey, eyes not dark nor light—sad though. When she smiled there was great charm but so it is true of many women. Her complexion was always pale and her voice, although it was sweet to those who loved her, was perhaps too quiet to be greatly remarked by strangers. I have known men who thought her an ordinary woman.... She had much humour but did not show it to every one. She was as still as that cloud there above the hill, full of colour; like, that is, to those who loved her; seen from another view, as perhaps that cloud may be, there was nothing wonderful.... Nothing wonderful, but so many loved her! There was never, I think, a woman so greatly beloved. And you may judge by me. I had led a life in which after my work women had always played the chief part, and as the months passed and I had grown proud I had vowed that women must be exceptional to please me. I had felt the eye of the world upon me. 'You'll see no ordinary women in Victor Leontievitch's company' I heard them say, and I was proud that they should say it. From the first instant of seeing Alexandra Pavlovna I loved her and I loved her in a new, an utterly new way. For the first time in my life I did not think of myself as a traveller who, passing for many years through countries that did not greatly interest him, feels his aches and pains, his money troubles, his discomforts and little personal irritations. Then suddenly he crosses the border and the new land so possesses him that he is only a vessel for its beauty, to absorb it, to hold it, to carry the burden of it in safety.... I crossed the border. For four years after that I pursued that enchanted journey. Why did I love her? Who can say? Andrey Vassilievitch adored her with an utter devotion and had done so since the first moment of meeting her. I have known many others, women and men, who felt that devotion. On that first evening we were very quiet—only another woman, a cousin of hers. After dinner I had half an hour's talk with her. I can see her—ah! how I can see you, my dear!—sitting back a little in her chair, resting, her hands folded very quietly in her lap, her eyes watching me gravely. I felt like a boy who has come into the world for the first time. I could not talk to her—I stammered over the simplest things. But I was conscious of a deep luxurious delight. I did not, as I had done before, lay plans, say that this-and-this would be so if I did this-and-this, I did not consciously try to influence or direct her. I felt no definite sensual attraction, did not say, as I had always done with other women, 'It is the hair, the eyes, the mouth.' If I thought at all it was only 'This is better than anything that I have known before; I had never dreamt of anything like this.'

"After I had left her that night I did not walk the streets, nor drink, nor find companions. I went home and slept the soundest sleep of my life. In the morning I knew tranquillity for the first time in all my days. I did not, as I had done after many earlier first meetings, hasten to see my friend. I did not know even that she liked me and yet I felt no doubt nor confusion. It was, perhaps, that I was ready to accept this new influence under any conditions, was ready for once to leave the rules to another. I felt no curiosity, knew no determination to discover the conditions of her life that I might bend them to my own purposes. I was quite passive, untroubled, and of a marvellous, almost selfish happiness.

"Our friendship continued very easily. It soon came to our meeting every day. In the summer they moved to their house in Finland and I went to stay with them. But it was not until her return to Petrograd in September that I told her that I loved her. Upon one of the first autumn days, upon an evening, when the little green tree outside their door was gold and there was a slip of an apricot moon, when the first fires were lighted (Andrey Vassilievitch had English fireplaces), sitting alone together in her little faded old-fashioned room, I told her that I loved her. She listened very quietly as I talked, her eyes on my face, grave, sad perhaps, and yet humorous, secure in her own settled life but sharing also in the life of others. She watched me rather as a mother watches her child.... I told her that it mattered nothing the conditions that she put upon me; that so long as I saw her and knew that she believed me to be her friend I asked for nothing. She answered, still very quietly but putting her hand on mine, that she had loved me from the first moment of our meeting. That she wondered that yet once again love should have come into her life when she had thought that that was all finished for her. She told me that love had been in her life nothing but pain and distress, and then she asked me, very simply, whether I would try to keep this thing so that it should be happy and should endure. I said that I would obey her in anything that she should command.... There followed then the strangest life for me. Lovers in the fullest sense we were and yet it was different from any love that I had ever known. When I ask myself why, in what, it differed I cannot answer. Two old grey middle-aged people who happened to suit one another.... Not romantic.... But I think in the end of it all the reason was that she never revealed herself to me entirely. I was always curious about her, always felt that other people knew more of her than I did, always thought that one day I should know all. It is 'knowing all' that kills love, and I never knew all. We were always together. She was a woman of very remarkable intelligence, loving music, literature, painting, with a most excellently critical love. Her friendship with me gave her, I do believe, a new youth and happiness. We became inseparable, and all my earlier life had passed away from me like worn-out clothes. I was happy—but of course I was not satisfied. I was jealous of that which Andrey Vassilievitch had—and I lacked. My whole relationship to Andrey Vassilievitch was a curious one. My friendship for his wife must I am sure have been torture to him. He knew that she had given me a great deal that she had never given to him. And yet, because he loved her so profoundly, he was only anxious that she should be happy. He saw that my friendship gave her new interests, new life even. He encouraged me, then, in every way, to stay with them, to be with them. He left us alone continually. During the whole of that four years he never once spoke in anger to me nor challenged my fidelity. My relationship to him was difficult. We were, quite simply as men, the worst-suited in the world. He had not a trick nor a habit that did not get on my nerves; he was intelligent only in those things that I despised a man for knowing. This would have been well enough had he not persisted in talking about matters of art and literature, of which, of course, he knew nothing. He did it, I believe, to please his wife and myself. I despised him for many things and yet, in my heart, I knew that he had much that I had not. He was, and is, a finer man than I.... And, last and first of all, he possessed part of his wife that I did not. After all, she did, in her own beautiful way, love him. She was a mother to him; she laughed tenderly at his foolishness, cared for him, watched over him, defended him. Me she would never need to defend. Our relationship was built rather on my defence of her. Sometimes I would wish that I were such a durak as Andrey Vassilievitch, that I might have her protection.... There were many, many times when I hated him—no times at all when he did not irritate me. I wished.... I wished.... I do not know what I wished. Only I always waited for the time when I should have all of her, when I should hold her against all the world. Then, after four years of this new life, she quite suddenly died. Again in that little house, on a 'white night,' just as when I had at first met her, the purple curtains hanging in the little street, the isvostchik sleeping, the clocks in the house chattering in their haste to keep up with time.... Only two months before the outbreak of the war she caught cold, for a week suffered from pneumonia and died. At the last Andrey Vassilievitch and I were alone with her. He had her hand in his but her last cry was 'Victor,' and as she died I felt as though, at last, after that long waiting, she had leapt into my arms for ever....

"After her death for many weeks, she was with me more completely than she had been during her lifetime. I knew that she was dead, but I thought that I also had died. I went into Finland alone, saw no one, talked to no one, saw only her. Then quite suddenly I came to life again. She withdrew from me.... Work seemed the only possible thing; but I was, during all this time, happy not miserable. She was not with me, but she was not very far away. Then Andrey Vassilievitch came back to me. He told me that he knew that she had loved me—that he had tried to speak of her to others who had known her, but they had, none of them, had real knowledge of her. Might he speak to me sometimes about her?

"I found that though he irritated me more than ever I liked to talk about her to him. As I spoke of her he scarcely was present at all and yet he had known her and loved her, and would listen for ever and ever if I wished.

"When the war had lasted some months the fancy came to me that I could get nearer to her by going into it. I might even die, which would be best of all. I did not wish to kill myself because I felt that to be a coward's death, and in such a way I thought that I would only separate myself from her. But in the war, perhaps, I might meet death in such a way as to show him that I despised him both for myself and her. By suicide I would be paying him reverence.... Some such thought also had Andrey Vassilievitch. I heard that he thought of attaching himself to some Red Cross Otriad. I told him my plans. He said no more, but suddenly, as you know, I found him on the platform of the Warsaw station. Afterwards he apologised to me, said that he must be near me, that he would try not to annoy me, that if sometimes he spoke of her to me he hoped that I would not mind.... And I? What do I feel? I do not know. He has some share in her that I have not. I have some share in her that he has not, and I think that it has come to both of us that the one of us who dies first will attain her. It seems to me now that she is continually with me, but I believe that this is nothing to the knowledge I shall have of her one day. Am I right? Is Andrey Vassilievitch right? Can it be that such a man—such men, I should say, as either I or he—will ever be given such happiness? I do not know. I only know that God exists—that Love is more powerful than man—that Death can fall before us if we believe that it will—that the soul of man is Power and Love.... I believe in God...."

CHAPTER V

FIRST MOVE TO THE ENEMY

It was during two nights in the forest of S—, about which I must afterwards write, that I had those long conversations with Trenchard, upon whose evidence now I must very largely depend. Before me as I write is his Diary, left to me by him. In this whole business of the war there is nothing more difficult than the varied and confused succession with which moods, impressions, fancies, succeed one upon another, but Trenchard told me so simply and yet so graphically of the events of these weeks that followed the battle of S— that I believe I am departing in no way from the truth in my present account, the truth, at any rate as he himself believed it to be....

The only impression that he brought away with him from the battle of S— was that picture, lighted by the horizon fires, of Marie Ivanovna kneeling with her hand on Semyonov's shoulder. That, every detail and colour of it, bit into his brain.

In understanding him it is of the first importance to remember that this was the one and only love business of his life. The effect of those days in Petrograd when Marie Ivanovna had shown him that she liked him, the thundering stupefying effect of that night when she had accepted his love, must have caught his soul and changed it as glass is caught by the worker and blown into shape and colour. There he was, fashioned and purified, ready for her use. What would she make of him? That she should make nothing of him at all was as incredible to him as that there should not be, somewhere in the world, Polchester town in Glebeshire county.

There had been with him, I think, from the first a fear that "it was all too good to be true"—Timeo Danaos et dona ferentes. It is not easy for any man, after thirty years' shy shrinking from the world, to shake himself free of superstitions, and such terrors the quiet and retired Polchester had bred in Trenchard's heart as though it had been the very epitome of life at its lowest and vilest. It simply came to this, that he refused to believe that Marie Ivanovna had been given to him only to be taken away again. About women he knew simply nothing and Russian women are not the least complicated of their sex. About Marie Ivanovna he of course knew nothing at all.

His first weeks in our Otriad had been like the painful return to drab reality after a splendid dream. "After all I am the hopeless creature I thought I was. What was there, in those days in Petrograd, that could blind me?" His shyness returned, his awkwardness, his mistakes in tact and resource were upon him again like a suit of badly made clothes. He knew this but he believed that it could make no difference to his lady. So sure was he of himself in regard to her—she might be transformed into anything hideous or vile and still now he would love her—that he could not believe that she would change. The love that had come to them was surely eternal—it must be, it must be, it must be....

He failed altogether to understand her youth, her inexperience, above all her coloured romantic fancy. Her romantic fancy had made him in her eyes for a brief hour something that he was not. After a month at the war I believe that she had grown into a woman. She had loved him for an instant as a young girl loves a hero of a novel. And although she was now a woman she must still keep her romantic fancy. He was no longer part of that—only a clumsy man at whom people laughed. She must, I think, have suffered at her own awakening, for she was honest, impetuous, pure, if ever woman was those things.

He did not see her as she was—he still clung to his confidence; but he began as the days advanced to be terribly afraid. His fears centred themselves round Semyonov. Semyonov must have seemed to him an awful figure, powerful, contemptuous, all-conquering. Any blunders that he committed were doubled by Semyonov's presence. He could do nothing right if Semyonov were there. He was only too ready to believe that Semyonov knew the world and he did not, and if Semyonov thought him a fool—it was quite obvious what Semyonov thought him—then a fool he must be. He clung desperately to the hope that there would be a battle—a romantic dramatic battle—and that in it he would most gloriously distinguish himself. He believed that, for her sake, he would face all the terrors of hell. The battle came and there were no terrors of hell—only sick headache, noise, men desperately wounded, and, once again, his own clumsiness. Then, in that final picture of Marie Ivanovna and Semyonov he saw his own most miserable exclusion.

In the days that followed there was much work and he was forgotten. He assisted in the bandaging-room; in later days he was to prove most efficient and capable, but at first he was shy and nervous and Semyonov, who seemed always to be present, did not spare him.

Then, quite suddenly, Marie Ivanovna changed. She was kinder to him than she had ever been, yes, kinder than during those early days in Petrograd. We all noticed the change in her. When she was with him in the bandaging-room she whispered advice to him, helped him when she had a free moment, laughed with him, put him, of course, into a heaven of delight. How happy at once he was! His clumsiness instantly fell away from him, he only smiled when Semyonov sneered, his Russian improved in a remarkable manner. She was tender to him as though she were much older than he. He has told me that, in spite of his joy, that tenderness alarmed him. Also when he kissed her she drew back a little— and she did not reply when he spoke of their marriage.

But for four days he was happy! He used to sing to himself as he walked about the house in a high cracked voice—one song I did but see her passing by—another Early one morning—I can hear him now, his voice breaking always on the high notes.

Early one morning   Just as the sun was rising   I heard a maid singing In the valley below: "Ah! don't deceive me! Pray never leave me,'   How could you treat a poor maiden so!"

His pockets were more full than ever of knives and string and buttons. His smile when he was happy lightened his face, changing the lines of it, making it if not handsome pleasant and friendly. He would talk to himself in English, ruffling his hands through his hair: "And then, at three o'clock I must go with Andrey Vassilievitch ..." or "I wonder whether she'll mind if I ask—" He had a large briar pipe at which he puffed furiously, but could not smoke without an endless procession of matches that afterwards littered the floor around him. "The tobacco's damp," he explained to us a hundred times. "It's better damp...."

Then, quite suddenly, the blow fell.

One evening, as they were standing alone together in the yard watching the yellow sky die into dusk, without any preparation, she spoke to him.

"John," she said, "I can't marry you."

He heard her as though she had spoken to another man. It was as though he said: "Ah, that will be bad news for so-and-so."

"I don't understand," he said, and instantly afterwards his heart began to beat like a raging beast and his knees trembled.

"I can't marry you," she told him, "because I don't love you. Ah, I've known it a long time—ever since we left Petrograd. I've often, often wanted to tell you ... I've been afraid."

"You can't marry me?" he repeated, "But you must...." Then hurriedly: "No, I shouldn't say that. You must forgive me ... you have confused me."

"I'm very unhappy ... I've been unhappy a long time. It was a mistake in Petrograd. I don't love you—but it isn't only that.... You wouldn't be happy with me. You think now ... but it's a mistake."

He has told me that as the idea worked through to his brain his only thought was that he must keep her at all costs, under any conditions, keep her.

"You can't—you mustn't," he whispered, staring as though he would hold her by her eyes. "Don't you see that you mustn't? What am I to do after all this? What are we both to do? It's breaking everything. I shan't believe in anything if you.... Ah! but no, you don't really mean anything...."

He saw that she was trembling and he bent forward, put his arm very gently round her as though he would protect her.

But she very strongly drew away from him, looked him in the face, then dropped her eyes, let her whole body droop as though she were most bitterly ashamed.

"I don't know," she said, "what I've been ... what I've done. During these last weeks I've been terrible to myself—and yet it's better too. I didn't live a real life before, and now I see things as they are. I don't love you, John, and so we mustn't marry."

He looked at her and then suddenly wild, furious, shouting at her:

"You mustn't.... You dare not.... Then go if you wish. I don't want you, do you hear?... I don't want.... I don't want you!"

She turned and walked swiftly into the house. He watched her go, then with quick stumbling steps hurried into the field below the farm.

There he stood, thinking of nothing, knowing nothing, seeing nothing. The dusk came up, there had been rain during the day, the mist was in grey sheets, the wet dank smell of the earth and of the vegetables amongst which he stood grew stronger as the light faded. He thought of nothing, nothing at all. He felt in his pocket for his pipe, something dropped—and he knelt down there on the soaking ground, searching. He searched furiously, raging to himself again and again: "Oh! I must find it! I must find it! I must find it!" His hands tore the wet vegetables, were thick with the soil. Other things fell from his pockets, Then the rain began to descend again, thin and cold. In some building he could hear a horse moving, stamping. He pulled up the vegetables by their roots in his search. As though a sword had struck him his brain was clear. He knew of his loss. He flung himself on the ground, rubbing the wet soil on to his face, whispering desperately: "Oh God!—Oh God!—Oh God!"

On the day following we did not know of what had happened. Trenchard was not with us, as he was sent about midday with some sanitars to bury the dead in a wood five miles from M—. That must have been, in many ways, the most terrible day of his life and during it, for the first time, he was to know that unreality that comes to every one, sooner or later, at the war. It is an unreality that is the more terrible because it selects from reality details that cannot be denied, selects them without transformation, saying to his victim: "These things are as you have always seen them, therefore this world is as you have always seen it. It is real, I tell you." Let that false reality be admitted and there is no more peace.

On this day there were the two sanitars, whose faces now he knew, walking solidly beside his cart, there were the little orchards with the soldiers' tents sheltering beneath them, the villages with the old men, the women, the children, watching, like ghosts, their passage, the fields in which the summer corn was ripening, the first trembling heat and beauty of a quiet day in early June. No sound in the world but peace, the woods opening around them as they advanced. He lay back on his bumping cart, watching the world as though he was seeing pictures of some place where he had once been but long left. Yes, long ago he had left it. His world was now a narrow burning chamber, in which dwelt with him a taunting jeering torturing spirit of reminiscence. He saw with the utmost clearness every detail of his relationship with Marie Ivanovna. He had no doubt at all that that relationship was finally, hopelessly closed. His was not a character that was the stronger for misfortune. He submitted, crushed to the ground. His mind now dwelt upon that journey from Petrograd, a journey of incredible, ironic ecstasy lighted with the fires of the wonderful spring that had accompanied it. He recalled every detail of his conversation with me. His confidence that life would now be fine for him—how could life ever be fine for a man who let the prizes, the treasures, slip from his fingers, without an attempt to clutch them? It was so now that he saw the whole of the affair—blame of Marie Ivanovna there was none, only of his own weakness, his imbecile, idiotic weakness. In that last conversation with her why could he not have said that he refused to let her go, held to her, dominated her, as a strong man would have done? No, without a word, except a cry of impotent childish rage, he had submitted.... So, all his life it had been—so, all his life it would be.

He could only wonder now at his easy ready belief that happiness would last for him. Had happiness ever lasted? As a man began so he ended. Life laughed at him and would always laugh. Nevertheless, he had that journey—five days of perfect unalloyed delight. Nobody could rob him of that. She had said to him that even at the beginning of the journey she had known that she did not love him—she had known but he had not, and even though he had cheated himself with the glittering bubble of an illusion the splendour had been there....

Meanwhile behind his despair there was something else stirring. He has told me that upon that afternoon he was only very dimly, very very faintly aware of it, aware of it only fiercely to deny it. He knew, however stoutly he might refuse to acknowledge it, that the events of the last weeks had bred in him some curiosity, some excitement that he could not analyse. He would like to have thought that his life began and ended only in Marie Ivanovna, but the Battle of S— had, as it were in spite of himself, left something more.

He found that he recalled the details of that battle as though his taking part in it had bound him to something. Even it was suggested to him that there was something now that he must do outside his love for Marie Ivanovna, something that had perhaps no connexion with her at all. In the very heart of his misery he was conscious that a little pulse was beating that was strange to him, foreign to him; it was as though he were warned that he had embarked upon some voyage that must be carried through to the very end. He was, in truth, less completely overwhelmed by his catastrophe than he knew.

As they now advanced and entered upon the first outworks of the Carpathians the day clouded. They stumbled down into a little narrow brown valley and drove there by the side of an ugly naked stream, wandering sluggishly through mud and weeds. Over them the woods, grey and sullen, had completely closed. The sun, a round glazed disk sharply defined but without colour, was like a dirty plate in the sky. Up again into the woods, then over rough cart tracks, they came finally to a standstill amongst thick brushwood and dripping undergrowth.

They could hear, very far away, the noise of cannon. The sanitars were inclined to grumble. "Nice sort of business, looking for dead men here, your Honour.... We must leave the carts here and go on foot. What's it wet for? It hasn't been raining."

Why was it wet, indeed? A heavy brooding inertia, Trenchard has told me, seemed to seize them all. "They were not pleasant trees, you know," I remember his afterwards telling me, "all dirty and tangled, and we all looked dirty too. There was an unpleasant smell in the air. But that afternoon I simply didn't care about anything, nothing mattered." I don't think that the sanitars at that time respected Trenchard very greatly. He wasn't, in any case, a man of authority and his broken stammering Russian wouldn't help him. Then there is nothing stranger than the fashion in which the Russian language will (if you are a timid foreigner), of a sudden wilfully desert you. Be bold with it and it may, somewhat haughtily, perhaps, consent to your use of it ... be frightened of it and it will despise you for ever. Upon that afternoon it deserted Trenchard; even his own language seemed to have left him. His brain was cold and damp like the woods around him.

They passed through the thickets and came, to their great surprise, upon a trench occupied by soldiers. This surprised them because they had heard that the Austrians were many versts distant. The soldiers also seemed to wonder. They explained their mission to a young officer who seemed at first as though he would ask them something, then checked himself, gave them permission to pass through and watched them with grave gaze. After they had crossed the barbed wire the woods suddenly closed about them as though a door had been softly shut behind them. The ground now squelched beneath their feet, the sky between the trees was like damp blotting-paper, and the smell that had been only faintly in the air before was now heavy around them, blown in thick gusts as the wind moved through the trees. Shrapnel now could be distinctly heard at no great distance, with its hiss, its snap of sound, and sometimes rifle-shots like the crack of a ball on a cricket bat broke through the thickets. They separated, spreading like beaters in a long line: "Soon," Trenchard told me, "I was quite alone. I could hear sometimes the breaking of a twig or a stumbling footfall but I might have been suddenly alone at the end of the world. It was obvious that the regimental sanitars had been there before us because there were many new roughly made graves. There were letters too and post cards lying about all heavy with wet and dirt. I picked up some of these—letters from lovers and sisters and brothers. One letter I remember in a large baby-hand from a boy to his father telling him about his lessons and his drill, 'because he would soon be a soldier.' One letter, too, from a girl to her lover saying that she had had a dream and knew now that her 'dear Franz, whom she loved with all her soul, would return to her!... I am quite confident now that we shall be happy here again very soon....' In such a place, those words."

As he walked alone there he felt, as I had felt before the battle of S—, that he had already been there. He knew those trees, that smell, that heavy overhanging sky. Then he remembered, as I had remembered, his dream. But whereas that dream had been to me only a reflected story, with him it had lasted throughout his life. He knew every step of that first advance into the forest, the look back to the long dim white house with shadowy figures still about it, the avenue with many trees, the horses and dogs down the first grey path, then the sudden loneliness, the quiet broken only by the dripping of the trees.

Always that had caught him by the throat with terror, and now to-day he was caught once again. He was watched: he fancied that he could see the eyes behind the thicket and hear the rustling movement of somebody. To-day he could hear nothing. If at last his dream was to be fashioned into reality let it be so. Did the creature wish to destroy him, let it be so. He had no strength, no hope, no desire....

"It was there," he told me, "when I scarcely knew what was real and what was not, that I saw that for which I was searching. I noticed first the dark grey-blue of the trousers, then the white skull. There was a horrible stench in the air. I called and the sanitars answered me. Then I looked at it. I had never seen a dead man before. This man had been dead for about a fortnight, I suppose. Its grey-blue trousers and thick boots were in excellent condition and a tin spoon and some papers were showing out of the top of one boot. Its face was a grinning skull and little black animals like ants were climbing in and out of the mouth and the eye-sockets. Its jacket was in good condition, its arms were flung out beyond its head. I felt sick and the whole place was so damp and smelt so badly that it must have been horribly unhealthy. The sanitars began to dig a grave. Those who were not working smoked cigarettes, and they all stood in a group watching the body with a solemn and serious interest. One of them made a little wooden cross out of some twigs. There was a letter just beside the body which they brought me. It began: 'Darling

Heinrich,—Your last letter was so cheerful that I have quite recovered from my depression. It may not be so long now before ...' and so on, like the other letters that I had read. It grinned at us there with a devilish sarcasm, but its trousers and boots were pitiful and human. The men finished the grave and then, with their feet, turned it over. As it rolled a flood of bright yellow insects swarmed out of its jacket, and a grey liquid trickled out of the skull. The last I saw of it was the gleam of the tin spoon above its boot...."

"We searched after that," he told me, "for several hours and found three more bodies. They were Austrians, in the condition of the first. I walked in a dream of horror. It was, I suppose, a bad day for me to have come with my other unhappiness weighing upon me, but I was, in some stupid way, altogether unprepared for what I had seen. I had, as I have told you, thought of death very often in my life but I had never thought of it like this. I did not now think of death very clearly but only of the uselessness of trying to bear up against anything when that was all one came to in the end. I felt my very bones crumble and my flesh decay on my body, as I stood there. I felt as though I had really been caught at last after a silly aimless flight and that even if I had the strength or cleverness to escape I had not the desire to try. I had been mocked with a week's happiness only to have it taken from me for my enemy's ironic enjoyment. I had a quite definite consciousness of my enemy. I had as a boy thought, you remember, of my uncle—and now, as I moved through the wood, I could hear the old man's chuckle just as he had chuckled in the old days, snapping his fingers together and twitching his nose...."

They searched the wood until late in the afternoon, trampling through the wet, peering through thickets, listening for one another's voices, finding sometimes a trophy in the shape of an empty shrapnel case, an Austrian cap or dagger. Then, quite suddenly, a sanitar noticed that the bursting of the shrapnel was much closer than it had been during the early afternoon. It was now, indeed, very near and they could sometimes see the flash of fire between the trees.

"There's something strange about this, your Honour," said one of the sanitars nervously, and they all looked at Trenchard as though it were his fault that they were there. Then close behind them, with a snap of rage, a shrapnel broke amongst the trees. After that they turned for home, without a word to one another, not running but hastening with flushed faces as though some one were behind them.

They came to the trench and to their surprise found it absolutely deserted. Then, plunging on, they arrived at the two wagons, climbed on to one of them, leaving Trenchard alone with the driver on the other. "I tell you," he remarked to me afterwards, "I sank into that wagon as though into my grave. I don't know that ever before or since in my life have I felt such exhaustion. It was reaction, I suppose—a miserable, wretched exhaustion that left me well enough aware that I was the most unhappy of men and simply forced me, without a protest, to accept that condition. Moreover, I had always before me the vision of the dead body. Wherever I turned there it was, grinning at me, the black flies crawling in and out of its jaws, and behind it something that said to me: 'There! now I have shown you what I can do.... To that you're coming.'..."

He must have slept because he was suddenly conscious of sitting up in his car, surrounded by an intense stillness. He looked about him but could see nothing clearly, as though he were still sleeping. Then he was aware of a sanitar standing below the cart, looking up at him with great agitation and saying again and again: "Borjé moi! Borjé moi! Borjé moi!"

"What is it?" he asked, rubbing his eyes. The sanitar then seemed to slip away leaving him alone with a vague sense of disaster. The sun had set, but there was a moon, full and high, and now by its light he could see that his wagon was standing outside the gate of the house at M—. There was the yard, the bandaging-room, the long faded wall of the house, the barn, but where? ... where?... He sat up, then jumped down on to the road. The big white tent on the further side of the yard, the tent that had, that very morning, been full of wounded, was gone. The lines of wagons, horses and tents that had filled the field across the road were gone. No voices came from the house—somewhere a door banged persistently—other sound there was none.

The sanitars then surrounded him, speaking all together, waving their arms, their faces white under the moon, their eyes large and frightened like the eyes of little children. He tried to push their babel off from him. He could not understand.... Was this a continuation of the nightmare of the afternoon? There was a roar just behind their ears as it seemed. They saw a light flash upon the sky and fade, flash again and fade. With their faces towards the horizon they watched.

"What is it?" Trenchard said at last. There advanced towards him then from out of the empty house an old man in a wide straw hat with a broom.

"What is it?" Trenchard said again.

"It's the Austrians," said the old man in Polish, of which Trenchard understood very little. "First it's the Russians.... Then it's the Austrians.... Then it's the Russians.... Then it's the Austrians. And always between each of them I have to clean things up"—and some more which Trenchard did not understand. The old man then stood at his gate watching them with a gaze serious, sad, reflective. Meanwhile the sanitars had discovered one of our own soldiers: this man, who had been sitting under a hedge and listening to the Austrian cannon with very uncomfortable feelings, told them of the affair. At three o'clock that afternoon our Otriad had been informed that it must retreat "within half an hour." Not only our own Sixty-Fifth Division, but the whole of the Ninth Army was retreating "within half an hour." Moreover the Austrians were advancing "a verst a minute." By four o'clock the whole of our Otriad had disappeared, leaving only this soldier to inform us that we must move on at once to T— or S—, twenty or thirty versts distant.

"Retreating!" cried Trenchard. "But we were winning! We'd just won a battle!"

"Tak totchno!" said the soldier gravely, "Twenty versts! the horses won't do it, your Honour!"

"They've got to do it!" said Trenchard sharply, and the echo of the Austrian cannon, again as it seemed quite close at hand, emphasised his words. Except for this the silence of the world around them was eerie; only far away they seemed to hear the persistent rumble of carts on the road.

"They're gone! They're all gone! We're left last of all!" and "The Austrians advancing a verst a minute!"

He took a last look at the house which had seemed yesterday so absolutely to belong to them and now was already making preparations for its new guests. As he gazed he thought of his agony in that field below the house. Only last night and now what years ago it seemed! What years, what years ago!

He climbed wearily again upon his wagon. There had entered into his unhappiness now a new element. This was a sensation of cold despairing anger that ground should be yielded so helplessly. About every field, every hedge and lane and tree, as slowly they jogged along he felt this. Only to-day this corn, these stones, these flowers were Russian, and to-morrow Austrian! This, as it seemed, simply out of the air, dictated by some whispering devil crouching behind a hedge, afraid to appear! This, too, when only a few hours ago there had been that battle of S— won by them after a struggle of many days; that position, soaked with Russian blood, to be surrendered now as a leaf blows in the wind.

When they arrived at T— and found our Otriad he was, I believe, so deeply exhausted that he was not conscious of his actions. His account to me of what then occurred is fantastic and confused. He discovered apparently the house where we were; it was then one o'clock in the morning. Every one was asleep. There seemed to be no place for him to be, he could find neither candles nor matches, and he wandered out into the road again. Then, it seems, he was standing beside a deep lake. "I can remember nothing clearly except that the lake was black and endless. I stood looking at it. I could see the bodies out of the forest, only now they were slipping along the water, their skulls white and gleaming. I had also a confused impression that Russia was beaten and the war over. And that for me too life was utterly at an end.... I remember that I deliberately thought of Marie because it hurt so abominably. I repeated to myself the incidents of the night before, all of them, talking aloud to myself. I decided then that I would drown myself in the lake. It seemed the only thing to do. I took my coat off. Then sat down in the mud and took off my boots. Why I did this I don't know. I looked at the water, thought that it would be cold, but that it would soon be over because I couldn't swim. I heard the frogs, looked back at the flickering fires amongst our wagons, then walked down the bank...."

Nikitin must for some time have been watching him, because at that moment he stepped forward, took Trenchard's arm, and drew him back. Nikitin has himself told me that he was walking up and down the road that night because he could not sleep. When he spoke to Trenchard the man seemed dazed and bewildered, said something about "life being all over for him and—death being horrible!"

Nikitin put his arm round him, took him back to his room, where he made him a bed on the floor, gave him a sleeping-draught and watched him until he slept.

That was the true beginning of the friendship between Nikitin and Trenchard.

CHAPTER VI

THE RETREAT

The retreat struck us as breathlessly as though we had been whirled by a wind-storm into midair on the afternoon of a summer day. At five minutes to three we had been sitting round the table in the garden of the house at M— drinking tea. We were, I remember, very gay. We had heard only the day before of the Russian surrender of Przemysl and that had for a moment depressed us; but as always we could see very little beyond our own immediate Division. Here, on our own Front, we had at last cleared the path before us. On that very afternoon we were gaily anticipating our advance. Even Sister K— who, for religious reasons, took always a gloomy view of the future, was cheerful. She sipped her cherry jam and smiled upon us. Anna Petrovna, imperturbably sewing, calmly sighed her satisfaction.

"Perhaps to-morrow we shall move. I feel like it. It will be splendid to go through the Carpathians— beautiful scenery, I believe." Molozov was absent in the town of B— collecting some wagons that had arrived from Petrograd. "He'll be back to-night, I believe," said Sister K—. "Dear me, what a pleasant afternoon!"

It was then that I saw the face of the boy Goga. I had turned, smiling, pleased with the sunshine, cherry jam, and a good Russian cigarette straight from Petrograd. The boy Goga stared across the yard at me, his round red cheeks pale, mouth open, and his eyes confused and unbelieving.

He seemed then to jump across the intervening space. Then he screamed at us:

"We're retreating.... We're retreating!" he shrieked in the high trembling voice peculiar to agitated Russians. "We have only half an hour and the Austrians are almost here now!"

We were flung after that into a hurry of movement that left us no time for reasoning or argument. Semyonov appeared and in Molozov's absence took the lead. He was, of course, entirely unmoved, and as I now remember, combed his fair beard with a little tortoiseshell pocket comb as he talked to us. "Yes, we must move in half an hour. Very sad ... the whole army is retreating. Why, God knows...."

There arose clouds of dust in the yard where we had had our happy luncheon. The tents had disappeared. The wounded were once more lying on the jolting carts, looking up through their pain and distress to a heaven that was hot and grey and indifferent. An old man whom we had not seen during the whole of our stay suddenly appeared from nowhere with a long broom and watched us complacently. We had our own private property to pack. As I pressed my last things into my bag I turned from my desolate little tent, looked over the fields, the garden, the house, the barns.... "But it was ours—OURS," I thought passionately. We had but just now won a desperately-fought battle; across the long purple misty fields the bodies of those fallen Russians seemed to rise and reproach us. "We had won that land for you—and now—like this, you can abandon us!"

At that moment I cursed my lameness that would prevent me from ever being a soldier. How poor, on that afternoon, it seemed to be unable to defend with one's own hand those fields, those rivers, those hills! "Ah but Russia, I will serve you faithfully for this!" was the prayer at all our hearts that afternoon....

Semyonov had wisely directed our little procession away from the main road to O— which was filled now with the carts and wagons of our Sixty-Fifth Division. We were to spend the night at the small village of T—, twenty versts distant; then, to-morrow morning, to arrive at O—.

The carts were waiting in a long line down the road, the soldiers, hot and dusty, carried bags and sacks and bundles. A wounded man cried suddenly: "Oh, Oh, Oh," an ugly mongrel terrier who had attached himself to our Otriad tried to leap up at him, barking, in the air. There was a scent of hay and dust and flowers, and, very faintly, behind it all, came the soft gentle rumble of the Austrian cannon.

Nikitin, splendid on his horse, shouted to Semyonov:

"What of Mr.? Hadn't some one better go to meet him?"

"I've arranged that!" Semyonov answered shortly.

It was of course my fate to travel in the ancient black carriage that was one of the glories of our Otriad, with Sister Sofia Antonovna, the Sister with the small red-rimmed eyes of whom I have spoken on an earlier page. She was a woman who found in every arrangement in life, whether made by God, the Germans, or the General of our Division, much cause for complaint and dismay. She had never been pretty but had always felt that she ought to be; she was stupid but comforted herself by the certain assurance that every one else was stupid too. She had come to the war because a large family of brothers and sisters refused to have her at home. I disliked her very much, and she hated myself and Marie Ivanovna more than any one else in the world. I don't know why she grouped us together—she always did.

Marie Ivanovna was sitting with us now in the carriage, white-faced and silent. Sofia Antonovna was very patronising.... "When you've worked a little more at the Front, dear, you'll know that these things must happen. Bad work somewhere, of course. What can you expect from a country like Russia? Everything mismanaged ... nothing but thieves and robbers. Of course we're beaten and always will be."

"How can you, Sofia Antonovna?" Sister Marie interrupted in a low trembling voice. "It is nobody's fault. It is only for a moment. We will return—soon—at once. I know it. Ah, we must, we must! ... and your courage all goes. Of course it would."

Sister Sofia Antonovna smiled and her eyes watched us both. "I'm afraid your Mr. will be left behind," she said.

"Dr. Semyonov," Marie Ivanovna began—then stopped. We were all of us silent during the rest of the journey.

And how is one to give any true picture of the confusion into which we flung ourselves at O—? O— had been the town at which, a little more than a month ago, we had arrived so eagerly, so optimistically. It had been to us then the quietest retreat in the world—irritating, provoking by reason of its peace. The little school-house, the green well, the orchard, the bees, the long light evenings with no sound but the birds and running water—those things had been a month ago.

We were hurled now into a world of dust and despair. The square market place, the houses that huddled round it were swallowed up by soldiers, horses, carts and whirling clouds. A wind blew and through the wind a hot sun blazed. Everywhere horses were neighing, cows and sheep were driven in thick herds through columns of soldiers, motor cars frantically pushed their way from place to place, and always, everywhere, covering every inch of ground flying, as it seemed, from the air, on to roofs, in and out of windows, from house to house, from corner to corner, was the humorous, pathetic, expectant, matter-of-fact, dreaming, stolid Russian soldier. He was to come to me, later on, in a very different fashion, but on this dreadful day in O— he was simply part of the intolerable, depressing background.

If this day were dreadful to me what must it have been to Trenchard! We were none of us aware at this time of what had happened to him two days before, nor did we know of his adventure of yesterday. O— seemed to him, he has told me, like hell.

We spent the day gathered together in a large white house that had formerly been the town-hall of O—. It had, I remember, high empty rooms all gilt and looking-glasses; the windows were broken and the dust came, in circles and twisting spirals, blowing over the gilt chairs and wooden floors.

We made tea and sat miserably together. Semyonov was in some other part of the town. We were to wait here until Molozov arrived from B—.

There can be few things so bad as the sense of insecurity that we had that afternoon. The very ground seemed to have been cut away from under our feet. We had gathered enough from the officers of our Division to know that something very disastrous "somewhere" had occurred. It was the very vagueness of the thing that terrified us. What could have happened? Only something very monstrous could have compelled so general a retirement. We might all of us be prisoners before the evening. That seemed to us, and indeed was afterwards proved in reality, to have been no slender possibility. There was no spot on earth that belonged to us. So firm and solid we had been at M—. Even we had hung pictures on the walls and planted flowers outside the dining-room. Now all that remained for us was this horrible place with its endless looking-glasses, its bare gleaming floors and the intolerable noise through its open windows of carts, soldiers, horses, the smell of dung and tobacco, and the hot air, like gas, that flung the dust into our faces.

Beyond the vague terrors of our uncertainty was the figure, seen quite clearly by all of us without any sentiment, of Russia. Certainly Trenchard and I could feel with less poignancy the appeal of her presence, and yet I swear that to us also on that day it was she of whom we were thinking. We had been, until then, her allies; we were now her servants.

By Russia every one of us, sitting in that huge room, meant something different. To Goga she was home, a white house on the Volga, tennis, long evenings, early mornings, holidays in a tangled wilderness of happiness. To Sister K— she was "Holy Russia," Russia of the Kremlin, of the Lavra, of a million ikons in a million little streets, little rooms, little churches. To Sister Sofia she was Petrograd with cafés, novels by such writers as Verbitzkaia and our own Jack London, the cinematograph, and the Islands on a fine evening in May. To the student like a white fish she was a platform for frantic speeches, incipient revolutions, little untidy hysterical meetings in a dirty room in a back street, newspapers, the incapacities of the Douma, the robberies and villainies of the Government. To Anna Petrovna she was comfortable, unspeculative, friendly "home." To Nikitin she was the face of one woman upon whose eyes his own were always fixed. To Marie Ivanovna she was a flaming glorious wonder, mystical, transplendent, revealed in every blade of grass, every flash of sun across the sky, every line of the road, the top of every hill.

And to Trenchard and myself? For Trenchard she had, perhaps, taken to herself some part of his beloved country. He has told me—and I will witness in myself to the truth of this—that he never in his life felt more burningly his love for England than at this first moment of his consciousness of Russia. The lanes and sea of his remembered vision were not far from that dirty, disordered town in Galicia—and for both of them he was rendering his service.

At any rate there we sat, huddled together, reflected in the countless looking-glasses as a helpless miserable "lot," falling into long silences, hoping for the coming of Molozov with later news, listening to the confusion in the street below. Marie Ivanovna with her hands behind her back and her head up walked, nervously, up and down the long room. Her eyes stared beyond us and the place, striving perhaps to find some reason why life should so continually insist on being a different thing from her imaginings of it.

Lighted by the hot sun, blown upon by the dust, her figure, tall, thin, swaying a little in its many reflections, had the determined valour of some Joan of Arc. But Joan of Arc, I thought to myself, had at least some one definite against whom to wave her white banner; we were fighting dust and the sun.

Trenchard and Nikitin had left us to go into the town to search for news. We were silent. Suddenly Marie Ivanovna, turning upon us all as though she hated us, cried fiercely:

"I think you should know that Mr. Trenchard and I are no longer engaged."

It was neither the time nor the place for such a declaration. I cannot suggest why Marie Ivanovna spoke unless it were that she felt life that was betraying her so basely that she, herself, at least, must be honest. We none of us knew what to say. What could we say? This appalling day had sunk for us all individualities. We were scarcely aware of one another's names and here was Marie Ivanovna thrusting all these personalities upon us. Sister Sofia's red-rimmed eyes glittered with pleasure but she only said: "Oh, dear, I'm very sorry." Sister K— who was always without tact made a most uncomfortable remark: "Poor Mr.!..."

That, I believe, was what we were all feeling. I had an impulse to run out into the street, find Trenchard, and make him comfortable. I felt furiously indignant with the girl. We all looked at her, I suppose, with indignation, because she regarded us with a fierce, insulting smile, then turned her back upon us and went to a window.

At that moment Molozov with Trenchard, Nikitin and Semyonov, entered. I have said earlier in this book that only upon one occasion have I seen Molozov utterly overcome, a defeated man. This was the occasion to which I refer. He stood there in the doorway, under a vulgar bevy of gilt and crimson cupids, his face dull paste in colour, his hands hanging like lead; he looked at us without seeing us. Semyonov said something to him: "Why, of course," I heard him reply, "we've got to get out as quickly as we can.... That's all."

He came over towards us and we were all, except Marie Ivanovna, desperately frightened. She cried to him: "Well, what's the truth? How bad is it?"

He didn't turn to her but answered to us all.

"It's abominable—everywhere."

I know that then the great feeling of us all was that we must escape from the horrible place in some way. This beastly town of O— (once cursed by us for its gentle placidity) was responsible for the whole disaster; it was as though we said to ourselves, "If we had not been here this would not have happened."

We all stood up as though we felt that we must leave at once, and while we stood thus there was a report that shook the floor so that we rocked on our feet, brought a shower of dust and whitewash from the walls, cracked the one remaining pane of glass and drove two mice scattering with terror wildly across the floor. The noise had been terrific. Our very hearts stood still. The Austrians were here then.... This was the end....

"It's the bridge," Semyonov said quietly, and of course ironically. "We've blown it up. There'll be the other in a moment."

There was—a second shock brought down more dust and a large scale of gilt wood from one of the cornices. We waited then for our orders, looking down from the windows on to what seemed a perfect babel of disorder and confusion.

"We must be at X— to-night," Molozov told us. "The Staff is on its way already. We should be moving in half an hour."

We made our preparations.

Trenchard, meanwhile, had had during this afternoon one driving compelling impulse beyond all others, that he must, at all costs, escape all personal contact with Marie Ivanovna. It seemed to him the most awful thing that could possibly happen to him now would be a compulsory conversation with her. He did not, of course, know that she had spoken to us, and he thought that it would be the easiest thing in all the confusion that this retreat involved that he should be flung up against her. He sought his chief refuge in Nikitin. I am aware that in the things I have said of Nikitin, in speaking both of his relation to Andrey Vassilievitch's wife and to Trenchard himself, I have shown him as something of a sentimental figure. And yet sentimental was the very last thing that he really was. He had not the "open-heartedness" that is commonly asserted to be the chief glory and the chief defect of the Russian soul. He had talked to me because I was a foreigner and of no importance to him—some one who would be entirely outside his life. He took Trenchard now for his friend I believe because he really was attracted by the admixture of chivalry and helplessness, of simplicity and credulity, of timidity and courage that the man's character displayed. I am sure that had it been I who had been in Trenchard's position he would not have stretched out one finger to help me.

Trenchard himself had only vague memories of the events of the preceding evening. He was aware quite simply that the whole thing had been a horrible dream and that "nothing so bad could ever possibly happen to him again." He had "touched the worst," and he undoubtedly found some relief to-day in the general distress and confusion. It covered his personal disaster and forced him to forget himself in other persons' misfortunes. He was, as it happened, of more use than any one just then in getting every one speedily out of O—. He ran messages, found parcels and bags for the Sisters, collected sanitars, even discovered the mongrel terrier, tied a string to him and gave him to one of our soldiers to look after. In what a confusion, as the evening fell, was the garden of our large white house! Huge wagons covered its lawn; horses, neighing, stamping, jumping, were dragged and pulled and threatened; officers, from stout colonels to very young lieutenants, came cursing and shouting, first this way and that. A huge bag of biscuits broke away from a provision van and fell scattering on to the ground; the soldiers, told that they might help themselves, laughing and shouting like babies, fell upon the store. But for the most part there was gloom, gloom, gloom under the evening sky. Sometimes the reflections of distant rockets would shudder and fade across the pale blue; incessantly, from every corner of the world, came the screaming rattle of carts, a sound like many pencils drawn across a gigantic slate—and always the dust rose and fell in webs and curtains of filmy gold, under the evening sun.

At last Trenchard found himself with Molozov and Ivan Mihailovitch, the student like a fish, in the old black carriage. Molozov had "flung the world to the devil," Trenchard afterwards said, "and I sat there, you know, looking at his white face and wondering what I ought to talk about." Trenchard suddenly found himself narrowly and aggressively English—and it is certain that every Englishman in Russia on Tuesday thanks God that he is a practical man and has some common sense, and on Wednesday wonders whether any one in England knows the true value of anything at all and is ashamed of a country so miserably without a passion for "ideas."

To-night Trenchard was an Englishman. He had been really useful at O— and he had felt a new spirit of kindness around him. He did not know that Marie Ivanovna had made her declaration to us and that we were therefore all anxious to show him that we thought that he had been badly treated. Moreover he suspected, with a true English distrust of emotions, that the Russians before him were inclined to luxuriate in their gloom. Molozov's despair and Ivan Mihailovitch's passionate eyes and jerking white hands irritated him.

He smiled a practical English smile and looked about him at the swaying procession of carts and soldiers with a practical eye.

"Come," he said to Molozov, "don't despair. There's nothing really to be distressed about. There must be these retreats, you know. There must be. The great thing in this war is to see the whole thing in proportion—the whole thing. France and England and the Dardanelles and Italy—everything. In another month or two—"

But Molozov, frowning, shook his head.

"This country ... no method ... no system. Nothing. It is terrible.... That's a pretty girl!" he added moodily, looking at a group of peasants in a doorway. "A very pretty girl!" he added, sitting up a little and staring. Then he relapsed, "No system—nothing," he murmured.

"But there will be," continued Trenchard in his English voice. (He told me afterwards that he was conscious at the time of a horrible priggish superiority.) "Here in Russia you go up and down so. You've no restraint. Now if you had discipline—"

But he was interrupted by the melancholy figure of an officer who hung on to our slowly moving carriage, walking beside it with his hand on the door. He did not seem to have anything very much to say but looked at us with large melancholy eyes. He was small and needed dusting.

"What is it?" asked Molozov, saluting.

"I've had contusion," said the little officer in a dreamy voice. "Contusion ... I don't feel very well. I don't quite know where I ought to go."

"Our doctors are just behind," said Molozov. "You can come on with them."

"Your doctors ..." the little officer repeated dreamily. "Very well...." But he continued with us. "I've had contusion," he said. "At M—. Yes.... And now I don't quite know where I am. I'm very depressed and unhappy. What do you advise?"

"There are our doctors," Molozov repeated rather irritably. "You'll find them ... behind there."

"Yes, I suppose so," the melancholy little figure repeated and disappeared.

In some way this figure affected Trenchard very dismally and drove all his English common sense away. We were moving now slowly through clouds of dust, and peasants who watched us from their doorways with a cold indifference that was worse than exultation.

When we arrived, at two or three in the morning, at X—, our destination, the spirits of all of us were heavily weighted. Tired, cross, dirty, driven and pursued, and always with us that harassing fear that we had now no ground upon which we might rest our feet, that nothing in the world belonged to us, that we were fugitives and vagabonds by the will of God.

As our carriage stopped before the door of the large white building in X— that seemed just like the large white building in O—, the little officer was again at our side.

"I've got contusion ..." he said. "I'm very unhappy, and I don't know where to go."

Trenchard felt now as though in another moment he would tumble back again into his nightmare of yesterday. The house at X— indeed was fantastic enough. I feel that I am in danger of giving too many descriptions of our various halting-places. For the most part they largely resembled one another, large deserted country houses with broken windows, bare walls and floors, a tangled garden and a tattered collection of books in the Polish language. But this building at X— was like no other of our asylums.

It was a huge place, a strange combination of the local town-hall and the local theatre. It was the theatre that at that early hour in the morning seemed to our weary eyes so fantastic. As we peered into it it was a huge place, already filled with wounded and lighted only by candles, stuck here and there in bottles. I could see, dimly, the stage at the back of the room, and still hanging, tattered and restless in the draught, a forgotten backcloth of some old play. I could see that it was a picture of a gay scene in an impossibly highly coloured town—high marble stairs down which flower-girls with swollen legs came tripping into a market-place filled with soldiers and their lovers—"Carmen" perhaps. It seemed absurd enough there in the uncertain candlelight with the wounded groaning and crying in front of it. There was already in the air that familiar smell of blood and iodine, the familiar cries of: "Oh, Sestritza—Oh, Sestritza!" the familiar patient faces of the soldiers, sitting up, waiting for their turn, the familiar sharp voice of the sanitar: "What Division? What regiment? bullet or shrapnel?"

I remember that some wounded man, in high fever, was singing, and that no one could stop him.

"He's dead," I heard Semyonov's curt voice behind me, and turning saw them cover the body on the stretcher with a sheet.

"Oh! Oh!... Oh! Oh!" shrieked a man from the middle of whose back Nikitin, probing with his finger, was extracting a bullet. The candles flared, the ladies from "Carmen" wavered on the marble steps, the high cracked voice of the soldier continued its song. I stood there with Trenchard and Andrey Vassilievitch. Then we turned away.

"We're not wanted to-night," I said. "We'd better get out of the way and sleep somewhere. There'll be plenty to do to-morrow!" Little Andrey Vassilievitch, whom during the retreat I had entirely forgotten, looked very pathetic. He was dusty and dirty and hated his discomfort. He did not know where to go and was in everybody's way. Nikitin was immensely busy and had no time to waste on his friend. Poor Andrey was tired and terribly depressed.

"What I say is," he confided to us in a voice that trembled a little, "that we are not to despair. We have to retreat to-day, but who knows what will happen to-morrow? Every one is aware that Russia is a glorious country and has endless resources. Well then.... What I say is ..."; an officer bundled into him, apologised but quite obviously cursed him for being in the way.

"Come along," said Trenchard, putting his arm on Andrey Vassilievitch's sleeve. "We'll find somewhere to sleep. Of course we're not in despair. Why should we be? You'll feel better to-morrow."

They departed, and as they went I wondered at this new side in Trenchard's character. He seemed strong, practical, and almost cheerful. I, knowing his disaster, was puzzled. My lame leg was hurting me to-night. I found a corner to lie down in, rolled myself in my greatcoat and passed through a strange succession of fantastic dreams in which Trenchard, Marie Ivanovna, Nikitin, and Semyonov all figured. Behind them I seemed to hear some voice crying: "I've got you all!... I've got you all!... You're caught!... You're caught!... You're caught!"

On the following day there happened to Trenchard the thing that he had dreaded. Writing of it now I cannot disentangle it from the circumstances and surroundings of his account of it to me. He was looking back then, when he spoke to me, to something that seemed almost fantastic in its ironical reality. Every word of that conversation he afterwards recalled to himself again and again. As to Marie Ivanovna I think that he never even began to understand her; that he should believe in her was a different matter from his understanding her. That he should worship her was a tribute both to his inexperience and to his sentiment. But his relation to her and to this whole adventure of his was confused and complicated by the fact that he was not, I believe, in himself a sentimental man. What one supposed to be sentiment was a quite honest and naked lack of knowledge of the world. As experience came to him sentiment fell away from him. But experience was never to come to him in regard to Marie Ivanovna; he was to know as little of her at the end as he had known at the beginning, and this whole conversation with her (of course, I have only his report of it) is clouded with his romantic conception of her. To that I might add also my own romantic conception; if Trenchard never saw her clearly because he loved her, I never saw her clearly because—because—why, I do not know.... She was, from first to last, a figure of romance, irritating, aggressive, enchanting, baffling, always blinding, to all of us.

During the morning after our arrival in M— Trenchard worked in the theatre, bandaging and helping with the transport of the wounded up the high and difficult staircase. Then at midday, tired with the heat, the closeness of the place, he escaped into the little park that bordered the farther side of the road. It was a burning day in June—the sun came beating through the trees, and as soon as he had turned the corner of the path and had lost the line of ruined and blackened houses to his right he found himself in the wildest and most glittering of little orchards. The grass grew here to a great height—the apple-trees were of a fine age, and the sun in squares and circles and stars of light flashed like fire through the thick green. He stepped forward, blinded by the quivering gold, and walked into the arms of Marie Ivanovna. He, quite literally, ran against her and put his arms about her for a moment to steady her, not seeing who she was.

Then he gave a little cry.

She was also frightened. "It was the only time," he told me, "that I had ever seen her show fear."

They were silent, neither of them knowing the way to speak.

Then she said: "John, don't r-run away. It is very good. I wanted to speak to you. Here, sit down here."

She herself sat down and patted the grass, inviting him. He at once sat down beside her, but he could say nothing—nothing at all.

She waited for a time and then, seeing him, I suppose, at a loss and helpless, regained her own courage. "Are you still angry with me?"

"No," he answered, not looking at her.

"You have a right to be; I behaved very badly."

"I don't understand," he replied, "why you thought in Petrograd that you loved me and then—so soon—found that you did not—so soon."

He looked at her and then lowered his eyes.

"What do you know or I know?" she suddenly asked him impetuously. "Are we not both always thinking that things will be so fine—seichass—and then they are not. How could we be happy together when we are both so ignorant? Ah, you know, John, you know that happy together we could never be."

He looked at her clearly and without hesitation.

"I was very stupid," he said. "I thought that because I had come into a big thing I would be big myself. It is not so; I am the same person as I was in England. I have not changed at all and I shall never change ... only in this one thing that whether you go from me or whether you stay I shall never love anybody but you. All men say that, I know," he added, "but there are not many men who have had so little in their lives as I, and so perhaps it means more with me than it does with others."

She made no reply to him. She had not, I believe, heard him. She said, as though she were speaking to herself: "If we had not come, John, if we had stayed in Petrograd, anything might have been. But here there is something more than people. I don't know whether I love or hate any one. I cannot marry you or any man until this is all over."

"And then," he interrupted passionately, touching her sleeve with his hand. "After the war? Perhaps—again, you will—"

She took his hand in hers, looking at him as though she were suddenly seeing him for the first time:

"No—you, John, never. In Petrograd I didn't know what this could be—no idea—none. And now that I'm here I can think of nothing else than what I'm going to find. There is something here that I'd be afraid of if I let myself be and that's what I love. What will happen when I meet it? Shall I feel fear or no? And so, too, if there were a man whom I feared...."

"Semyonov!" Trenchard cried.

She looked at him and did not answer. He caught her hand urgently. "No, Marie, no—any one but Semyonov. It doesn't matter about me. But you must be happy—you must be. Nothing else—and he won't make you. He isn't—"

"Happy!" she answered scornfully. "I don't want to be happy. That isn't it. But to be sure that one's not afraid—" (She repeated to herself several times Hrabrost—the Russian for "bravery.") "That is more than you, John, or than I or than—"

She broke off, looked at him suddenly as he told me "very tenderly and kindly as though she liked me."

"John, I'm your friend. I've been bad to you, but I'm your friend. I don't understand why I've been so bad to you because, I would be fur-rious—yes, fur-rious—if any one else were bad to you. And be mine, John, whatever I do, be mine. I'm not really a bad character—only I think it's too exciting now, here—everything—for me to stop and think."

"You know," he answered with a rather tired gesture (he had worked in that hot theatre all the morning) "that I am always the same—but you must not marry Semyonov," he added fiercely.

She did not answer him, looked up at the sunlight and said after a time:

"I hate Sister K—. She is not really religious. She doesn't wash either. Let us go back. I was away, I said, only for a little."

They walked back, he told me, in perfect silence. He was more unhappy than ever. He was more unhappy because he saw quite clearly that he did not understand her at all; he felt farther away from her than ever and loved her more devotedly than ever: a desperate state of things. If he had taken that sentence of hers—"I think it's too exciting—now—here—for me to stop and think," he would, I fancy, have found the clue to her, but he would not believe that she was so simple as that. In the two days that followed, days of the greatest discomfort, disappointment and disorder, his mind never left her for a moment. His diary for these four days is very short and unromantic.

"June 23rd. In X—. Morning worked in the theatre. Bandaged thirty. Operation 1—arm amputated. Learn that there has been a battle round the school-house at O— where we first were. Wonderful weather. Spent some time in the park. Talked to M. there. Evening moved—thirty versts to P—. Much dust, very slow, owing to the Guards retreating at same time. Was with Durward and Andrey Vassilievitch in a Podvoda—Like the latter, but he's out of place here. Arrived 1.30.

"June 24th. Off early morning. This time black carriage with Sisters K— and Anna Petrovna. More dust—thousands of soldiers passing us, singing as though there were no retreat. News from L— very bad. Say there's no ammunition. Arrived Nijnieff evening 7.30. Very hungry and thirsty. We could find no house for some hours; a charming little town in a valley. Nestor seems huge—very beautiful with wooded hills. But whole place so swallowed in dust impossible to see anything. Heaps of wounded again. I and Molozov in nice room alone. Have not seen M. all day.

"June 25th. This morning Nikitin, Sister K—, Goga, and I attempted to get back to P— to see whether there were wounded. Started off on the carts but when we got to the hill above the village met the whole of our Division coming out. The village abandoned, so back we had to go again through all the dust. Evening nothing doing. Every one depressed.

"June 26th. Very early—half-past five in the morning—we were roused and had to take part in an exodus like the Israelites. Most unpleasant, moving an inch an hour, Cossacks riding one down if one preferred to go on foot to being bumped in the haycart. Every one in the depths of depression. Crossed the Nestor, a perfectly magnificent river. Five versts further, then stopped at a farmhouse, pitched tents. Instantly hundreds of wounded. Battle fierce just other side of Nijnieff. Worked like a nigger—from two to eight never stopped bandaging. About ten went off to the position with Molozov. Strange to be back in the little town under such different circumstances. Dark as pitch—raining. Much noise, motors, soldiers like ghosts though—shrapnel all the time. Tired, depressed and nervous. Horrid waiting doing nothing; two houses under the shrapnel. Expected also at every moment bridge behind us to be blown up. At last wagons filled with wounded, started back and got home eventually, taking two hours over it. Very glad when it was over...."

We had arrived, indeed, although we did not then know it and were expecting, every moment, to move back again, at the conclusion of our first exodus. Our only other transition, after a day or two longer at our farmhouse, was forward four versts to a tiny village on a high hill overlooking the Nestor, to the left of Nijnieff. This village was called Mittövo. Mittövo was to be our world for many weeks to come. We inhabited once again the large white deserted country-house with the tangled garden, the dusty bare floors, the broken windows. At the end of the tangled garden there was a white stone cross, and here was a most wonderful view, the high hill running precipitously down to the flat silver expanse of the Nestor that ran like a gleaming girdle under the breasts of the slopes beyond. These further slopes were clothed with wood. I remember, on the first day that I watched, the forest beyond was black and dense like a cloud resting on the hill; the Nestor and our own country was soaked with sun.

"That's a fine forest," I said to my companion.

"Yes, the forest of S—, stretches miles back into Galicia." It was Nikitin that day who spoke to me. We turned carelessly away. Meanwhile how difficult and unpleasant those first weeks at Mittövo were! We had none of us realised, I suppose, how sternly those days of retreat had tested our nerves. We had been not only retreating, but (at the same time) working fiercely, and now, when for some while the work slackened and, under the hot blazing sun, we found nothing for our hands to do, a grinding irritable reaction settled down upon us.

I had known in my earlier experience at the war the troubles that inevitably rise from inaction; the little personal inconveniences, the tyrannies of habits and manners and appearances, when you've got nothing to do but sit and watch your immediate neighbour. But on that earlier occasion our army had been successful; it seemed that the war would soon find its conclusion in the collapse of Germany, and good news from Europe smiled upon us every morning at breakfast. Now we were tired and over-wrought. Good news there was none—indeed every day brought disastrous tidings. We, ourselves, must look back upon a hundred versts of fair smiling country that we had conquered with the sacrifice of many thousands of lives and surrendered without the giving of a blow. And always the force that compelled us to this was sinister and ironical by its invisibility.

It was the Russian temperament to declare exactly what it felt, to give free rein to its moods and dislikes and discomforts. The weather was beginning to be fiercely hot, there were many rumours of cholera and typhus—we, all of us, lost colour and appetite, slept badly and suffered from sudden headaches.

Three days after our arrival at Mittövo we had all discovered private hostilities and resentments. I was as bad as any one. I could not endure the revolutionary student, Ivan Mihailovitch. I thought him most uncleanly in his habits, and I was compelled to sleep in the same room with him. Certainly it was true that washing was not one of the most important things in the world to him. In the morning he would lurch out of bed, put on a soiled shirt and trousers, dab his face with a decrepit sponge, take a tiny piece of soap from an old tin box, look at it, rub it on his fingers and put it hurriedly away again as though he were ashamed of it. Sometimes, getting out of bed, he would cry: "Have you heard the latest scandal? About the ammunition in the Tenth Army! They say—" and then he would forget his washing altogether. He did not shave his head, as most of us had done, but allowed his hair to grow very long, and this, of course, was often a subject of irritation to him. He had also a habit of sitting on his bed in his nightclothes, yawning and scratching his body all over, very slowly, with his long (and I'm afraid dirty) finger-nails, for the space, perhaps, of a quarter of an hour. This I found difficult to endure. His long white face was always a dirty shade of grey and his jacket was stained with reminiscences of his meals. His habits at table were terrible; he was always so deeply interested in what he was saying that he had not time to close his mouth whilst he was eating, to ask people to pass him food (he stretched his long dirty hand across the table) or to pass food to others. He shouted a great deal and was in a furious passion every five minutes. I also just at this time found the boy Goga tiresome; the boy had not been taught by his parents the duty that children owe to their elders and I am inclined to believe that this duty is almost universally untaught in Russia. To Goga a General was as nothing, he would contradict our old white-haired General T—, when he came to dine with us, would patronise the Colonel and assure the General's aide-de-camp that he knew better. He would advance his father as a perpetual and faithful witness to the truth of his statements. "You may say what you like," he would cry to myself or a Sister, "but my father knows better than you do. He has the front seat in the Moscow Opera all through the season and has been to England three times." Goga also had been once to England for a week (spent entirely on the Brighton Pier) and he told me many things. He would forget, for a moment, that I was an Englishman and would assure me that he knew better than I did. He was a being with the best heart in the world, but his parents loved him so much that they had neglected his education.

These things may seem trifling enough, but they had, nevertheless, their importance. Among the Sisters, Sister K— was the unpopular one. I myself must honestly confess that she was a woman ill-suited to company less worthy than herself. She had an upright virtuous character but she was narrow (a rare fault in a Russian), superstitious, dogmatically religious, and entirely without tact. She quite honestly thought us a poor lot and would say to me: "I hope, Mr. Durward, you don't judge Russia by the specimens you find here," and was, of course, always overheard. She was a strict moralist, but was also generous with all the warmth of Russian generosity in money matters. She was a marvellous hard worker, quite fearless, accurate, and punctual in all things. She fought incessant battles with Anna Petrovna who hated her as warmly as it was in her quiet, unruffled heart to hate any one. The only thing stranger than the fierceness of their quarrels was the suddenness of their conclusion. I remember that at dinner one day they fought a battle over the question of a clean towel with a heat and vigour that was Homeric. A quarter of an hour later I found them quietly talking together. Anna Petrovna was showing Sister K— a large and hideous photograph of her children.

"How sympathetic! How beautiful!" said Sister K—.

"But I thought you hated her?" I said afterwards in confusion to Anna Petrovna.

"She was very sympathetic about my children," said Anna Petrovna placidly.

Then, of course, Sister Sofia Antonovna, the sister with the red eyes, made trouble when she could. She was, as I discovered afterwards, a bitterly disappointed woman, having been deserted by her fiancé only a week before her marriage. That had happened three years ago and she still loved him, so that she had her excuse for her view of the world. My friends seemed to me, during those first weeks at Mittövo, simply a company of good-hearted, ill-disciplined children. I had gone directly back to my days in the nursery. Restraint of any kind there was none, discipline as to time or emotions was undreamed of, and with it all a vitality, a warmth of heart, a sincerity and honesty that made that Otriad, perhaps, the most lovable company I have ever known. Russians are fond of sneering at themselves; for him who declares that he likes Russia and Russians they have either polite disbelief or gentle contempt. In England we have qualities of endurance, of reliability, of solidity, to which, often enough, I long to return—but that warmth of heart that I have known here for two long years, a warmth that means love for the neglected, for the defeated, for the helpless, a warmth that lights a fire on every hearth in every house in Russia—that is a greater thing than the possessors of it know.

Through all the little quarrels and disputes of our company there ran the thread of the affair of Trenchard, Marie Ivanovna and Semyonov. Trenchard was lighted now with the pleasure of their affection, and Marie Ivanovna, who had been at first so popular amongst them, was held to be hard and capricious. She, at least, did not make it easy for them to like her. She had seemed in those first days in O— as though she wished to win all their hearts, but now it was as though she had not time to consider any of us, as though she had something of far greater importance to claim her attention. She was now very continually with Semyonov and yet it seemed to me that it was rather respect for his opinion and admiration of his independence than liking that compelled her. He was, beyond any question, in love with her, if the name of love can be given to the fierce, intolerant passion that governed him.

He made no attempt to disguise his feelings, was as rude to the rest of us as he pleased, and, of course, flung his scorn plentifully over Trenchard. But now I seemed to detect in him some shades of restlessness and anxiety that I had never seen in him before. He was not sure of her; he did not, I believe, understand her any more than did the rest of us. With justice, indeed, I was afraid for her. His passion, I thought, was as surely and as nakedly a physical one as any other that I had seen precede it, and would as certainly pass as all purely physical passions do. She was as ignorant of the world as on the day when she arrived amongst us; but my feeling about her was that she would receive his love almost as though in a dream, her thoughts fixed on something far from him and in no way depending on him. At any rate she was with him now continually. We judged her proud and hard-hearted, all of us except Trenchard who loved her, Semyonov who wanted her, and Nikitin, who, as I now believe, even then understood her.

Trenchard meanwhile was confused and unsettled: inaction did not suit him any better than it did the rest of us. He had too much time to think about Marie Ivanovna.

He was undoubtedly pleased at his new popularity. He expanded under it and became something of the loquacious and uncalculating person that he had shown himself during his confession to me in the train. To the Russians his loquacity was in no way strange or unpleasant. They were in the habit of unburdening themselves, their hopes, their disappointments, their joys, their tragedies, to the first strangers whom they met. It seemed quite natural to them that Trenchard, puffing his rebellious pipe, should talk to them about Glebeshire, Polchester, Rafiel, Millie and Katherine Trenchard.

"I'd like you to meet Katherine, Anna Petrovna," he would say. "You would find her delightful. She's married now to a young man she ran away with, which surprised every one—her running away, I mean, because she was always considered such a serious character."

"I forget whether you've seen my children, 'Mr.'" Anna Petrovna would reply. "I must show you their photograph."

And she would produce the large and hideous picture.

He was the same as in those first days, and yet how immensely not the same. He bore himself now with a chivalrous tact towards Marie Ivanovna that was beyond all praise. He always cherished in his heart his memory of their little conversation in the orchard. "How I wish," he told me, "that I had made that conversation longer. It was so very short and I might so easily have lengthened it. There were so many things afterwards that I might have said—and she never gave me another chance."

She never did—she kept him from her. Kind to him, perhaps, but never allowing him another moment's intimacy. He had almost the air, it seemed to me, of patiently waiting for the moment when she should need him, the air too of a man who was sure, in his heart, that that moment would come.

And the other thing that stiffened him was his hatred for Semyonov. Hatred may seem too fierce a word for the emotion of any one as mild and gentle as Trenchard—and yet hatred at this time it was. He seemed no longer afraid of Semyonov and there was something about him now which surprised the other man. Through all those first days at Mittövo, when we seemed for a moment almost to have slipped out of the war and to be leading the smaller more quarrelsome life of earlier days, Trenchard was occupied with only one question—"What was he feeling about Semyonov?"—"I felt as though I could stand anything if only she didn't love him. Since that awful night of the Retreat I had resigned myself to losing her; any one should marry her who would make her happy—but he—never! But it was the indecision that I could not bear. I didn't know—I couldn't tell, what she felt."

The indecision was not to last much longer. One evening, when we had been at Mittövo about a week, he was at the Cross watching the sun, like a crimson flower, sink behind the dim grey forest. The Nestor, in the evening mist, was a golden shadow under the hill. This beauty made him melancholy. He was wishing passionately, as he stood there, for work, hard, dangerous, gripping work. He did not know that that was to be the last idle minute of his life. Hearing a step on the path he turned round to find Semyonov at his side.

"Lovely view, isn't it?" said Semyonov, watching him.

"Lovely," answered Trenchard.

Semyonov sat down on the little stone seat beneath the Cross and looked up at his rival. Trenchard looked down at him, hating his square, stolid composure, his thick thighs, his fair beard, his ironical eyes. "You're a beastly man!" he thought.

"How long are you going to be with us, do you think?" asked Semyonov.

"Don't know—depends on so many things."

"Why don't you go back to England? They want soldiers."

"Wouldn't pass my eyesight."

"When are they going to begin doing something on the other Front, do you think?"

"When they're ready, I suppose."

"They're very slow. Where's all your army we heard so much about?"

"There's a big army going to be ready soon."

"Yes, but we were told things would begin in May. It's only the Germans who've begun."

"I don't know; I've seen no English papers for some weeks."

There was a pause. Semyonov smiled, stood up, looked into Trenchard's eyes.

"I must go to England," he said slowly, "after the war. Marie Ivanovna and I will go, I hope, together. She told me to-day that that is one of the things that she hopes we will do together—later on."

Trenchard returned Semyonov's gaze. After a moment he said:

"Yes—you would enjoy it." He waited, then added: "I must be walking back now. I'm late!" And he turned away to the house.

CHAPTER VII

ONE NIGHT

Marie Ivanovna herself spoke to me of Semyonov. She found me alone waiting for my morning tea. We were before the others, and could hear, in the next room, Molozov splashing water about the floor and crying to Michail, his servant, to pour "Yestsho! Yestsho!" "Yestsho! Yestsho!"—"Still more! Still more," over his head.

She stood in the doorway looking as though she hated my presence.

"The others have not arrived," I said. "It's late to-day."

"I can see," she answered. "Every one is idle now."

Then her voice changed. She came across to me. We talked of unimportant things for a while. Then she said: "I'm very happy, Mr. Durward.... Be kind about it. Alexei Petrovitch and I...." She hesitated.

I looked at her and saw that she was again the young and helpless girl whom I had not seen since that early morning before our first battle. I said, very lamely, "If you are happy, Marie Ivanovna, I am glad."

"You think it terrible of me," she said swiftly. "And why do you all talk of being happy? What does that matter? But I can trust him. He's strong and afraid of nothing."

I could say nothing.

"Of course you think me very bad—that I have treated—John—shamefully—yes?... I will not defend myself to you. What is there to defend? John and I could never have lived together, never. You yourself must see that."

"It does not matter what I think," I answered. "I am Trenchard's friend, and he has no knowledge of life nor human nature. He has made a bad start. You must forgive me if I think more of him than of you, Marie Ivanovna."

"Yes," she said fiercely. "It is John—John—John, you all think of. But John would not have loved me if he knew me as I truly am. And now, at last, I can be myself. It does not matter to Alexei Petrovitch what I am."

"But you have known him so short a time—and you have been so quick. If you had waited...."

"Waited!" she caught me up. "Waited! How can one wait when one isn't allowed to wait? It must be finished here, at once, and I'm not going to finish alone. I'm frightened, Mr. Durward, but also I must see it right through. He makes me brave. He's afraid of nothing. I couldn't leave this, and yet I was frightened to go on alone. With him beside me I'm not afraid."

Anna Petrovna interrupted us.

"It's Goga's stomach again," she said placidly. "He's had great pain all night. It was those sweets yesterday. Just give me that glass, my dear. Weak tea's the only thing he can have."

Well, I had said nothing to Marie Ivanovna. What was there I could have said?

And the next thing about Trenchard was that he had got his wish, and was lying on his back once more, in one of our nice, simple, uncomfortable haycarts, looking up at the evening sky. This was the evening after his conversation with Semyonov. Quite suddenly the battle had caught us into its arms again. It was raging now in the woods to the right of us, woods on the further side of the Nestor, situated on a tributary. I will quote now directly from his diary:

As our line of carts crossed the great river I could hear the muffled "brum-brum" of the cannons and "tap-tap-tap" of the machine-guns now so conventionally familiar. Nikitin was lying in silence at my side. Behind us came twenty wagons with the sanitars; the evening was very still, plum-colour in the woods, misty over the river; the creaking of our carts was the only sound, save the "brum-brum" and the "tap-tap-tap"....

I lay on my back and thought of Semyonov and myself. I had in my mind two pictures. One was of Semyonov sitting on the stone under the cross, looking up at me with comfortable and ironical insolence, Semyonov so strong and resolute and successful. Semyonov who got what he wanted, did what he wanted, said what he wanted.

The other picture was of myself, as I had been the other night when I had gone with the wagons to Nijnieff to fetch the wounded. I saw myself standing in a muddy little lane just outside the town, under pouring rain. The wagons waited there, the horses stamping now and then, and the wounded men on the only wagon that was filled, moaned and cried. Shrapnel whizzed overhead—sometimes crying, like an echo, in the far distance, sometimes screaming with the rage of a hurt animal close at hand. Groups of soldiers ran swiftly past me, quite silent, their heads bent. Somewhere on the high road I could hear motor-cars spluttering and humming. At irregular intervals Red Cross men would arrive with wounded, would ask in a whisper that was inhuman and isolating whether there were room on my carts. Then the body would be lifted up; there would be muttered directions, the wounded man would cry, then the other wounded would also cry—after that, there would be the dismal silence again, silence broken only by the shrapnel and the heavy plopping smothers of the rain. But it was myself upon whom my eyes were fixed, myself, a miserable figure, the rain dripping from me, slipping down my neck, squelching under my boots. And as I stood there I was afraid. That was what I now saw. I had been terribly afraid for the first time since I had come to the war. I had worked all day in the bandaging room, and perhaps my physical weariness was responsible; but whatever it might be there I was, a coward. At the threat of every shrapnel I bent my head and shrugged my shoulders, at every cry of the wounded men—one man was delirious and sang a little song—a shudder trembled all down my body. I thought of the bridge between myself and the Otriad—how easily it might be blown up! and then, if the Division were beaten back what massacre there would be! I wanted to go home, to sleep, to be safe and warm—above all, to be safe! I saw before me some of the wounded whom I had bandaged to-day—men without faces or with hanging jaws that must be held up with the hand whilst the bandage was tied. One man blind, one man mad (he thought he was drowning in hot water), one man holding his stomach together with his hands. I saw all these figures crowding round me in the lane—I also saw the dead men in the forest, the skull, the flies, the strong blue-grey trousers.... I shook so that my teeth chattered—a very pitiful figure.

Well, that was the other night. It was true that to-night I did not feel frightened—at least not as yet. But then it was a beautiful evening, very peaceful, still and warm—and there was Nikitin. In any case there were those two figures whom I must consider—Semyonov and myself. That brief conversation last night had brought us quite sharply face to face. I found to my own surprise that Semyonov's declaration of his engagement had not been a great shock to me, had not indeed altered very greatly the earlier situation. But it had shown me quite clearly that my own love for Marie Ivanovna was in no way diminished, that I must protect her from a man who was, I felt, quite simply a "beastly" man.

Well, then if Semyonov and I were to fight it out, I would need to be at my best. Did that little picture of the other evening show me at my best? This business presented a bigger fight than the simple one with Semyonov. I knew, quite clearly, as I lay on my back in the cart, that the fight against Semyonov and the fight against ... was mingled together, depended for their issue one upon the other—that the dead men in the forest had no merely accidental connexion with Marie Ivanovna's safety and Semyonov's scornful piracies.

Well, then ... Semyonov and I, I and my old dead uncle, myself shaking in the road the other night under the rain! What was to be the issue of all of it?

I, on this lovely evening, saw quite clearly the progress of events that had brought me to this point. One: that drive with Durward on the first day when we had stopped at the trench and heard the frogs. Two: the evening at O—, when Marie Ivanovna had been angry and we had first heard the cannon. Three: the day at S— and Marie kneeling on the cart with her hand on Semyonov's shoulder. Four: her refusal of me, the bodies in the forest, the Retreat, that night Nikitin (getting well into the thick of it now). Five: the talk with Marie in the park. Six: the wet night at Nijnieff. Seven: last night's little talk with Semyonov.... Yes, I could see now that I had been advancing always forward into the forest, growing ever nearer and nearer, perceiving now the tactics of the enemy, beaten here, frightened there, but still penetrating—not, as yet, retreating ... and always, my private little history marching with me, confused with the private little histories of all of the others, all of them penetrating more deeply and more deeply....

And if I lost my nerve I was beaten! If I had lost my nerve no protecting of Marie, no defiance of Semyonov—and, far beyond these, abject submission to my enemy in the forest. If I had lost my nerve!... Had I? Was it only weariness the other night? But twice now I had been properly beaten, and why, after all, should I imagine that I would be able to put up a fight—I who had never in all my life fought anything successfully? I lay on my back, looked at the sky. I sat up, looked at the country, I set my teeth, looked at Nikitin.

Nikitin grunted. "I've had a good nap," he said. "You should have had one. There'll be plenty of work for us to-night by the sound of it." We turned a corner of the road through the wood and one of our own batteries jumped upon us.

"I'm glad it's not raining," I said.

"We've still some way to go," said Nikitin, sitting up. "What a lovely evening!" Then he added, quite without apparent connexion, "Well, you're more at home amongst us all now, aren't you?"

"Yes," said I.

"I'm glad of that. And what do you think of Andrey Vassilievitch?"

I answered: "Oh! I like him! ... but I don't think he's happy at the war," I added.

"I want you to like him," Nikitin said. "He's a splendid man ... I have known him many years. He is merry and simple and it is easy to laugh at him, but it is always easy to laugh at the best people. You must like him, 'Mr.'... He likes you very much."

I felt as though Nikitin were here forming an alliance between the three of us. Well, I liked Nikitin, I liked Andrey Vassilievitch. I listened to the battery, now some way behind us, then said:

"Of course, I am his friend if he wishes."

Nikitin repeated solemnly: "Andrey Vassilievitch is a splendid fellow."

Then we arrived. Here, beside the broad path of the forest there was a clearing and above the clearing a thick pattern of shining stars curved like the top of a shell. Here, in the open, the doctors had made a temporary hospital, fastening candles on the trees, arranging two tables on trestles, all very white and clean under a brilliant full moon. There were here two Sisters whom I did not know, several doctors, one of them a fat little army doctor who had often been a visitor to our Otriad. The latter greeted Nikitin warmly, nodded to me. He was a gay, merry little man with twinkling eyes. "Noo tak. Fine, our hospital, don't you think? Plenty to do this night, my friend. Here, golubchik, this way.... Finger, is it? Oh! that's nothing. Here, courage a moment. Where are the scissors?... scissors, some one. One moment.... One ... moment. Ah! there you are!" The finger that had been hanging by a shred fell into the basin. The soldier muttered something, slipped on to his knees, his face grey under the moon, then huddled into nothing, like a bundle of old clothes, fainted helplessly away.

"Here, water!... No, take him over there! That's right. Well, 'Mr.'—how are you? Lovely night.... Plenty of work there'll be, too. Oh! you're going down to the Vengerovsky Polk? Yes, they're down to the right there somewhere—across the fields.... Warm over there."

The noise just then of the batteries was terrific. We were compelled to shout at one another. A battery behind us bellowed like a young bull and the shrapnel falling at some distance amongst the trees had a strange splashing sound as of a stone falling into water.[A] The candles twinkled in the breeze and the place had the air of a Christmas-tree celebration, the wounded soldiers waiting their turn as children wait for their presents. The starlight gave the effect of a blue-frosted crispness to the pine-strewn ground. We arranged our wagons safely, then, followed by the sanitars, walked off, Nikitin almost fantastically tall under the starlight as he strode along. The forest-path stopped and we came to open country. Fields with waving corn stretched before us to be lost in the farther distance in the dark shadows of the forest.

[Footnote A: It must be remembered that this account is Trenchard's—taken from his diary. In my own experience I have never known the bursting of shell to sound in the least like a stone in water. But he insists on the accuracy of this. Throughout this and the succeeding chapters there are many statements for which I have only his authority.—P.D.]

A little bunch of soldiers crouched here, watching, Nikitin spoke to them.

"Here, golubchik ... tell me! what polk?"

"Moskovsky, your Honour."

"And the Vengerovsky ... they're to the right, are they?"

"Yes, your Honour. By the high road, when it comes into the forest."

"What? There where the road turns?"

"Tak totchno."

"How are things down there just now? Wounded, do you think?"

"Ne mogoo znat. I'm unable to say, your Honour ... but there's been an attack there an hour ago."

"Are those ours?"—listening to a battery across the fields.

"Ours, your Honour."

"Well, we'll go on and see."

I had listened to this conversation with the sensation of a man who has stopped himself on the very edge of a precipice. I thought in those few moments with a marvellous and penetrating clarity. I had, after all, been always until now at the battle of S—, or when I had gone with the wagons to Nijnieff, on the outskirts of the thing. I knew that to-night, in another ten minutes, I would be in the middle—the "very middle." As I waited there I recalled the pages of the diary of some officer, a diary that had been shown me quite casually by its owner. It had been a miracle of laconic brevity: "6.30 A. M., down to the battery. All quiet. 8.0, three of their shells. One of ours killed, two wounded. Five yards' distance. 8.30, breakfasted; K. arrived from the 'Doll's House'—all quiet there," and so on. This, I knew, was the proper way to look at the affair: "6.0 A. M., down to the battery. 7.0 A. M., breakfasted. 8.0 A. M., dead...." For the life of me now I could not look at it like that. I saw a thousand things that were, perhaps, not really there, but were there at any rate for me. If I was beaten to-night I was beaten once and for all.... I saw the shining road under the starlight and shadows of wounded men, groaning and stumbling, whispering their way along.

"Let's go," said Nikitin.

I drew a breath and stepped out into the moonlight. A shell burst with a delicate splash of fire amongst the stars. The road looked very long and very, very lonely.

However, soon I found myself walking along it quite casually and talking about unimportant peaceful things. "Come," I thought to myself. "This really isn't so bad."

"It's a great pity," Nikitin said, "that I can't read English. Have to take your novelists as they choose to give them us. Who is there now in England?"

"Well," said I as one talks in a dream, "there's Hardy, and Henry James, and Conrad. I've seen translations of Conrad in Petrograd. And then there's Wells—"

"Yes, Wells I know. But he writes stories for boys.... There's Jack London, but his are American. I like to read an English novel sometimes. Your English life is so cosy. You have tea before the fire and everything is comfortable. We don't know what comfort is in Russia."

A machine gun "rat-tat-tat-tated" close to us, and three rockets, like a flight of startled birds, rose suddenly together on the far horizon.

"No, we have no comfort in Russia," repeated Nikitin. "Now I fancy that an English country-house...."

We had reached the further wood; the moonlight fell away from us and the shadows shifted and trembled under the reflection of rockets and a projector that swung lazily and unsteadily, like something nodding in its sleep.

On the left of the road there was a house standing back in its own garden. I could see dimly that this was a row of country villas.

"Stand by this gate five minutes," Nikitin whispered to me. "I must find the Colonel. The sanitars will come and fetch you when I've settled the spot for our bandaging."

Nikitin disappeared and I was quite alone. I felt terribly desolate. I stood back against the gate of the villa watching soldiers hurry by, seeing high mysterious hedges, the roofs of houses, a line of lighted sky, the tops of trees, all these things rising and falling as the glare in the heavens rose and fell. There was sometimes a terrible noise and sometimes an equally terrible stillness. Somewhere in the darkness a man was groaning, "Oh! ah!—Oh! ah!" without cessation. Somewhere the gate of one of the villas swung to and fro, creaking. Sometimes soldiers would stare at my motionless figure and then pass on.

All this time, as in one's dreams sometimes one holds off a nightmare, I was keeping my fear at bay. I had now exactly the sensation that I had known so often in my dream, that I was standing somewhere in the dark, that the Enemy was watching me and waiting to spring. But to-night I was only nearly afraid. One step on my part, one extra noise, one more flare of light, and I would abandon myself to panic, but, although the perspiration was wet on my forehead, my heart thumping, and my hands dry and hot, I was not yet quite afraid.

I had a strange sensation of suffocation, as though I were at the bottom of a well, a well black and damp, with the stars of the sky miles away. There came to me, with a kind of ironic sentimentality, the picture of the drawing-room at home in Polchester, the corner where the piano stood with a palm in an ugly brass pot just behind it, the table near the door with a brass Indian tray and a fat photograph-book with, gilt clasps, the picture of "Christ being Scourged" above the fireplace, and the green silk screen that stood under the picture in the summer.

A soldier stopped and spoke to me: "Your Honour, it's on the right—the next gate." I followed him without attention, having no doubt but that this was one of our own sanitars, and accompanied a group of soldiers that surrounded a bobbing kitchen on wheels. I was puzzled by the kitchen because I knew that one had not been brought by our Otriad, but I thought that the doctors of the Division had perhaps begged our men to aid the army sanitars.

We hurried through a gate to the right, where in what appeared to be a yard of some kind, the kitchen was established and then, from out of the very earth as it seemed, soldiers appeared, clustering around it with their tin cans. The soldier who was in charge of the party said to me in a confidential whisper: "There's plenty of Kasha, your Honour, and the soup will last us, too."

"Very good," said I in a bewildered voice. At the strange accent the soldier looked at me, and then I looked at the soldier. The soldier was a stranger to me (a pleasant round man with a huge smiling mouth and two chins) and I was a stranger to the soldier.

"Well," said the soldier, looking, "I thought...."

"I thought—" said I, most uncomfortable.

The soldiers vanished back into the darknesses round the kitchen. Voices, whispering, could be heard.

"Now, that's the end," thought I. "I'm shot as a German spy."

I looked at the soldiers, clustered like bees round the kitchen, then I slipped through the gate into the dark road. I stood there listening. The battle seemed to have drawn away, because I could hear rifles, machine-guns, cannon muffled round a corner of the hill. Here there was now silence, broken only by soldiers who hurried up the road or went in and out at the villa gates. I felt abandoned. How was I to discover Nikitin again? Before what gate had I stood? I did not know; I seemed to know nothing.

I moved down the road, very miserable and very cold. I had stupidly left my coat in one of the wagons. I walked on, my boots knocking against one another, thinking to myself: "If I'm not given something to do very soon I shall be just as I was the other night at Nijnieff—and then I shall suddenly take to my heels down this road as hard as I can go!"

It was then that I tumbled straight into the arms of Nikitin, who was standing at the edge of the forest, watching for me. I was so happy that I felt now afraid of nothing. I held Nikitin's arm, babbling something about kitchens and Germans.

"Well, I don't understand what you say," I remember Nikitin replied; "but you must come and work. There's plenty of it."

We moved to a cottage on the very boundary of the forest, where a little common ran down to the moonlight. Passing through a narrow passage, I entered into a little room with a large white stove. On the top of the stove, under the roof, crouched a boy or a young man with long black hair and a white face. This youth wore what resembled a white shirt over baggy white trousers. His feet were bare and very dirty. Nothing moved except his eyes. He sat there, in exactly that position, all night.

The room was small but was the best that could be obtained. Within the space of ten minutes it became a perfect shambles. The wounded were brought in without pause and under the candlelight Nikitin, two sanitars, and I worked until the sweat ran down our backs and arms in streams. It dripped from my nose, into my mouth, into my eyes. The wounds were horrible. No man seemed to come into the room with an unmangled body. The smell rose higher and higher, the bloody rags lay about the kitchen floor, torn arms, smashed legs, heads with gaping wounds, the pitiful crying and praying, the shrill voices of the delirious, Nikitin, his arms steeped in blood to the elbows, probing, cutting, digging, I myself bandaging until I did not know what my hands were doing.... Then suddenly the battle coming right back to us again, overhead now as it seemed; the cannon shaking three silly staring china dogs on the kitchen dresser, the rifle fire clattering like tumbling crockery about the walls of the cottage—and through it all the white youth, crouched like a ghost on the stove, watching without pause....

"Ah, no, your Honour.... Ah, no! ... I can't! I can't! Oh, oh, oh, oh!" and then sobs, the man breaking down like a child, hiding his face in his arms, his wounded leg twitching convulsively. I paused, wiped the sweat from my eyes, stood up. Nikitin looked at me.

"Take some fresh air!" he said. "Go out with the stretcher for half an hour. I can manage here."

I wiped my forehead.

"Sure you can manage?" I asked.

"Quite," said Nikitin. "Here, hold his back!... No, durak, his back. Bojé moi, can't you get your arm under? There—like that. Horosho, golubchik, horosho ... only a minute! There! There!"

I washed my hands and went out. The air caressed my forehead like cold water; from the little garden at the back there came scents of flowers; the moonlight was blue on the common. Eight sanitars were waiting to start. The Feldscher in charge of them did not, I thought, seem greatly pleased when he saw me, but then I am often stupidly sensitive; no one said anything and we started. We carried two stretchers and a soldier from the trenches was with us to guide us.

I could see that the men were not happy. I heard one of them mutter to another that they should not have been sent now; that they should have waited until the attack was over ... "and the full moon.... Did any one ever see such a moon?"

We came to cross-roads and advanced very carefully.

As we crossed the road I was conscious of great excitement. The noise around us was terrific and different from any noise that I heard before. I did not think at the time, but was informed afterwards that it was because we were almost directly under a high-wooded cliff (the actual position about whose possession the battle was being fought), that the noise was so tremendous. The echo flung everything back so that each report sounded three or four times. This certainly had the strangest effect—a background as it were of rolling thunder, sometimes distant, sometimes very close and, in front of this, clapping, bellowing, stamping, and then suddenly an absolutely smashing effect as though some one cried: "Well, this will settle it!" In quieter intervals one heard the birdlike flight of bullets above one's head and the irritated bad temper of the machine-guns. At every smashing noise the sanitars, who were, I believe, schoolmasters and little clerks, and therefore of a more sensitive head than the peasant soldier, ducked their heads, and one fat red-faced man tried to lie down flat on two occasions and was cursed heartily by the Feldscher. I myself felt no fear but only a pounding exhilarating excitement, because I was at last "really in it." We found one wounded man very soon, lying under the hedge with the top of his head gone. Four sanitars (their relief showed very plainly in their faces) returned with him. We advanced again, skirting now a little orchard and keeping always in the shadow under the hedge. Our guide, the soldier, assured us that the wounded man was "very near—quite close." Then we came to a large barn on the edge of what seemed a silver lake but was in reality a long field under the full light of the moon. As we paused I saw, on the further side of the field, two shells burst, very quickly, one after the other.

We all stopped under the shelter of the barn.

"Well," said the Feldscher to the soldier, "where's your man?"

"Only a short way," said the soldier. "Quite close."

"Across that field?" asked the Feldscher, pointing to the moonlight.

"Yes, certainly," said the soldier.

The Feldscher scratched his head. "We can't go further without orders," he said. "That's very dangerous in front there. I'm responsible for these men. We must return and ask, your Honour," he said, turning to me.

"We shall be nearly an hour returning," I said. "Is your friend badly wounded?" I asked the soldier.

"Very," said he.

"You see ..." I said to the Feldscher. "We can't possibly leave him like that. It's only a little way."

The Feldscher shook his head. "I can't be responsible. I had my orders to go so far and no further. I must see that my men are safe."

The sanitars who were sitting in a row on their haunches under the shadow of the barn all nodded their heads.

"I didn't know Russians were cowards," I said fiercely.

The Feldscher shook his head quite unmoved: "Your Honour must understand that I had my orders." Then he added slowly: "but of course if your Honour wishes to go yourself ... I would come with you. The others ... they must do as they please. They are in their right to return. But I should advise that we return."

"I'm going on," I said.

I must say here that I felt no other sensation than a blind and quite obstinate selfishness. I had no thought of Nikitin or of the sanitars. I did not (and this I must emphasise) think, for a moment, of the wounded man. If the situation had been that by returning I should save many lives and by advancing should save only my own I should still have advanced. If the only hope for the wounded man was my instant speech with Nikitin I would not have gone back to speak with him. I was at this moment neither brave nor fearful. I repeat that I had no sensation except an absolutely selfish obstinate challenge that I, myself, was addressing to Something in space. I was saying: "At last, my chance has come. Now you shall see whether I fly from you or no. Now you shall do your worst and fail. I'm the hunter now, not the hunted."

I was conscious of nothing but this quite childish preoccupation with myself. I was, nevertheless, pleased with myself. "There, you see," some one near me seemed to say, "he's not quite so unpractical after all. He's full of common sense." I looked at the row of sanitars squatting on the ground, and felt like a schoolmaster with his children.

"You'd better go home then," I said scornfully. The Feldscher, who was a short stocky man, with a red face and melancholy eyes (something like a prize-fighter turned poet), dismissed them. They went off in a line under the hedge.

The man obviously thought me a tiresome prig. He had no romantic illusions about the business; he had not been a Feldscher during twenty years for nothing and knew that a wound was a wound; when a man was dead he was dead.

However.... "Truly it's not far?" he asked the soldier.

"Tak totchno," the man answered, his face quite without expression.

We crossed the moonlit field and for a brief moment silence fell, as though an audience were holding its breath watching us. On the other side were cottages, the outskirts of a tiny village. Here beside these cottages we fell into a fantastic world. That small village must in other times have been a pretty place, nestling with its gardens by the river under the hill. It seemed now to rock and rattle under the noise of the cannon. All the open spaces were like white marble in the moonlight and in these open spaces there was utter silence and emptiness. The place seemed deserted—and yet, in every shadow, in long lines under the cottage wells, in little clumps and clusters round trees or ruins there were eyes staring, the gleam of muskets shone, little specks of light, dancing from wall to wall. Everywhere there were bodies, legs, boots, arms, heads, sudden caps, sudden fingers, sudden hot and streaming breaths. And over everything this infernal noise and yet no human sound. A nightmare of the true nightmare of dreams. The open silver spaces, the little gardens thick with flowers, the high moon and the starry sky, not a living soul to be seen—and nevertheless watchers everywhere. "Step forward on to that little plot of grass in front of the cottage windows and you're a dead man"—the moonlight said. There were men in the body of the earth, not in trenches, but in holes—my foot stepped on a head of hair and some low voice cursed me. I was, I suppose, by this time, a little delirious with my adventure. I know that I could now distinguish no separate sounds—shells and bullets had vanished and in their stead were whispers and screams and shouts of triumph and bursts of laughter. Songs in chorus, somewhere miners hammering below the earth, somewhere storm at sea with the crash of waves on rocks and the shriek of wind through rigging, somewhere some one who dropped heavy loads of furniture so carelessly that I cursed him—and always these little patches of moonlight, so tempting just because one was forbidden....

We were not popular here. Husky, breathless voices whispered to us "to be away from here, quick. We would draw the fire. What did we want here now?"

"Have you any wounded?" we whispered in return.

"No, no," the answer came. "Keep away from the moonlight." The voices came to us connected sometimes with a nose, an eye, or a leg, often enough out of the heaven itself.

"There's a man wounded behind the next lines," some voice murmured.

We stumbled on and suddenly came to a river with very steep banks and a number of narrow and slender bridges. If this had in reality been a nightmare this river could not have obtruded itself more often than it did. We discovered to our dismay that our soldier-guide had disappeared (exactly as in a nightmare he would have done). We crossed the river (bathed of course in moonlight), the plank bridge shaking and quivering beneath us.

We had then a difficult task. Here a row of cottages beneath the very edge of the bank and in the cottage shadow the soldiers were ranged in a long line. Their boots stretched to the verge of the bank, which was slippery and uncertain. We had to walk on this with our stretchers, stepping between the boots, stumbling often and slipping down towards the water.

"Any wounded?" we whispered again and again.

"No," the whisper came back. "Hasten.... Take care of the moonlight."

And then, to my infinite relief and comfort, behind the cottages we found our wounded man. There was a dark yard here, apparently quite deserted. The Feldscher made an exclamation and stepped forward. Three bodies lay together, over one another; two men were dead and cold, the third stirred, very faintly, as we came up, opened his eyes, smiled and said:

"Eh, Bojé moi ... at last!"

As we moved him on to the stretcher, with a little sigh he fainted again. He had a bad stomach-wound. Before picking up the stretcher, the Feldscher wiped his forehead and crossed himself.

"It's a heavy thing for two," he said. "He's a big man," looking at the soldier. There was now somewhere, apparently not very far away, hot rifle fire. The crackle sparkled in the air, as though one were living in a world in which all the electricity was loose. The other firing seemed to have drawn away, and the "Boom—Boom—boom" in front of us was echo from the hill....

We picked up the stretcher and started. It was fortunate for us that we had that difficult bit beside the river at the beginning of our journey. I don't know how we managed it, stepping over the endless row of legs, with every side step the stretcher lurching over to the left and threatening to pitch us into the river. So slippery too was the ground that our boots refused to grip. The man on the stretcher was dreaming, making a little sound like an unceasing lullaby on two notes—"Na ... na! Na ... na! Na ... na!"

We were compelled to cross the river twice, and the planks bent under our weight until I was assured that they would snap. My arms were beginning to ache and the sweat to trickle down my spine. My right boot had rubbed my heel. We left the river behind us and then, suddenly, my right hand began to slip off the iron handle of the stretcher.

"We'll have to put it down a moment," I said. We laid it on the ground and at the same instant a bullet sang so close to my ear that I felt it as though an insect had bitten me. Then a shell, exploding, as it seemed to us, amongst the very cottages where we had just been, startled us.

"We saved our man," said the Feldscher, looking at the soldier, "but we'd better move on. It's uncomfortable here."

We picked the thing up and started again, and at once my hand began to slip away from its hold (nightmare sensation exactly). I bent my head down, managed to lick my hand without raising it, and stiffened the muscles of my arm. We were watched, once more, by a million eyes—again I stepped on a head of hair buried somewhere in the ground. Then some voice cried shrilly: "Ah! Ah!" ... some man hit.

Every bone in my body began to ache. I was, of course, rottenly trained, without a sound muscle in my body, and my legs threatened cramp, my heel grated against my boot and sent a stab to my stomach with every movement, my shoulders seemed to pull away from the stretcher as though they would separately rebel against my orders ... and my hand began again to slip. The Feldscher also began to feel the strain. Once he asked me to stop. He apologised; I could see the sweat pouring down his face: "A very big man'" he said.

Whether it were the echo, whether my ears had by this time been utterly deafened and confused I do not know, but now the shock and rumble of the cannon seemed to come directly from under my feet. I felt perhaps as though I were on one of those railways that I have seen in London at a fair when the ground shakes and quivers beneath you. It really would not have surprised me had the earth suddenly yawned and swallowed me. Every plague now beset me. My hand refused to hold the stretcher, my body was wet with perspiration, my face was for some reason covered with mud.... There was a snap and my braces burst. My belt was loose and my trousers, as though they had waited for their opportunity, slipped down over my knees. I felt the cold night wind on my flesh. Neither decency nor comfort mattered to me now—I would have walked gladly naked through the world. The Feldscher was making a grinding noise between his teeth. I was no longer conscious of shell or bullets. I heard no noise. I was aware of neither light nor darkness. I could not have told my name had any one asked me it. I did not recognise trees nor houses, nor was I at all aware that with a muddy face and my trousers down to my knees I was a strange figure. I was aware of one thing only—that I must keep my right hand on the stretcher. My left behaved decently enough, but my right was a rebel. I felt a personal fury against it, as though I said to it: "Ah! but I'll punish you when I get back!" I with all my mental consciousness "willed" it to remain on the handle. It slipped. I drove it back. It slipped further, it was almost gone.... With a supreme effort I drove it back again, "I will fall off," said my hand. "You shall not," said I. "I have!" cried my hand triumphantly. "Back!" I swore, driving it.

We were now, I believe, both stumbling along, the wounded man pitching from side to side. Of the rest of our journey I have the most confused memory. The firing had no longer any effect upon me. I was thinking of my rebellious hand, my aching heel, and the irritation of my trousers clustered about my legs. "Another step and I shall fall!" I thought.... "I shall sleep." I heard, from a great distance as it seemed, the soldier's "Na ... Na! Na ... na!" I replied to him as a nurse to her child. "Na ... na! Na ... na!" ... Then I heard Nikitin's voice....

Half an hour after my adventure I was watching the dawn flood the sky from the little garden at the back of the cottage. It seemed that those stretchers are really heavy things for any two men to carry.... We had been three hours on our journey!

Well—I sat in the garden watching the sun rise. To my right were four dead men neatly laid out in a row under a tree. Their faces had not been covered but their eyes were closed, their cheeks, hands, and feet like wax. In front of them the young man who had sat on the stove in the kitchen all night and watched us at work was mowing the tall grass with a scythe. He was going to dig graves. He wore a white shirt and white trousers and had long black hair.

"Why didn't they take you for a soldier?" I asked him.

"Consumptive," he said.

I had washed my face, hitched up my trousers. I sat on the trunk of a tree, watched the dew on the grass and the faint blue like the colour of a bird's egg flood the sky, staining it pale yellow. All firing had utterly ceased. There was not a sound except the birds in the trees who were beginning to sing. A soldier, a fine grave figure with a black beard, was washing in a little pool at the end of the garden. He was naked save for his white drawers. There was, I repeat, not a sound. Our cottage looked so peaceful—smoke coming from the chimney. No sign of the shambles, no sign except the four dead men, all so grave and quiet. The blue in the sky grew deeper. Then the sun rose, a jolly gold ball with red clouds swinging in streamers away from it.

The birds sang above my head so loudly that the boy who was mowing looked up at them. The soldier finished his washing, put on his shirt. He was a Mahommedan, I perceived, because he prayed, very solemnly, his face to the sun, bowing to the ground. The grass fell before the flashing scythe, the sun flamed behind the trees, and I was happy as I had never known happiness in my life before.

I had done only what all the soldiers are doing every day of their lives. I had been only where they always were.... But I felt that I need never be afraid again. Every one knows how an early summer morning can give one confidence; in my happiness, God forgive me, I thought that my struggles were at an end, that I had met my enemy and defeated him ... that I was worthy and able to defend Marie.

These things may seem foolish now when one knows what followed them, but the happiness of that morning at least was real. Perhaps all over Europe there were men, at that moment, happy as I was, because they had proved something to themselves. Then Nikitin called to me, laughing.

"Tea, 'Mr.' and bulki (white bread) and sausage?"

"All right, I'm coming," I answered. "Listen, golubchik," I called to the soldier. "Bring me some water in your kettle. I'll wash my hands."

He came, smiling, towards me.

I have given the incidents of this night in great detail for my own satisfaction, because I wish to forget nothing. To others the little adventure must seem trivial, but to myself it represented the climax of a chain of events.

PART TWO

CHAPTER I

THE LOVERS

Semyonov and Marie Ivanovna did not offer us a picture of idealised love—they did not offer us a picture of anything, and although they were, both of them, most certainly changed, they could not be said in any way to do what the Otriad expected of them. The Otriad quite frankly expected them to be ashamed of themselves. To expect that of Semyonov at any time showed a lamentable lack of interest in human character, but, as I have already said, our Otriad was always excited by results rather than causes. Semyonov had never shown himself ashamed of anything, and he most certainly did not intend to begin now. He had never disguised his love for Marie Ivanovna and now she was his "spoils"—won by his own strong piratical hand from the good but rather feeble bark Trenchard—he manifested his scorn of us more openly than ever.

He seemed to have grown rather stronger and stouter during these last months, and his square stolidity was a thing at which to marvel. Had he been taller, had his beard been pointed rather than square, he would have been graceful and even picturesque—but his figure, as he strode along, showed foursquare, as though it had been hewn out of wood; one of those pale, almost white, honey-coloured woods would give the effect of his fair beard and eyebrows. His thick red lips were more startling than ever, curved as they usually were in cynical contempt of some foolish victim. How he did despise us!

When one of our childish quarrels arose at meal-times he would say nothing, but would continue stolidly his serious business of eating. He was very fond of his food, which he ate in the greediest manner. When the quarrel was subsiding, as it usually did, into the first glasses of tea, he would look up, watch us with his contemptuous blue eyes, laugh and say: "Well, and now?... Who is it next?"—and every one would be clumsily embarrassed.

We were often, as are all Russian companies, ridiculously amused about nothing. At the most serious crises we would, like Gayeff in "The Cherry Orchard," suddenly break into stupid bursts of laughter, quite aimless but with a great deal of sincerity. Whirls of laughter would invade our table. "Oh, do look at Goga!" some one would say, and there we all were, perhaps for a quarter of an hour! Semyonov, strangely enough, shared this childish habit, and there was nothing odder than to see the man lose control of himself, double himself up, laugh until the tears ran down his face—simply at nothing at all!

The truth is that now I was very far from hating him. There were moments, certainly, when he was rude to the Sisters, when he was abominably greedy, when he was ruthlessly selfish, when he poured scorn upon me; at such times I thought him, as Trenchard has expressed it, a "beastly" man. He certainly had no great opinion of myself. "You think yourself very clever, Ivan Andreievitch. Yes, you think you're watching all of us and studying all our characters. And I suppose there'll be a book one day, another of those books by Englishmen about poor Russians—and you'll flatter yourself that now at last one true picture has been given ... but let me tell you that you'll never know anything really about us so long as you're a sentimentalist!"

Yes, there were moments when I hated him, but those moments never continued for long. For one thing one could not hate so magnificent, so honest, so uncompromising, so efficient a worker! He was worthy of some very high position in the army, and he could certainly have attained any height had he chosen. He had a genius for compelling other men to obey him, he was never perturbed by unexpected mischance, he paid no attention at all to what other people thought of him, and he seemed incapable of fatigue. I often wondered what he was doing here, why he had chosen so small an Otriad as ours in which to work, why he stayed with us when he, so openly, despised us all. Until the arrival of Marie Ivanovna there was no answer to these questions—after that the answer was obvious enough. Again, one could not hate a man of his sterling independence of character. We were, all of us I think, emotionalists, of one kind or another, and went up and down in our feelings, alliances, severances, trusts and distrusts, as a thermometer goes up and down. We were good enough people in our way, but we were most certainly not "a strong lot." Even Nikitin, the best of the rest of us, was a dreamy idealist, far enough from life as it was and quite unprepared to come down from his dreams and see things as they were.

But Semyonov never relaxed for an instant from his position. He asked no man's help nor advice, minded no man's scorn, sought no man's love. During my experience of him I saw him moved only once by an overmastering emotion, and that was, of course, his love for Marie Ivanovna. That, I believe, did master him, but deep down, deep down, he kept his rebellions, his anxieties, his surmises; only as the light of a burning house is seen by men, pale and faint upon the sky many miles from the conflagration, did we catch signs of his trouble. If I had not had those talks with Trenchard and read his diary I should have known nothing. Even now I can offer no solution....

Meanwhile he showed fiercely and openly enough his love for Marie Ivanovna. He behaved to her with the vulgarest ostentation, as a rich merchant behaves when he has snatched some priceless picture from a defeated rival. As he laughed at us he seemed to say: "Now, I have really a thing of value here. You are, all of you, too stupid to realise this, but you must take my word for it. Show yourself off, my dear, and let them all see!"

Marie Ivanovna most certainly did not "show herself off." The beginning of his trouble was that he could not do with her as he pleased. She had fallen into his hands so easily that he thought, I suppose, that "she had been dying of love for him" from the first moment of seeing him. But this was I believe very far from the truth. My impression of her acceptance of him was that she had done it "with her eyes fixed upon something else." That she had not realised all the consequences of accepting him any more than she had realised the consequences of her accepting Trenchard was obvious from the first. She simply was ignorant of life, and at the same time wanted to cram into her hands the full sense of it (as one crushes rose-leaves) as quickly as possible. She admired Semyonov—it may be that she loved him; but she certainly had not surrendered herself to him, and in her lively ignorant way she was as strong as he.

During the first weeks of her engagement she was, as she had been at her first arrival amongst us, as happy and light-hearted as a child. She knew that we disapproved of her treatment of Trenchard, but she thought that we must see, as she did, that "she had behaved in the only possible way." Once again she was straight and honest to the world—and she could behave now like a real friend of her John. That strange irrational temper that she had shown during the Retreat had now entirely disappeared. She approved of us all and wished us to approve of her—which we, as we were Russians and could not possibly dislike pleasant agreeable people whatever there might be against them, speedily did. She was charming to us. I can see her now, leaning her chin on her hands; looking at us, the colour, shell-pink, coming and going delicately in her cheek, like flame behind china. Her delicacy, her height, her slender figure, her wide childish eyes, her charmingly ugly large mouth and short nose, her black hair, the appeal of her ignorance and strength and credulity—ah! she won our hearts simply whenever she pleased! Of course we disliked her when she was rude to us, our self-respect demanded it, but let her "come round" and round we came too.

Her treatment of Semyonov was strange. She was quite fearless, laughing at his temper, his sarcasm, rebuking his selfishness and bad manners, avoiding his coarse and unhesitating love-making, and above all, trusting him in the oddest way as though, in spite of his faults, she placed all her reliance on him and knew that he would not fail her. Nothing annoyed him more than her behaviour to Trenchard. It would, of course, be absurd to say that he was jealous of Trenchard; he despised the man too deeply and was, himself, too sure of his lady to know jealousy; but he was irritated by the attention paid to him, irritated even by the attention he himself paid to him.

"Wherever I go there's that man," he said once to me. "Why doesn't he go back to his own country?"

"I suppose," I would answer hotly, "he has other things to do than to consider your individual wishes, Alexei Petrovitch."

Then he would laugh: "Well, well, Ivan Andreievitch, you sentimentalists all hang together."

"Why can't you leave him alone?" I remember that I continued.

"Because he doesn't leave me alone," he answered shortly.

It was, of course, Marie Ivanovna who brought them together. She could not see, or rather she would not see, that friendship between two such men was an impossibility. For herself she liked Trenchard better than she had ever done. She had now no responsibility towards him; we were all fond of him, pleased ourselves by saying that "he was more Russian than English." The Sisters mended his clothes, cared for his stomach, and listened with pleased gravity to his innocent chatter. Marie Ivanovna was now really proud of him. There were great stories of the courage and enterprise he had shown during the night when he had been with Nikitin. Nikitin, in his lofty romantic fashion, spoke of him as though he had been the hero of the Russian army. Trenchard was, of course, quite unspoiled by this praise and popularity. He remained for me at least very much the same innocent, clumsy, pathetic, and frequently irritating figure that he had been at the beginning. I will honestly confess that I was often heartily tired of his Glebeshire stories, tired too of a certain childish obstinacy with which he clung to his generally crude and half-baked opinions.

But then I do not care to be contradicted by people of whom, intellectually, I have a low estimation; it is one of my most unfortunate weaknesses. I had no opinion of Trenchard's intellect at all, and in that I was quite wrong. Semyonov at this time flung Nikitin, Andrey Vassilievitch, Trenchard and myself into one basket. We were all "crazy romantics" and there came an occasion, which I have reason most clearly to remember, when he told us what he thought of us. We were together, Semyonov, Nikitin, Trenchard and I, after breakfast, smoking cigarettes, enjoying half an hour's idleness before setting about our various business. It was a blazing hot morning and the air quivered, like a silver curtain before our eyes, separating us from the dim blue forest of S— beyond the river, the Nestor itself, the deep green slopes of our own hill. We had been silent, then Trenchard said a foolish thing: "War brings all the best out of people, I think," he said. God knows what private line of thought he had been pursuing, some sentimental reflections, I suppose, that were in him perfectly honest and sincere. But he did not look his best that morning, sitting back in his chair with his mouth open, his forehead damp with the heat, his tunic up about his neck and a rather dirty blue pocket-handkerchief in his hand.

I saw Semyonov's lip curl.

"Yes. That's very interesting, Mr.," he said. "I'm glad at any rate that we've had the honour of seeing the best of you. That's very pleasant to know."

"What I mean—" said Trenchard, blushing and stammering. "What ... that is—"

"I agree with Mr.," suddenly said Nikitin, who had been dreamily watching the blue forest. "War does bring out the best in the human character—always."

Semyonov turned smilingly to him. "Yes, Vladimir Stepanovitch, we know your illusions. Forgive me for insisting that they are illusions. I would not disturb your romantic happiness for the world."

"You can't disturb me, Alexei Petrovitch," Nikitin answered sleepily. "What a hot morning!"

"No," said Semyonov. "I would be very wrong to disturb you. Believe me, I've never tried. It's very agreeable to me to see you and Mr. so happy together and it must be pleasant for both of you to feel that you've got a nice God all of your own who sleeps a good deal but still, on the whole, gives you what you want. We may wonder a little what Mr. has done to be so favoured—never very much I fancy—but still I like the friendliness and comfort of it and I'm really lucky to have the good fortune of your acquaintance. So nice for Russia too to have plenty of people about who don't do any work nor take any trouble about anything because they've got a nice fat God who'll do it all for them if they'll only be patient. Thats why we're beating the Germans so handsomely—the poor Germans, who only, ignorant heathens as they are, believe in themselves."

He looked at us all with a friendly patronising contempt.

"That's your point of view, Alexei Petrovitch," Nikitin answered rather hotly. "Think as you please of course. But there's more in life than you can see—there is indeed."

"Of course there is," said Semyonov lazily, "much more. I'm an ignorant, rough man. I like things as they are and make the best of them, so, of course, I'm not clever. Mr.'s clever, aren't you, Mr.? All the same he doesn't know how to put his boots on properly. If he put his boots on better and knew less about God he might be of more use at the Front, perhaps. That's only my idea, and I daresay I'm wrong.... All the same, for the sake of the comfort and the pockets of all of us I do hope you'll really rouse your God and ask Him to do something sensible—something with method in it and a few more bullets in it and a little more efficiency in it. You might ask Him to do what He can...."

He looked at us, laughing; then he said to Trenchard, "But don't you fear, Mr. You'll go to heaven all right. Even though it's the wise men who succeed in this world, I don't doubt it's the fools who have their way in the next."

He left us.

Semyonov was with every new day more baffled by Marie Ivanovna. In the first place she quietly refused to obey him. We were now much occupied with the feeding of the peasants in a village stricken with cholera on the other side of the river. A gloomy enough business it was and I shall have, very shortly, to speak of it in detail. For the moment it is enough to say that two of us went off every morning with a kitchen on wheels, distributed the food, and returned in the afternoon. Semyonov intensely disliked Marie Ivanovna's share in this work, but he could not, of course, object to her taking, with the other Sisters, the risks and unpleasantness of it. He made, whenever it was possible, objections, found her work at the hospital where he himself was, occupied her in every possible way. But he did this against her will. She seemed to find a very especial pleasure and excitement in the cholera work; she wished often to take the place of some other Sister. Indeed everything on the other side of the river seemed to have a great fascination for her. She herself told me: "The moment I cross the bridge I feel as though I were on enchanted ground." On the occasions when I accompanied her to the cholera village she was radiant, so happy that she seemed to have nothing further in the world to desire. She herself was puzzled. "What is it?" she said to me. "Is it the forest? It must be, I think, the forest. I would remain on this side for ever if I had my way."

When I saw Semyonov's anxiety about her I could not but remember that little scene at the battle of S— when he had taken her off with him, leaving Trenchard in so pitiful a condition. Certainly Time brings in his revenges! And Marie Ivanovna would listen to nothing that he said.

"I want you at the hospital this morning," he would say.

"Do you really want me?" she would ask, looking up, laughing, in his face.

"Of course I do."

"Well, you should have told me last night. This morning I go with Anna Petrovna to the cholera. All is arranged."

"I'm afraid you must change your plans."

"I'm afraid not."

"Goga may go...."

"No, I wish to go."

And she went. He had certainly never before in his life been thus defied. He simply did not know what to do about it. If he had thought that bullying would frighten her he would, I believe, have bullied her, but he knew quite well that it wouldn't. And then, as I now began to perceive (I had at first thought otherwise), he was for the first time in his life experiencing something deeper and more confusing than his customary animal passions. He may at first have wanted Marie Ivanovna as he wanted his dinner or his supper ... now he wanted her differently. New emotions, surprising confusing emotions stirred in him. At least that is how I interpret the uneasiness, the hesitation, which I now seemed to perceive in him. He was no longer sure of himself.

I witnessed just at this time a little scene that surprised me. I had been in the bandaging room alone one evening, cutting up bandages. I was going through the passage into the other part of the house when a sound stopped me. I could not avoid seeing beyond the open door a little scene that happened so swiftly that I could neither retire nor advance.

Marie Ivanovna and Semyonov were coming together towards the bandaging room. She was in front of him when he put his hand on her arm.

"Do you love me?" he said in a low voice.

She turned round to him, laughing.

"Yes," she said, looking at him.

"Then kiss me."

"No, not now."

"Why not now?"

"I don't want to."

"Why don't you want to?"

She shook her head, still laughing into his eyes.

"But if I command you?"

"Ah! command!... Then I certainly will not."

His hand tightened on her arm and she did not draw away.

"Kiss me."

"No."

"I say yes."

"I say no."

He suddenly caught her, held her to him as though he would kill her and kissed her furiously, on her eyes, her mouth, her hair. With his violence he pushed back her head-dress. I could see his back bent like a bow, and his thick short legs wide apart, every muscle taut. She lay quite motionless, as though asleep in his arms, giving him no response—then quite suddenly she flung her hands round his neck and kissed him as passionately as he had kissed her. At last they parted, both of them laughing.

He looked at her, and then with a gentleness and courtesy that I had never seen in him before nor dreamed that he possessed, very softly kissed her hand.

"I love you and—and you love me," he said.

"Yes ... I love you," she answered gravely. "At least, part of me does."

"It shall be all of you soon," he answered.

"If there's time enough," she replied.

"Time!... I'll follow you wherever you go—"

"I really believe you will," she answered, laughing again. They waited then, looking at one another. A bell rang. "Ah! I'm hungry.... Supper time...." To my relief they passed away from the bandaging room towards the other part of the house.

Meanwhile his irritation at Marie Ivanovna's kindness to Trenchard increased with every hour. His attitude to the man had changed since Trenchard's night at the Position; he was vexed, I think, to hear that the fellow had proved himself a man—and a practical man with common sense. Semyonov was honest about this. He did not doubt Nikitin's word, he even congratulated Trenchard, but he certainly disliked him more than ever. He thought, I suppose, as he had thought about Nikitin: "How can a man with his wits about him be at the same time such a fool?" And then he saw that Marie Ivanovna was delighted with Trenchard's little piece of good luck. She laughed at Semyonov about it. "We all know you're a very brave man," she cried. "But you're not so brave as Mr." And Semyonov, because he knew that Trenchard was a fool and that he himself was not, was vexed, as a bull is vexed by a red flag. These things made him think a great deal about Trenchard. I have seen him watching him with angry and puzzled gaze as though he would satisfy himself why this gnat of a man worried him!

Then, finally, was Andrey Vassilievitch.... The little man had not given me much of his company during these last weeks. I fancy that since that night at the battle of S— when he had revealed his terror he had been shy of me although, God knows, he had no need to be. He never forgot if any one had seen him in an unfortunate position, and, although he bore me no grudge, he was nervous and embarrassed with me. It happened, however, that during this same week of which I have been speaking I had a conversation with him. I was standing alone by the Cross watching a long trail of wagons cross the bridge far beneath me, watching too a high bank of black cloud that was passing away from the sky above the forest, blown by a wind that rolled the surface of the river into silver. He too had come to look at the view and was surprised and disturbed at finding me there. Of course he was exaggerated in expressions of pleasure: "Why, Ivan Andreievitch, this is delightful!" he cried. "If I only had known we might have walked here together!"

We sat down on the stone seat.

"You don't think it will rain?" he asked anxiously. "No, those clouds are going away, I see. Well ... this is delightful ..." and then sat there gloomily looking in front of him.

I could see that he was depressed.

"Well, Andrey Vassilievitch," I said to him. "You're depressed about something?"

"Yes," he said very gloomily indeed. "I have many unhappy hours, Ivan Andreievitch."

I did not get up and leave him as I very easily might have done. I had had, since the night when Nikitin had spoken to me so frankly, a desire to know the little man's side of that affair. In some curious fashion that silent plain wife of his had been very frequently in my thoughts; there had not been enough in Nikitin's account to explain to me his passion for her, and yet her ghost, as though evoked by the memories both of Nikitin and her husband, had seemed to me, sometimes, to be present with us....

I waited.

"Tell me frankly," Andrey Vassilievitch said at last, "am I of any use here?"

"Of use?" I repeated, taken by surprise.

"Yes. Am I doing only what any one else can do as well? Would it be better perhaps if another were here?"

"No, certainly not," I answered warmly. "Your business training is of the greatest value to us. Molozov has said to me 'that he does not know what we should do without you.'"

(This was not strictly true.)

"Ah!" the little man was greatly pleased. "I am glad, very glad—to hear what you say. Semyonov made me feel—"

"You should not be influenced," I hurriedly interrupted him, "by what Semyonov thinks. It is of no importance."

"He has a bad character," Andrey Vassilievitch said suddenly with great excitement, "a bad character. And why cannot he leave me alone? Why should he laugh always? I do my best. I am quiet and not in his way. I can do things that he cannot. I am not big as he but at least I do not rob men of their women."

He was shaking with anger, his head trembling and his hands quivering—it was difficult not to smile.

"You must not listen nor notice nor think of it," I said firmly. "We are grateful for your work—all of us. Semyonov laughs at us all."

"That poor Marie Ivanovna," he burst out. "She does not know. She is ignorant of life. At first I was angry with her but now I see that she is helpless. There will be terrible things afterwards, Ivan Andreievitch!" he cried.

"I think she understands him better than we do."

"I have never," he said vehemently, "hated a man in my life as I hate him." But in spite of his passionate declaration he was obviously reassured by my defence of him. He was quiet suddenly, looked at the view mildly and, in a moment, thought me the best friend he had in the world—in the Russian manner.

"You see, Ivan Andreievitch," he said, looking at me with the eyes of an unnaturally wise baby, "that I cannot help wishing that my wife were here to advise Marie Ivanovna. She would have loved my wife very much, as every one did, and would have confided in her. That would have helped a girl who, like Marie Ivanovna, is ignorant of the world and the loves of men."

"You miss your wife very much?" I asked.

"There is not a moment of the day but I do not think of her," he answered very solemnly, staring in front of him. "That must seem strange to you who did not know her, and even I sometimes think it is not good. But what to do? She was a woman so remarkable that no one who knew her can forget."

"I have often been told that every one who knew her loved her," I said.

"Ah! you have heard that.... They talk of her, of course. She will always be remembered." His eyes shone with pleasure. "Yes, every one loved her. I myself loved her with a passion that nothing can ever change. And why?... I cannot tell you—unless it were that she was the only person I have known who did not wish me another kind of man. I could be myself with her and know that she still cared for me.... I will not pretend to you, Ivan Andreievitch, that I think myself a fine man," he continued. "I have never thought myself so. When I was very young I envied tall men and handsome men and men who knew what was the best thing to do without thinking of it. I have always known that people would only come to me for what I have got to give and I have pretended that I do not care. And once I had an English merchant as my guest. He was very agreeable and pleasant to me—and then by chance I overheard him say: 'Ah, Andrey Vassilievitch! A vulgar little snob!' That is perhaps what I am—I do not know—we are all what God pleases. But I had mistresses, I had friends, acquaintances. They despised me. They left me always for some one finer. They say that we Russians care too much what others think of us—but when in your own house people—your friends—say such things of you...."

He broke off, then, smiling, continued:

"My wife came. There was something in me, just as I was, that she cared for. She did not passionately love me, but she loved me with her heart because she saw that I needed love. She always saw people just as they were.... And I understood. I understood from the beginning exactly what I was to her...."

He paused again, put his hand on my knee, then spoke, looking very serious with his comic little nose and mouth like the nose and mouth of a poodle. "I had a friend, Ivan Andreievitch. A fine man.... He loved my wife and my wife loved him. He was not vulgar. He had a fine taste, he was handsome and clever. What was I to do? I knew that my wife loved him, and she must be happy. I knew that I owed her everything because of all that she had done for me. I helped them in their love.... For five years I wished them well. Do you think it was easy for me? I suffered, Ivan Andreievitch, the tortures of hell. I was jealous, God forgive me! How jealous! Sometimes alone in my room I would cry all night—not a fine thing to do. But then how should I act? She gave him what she could never give to me. She loved him with passion—for me she cared as good women care for the poor. I was foolish perhaps. I tried to be as they were, with their taste and easy judgments ... I failed, of course. What could I do all at once? One is as God has pleased from the beginning. Ah! how I was unhappy those five years! I wished that he would die and then cursed myself for wishing it. And yet I knew that I had something that he had not. I needed her more than he, and she knew that. Her charm for him would fade perhaps as the years passed. He was a passionate man who had loved many women. For me, as she well knew, it would never pass.

"She died. For a time I was like a dead man. And she was not enough with me. I talked to her friends, but they had not known her—not as she was. Only one had known her and he was the friend whom she had loved.

"Of course he found me as he had always done—tiresome, irritating, of vulgar taste. But he, too, wanted to speak of her. And so we were drawn together.... Now ... is he my friend? I say always that he is. I say to myself: 'Andrey Vassilievitch, he is your best friend'—but I am jealous. Yes, Ivan Andreievitch, I am jealous of him. I think that perhaps he will die before me and that then—somewhere—together—they will laugh at me. And he has such memories of her! At the last she cried his name! He is so much a grander man than I! Fine in every way! Did I say that she would laugh? No, no ... that never. But she will say: 'Poor Andrey Vassilievitch!' She will pity me!... I think that I would be happier if I did not see my friend. But I cannot leave him.... We talk of her often. And yet he despises me and wonders that she can have loved me...."

I had a fear lest Andrey Vassilievitch should cry. He seemed so desolate there, giving strange little self-important coughs and sniffs, beating the ground with his smart little military boot.

Across the river the black wall of cloud had returned and now hung above the forest of S—, that lay sullenly, in its shadow, forbidding and thick, itself like a cloud. The world was cold, the Nestor like a snake.... I shivered, seized by some sudden sense of coming disaster and trouble. The evenings there were often strangely chill.

"Look," cried Andrey Vassilievitch, starting to his feet "There's Marie Ivanovna!"

I turned and saw her standing there, smiling at us, silently and without movement, like an apparition.

CHAPTER II

MARIE IVANOVNA

It was on July 23 that I first entered the Forest of S—. I did not, I remember, pay the event any especial attention. I went with Anna Petrovna to the cholera village that is on the outskirts of the forest, and I recollect that we hastened back because that evening we were to celebrate the conclusion of the first six months' work of our Otriad. Of my entrance into the forest I remember absolutely nothing; it seemed, I suppose, an ordinary enough forest to me. Of the festivities in the evening I have a very clear recollection. I remember that it was the loveliest summer weather, not too hot, with a little breeze coming up from the river, and the green glittering on every side of us with the quiver of flashing water. In the little garden outside our house a table had been improvised and on this were a large gilt ikon, a vase of flowers in a hideous purple jar, and two tall candles whose flames looked unreal and thin in the sunlight. There was the priest, a fine stout man with a long black beard and hair falling below his shoulders, clothed in silk of gold and purple, waving a censer, monotoning the prayers in a high Russian tenor, with one eye on the choir of sanitars, one eye on the candles blown by the wind, the breeze meanwhile playing irreverent jests on his splendid skirts of gold. Then there was the congregation in three groups. The first group—two generals, two colonels, four or five other officers, the Sisters (Sister K— bowing and crossing herself incessantly, Anna Petrovna with her attention obviously on the dinner cooking behind a tree in the garden, Marie Ivanovna looking lovely and happy and good), ourselves— Molozov official, Semyonov sarcastic, Nikitin in a dream, Andrey Vassilievitch busy with his smart uniform, Trenchard (forgotten his sword, his blue handkerchief protruding from his pocket) absorbed by the ceremony, myself thinking of Trenchard, Goga—and the rest. The second group—the singing sanitars, some ten of them, stout and healthy, singing as Russians do with complete self-forgetfulness and a rapturous happiness in front of them, a funny little man with spectacles and a sharp-pointed beard, once a schoolmaster, now a sanitar, conducting their music with a long bony finger—all of them chanting the responses with perfect precision and harmony. Third group, the other sanitars, the strangest collection of faces, wild, savage and eastern: Tartars, Lithuanians, Mongolian, mild and northern, cold and western, merry and human from Little Russia, gigantic and fierce from the Caucasus, small and frozen from Archangel, one or two civilised and superior and uninteresting from Petrograd and Moscow.

Over the wall a long row of interested Galician peasants and soldiers passing in carts or on horseback. Seeing the ikon, the priest, the blowing candles, hearing the singing they would take off their hats, cross themselves, for a moment their eyes would go dreamy, mild, forgetful, then on their hats would go again, back they would turn their horses, cursing them up the hill, chaffing the Galician women, down deep in the everyday life again.

The service ended. The priest turns to us, the gold Cross is raised, we advance one by one: the generals, the colonels, the lieutenants, the Sisters, Semyonov, Nikitin, Goga, then the choir, then the sanitars, even to hunch-backed Alesha, who is always given the dirtiest work to do and is only half a human being; one by one we kiss the Cross, the candles are blown out, the ikon folded up and put away in a cardboard box, we are introduced to the generals, there is general conversation, and the stars and the moon come out "blown straight up, it seems, out of the bosom of the Nestor...."

It was a very happy and innocent evening. For extracting the utmost happiness possible out of the simplest materials the Russians have surely no rivals. How our generals and our colonels enjoyed that evening! A wonderful dinner was cooked between two stones in the garden—little pig, young chickens, borshtsh, that most luxurious of soups, and ices—yes, and ices. Then there were speeches, many, many glasses of tea, strawberry and cherry jam, biscuits and cigarettes. We were all very, very happy....

It was arranged on the morning after the feast that I should go again to the cholera village with Marie Ivanovna and Semyonov. Under a morning of a blazing relentless heat, bars of light ruling the sky, we started, the three of us, at about ten o'clock, in the little low dogcart, followed by the kitchen and the boiler. Marie Ivanovna sat next to Semyonov, I facing them. Semyonov was happier than I had ever seen him before. Happiness was not a quality with which I would ever have charged him; he had seemed to despise it as something too simple and sentimental for any but sentimental fools—but now this morning (I had noticed something of the same thing in him the evening before) he was quite simply happy, looking younger by many years, the ironical curve of his lip gone, his eyes smiling, his attitude to the world gentle and almost benevolent. Of course she, Marie Ivanovna, had wrought this change in him. There was no doubt this morning that she loved him. She had in her face and bearing all the pride and also all the humility that a love, won, secured, ensured, brings with it. She did not look at him often nor take his hand. She spoke to me during the drive and only once and again smiled up at him; but her soul, shining through the thin covering of her body, laughed to me, crying: "I am happy because I have my desire. Of yesterday I remember nothing, of to-morrow I can know nothing, but to-day is mine!"

He was very quiet. When he looked at her his eyes took complete possession of her. I did not, that morning, count at all to either of them, but I too felt a kind of pride as though I were sharing in some triumphal procession. She chattered on, and then at last was silent. I remember that the great heat of the morning wrought in us all a kind of lethargy. We were lazily confident that day that nothing evil could overtake us. We idly watched the sky, the river, the approaching forest, with a luxurious reliance on the power of man, and I caught much of my assurance from Semyonov himself. He did really seem to me, that morning, a "tremendous" figure, as he sat there, so still, so triumphant. He had never before, perhaps, been quite certain of Marie Ivanovna, had been alarmed at her independence, or at his own passionate love for her. But this morning he knew. She loved him. She was his—no one could take her from him. She was the woman he wanted as he had never wanted a woman before, and she was his— she was his!

I do not remember our entering the forest. I know that first you climb a rough, rather narrow road up from the river, that the trees close about you very gradually, that there is a little church with a green turret and a fine view of the Nestor, and that there a broad solemn avenue of silver birch leads you forward, gently and without any sinister omens. Then again the forest clears and there are fields of corn and, built amongst the thin scattering of trees, the village of N—. It was here, on passing the first houses of the village, that I felt the heat to be almost unbearable; it seemed strange to me, I remember, that they (whoever "they" were), having so many trees here, a forest that stretched many miles behind them, should have chosen to pitch their village upon the only exposed and torrid bit of ground that they could find. Behind us was the forest, in front of us also the forest, but here, how the sun blazed down on the roofs and little blown patches of garden, how it glared in through the broken windows, and penetrated into the darkest corners of the desolate rooms!

Poor N—! In the second month of the war it had been shelled and many of the houses destroyed. The buildings that remained seemed to have given up the struggle and abandoned themselves to inevitable degradation. Moreover, down the principal street, at every other door there hung the sinister black flag, a piece of dirty black cloth fastened to a stick, and upon the filthy wall was scrawled in Russian "cholera." Dead, indeed, under the appalling heat of the morning the whole place lay. No one was to be seen until we neared the ruins of what had once been a little town-hall or meeting-place, a procession turned the corner—a procession of a peasant with a tall lighted candle, another peasant with a tattered banner, a priest in soiled silk, a coffin of white wood on a haycart, and four or five white-faced and apathetic women. A doleful singing came from the miserable party. They did not look at us as we passed....

A rumble of cannon, once and again, sounded like the lazy snore of some sleeping beast.

Near the town-hall we found a company of fantastic creatures awaiting us. They were pressed together in a dense crowd as though they were afraid of some one attacking them. There were many old men, like the clowns in Shakespeare, dirty beyond belief in tattered garments, wide-brimmed hats, broad skirts and baggy trousers; old men with long tangled hair, bare bony breasts and slobbering chins. Many of the women seemed strong and young; their faces were on the whole cheerful—a brazen indifference to anything and everything was their attitude. There were many children. Two gendarmes guarded them with rough friendly discipline. I thought that I had seen nothing more terrible at the war than the eager pitiful docility with which they moved to and fro in obedience to the gendarmes' orders. A dreadful, broken, creeping submission....

But it was their fantasy, their coloured incredible unreality that overwhelmed me. The building, black and twisted against the hard blue sky, raised its head behind us like a malicious monster. Before us this crowd, all tattered faded pieces of scarlet and yellow and blue, men with huge noses, sunken eyes, sharp chins, long skinny hands, women with hard, bright, dead faces, little children with eyes that were afraid and indifferent, hungry and mad, all this crowd swaying before us, with the cannon muttering beyond the walls, and the thin miserable thread of the funeral hymn trickling like water under our feet.... I looked from these to Semyonov and Marie Ivanovna, they in their white overalls working at the meat kitchen and the huge bread-baskets, radiant in their love, their success, their struggle, confident, both of them, this morning that they had the fire of life in their hands to do with it as they pleased.

I have not wished during the progress of this book, which is the history of the experiences of others rather than of myself, to lay any stress on my personal history, and here I would only say that any one who is burdened with a physical disease or encumbrance that will remain to the end of life must know that there are certain moments when this hindrance leaps up at him like the grinning face of a devil— despairing hideous moments they are! I have said that during our drive I had felt a confident happy participation in the joy of those others who were with me ... now as we stood there feeding that company of scarecrows, a sudden horror of my own lameness, a sudden consciousness that I belonged rather to that band of miserable diseased hungry fugitives than to the two triumphant figures on the other side of me, overwhelmed and defeated me. I bent my head; I felt a shame, a degradation as though I should have crept into some shadow and hidden.... I would not mention this were it not that afterwards, in retrospect, the moment seemed to me an omen. After all, life is not always to the victorious!...

Our scarecrows wanted, horribly, their food. It was dreadful to see the anxiety with which they watched the portioning of the thick heavy hunks of black bread. They had to show Marie Ivanovna their dirty little scraps of paper which described the portions to which they were entitled. How their bony fingers clutched the paper afterwards as they pressed it back into their skinny bosoms! Sometimes they could not wait to return home, but would squat down on the ground and lap their soup like dogs. The day grew hotter and hotter, the world smelt of disease and dirt, waste and desolation. Marie Ivanovna's face was soft with tenderness as she watched them. Semyonov had always his eye upon her, seeing that she did not touch them, sometimes calling out sharply: "Now! Marie! ... take care! Take care!" but this morning he also seemed kind and gentle to them, leading a small girl back to her haggard bony old guardian, carrying her heavy can of soup for her, or joking with some of the old men.... "Now, uncle ... you ought to be at the war! What have they done, leaving you? So young and so vigorous! They'll take you yet!" and the old man, a toothless trembling creature, clutching his hunk of bread with shaking hands, would grin like the head of Death himself! How close to death they all seemed! How alive were my friends, strong in the sun, compassionate but also perhaps a little despising this poor gathering of wastrels.

The work went on; then at last the final scraps of meat and bread had been shared, the kitchen closed its oven, we took off our overalls, shook ourselves, and bade farewell to the scarecrows. The kitchen was then sent home and we moved forward with the tea boiler and two sanitars further into the forest. Our destination was a large empty house behind the trenches. From here we were to take tea in the boiler to certain regiments, tea with wine in it as preventative against cholera. It was the early afternoon now, and we moved very slowly. The heat was intense and although the trees were thick on every side of us there seemed to be no shade nor coolness, as though the leaves had been made of paper.

"This is a strange forest," I said. "Although there are trees there's no shade. It burns like a furnace."

No one replied. We passed as though in a dream, meeting no one, hearing no sound, the light dancing and flickering on our path. I nodded on my seat. I was half asleep when we arrived at our destination. This was the accustomed white deserted house standing in a desolate tangled garden. There was no one there on our arrival. All the doors were open, the sun blazing along the dusty passages. It was inhabited, just then, I believe, by some artillery officers, but I saw none of them. Semyonov went off to find the Colonel of the regiment to whom we were to give tea; Marie Ivanovna and I remained in one of the empty rooms, the only sound the buzzing flies. Every detail of that room will remain in my heart and brain until I die. Marie Ivanovna, looking very white and cool, with the happiness shining in her large clear eyes, sat on an old worn sofa near the window. In the glass of the window there were bullet holes, and beyond the window a piece of blazing golden garden. The room was very dirty, dust lay thick upon everything. Some one had eaten a meal there, and there was a plate, a knife, also egg-shells, an empty sardine-tin, and a hunk of black bread. There was a book which I picked up, attracted by the English lettering on the faded red cover. It was a "Report on the Condition of New Mexico in 1904"—a heavy fat volume with the usual photographs of water-falls, cornfields and enormous sheep. On the walls there was only one picture, a torn supplement from some German magazine showing father returning to his family after a long absence—welcomed, of course, by child (fat and ugly), wife (fatter and uglier), and dog (a mongrel). There was the usual pile of fiction in Polish, translations I suspect of Conan Doyle and Jerome; there was a desolate palm in a corner and a chipped blue washing stand. A hideous place: the sun did not penetrate and it should have been cool, but for some reason the air was heavy and hot as though we were enclosed in a biscuit-tin.

I leaned against the table and looked at Marie Ivanovna.

"Isn't it strange?" I said, "we're only a verst or two from the Austrians and not a sound to be heard. But the gendarme told me that we must be careful here. A good many bullets flying about, I believe."

"Ah!" she said laughing. "I don't feel as though anything could touch me to-day. I never loved life before as I love it now. Is it right to be so happy at such a time as this and in such a place?... And how strange it is that through all the tragedy one can only truly see one's own little affairs, and only feel one's own little troubles and joys. That's bad ... one should be punished for that!"

I loved her at that moment; I felt bitterly, I remember, that I, because I was plain and a cripple, silent and uninteresting, would never win the love of such women. I remembered little Andrey Vassilievitch's words about his wife: "For me she cared as good women care for the poor." In that way for me too women would care—when they cared at all. And always, all my life, it would be like that. How unfair that everything should be given to the Semyonovs and the Nikitins of this world, everything denied to such men as Trenchard, Andrey Vassilievitch and I!...

But my little grumble passed as I looked at her.

How honest and straight and true with her impulses, her enthusiasms, her rebellions and ignorances she was! Yes, I loved her and had always loved her. That was why I had cared for Trenchard, why now I was attracted by Semyonov, because, shadow of a man as I was, not man enough to be jealous, I could see with her eyes, stand beside her and share her emotion.... But God! how that day I despised myself!

"You're tired!" she said, looking at me. "Is your leg hurting you?"

"Not much," I answered.

"Sit down here beside me." She made way for me on the sofa. "Ivan Andreievitch, you will always be my friend?"

"Always," I answered.

"I believe you will. I'm a little afraid of you, but I think that I would rather have you as a friend than any one—except John. How fortunate I am! Two Englishmen for my friends! You do not change as R-russians do! You will be angry with me when you think that I am wrong, but then I can believe you. I know that you will tell me the truth."

"Perhaps," I said slowly, "Alexei Petrovitch will not wish that I should be your friend!"

"Alexei?" she said, laughing. "Oh, thank you very much, I shall choose my own friends. That will always be my affair."

I had an uneasy suspicion that perhaps she knew as little about Semyonov as she had once known about Trenchard. It might be that all her life she might never learn wisdom. I do not know that I wished her to learn it.

"No," she continued. "But you forgive me now? Forgive me for all my mistakes, for thinking that I loved John when I did not and treating him so badly. Ah! but how unhappy I was! I wished to be honourable and honest—I wished it passionately—and I seemed only to make mistakes. And then because I was ashamed of myself I was angry with every one—at least it seemed that it was with every one, but it was really with myself."

"I did you injustice," I said. "And I did Alexei Petrovitch an injustice also. I know now that he truly and deeply loves you.... I believe that you will be very happy ... yes, it is better, much better, than that you should have married Trenchard."

Her face flushed with happiness, that strange flush of colour behind her pale cheeks, coming and going with the beats of her heart.

She continued happily, confidently: "When I was growing up I was always restless. My mother allowed me to do as I pleased and I had no one in authority over me. I was restless because I knew nothing and no one could tell me anything that seemed to me true. I would have, like other girls, sudden enthusiasms for some one who seemed strong and wonderful—and then they were never wonderful—only like every one else. I would be angry, impatient, miserable. Russian girls begin life so early.... After a time, mother began to treat me as though I was grown up. We went to Petrograd and I thought about clothes and theatres. But I never forgot—I always waited for the man or the work or the friend that was to make life real. Then suddenly the war came and I thought that I had found what I wanted. But there too there were disappointments. John was not John, the war was not the war ... and it's only to-day now that I feel as though I were r-right inside. I've been so stupid—I've made so many mistakes." She dropped her voice: "I've always been afraid, Ivan Andreievitch, that is the truth. You remember that morning before S—?"

"Yes," I said. "I remember it."

"Well, it has been often, often like that. I've been afraid of myself and—of something else—of dying. I found that I didn't want to die, that the thought of death was too horrible to me. That day of the Retreat how afraid I was! John could not protect me, no one could. And I was ashamed of myself! How ashamed, how miserable. And I was afraid because I thought of myself more than of any one else—always. I had fine ideals but—in practice—it was only that—that I always was selfish. Now, for the first time ever, I care for some one more than myself and suddenly I am afraid of death no longer. It is true, Ivan Andreievitch, I do not believe that death can separate Alexei from me; I have more reason now to wish to live than I have ever had, but now I am not afraid. Wherever I am, Alexei will come—wherever he is, I will go...."

She broke off—then laughed. "You think it silly in England to talk about such things. No English girl would, would she? In Russia we are silly if we like. But oh! how happy it is, after all these weeks, not to be afraid—not to wake up early and lie there and think—think and shudder. They used to say I was brave about the wounded, brave at S—, brave at operations ... if they only knew! You only, Ivan Andreievitch, have seen me afraid, you only!..." She looked at me, her eyes searching my face: "Isn't it strange that you who do not love me know me, perhaps, better than John—and yes, better than Alexei. That's why I tell you—I can talk to you. I never could talk to women—I never cared for women. You and John for my friends—yes, I am indeed happy!"

She got up from the old sofa, walked a little about the room, looked at the remains of the meal, at the book, then turned round to me:

"Don't ever tell any one, Ivan Andreievitch, that I have been afraid.... I'm never to be afraid again. And I'm not going to die. I know now that life is wonderful—at last all that when I was young I expected it to be.... Do you know, Ivan Andreievitch, I feel to-day as though I would live for ever!..."

Semyonov came in. He was in splendid spirits; I had never seen him so gay, so carelessly happy.

"Well," he cried to me, "we're to go now—at once ... and the next time at eight. We'll leave you this time. We'll be back by half-past six. We'll do the Third and Fourth Roti now. The Eighth and Ninth afterwards. Can you wait for tea until we return? Good.... Half-past six, then!"

They departed. As she went out of the door she turned and gave me a little happy smile as though to bind me to an intimate enduring confidence. I smiled back at her and she was gone.

After they had left me I felt very lonely. The house was still and desolate, and I took a book that I had brought with me—the "Le Deuil des Primeveres" of François Jammes. I had learnt the habit during my first visit to the war of always taking a book in my pocket when engaged upon any business; there were so many long weary hours of waiting when the nerves were stretched, and a book—quiet and real and something apart from all wars and all rumours of wars—was a most serious necessity. What "Tristram

Shandy" was to me once under fire near Nijnieff, and "Red-gauntlet" on an awful morning when our whole Otriad meditated on the possibility of imprisonment before the evening—with nothing to be done but sit and wait! I went into the garden with M. Jammes.

As I walked along the little paths through a tangle of wood and green that might very well have presented the garden of the Sleeping Beauty, I heard now and then a sound that resembled the swift flight of a bird or the sudden "ting" of a telegraph-wire. The Austrians were amusing themselves; sometimes a bullet would clip a tree in its passing or one would see a leaf, quite suddenly detached, hover for a moment idly in the air and then circle slowly to the ground. Except for this sound the garden was fast held in the warm peace of a summer afternoon. I found a most happy little neglected orchard with old gnarled apple-trees and thick waving grass. Here I lay on my back, watching the gold through the leaves, soaked in the apathy and somnolence of the day, sinking idly into sleep, rising, sinking again, as though rocked in a hammock. I was in England once more—at intervals there came a sharp click that exactly resembled the sound that one hears in an English village on a summer afternoon when they are playing cricket in the field near by—oneself at one's ease in the garden, half sleeping, half building castles in the air, the crack of the ball on the bat, the cooing of some pigeons on the roof.... Once again that sharp pleasant sound, again the flight of the bird above one's head, again the rustle of some leaves behind one's head ... soon there will be tea, strawberries and cream, a demand that one shall play tennis, that saunter through the cool dark house, up old stairs, along narrow passages to one's room where one will slowly, happily change into flannels—hearing still through the open window the crack of the bat upon the ball from the distant field....

But as I lay there I was unhappy, rebellious. The confidence and splendour of Marie Ivanovna and Semyonov had driven me into exile. I hated myself that afternoon. That pursuit—the excitement of the penetration into the dark forest—the thrill of the chase—those things were for the strong men, the brave women—not for the halt and maimed ... not love nor glory, neither hate nor fierce rebellion were for such men as I.... I cursed my fate, my life, because I loved, not for the first time, a woman who was glad that I did not love her and was so sure that I did not and could not, that she could proclaim her satisfaction openly to me!

I had an hour of bitterness—then, as I had so often done before, I laughed, drove the little devil into his cage, locked it, dropped the thick curtain in front of it.

I claimed the company of M. François Jammes.

He has a delightful poem about donkeys and as I read it I regained my tranquillity. It begins:

Lorsqu'il faudra aller vers Vous, ô mon Dieu, faites   Que ce soit par un jour ou la campagne en fete Poudroiera. Je désire, ainsi que je fis ici-bas,   Choisir un chemin pour aller, comme il me plaira,   Au Paradis, où sont en plein jour les étoiles.   Je prendrai mon bâton et sur la grande route   J'irai et je dirai aux ânes, mes amis: Je suis Francois Jammes et je vais au Paradis,   Car il n'y a pas d'enfer au pays du Bon Dieu.   Je leur dirai: Venez, doux amis du ciel bleu,   Pauvres bêtes chéries qui d'un brusque mouvement d'oreilles,   Chassez les mouches plates, les coups et les abeilles....

That brought tranquillity back to me. I found another poem—his "Amsterdam."

Les maisons pointues ont l'air de pencher. On dirait   Qu'elles tombent. Les mâts des vaisseaux qui s'embrouillent   Dans le ciel sont penchés comme des branches sèches   Au milieu de verdure, de raye, de rouille,   De harengs saurs, de peaux de moutons et de bouille.

Robinson Crusoë passa par Amsterdam   (Je crois du moins qu'il y passa) en revenant   De l'île ombreuse et verte aux noix de coco fraîches.   Quelle émotion il dut avoir quand il vit luire   Les portes énormes, aux lourds marteaux, de cette ville!...

Regardait-il curieusement les entresols   Ou les commis écrivent les livres de comptes?   Eut-il envie de pleurer en resongeant   A son cher perroquet, à son lourd parasol,   Qui l'abritait dans l'île attristée et clémente?...

I was asleep; my eyes closed; the book fell from my hand. Some one near me seemed to repeat in the air the words:

Robinson Crusoë passa par Amsterdam   (Je crois, du moins, qu'il y passa) en revenant   De l'île ombreuse.... "De l'île ombreuse" ... "Robinson Crusoë passa" ...

I was rocked in the hot golden air. I slept heavily, deeply, without dreams....

I was awakened by a cold fierce apprehension of terror. I sat up, stared slowly around me with the sure, certain conviction that some dreadful thing had occurred. The orchard was as it had been—the sun, lower now, shone through the green branches. All was still and even, as I listened I heard the sharp crack of the ball upon the bat breaking the evening air. My heart had simply ceased to beat. I remember that with a hand that trembled I picked up the book that was lying open on the grass and read, without understanding them, the words. I remember that I said, out aloud: "Something's happened," then turning saw Semyonov's face.

I realised nothing save his face with its pale square beard and red lips, framed there by the shining green and blue. He stood there, without moving, staring at me, and the memory of his eyes even now as I write of it hurts me physically so that my own eyes close.

That was perhaps the worst moment of my life, that confrontation of Semyonov. He stood there as though carved in stone (his figure had always the stiff clear outline of stone or wood). I realised nothing of his body—I simply saw his eyes, that were staring straight in front of him, that were blazing with pain, and yet were blind. He looked past me and, if one had not seen the live agony of his eyes, one would have thought that he was absorbed in watching something that was so distant that he must concentrate all his attention upon it.

I got upon my feet and as my eyes met his I knew without any question at all that Marie Ivanovna was dead.

When I had risen we stood for a moment facing one another, then without a word he turned towards the house. I followed him, leaving my book upon the grass. He walking slowly in front of me with his usual assured step, except that once he walked into a bush that was to his right; he afterwards came away from it, as a man walking in his sleep might do, without lowering his eyes to look at it. We entered by a side-door. I, myself, had no thoughts at all at this time. I felt only the cold, heavy oppression at my heart, and I had, I remember, no curiosity as to what had occurred. We passed through passages that were strangely dark, in a silence that was weighted and mysterious. We entered the room where we had been earlier in the afternoon; it seemed now to be full of people, I saw now quite clearly, although just before the whole world had seemed to be dark. I saw our two soldiers standing back by the door; a doctor, whose face I did not know, a very corpulent man, was on his knees on the floor—some sanitars were in a group by the window. In the middle of the room lay Marie Ivanovna on a stretcher. Even as I entered the stout doctor rose, shaking his head. I had only that one glimpse of her face on my entry, because, at the shake of the doctor's head, a sanitar stepped forward and covered her with a cloth. But I shall see her face as it was until I die. Her eyes were closed, she seemed very peaceful.... But I cannot write of it, even now....

My business here is simply with facts, and I must be forgiven if now I am brief in my account.

The room was just as it had been earlier in the afternoon; I saw the sardine-tin, the dirty plate that had a little cloud of flies upon it; the room seemed under the evening sun full of gold dust. I crossed over to our soldiers and asked them how it had been. One of them told me that they had gone with the boiler to the trenches. Everything had been very quiet. They had taken their stand behind a small ruined house. Semyonov had just returned from telling the officers of the Rota that the tea was ready when, quite suddenly, the Austrians had begun to fire. Bullets had passed thickly overhead. Marie Ivanovna had seemed quite fearless, and laughing, had stepped, for a moment, from behind the shelter to see whether the soldiers were coming for their tea. She was struck instantly; she gave a sharp little cry and fell. They rushed to her side, but death had been instantaneous. She had been struck in the heart.... There was nothing to be done.... The soldiers seemed to feel it very deeply, and one of them, a little round fellow with a merry face whom I knew well, turned away from me and began to cry, with his hand to his eyes.

Semyonov was standing in the room with exactly that same dead burning expression in his eyes. His mouth was set severely, his legs apart, his hands at his sides.

"A terrible misfortune," I heard the stout doctor say.

Semyonov looked at him gravely.

"Thank you very much for your kindness," he said courteously. Then, by a common instinct, without any spoken word between us, we all went from the room, leaving Semyonov alone there.

I remember very little of our return to Mittövo. We borrowed a cart upon which we laid the body. I sat in the trap with Semyonov. I was, I remember, afraid lest he should suddenly go off his head. It seemed quite a possible thing then, he was so quiet, so motionless, scarcely breathing. I concentrated all my thought upon this. I had my hand upon his arm and I remember that it relieved me in some way to feel it so thick and strong beneath his sleeve. He did not look at me once.

I do not know what my thoughts were, a confused incoherent medley of nonsense. I did not think of Marie Ivanovna at all. I repeated again and again to myself, in the silly, insane way that one does under the shock of some trouble, the words of the poem that I had read that afternoon:

Robinson Crusoë passa par Amsterdam   (Je crois du moins qu'il y passa) en revenant   De l'île ombreuse et verte—ombreuse et verte—ombreuse et verte....

It was dark, or at any rate, it seemed to me dark. The weather was still and close; every sound echoed abominably through the silence. When we arrived at Mittövo I suddenly thought of Trenchard. I had utterly forgotten him until that moment. I got out of the trap and when Semyonov climbed out he put his hand on my arm. I don't know why but that touched me so deeply and sharply that I felt, suddenly, as though in another instant I should lose my self-control. It was so unlike him, so utterly unlike him, to do that. I trembled a little, then steadied myself, and we walked together into the house. They must all instantly have known what had occurred because I heard running steps and sharp anxious voices.

I felt desperately, as a man runs when he is afraid, that I must be alone. I slipped away into the passage that leads from the hall. This passage was quite dark and I was feeling my direction with my hands when some one, carrying a candle, turned the corner. It was Trenchard. He raised the candle high to look at me.

"Hallo, Durward," he cried. "You're back. What sort of a time?..."

I told him at once what had occurred. The candle dropped from his hand, falling with a sharp clatter. There was a horrible pause, both of us standing there close to one another in the sudden blackness. I could hear his fast nervous breathing. I was myself unstrung I suppose, because I remember that I was dreadfully afraid lest Trenchard should do something to me, there, as we stood.

I felt his hand groping on my clothes. But he was only feeling his way. I heard his steps, creeping, stumbling down the passage. Once I thought that he had fallen.

Then there was silence, and at last I was alone.

CHAPTER III

THE FOREST

And now I am confronted with a very serious difficulty. There is nothing stranger in this whole business of the life and character of war than the fashion in which an atmosphere that has been of the intensest character can, by the mere advance or retreat of a pace or two, disappear, close in upon itself, present the blindest front to the soul that has, a moment before, penetrated it. It is as though one had visited a house for the first time. The interior is of the most absorbing and unique interest. There are revealed in it beauties, terrors, of so sharp a reality that one believes that one's life is changed for ever by the sight of them. One passes the door, closes it behind one, steps into the outer world, looks back, and there is only before one's view a thick cold wall—the windows are dead, there is no sound, only bland, dull, expressionless space. Moreover this dull wall, almost instantly, persuades one of the incredibility of what one has seen. There were no beauties, there were no terrors.... Ordinary life closes round one, trivial things reassume their old importance, one disbelieves in fantastic dreams.

I believe that every one who has had experience of war will admit the truth of this. I had myself already known something of the kind and had wondered at the fashion in which the crossing of a mere verst or two can bring the old life about one. I had known it during the battle of S—, in the days that followed the battle, in moments of the Retreat, when for half an hour we would suddenly be laughing and careless as though we were in Petrograd.

And so when I look back to the weeks of whose history I wish now to give a truthful account, I am afraid of myself. I wish to give nothing more than the facts, and yet that something that is more than the facts is of the first, and indeed the only, importance. Moreover the last impression that I wish to convey is that war is a hysterical business. I believe that that succession of days in the forest of S—, the experience of Nikitin, Semyonov, Andrey Vassilievitch, Trenchard and myself—might have occurred to any one, must have occurred to many other persons, but from the cool safe foundation on which now I stand it cannot but seem exceptional, even exaggerated. Exaggerated, in very truth, I know that it is not. And yet this life—so ordered, so disciplined, so rational, and THAT life—where do they join?... I penetrated but a little way; my friends penetrated into the very heart ... and, because I was left outside, I remain the only possible recorder: but a recorder who can offer only signs, moments, glimpses through a closing door....

I am waiting now for the return of my opportunity.

On the night of the death of Marie Ivanovna I slept a heavy, dreamless sleep. I was wakened between six and seven the next morning by Nikitin, who told me that he, Trenchard, Andrey Vassilievitch and I were to return at once to the forest. I realised at once that indescribable quiver in the air of momentous events. The house was quite still, the summer morning very fresh and clear, but the air was weighted with some crisis. It was not only the death of Marie Ivanovna that was present with us, it was rather something that told us that now no individual life or death counted ... individualities, personalities, were swallowed up in the sweeping urgency of a great climax. Nikitin simply told me that a furious battle was raging some ten versts on the other side of the river, that we were to go at once to form a temporary hospital behind the lines in the Forest; that the nurses and the rest of the Otriad would remain in Mittövo to wait for the main tide of the wounded, but that we were to go forward to help the army doctors. He spoke very quietly. We said nothing of Marie Ivanovna.

I dressed quickly and on going out found the wagons waiting, some fifteen or twenty sanitars and Trenchard and Andrey Vassilievitch. The four of us climbed into one of the wagons and set off. I did not see Semyonov. Trenchard was pale, there were heavy black lines under his eyes—but he seemed calm, and he stared in front of him as though he were absorbed by some concentrated self-control. For the first time in my experience of him he seemed to me a strong independent character.

We did not speak at all. I could see that Andrey Vassilievitch was nervous: his eyes were anxious and now and then he moistened his lips with his tongue. When we had crossed the river and began to climb the hill I knew that I hated the Forest. It was looking beautiful under the early morning sun, its green so delicate and clear, its soft shadows so cool, its birds singing so carelessly, the silver birches, lines of light against the dark spaces; but this was all to me now as though it had been arranged by some ironic hand. It knew well enough who had died there yesterday and it was preparing now, behind its black recesses, a rich harvest for its malicious spirit. We passed through the cholera village and reached the white house of yesterday at about ten o'clock. As we clattered up to the door I for a moment closed my eyes. I felt as though I could not face the horrible place, then summoning my control I boldly challenged it, surveying its long broken windows, its high doorway, its sunny, insulting garden. We were met by the stout doctor, whom I had seen before. As he is of some importance in the events that followed I will mention his name—Konstantine Feôdorovitch Krylov. He was large and stout, a true Russian type, with a merry laughing face. He had the true Russian spirit of unconquerable irrational merriment. He laughed at everything with the gaiety of a man who finds life too preposterous for words. He had all the Russian untidyness, kindness of heart, gay, ironical pessimism. "To-morrow" was a word unknown to him:

nothing was sacred to him, and yet at times it seemed as though life were so holy, so mysterious, that the only way to keep it from careless eyes was by laughing at it. He had no principles, no plans, no prejudices, no reverences. If he wished to sleep for a week he would do so, if he wished to eat for a week he would do so. If he died to-morrow he did not care ... it was all so absurd that it was not worth while to give it any attention. He would grow very fat, he would die—he would love women, play cards, drink, quarrel, give his life for a sentimental moment, pour every farthing of his possessions into the lap of a friend, incur debts which he would not pay, quarrel wildly with a man about a rouble, remember things that you would expect him to forget, forget everything that he should remember—a pagan, a saint, a blackguard, a hero—anything you please so long as you do not take it seriously.

This morning he was dirty and looked as though he had slept for many nights without taking off his clothes—unshaven, his shirt open showing his hairy chest, his eyes blinking in the light.

"That's good," he said, seeing us. "I've got to be off, leaving the place to you.... Fearful time they're having over there," pointing across the garden. "Yes, five versts away. Plenty of work in a minute. Brought food with you? Very little here." Then I heard him begin, as he walked into the house with Nikitin, "Terrible thing, Doctor, about your Sister yesterday.... Terrible.... I—"

I remember that my great desire was that I should not be left alone with Trenchard. I clung to Andrey Vassilievitch, and a poor resource he was, watching with nervous eyes the building and the glimmering forest, dusting his clothes and beginning sentences which he did not finish, Trenchard was quite silent. We entered the horrible room of yesterday. The dirty plate and the sardine-tin were still there with the flies about them: the highly coloured German supplement watched us from its rakish position on the wall, the treatise on New Mexico was lying on the table. I picked up the book and it opened naturally at a place where the last reader had turned down the corner of the page. The same page happens to be quoted exactly in Trenchard's diary on an occasion about which afterwards I shall have to speak. There is an account of the year's work of some New Mexican school and it runs:

"Besides the regular class work there have been other features of special merit, programmes of which we append:

"Lectures: Rev. H. W. Ruffner, Titles and Degrees; Mr. Fred A. Bush, What the Community owes the Newspaper and what the Newspaper owes the Community; Dr. E. H. Woods, Tuberculosis; Rev. I. R. Glass, Fools; Mr. Eugene Warren, Blood of the Nation; Dr. L. M. Strong, Orthopedics; Hon. S. M. Ashenfelter, Freedom of Effort; Hon. W. T. Cessna, Don't Pay too dearly for the Whistle; Dr. O. S. Westlake, The Physician and the Laity; Prof. Wellington Putman, Rip Van Winkle; Rev. E. S. Hanshaw, The Mind's Picture Gallery; Hon. R. M. Turner, Opportunities.

"Othello. For the first time the normal students presented for the class-day exercise a Shakespearian play, Othello. Cast of characters: Othello, E. F. Dunlavey; Iago, Douglas Giffard; Duke of Venice, Charles Harper; Brabantio, Eugene Cosgrove; Cassio, Arnold Rosenfeld; Roderigo, Erwin Moore; Montano, Wilson Portherfield; Lodovico, Henry Geitz; Gratiano, William Fleming; Desdemona, Carrie Whitehill; Emilia, Gussie Rodgers; Bianca, Florence Otter; senators, officers, messengers and attendants.

"Graduating Programme. Music: the Anglo-Saxon in History, Douglas Giffard; the Anglo-Saxon in Science, Florence Otter; the Anglo-Saxon in Literature, Gussie Rodgers; Music; annual address, Hon. R. M. Turner; Music; presentation of diplomas.

"Doubtless among the most interesting and most profitable events of the institution was the annual society contest between the two societies, the Literati and the Lyceum. The Silver City Commercial Club offered a costly cup to the winning society and it was won by the Lyceum. The contest was in oration, elocution, debate, parliamentary usage and athletics.

"The inside adornment of the hall has not been neglected. A number of portraits and a large number of carbon prints of celebrated paintings have been added, the class picture being the most important and costing in the neighbourhood of $100; this is the hunting scene of Ruysdael. Some of the others are 'The Parthenon,' 'The Immaculate Conception' by Murillo, and 'The Allegorie du Printemps' by Botticelli. Many valuable specimens have been added to the museum: among these are minerals, animals and vegetable products, and manufactured articles from abroad illustrative of the habits and customs of foreigners."

I give this page in full because it was afterwards to have importance, though at the time I glanced at it only carelessly. But I remember that I speculated on the lecture by the Rev. I. R. Glass about "Fools," that I admired a contest so widely extended as to embrace oration, parliamentary usage and athletics, that I liked very much the "class Ruysdael," "costing in the neighbourhood of $100," and the "manufactured articles from abroad, illustrative of the habits and customs of foreigners."

Nikitin came up to me. "Will you please set off at once with Mr. to Vulatch?" he said. "Find there Colonel Maximoff and get direct orders from him. Return as soon as possible. They say we're not likely to have wounded until late this afternoon—a good thing as a lot wants doing to this place. Hasten, Ivan Andreievitch. No time to lose."

Vulatch was a little town situated ten versts to our right in the Forest. I had heard of its strange position before, quite a town and yet lying in the very heart of the Forest, as though it had been the settlement of some early colonists. It had running through it a good high road, but otherwise was far removed from the outer world. It had during the war been twice bombarded and was now, I believed, ruined and deserted. For the moment it was the headquarters of the Sixty-Fifth Staff. I was frankly frightened of going alone with Trenchard—frightened both of myself and of him. I told him and without a word he went with me. When we started off in the wagon I looked at him. He was sitting on the straw, very quietly, his hands folded, looking in front of him. He seemed older: the sentimental naïveté that had been always in his face seemed now entirely to have left him. He had always looked before as though he wanted some one to help him out of a position that was too difficult for him; now he was alone in a world where no one could reach him. During the whole drive to Vulatch we exchanged no word. The sound of the cannon was distant but incessant, and strangely, as it seemed to me, we were alone. Once and again soldiers passed us, sometimes wagons with kitchens or provisions met us on the road, sometimes groups of men were waiting by the roadside, once we saw them setting up telegraph wires, once a desolate band of Austrian prisoners crossed our path, twice wagons with wounded rumbled along—but for the most part we were alone. We were out of the main track of the battle. It was as though the Forest had arranged this that it might the more impress us. Our road, although it was the high road, was rough and uneven and we advanced slowly: with every step that the horses took I was the more conscious of a sinister and malign influence. I know how easily one's nerves can lend atmosphere to something that is in itself innocent and harmless enough, but it must be remembered that (at this time), in spite of what had happened yesterday, neither Trenchard's nerves nor mine were strained. My sensation must, I think, have closely resembled the feelings of a diver who, for the first time, descends below the water. I had never felt anything like this before and there was quite definitely about my eyes, my nose, my mouth, a feeling of suffocation. I can only say that it was exactly as though I were breathing in an atmosphere that was strange to me. This may have been partly the effect of the sun that was beating down very strongly upon us, but it was also, curiously enough, the result of some dimness that obscured the direct path of one's vision. On every side of our rough forest road there were black cavernous spaces set here and there like caves between sheets of burning sunlight. Into these caves one's gaze simply could not penetrate, and the light and darkness shifted about one with exactly the effect of stirring, swaying water. Although the way was quite clear and the road broad I felt as though at any moment our advance would be stopped by an impenetrable barrier, a barrier of bristled thickets, of an iron wall, of a sudden, fathomless precipice. Of course to both Trenchard and myself there were, during this drive, thoughts of his dream. We both recognized, although at this time we did not speak of it, that this was the very place that had now grown so vivid to us. "Ah, this is how it looks in sunlight!" I would think to myself, having seen it always in the early morning and cold. Behind me the long white house, the hunters, the dogs.... No, they were not here in the burning suffocating sunlight, but they would come—they would come!

The monotony of the place emphasised its vastness. It was not, I suppose, a great Forest, but to-day it seemed as though we were winding further and further, through labyrinth after labyrinth of clouding obscurity, winding towards some destination from which we could never again escape. "Pum—pum—pum," whispered the cannon; "Whirr—whirr—whirr," the shadowy trembling background echoed. Then with a sudden lifting of the curtain Vulatch was revealed to us. Ruined towns and villages were, by this time, no new sight to me, but this place was different from anything that I had ever seen before. From the bend of the little hill we looked down upon it and the sight of it made me shudder. It was the deadest place, the deadest place in the world—all white under the sun it lay there like the bleached bones of some animal picked clean long ago by the birds.

Not a sound came from it, not a movement could be discerned in it. I could see, standing out straight from the heart of it, what must have been once a fine church. It had had four green turrets perched like little green bubbles on white towers; three of these were still there, and between them stood the white husk of the place; from where we watched we could see little fires of blue light sparkling like jewels between the holes. Over it all was a strange metallic glitter as though we were seeing through glass, glass shaded very faintly green. Under this green shadow, which seemed very gently to stain the air, the town was indeed like a lost city beneath the sea. Catching our breaths we plunged down into the fantastic depths....

As we descended the hill we were surprised by the silence—not a soul to be seen. We had expected to find the place filled with the soldiers of the Sixty-Fifth Division. Our driver on this day was the man Nikolai whom I have mentioned before as attaching himself from the very beginning to Trenchard's service. He had been Trenchard's unofficial servant now for a long time, saying very little, always succeeding, in some quiet fashion of his own, in accompanying Trenchard on his expeditions. Nikolai was one of the quietest human beings I have ever known. His charming ugly face was in repose a little gloomy, not thoughtful so much as expectant, dreamy perhaps but also very practical and unidealistic. His smile changed all that; in a moment his face was merry, even good-humouredly malicious, suspicious, and a little ironical. He had the thick stolid body of the Russian peasant who is trained to any endurance, any misfortune that God might choose to send it. His attachment to Trenchard had been so unobtrusive that Molozov had officially permitted it without realising that he had permitted anything. It was so unobtrusive that I myself had not, during these last weeks, noticed it. To-day I saw Nikolai glance many times at Trenchard. His eyes were anxious and inquiring; he looked at him rather as a dog may look at his master, although there was here no dumb submission, nor any sentimental weakness.... I should rather say that Nikolai looked at Trenchard as one free man may look at another. "What is the matter with you?" his eyes seemed to say. "But I know ... a terrible thing has happened to you. At any rate I am here to be of any use that I can."

"Nikolai," I said, "why is there no one here?"

"Ne mogoo znat, your Honour."

"Well, the first soldier you see you must ask."

"Tak totchno."

"Who said you were to drive us?"

"Vladimir Stepanovitch, your Honour."

"Are you going to remain with us?"

"Tak totchno."

His eyes rested for a moment on Trenchard, then he turned to his horses.

We were entering the town now and it did, indeed, present to us a scene of desperate desolation. The place had been originally built in rising tiers on the side of the valley, and the principal street had leading out of it, up the hill, steps rising to balconied houses that commanded a view of the opposite hill. Almost every house in this street was in ruins; sometimes the ruins were complete—only an isolated chimney of broken stone wall remaining, sometimes the shell was standing, the windows boarded up with wood, sometimes almost the whole building was there, a gaping space in the roof the only sign of desolation. And there remained the ironical signs of its earlier life. Many of the buildings had their titles still upon them. In one place I saw the blackened and almost illegible plate of a lawyer, in another a large still fresh-looking advertisement of a dentist, here there was the large lettering "Tobacconist," there upon a trembling wall the tattered remains of an announcement of a sale of furniture. Once, most ironical of all, a gaping and smoke-stained building showed the half-torn remnant of a cinematograph picture, a fat gentleman in a bowler hat entering with a lady on either arm a gaily painted restaurant. Over this, in big letters, the word "FARCE."

Although we saw no soldiers we were not entirely alone. In and out of the sunny caverns, appearing outlined against the darkness, vanishing in a sudden blaze of light, were shadows of the citizens of Vulatch. They seemed to me, without exception, to be Jews. From most of the Galician towns and villages the Jews had been expelled—here they only, apparently, had been left. Of women I saw scarcely any—old men, with long dirty black or grizzled beards, yellow skins, peaked black caps, and filthy black gowns clutched about their thin bodies. They watched us, silently, ominously, maliciously. They crept from door to door, stole up the stone steps and vanished, appeared, as it seemed, right beneath our horses' feet and disappeared. If we caught them with our eyes they bowed with a loathsome, trembling subservience. There were many little Jewish children, with glittering eyes, naked feet, bare scrubby heads and white faces. Nikolai at length caught an old man and asked him where the soldiers were. The old man replied in very tolerable Russian that all the soldiers had gone last night—not one of them remained—but he believed that some more were shortly to arrive. They were always coming and going, he said.

We stayed where we were, under the blazing sun, and held council. In every doorway, in every shadow, there were eyes watching us. The whole town was overweighted, overwhelmed by the brooding Forest. From where we stood I could see it rising on every side of us like a trembling, threatening green wave; in the furious heat of the sun the white ruins seemed to jump and leap.

"Well," I said to Trenchard, "what's to be done?"

He pulled himself back from his thoughts.

He had been sitting in the cart, quite motionless, his face white and hidden, as though he slept. He raised his tired, heavy eyes to my face.

"Do?" he said.

"Yes," I answered impatiently. "Didn't you hear what Nikolai said? There are no soldiers here. We can't find Maximoff because he isn't here. We must go back, I suppose."

"Very well," he answered indifferently.

"I'm not going back," I said, "until I've had something to drink—tea or coffee. I wonder whether there's anything here—any place we could go to."

Nikolai inquired. Old Shylock pointed with his bony finger down the street.

"Very fine restaurant there," he said.

"Will you come and see?" I asked Trenchard.

"Very well," said Trenchard.

I told Nikolai to stay there and wait for us. I walked down the street, followed by Trenchard. I found on my left, at the top of a little flight of steps, a house that was for the most part untouched by the general havoc around and about it. The lower windows were cracked and the door open and gaping, but there stood, quite bravely with new paint, the word "Restoration" on the lintel and there were even curtains about the upper windows. Passing through the door we found a room decently clean, and behind the little bar a stout red-faced Galician in white shirt and grey trousers, a citizen of the normal world. We were just then his only customers. We asked him for tea and sat down at a little table in the corner of the room. He did not talk to us but stood in his place humming cheerfully to himself and cleaning glasses. He was a rogue, I thought, looking at his little eyes, but at any rate a merry rogue; he certainly had kept off from him the general death and desolation that had overwhelmed his neighbours. I sat opposite to Trenchard and wondered what to say to him. His expression had never varied. As I looked at him I could not but think of the strength of his eyes, of his mouth, the quiet concentration of his hands ... a different figure from the smiling uncertain man on the Petrograd station—how many years ago?

Our tea was brought to us. Then quite suddenly Trenchard said to me:

"Did she say anything before she died?"

"No," I answered quietly. "She died instantly, they told me."

"How exactly was she killed?"

His eyes watched my face without falter, clearly, gravely, steadfastly.

"She was killed by a bullet. Stepped out from behind her shelter and it happened at once. She can have suffered nothing."

"And Semyonov let her?"

"He could not have prevented it. It might have happened to any one."

"I would have prevented it," he said, nodding his head gravely.

He was silent for a little; then with a sudden jerk he said:

"Where has she gone?"

"Gone?" I repeated stupidly after him.

"Yes—that's not death—to go like that. She must be somewhere still—somewhere in this beastly forest. What—afterwards—when you saw her—what? ... her face?..."

"She looked very peaceful—quite happy."

"No restlessness in her face? No anxiety?"

"None."

"But all that life—that energy. It can't have stopped. Quite suddenly. It can't. She can't have wanted not to know all those things that she was so eager about before." He was suddenly voluble, excited, leaning forward, staring at me. "You know how she was. You must have seen it numbers of times—how she never looked at any of us really, how we were none of us—no, not even Semyonov—anything to her really; always staring past us, wanting to know the answer to questions that we couldn't solve for her. She wouldn't give it all up simply for nothing, simply for a bullet ..." he broke off.

"Look here, Trenchard," I said, "try not to think of her just now more than you can help, just now. We're in for a stiff time, I believe. This will be our last easy afternoon, I fancy, and even now we ought to be back helping Nikitin. You've got to work all you know. One's nerves get wrong easily enough in a place like this—and after what has happened I feel this damned Forest already. But we mustn't let our nerves go. We've simply got to work and think about nothing at all—think about nothing at all."

I don't believe that he heard me.

"Semyonov?" he said slowly. "What did he do?"

"He was very quiet," I answered. "He didn't say anything. He looked awful."

"Yes. She snapped her fingers at him anyway. He couldn't keep her for all his bullying."

"It pretty well killed him," I said rather fiercely. "Look here, Trenchard. Don't think of yourself—or of her. Every one's in it now. There isn't any personality about it. We've simply got to do our best and not think about it. It's thinking that beats one if one lets it."

"Semyonov ... Semyonov," he repeated to himself, smiling. "No, he had not power over her." Then looking at me very calmly, he remarked: "This Death, you know, Durward.... It simply doesn't exist. It can't stop her. It can't stop any one if they're determined. I'll find her before Semyonov does, too."

Then, as though he had waked from sleep, he said to me, his voice trembling a little: "Am I talking queerly, Durward? If I am, don't think anything of it. It's this heat—and this place. Let's get back." He only spoke once more. He said: "Do you remember that first drive—ages ago, when we saw the trenches and heard the frogs and I thought there was some one there?"

"Yes," I said. "I remember."

"Well, it's rather like that now, isn't it?"

A pretty girl, twenty-two or twenty-three years of age, obviously the daughter of the red-faced proprietor, came up to us and asked us if we would like any more tea. She would be stout later on, her red cheeks were plump and her black hair arranged coquettishly in little shining curls. She smiled on us.

"No more tea?" she said.

"No more," I answered.

"You will not be staying here?"

"Not to-night."

"We have a nice room here."

"No, thank you."

"Perhaps one of you—"

"No. We are returning to-night,"

"Perhaps, for an hour or two." Then smiling at me and laughing a little, "I have known many officers ... very many."

"No, thank you," I said sternly.

"I have a sister," she said. She turned, crying: "Marie, Marie!"

A little girl, who could not have been more than fourteen years of age, appeared from the background. She also was red-cheeked and plump; her hair also was arranged in black, shining curls. She stood looking at us, half smiling, half defiant, sucking her finger.

"She also has known officers," said the girl. "She would be very glad, if you cared—"

I heard their father behind the bar humming to himself.

"Come out of this!" I said to Trenchard. "Come away!"

He followed me quietly, bowing very politely to the staring sisters....

"Go on," I said to Nikolai. "Drive on. No time to waste. We've got work to do."

On our return we found that the press of work was not as yet severe. Half the building belonged to us, the remaining half being used by the officers of the battery. Nikitin had arranged a large room, that must I think have been a dining-room in happier days, with beds; to the right was the operating-room, overhead were our bedrooms and the room where originally I had sat with Marie Ivanovna was a general meeting place. The officers of the battery, two middle-aged and two very young indeed, were extremely courteous and begged us to make use of them in any way possible. They were living in the raggedest fashion, a week's growth of beard on their chins, their beds unmade, the floor littered with ends of cigarettes, pieces of paper, journals.

"Been here weeks," they apologetically explained to us. "Come in and have a meal with us whenever you like." They resembled animals in a cave. When they were not on duty they played chemin-de-fer and slept. Meanwhile for three days and nights our work was slight. The battle drew further away into the Forest. Wagons with wounded came to us only at long intervals.

The result of these three days was a strange new intimacy between the four of us. I have never in all my life seen anything more charming than the behaviour of Nikitin and Andrey Vassilievitch to Trenchard. There is something about Russian kindness that is both simpler and more tactful than any other kindness in the world. Tact is too often another name for insincerity, but Russian kindheartedness is the most honest impulse in the Russian soul, the quality that comes first, before anger, before injustice, before prejudice, before slander, before disloyalty, and overrides them all. They were, of course, conscious that Trenchard's case was worse than their own. Marie Ivanovna's death had shocked them, but she had been outside their lives and already she was fading from them. Trenchard was another matter. Nikitin seemed to me for the first time in my knowledge of him to come down from his idealistic dreaming. He cared for Trenchard like a child, but never obtrusively. Trenchard seemed to appreciate it, but there was something about him that I did not like. His nerves were tensely strained, he did his work with his eyes fixed upon some impossible distance, he often did not hear us when we spoke to him.

And so the three of us formed a kind of hedge about him to protect him, a hedge of which he was perfectly unconscious. He was very silent and I would have given a great deal to hear again one of those Glebeshire stories that I had once found so tiresome. That some plan or purpose was in his head one could not doubt.

We had, all of us, much in common in our characters. We liked the sentimental easy coloured view of life. We suddenly felt a strange freedom here in this place. For myself, on the third day, I found that

Marie Ivanovna was most strangely present with me, and on the afternoon of that day, our wounded quiet on their beds, our wagons sent into the tent with no prospect of their return for several hours, we sat together, Nikitin, Andrey Vassilievitch and I, looking out through a break in the garden towards the Forest, and talked about her. The weather was now very heavy—certainly a thunderstorm was coming. I was also weighted down by an intense desire for sleep, at the same time knowing that if I were to fling myself on my bed sleep would not come to me. This is an experience that is not unusual at the Front, and officers have told me that in the middle of a battle when there comes a sudden lull, their longing for sleep has been so overpowering that no imminent danger could lift it from their eyes.

We sat there then and talked in low voices of Marie Ivanovna. I was aware of the buzzing of the flies, of the dull yellow light beyond the windows, of the Forest crouching a little as it seemed to me like a creature who expects a blow. We were all half asleep perhaps, the room dark behind us, and we talked of her as we might talk of a picture, a book, an experience ended and dismissed—something outside our present affairs. And yet I knew that for me at any rate she was not outside them. I felt as though at any moment she might enter the room. We discussed her aloofness, her sudden happiness and her sudden distress, her intimacies and withdrawals, Nikitin and Andrey Vassilievitch slowly elaborating her into a high romantic figure. Behind her, behind all our thoughts of her, there was the presence of Semyonov. Nothing was stranger during our time here than the way that Semyonov had always kept us company.

Our consciousness of relief from him had begun it. We had been more under his influence than any of us had cared to confess and, in his presence, had checked our natural impulses. I also was strongly aware of him through Trenchard. Trenchard seemed now to have a horror of him that could be explained only by the fact that he held him responsible for Marie Ivanovna's death. "It's a good thing," I thought to myself, "that Semyonov's not here."

These hours of waiting, when there was nothing to do, was bad for all our nerves. Upon this afternoon I remember that after a time silence fell between us. We were all staring in front of us, seeing pictures of other places and other people. I was aware, as I always was, of the Forest, seeing it shine with its sinister green haze, seeing the white bleached town, the huddled villagers waiting for their food, but seeing yet more vividly the deep silences, the dark hollows, the silent avenues of silver birch. Against this were the figures of the people who were dear to me. It is strange how war selects and brings forward as one's eternal company the one or two souls who have been of importance in one's life. One knows then, in those long, long threatening pauses, when the battle seems to gather itself together before it thunders its next smashing blow, those who are one's true companions. Certain English figures were now with me outlined against the Forest—and joined together with them Marie Ivanovna as I had last seen her, turning round to me by the door and smiling upon me. I did truthfully feel, as Trenchard had said to me, that she was not dead; I sat, staring before me, conjuring her to appear. The others also sat there, staring in front of them. Were they also summoning some figure? I knew, as though Andrey Vassilievitch had told me, that he was thinking of his wife. And Nikitin?...

He sat there, lying back on the old sofa that Marie had used, his black beard, his long limbs, his dark eyes giving him the colour of some Eastern magician. He did indeed, with his intense, absorbed gaze, seem to be casting a spell As I looked Andrey Vassilievitch caught his glance—they exchanged the strangest flash—something that was intimate and yet foreign, something appealing and yet hostile. It was as though Andrey Vassilievitch had said: "I know you are thinking of her. Leave her to me," and Nikitin had replied: "My poor friend. What can you do?... I do as I please."

I know at least that I saw Andrey Vassilievitch frown, make as though he would get up and leave the room, then think better of it, and sink back into his chair.

I remember that just at that moment Trenchard entered. He joined us and sat on the sofa near Nikitin without speaking, staring in front of him like the rest of us. His face was tired and old, his cheeks hollow.

I waited and the silence began to get on my nerves. Then there came an interruption. The door opened quite silently: we all turned our eyes towards it without moving our heads. In the doorway stood Semyonov.

We were startled as though by a ghost. I remember that Andrey Vassilievitch jumped to his feet, crying. Trenchard never moved. Semyonov with his usual stolid self-possession came towards us, greeted us, then turning to me said:

"I've come to take your place, Ivan Andreievitch."

"My place?" I stammered.

"Yes. You're wanted there. You're to return at once in the britchka.... In half an hour, if you don't mind."

"And you'll stay?"

"And I'll stay."

No one else said anything. I remember that I had some half-intention of protesting, of begging to be allowed to remain. But I was no match for Semyonov. I could fancy the futility of my saying: "But really, Alexei Petrovitch, we don't want you here. It's much better to leave me. You'll upset them all. It's a nervous place, this." I said nothing, except: "All right. I'll go." He watched me. He watched us all. I fancy that he smiled.

Outside I had a desperate absurd thought that I would return and ask him to be kind to Trenchard. As I turned away some one seemed to whisper in my ear:

"He's come, you know, to find Marie Ivanovna."

CHAPTER IV

FOUR?

Before I give the extracts from Trenchard's diary that follow I would like to say that I do not believe that Trenchard had any thought whatever, as he wrote, of publication. He says quite clearly that he wrote simply for his own satisfaction and later interest. At the same time I am convinced that he would not now object to their publication. If he had been here he would, I know, have supported my intention. The diary lies before me, here on my table, written in two yellow, stiff-covered manuscript books without lines. They are written very unevenly and untidily, with very few erasures, but at times incoherently and with gaps. In one place he has cut from the newspaper Rupert Brooke's sonnet, beginning:

"Blow out, you Bugles, over the rich Dead!"

and pasted it on to the blank page.

At times he sticks on to the other pages newspaper descriptions that have pleased him. His own descriptions of the Forest seem to me influenced by my talks with him, and I remember that it was Nikitin who spoke of the light like a glass ball and of the green-like water. For the most part he exhibits, from the beginning of the diary to the end, extreme practical common sense and he makes, I fancy, a very strong effort to record quite simply and even naïvely the truth as he sees it. At other times he is quite frankly incoherent....

I will give, on another page, my impression of him when I saw him on my return to the Forest. I am, of course, in no way responsible for inconsistencies or irrelevances. He had kept a diary since his first coming to the war and I have already given some extracts from it. The earlier diary, in one place only, namely his account of his adventure during his night with Nikitin, is of the full descriptive order. That one occasion I have already quoted in its entirety. With that exception the early diary is brief and concerned only with the dryest recital of events. After the death of Marie Ivanovna, however, its character entirely changes for reasons which he himself shows. I would have expected perhaps a certain solemnity or even pomposity in the style of it; he had never a strong sense of humour. But I find it written in the very simplest fashion; words here and there are misspelt and his handwriting is large and round like a schoolboy's.

Thursday, July 29th. I intend to write this diary with great fulness for two reasons—in the first place because I can see that it is of the greatest importance, if one is to get through this business properly, to leave no hours empty. The trying thing in this affair is having nothing to do—nothing one can possibly do. They all, officers, soldiers, from Nikolai Nikolaievitch to my Nikolai here, will tell you that. No empty hours for me if I can help it.... Secondly, I really do wish to record exactly my experiences here. I am perfectly aware that when I'm out of it all, when it's even a day's march behind me, I shall regard it as frankly incredible—not the thing itself but the way I felt about it. When I come out of it into the world again I shall be overwhelmed with other people's impressions of it, people far cleverer than I. There will be brilliant descriptions of battles, of what it feels like to be under fire, of marches, victories, retreats, wounds, death—everything. I shall forget what my own little tiny piece of it was like—and I don't want to forget. I want intensely to remember the truth always, because the truth is bound up with Marie, and Marie with the truth. Why need I be shy now about her? Why should I hesitate, under the fear of my own later timidity, of saying exactly now what I feel? God knows what I do feel! I am confused, half-numb, half-dead, I believe, with moments of fiery biting realisation. I'm neither sad, nor happy—only breathlessly expectant. The only adventure I have ever had in my life is not—no, it is not—yet ended. And I know that Marie could not have left me like that, without a word, unless she were returning or were going to send for me.

Meanwhile to-day a beastly thing has happened, a thing that will make life much harder for me here. All the morning there was work. Bandaged twenty—had fifty in altogether—sent thirty-four on, kept the rest. Two died during the morning. This isn't really a good place to be, it's so hemmed in with trees. We ought to be somewhere more open. The Forest is unhealthy, too. There's been fighting in and out of it almost since the war began—it can't be healthy. In this hot weather the place smells.... Then there are the Flies. I write them with a capital letter because I've got to keep my head about the Flies. Does any one at home or away from this infernal strip of fighting realise what flies are? Of course one's read of the tropical sorts, all red and stinging, or white and bloated—what you like, evil and horrid, but these here are just the ordinary household kind. Quite ordinary, but sheets, walls of them. I came into the little larder place near our sitting-room this morning. I thought they'd painted the walls black during the night. Then, at my taking the cover off some sugar, it was exactly as though the walls hovered and then fell inward breaking into black dust as they fell. They'll cluster over a drop of wine on the table just like an evil black flower with grey petals. With one's body they can play tricks beyond belief. They laugh at one, hovering at a distance, waiting. They watch one with their wicked little eyes ... yes, I shall have to be careful about flies.

I've had a headache all day, but then in the afternoon there was a thunderstorm hovering somewhere near and there was no work to do. I feel tired, too, and yet I can't sleep. Later in the afternoon we were all sitting together, very quiet, not talking. I was thinking about Semyonov then. I wondered whether he felt her death. How had he taken it? Durward would tell me so little. I was so glad, all the same, that he wasn't here. And yet, in the strangest way, I would like to have spoken to him, to have asked him, if I had dared, a little about her. He was the only man to whom she really gave herself. I don't grudge him that—but there's so much that I want to know—and yet I'd die rather than ask him. Die! That's an old phrase now—death would tell me much more than Semyonov ever could. Just when we were sitting there he came in. It was the most horrible shock. I don't want to put it melodramatically but that was exactly what it was. I had been thinking of him, thinking even of speaking to him, but I had known at the time that he wasn't here, that he couldn't be here—then there he was in the doorway—square and solid and grave and scornful. Now the horrible thing is that the moment I realised him I felt afraid. I didn't feel anger or hatred or fine desires for revenge—anything like that—simply a miserable contemptible fear. It seems that as soon as I climb out of one fear I tumble into another. They are not physical now, but worse!

Later. The last bit seems rather silly. But I'll leave it.... As to Semyonov. Of course he was very quiet and scornful with all of us. He told Durward that he'd come to take his place and Durward went without a word, Semyonov went off then with Nikitin, looking about, and making suggestions! He changed some things but not very much. We had been pretty intimate, all of us, before he came. I had really felt this last day that Vladimir Stepanovitch and Andrey Vassilievitch were understood by me. Russians come and go so. At one moment they are close to you, intimate, open-hearted, then suddenly they shut up, are miles away, look at you with distrust and suspicion. So with these two. On Semyonov's arrival they changed absolutely. He shut them up of course. We were all as gloomy at supper as though we were deadly enemies. But the worst thing was at night. Durward and I had slept in one little room, Vladimir Stepanovitch and Andrey Vassilievitch in another. Of course Semyonov took Durward's bed. There was nowhere else for him to go. I don't know what he thought about it. Of course he said nothing. He talked a little about ordinary things and I answered stupidly as I always do with him. I hated the solemn way he undressed. He was a long time cleaning his teeth, making noises in his mouth as though he were laughing at me. Then he sat on his bed, naked except for his shirt, combing his moustache and beard very carefully with a pocket-comb. He was so thick and solid and scornful, not looking at me exactly, just staring in front of him. There was no sound except his comb scraping through his beard. The room was so small and he seemed absolutely to fill it, so that I felt really flattened against the wall. It was as though he were showing me deliberately how much finer a man he was than I, how much stronger his body, that he could do anything with me if he liked. He asked me, very politely, whether I'd mind blowing out the candle and I did it at once. He watched me as I walked across the floor and I felt ashamed of my thinness and my ugliness and I know that he knew that I was ashamed. After the light was blown out I heard him settle into his bed with a great heavy plop. I couldn't sleep for a long time, and at every movement that he made I felt as though he were laughing at me. And yet with all this I had also the strangest impulse to get up, there in the dark, to walk across the room, to put my hand on his shoulder and to ask him about her. What would he do? He'd refuse to speak, I suppose. I should only get insulted—and yet.... He must be thinking of her—all the time just as I am. He must want to talk of her and I know her better than any one else did. And perhaps if I once broke down his pride ... and yet every time that his body moved and the bed creaked I felt that I hated him, that I never wanted to speak to him again, that.... Oh! but I'm ashamed of myself. He is right to despise me....

Saturday, July 31st. It is just midnight. I am on duty to-night. Everything is quiet and there are not likely I think to be any more wounded until the morning. I am sitting in the room where they brought Marie. It's strange to think of that, and when you're sitting with a candle in a dark room you can imagine anything. It's odd in this affair how little things affect one. There's a book here, a "Report on New Mexico." I looked at it idly the other day and now I'm for ever picking it up. It always opens at the same page and I find myself thinking, speculating about it in a ridiculous manner. I shall throw the thing away to-morrow, but I know the page by heart anyway. It's an account of the work of some school or other. Here are a few of the lectures that were given:

Mr. Fred. A. Bush. What the Community owes the Newspaper and what the Newspaper owes the Community.—Rev. I. R. Glass. Fools.—Hon. W. T. Cessna. Don't Pay too dearly for the Whistle.—Prof. Wellington Putman. Rip van Winkle.—Rev. R. S. Hanshaw. The Mind's Picture Gallery.

Then they acted Othello—The "Normal Students," whoever they may be. Othello, E. F. Dunlavey. Iago—Douglas Giffard. Desdemona—Carrie Whitehill. Emilia—Gussie Rodgers.... Afterwards I see that Miss Gussie Rodgers gave a lecture on the Anglo-Saxon in Literature. She must have been a clever young woman. Then I see that they decorated one of their rooms with "a large number of carbon prints of celebrated paintings," "the class picture being the most important and costing in the neighbourhood of $100—this is the hunting scene of Ruysdael...." Also they added to their Museum "manufactured articles from abroad illustrative of the habits and customs of foreigners."

Now isn't that all incredible after the day that I've had? Where do the things join? What's all that got to do with the horrors I've been through to-day, with the Forest, the cholera, Marie, Semyonov.... With all that's happening in Europe? With this mad earthquake of a catastrophe? And yet one thinks of such silly things. I can see them doing Othello with their cheap ermine, bad jewellery and impossible wigs. I expect Othello's black came off as he got hotter and hotter; and the Rev. I. R. Glass on "Fools".... There'd be all the cheap morality—"It's better, my young friends, to be good than to be bad. It pays better in the end"—and there'd be little stories, sentimental some of them and humorous some of them. There'd be a general titter of laughter at the humorous ones.... And the carbon prints, the "Ruysdael" always pointed out to visitors ... and after the war it will all be going on again. At Polchester, too, they'll be having cheap lectures in the Town-Hall and Shakespeare Readings and High-School Prize-givings.... Where's the Connexion between That and This? Where's the permanent thing in us that goes on whatever life may do to us? Is life still beautiful and noble in spite of whatever man may do with it, or is Semyonov right and there is no meaning in my love for Marie, nothing real and true except the things we see with our eyes, hear with our ears? Is Semyonov right, or are Nikitin, Andrey Vassilievitch and I?... And now let me stick to facts. I left this morning about six with twenty wagons to fetch wounded. Such a wonderful summer morning—the Forest quite incredibly beautiful, birds singing in thousands, and that strange little stream that runs near our house and can look so abominable when it pleases, was trembling and lovely as though it didn't know what evil was. We got to the first Red Cross place about eight. Here was Krylov. What a good fellow! Always cheerful, always kindhearted, nothing can dismay him. A Russian type that's common enough in spite of all the "profound pessimism of the Russian heart" that we're always hearing of. There he was anyway, working like a butcher before a feast-day. Dirty looking barn they were working in and it smelt like hell. Cannon pretty close too. They say the Austrians are fearfully strong just here and of course our ammunition is climbing down to less than nothing—looks as though we were going to have a hot time soon. I turned in and helped Krylov all the morning and somehow his fat, ugly face, his little exclamations, his explosive comical rages, his sudden rough kindnesses did one a world of good. We filled the wagons and sent them back, then about midday, under a blazing hot sun, we went on with the others. Is there any place in the globe hot and suffocating quite as this Forest is? Even in the open spaces one can't breathe and there's never any proper shade under the trees. At first we were at a loss, No one seemed quite to know where the Vengrovsky Polk were. I had to go on alone and reconnoitre. I was right out in the open then and more alone than one could believe. Cannon were blazing away and one battery seemed just behind me—and yet I couldn't see it. I could see nothing—only great ridges of hills with the Forest like gigantic torrents of green water under the mist, and just at my feet cornfields thick with cornflowers. Then I saw rather a wonderful thing. I came to the edge of my hill and looked down into a cup of a valley, quite a little valley with the green waves towering on every side of it. Through the mist there shimmered below me a blue lake. I was puzzled—there was no water here that I knew, but by this time the Forest has so bewitched my senses that I'm ready to believe anything of it. There it was, anyway, a blue lake, shifting a little under gold haze. I climbed down the hill a yard or two and then you can believe that I jumped! My blue lake was Austrian prisoners, nothing more nor less! Has any one quite seen them like that before, I wonder, and isn't this Forest really the old witch's forest, able to do what it pleases with anything? There they were, hundreds of them, covering the whole floor of the little valley. I walked down into the middle of them, found an officer, asked him about wounded, and got directed some two versts in front of me. Then I climbed up the hill back to my wagons and we started off. We went down the hill round by the road and came to the prisoners, crossed a stream and plunged into a shining dazzling nightmare. Where the cannon were I don't know—all a considerable distance away, I suppose, because the only sign of shell were the little breaking puffs of smoke in the blue sky with just a pin-flash of light as they broke; but really amongst that welter of wooded hill the sounds were uncanny. They'd be under one's feet, over one's head, in one's ear, up against one's stomach, straight in the small of one's back. Since my night with Nikitin physical fear really seems to have left me—the whole outward paraphernalia of the war has become an entirely commonplace thing, but it was the Forest that I felt—exactly as though it were playing with me. Wasn't there an old mediæval torture when they shot arrows at their victim, always just missing him, first on one side, then on another, until at last, tired of the game, they fixed him through the head? Well, that's what the old beast was trying to do to me, anything to doubt what's real and what is not, anything to make me question my senses.... We tumbled quite suddenly on to some men, a small Red Cross shelter and two or three hundred soldiers sitting under the trees by the road resting—most of them sleeping. The doctor in the Red Cross place—a small fussy man—was ill-tempered and overworked. There were at least thirty dead men lying in a row outside the shelter, and the army sanitars were bringing in more wounded every minute. "Why weren't there more wagons? What was the use of coming with so few? Where was the other doctor, some one or other who ought to have relieved him?" There he was, like a little monkey on wires, dancing up and down in the blazing road, his arms covered with blood, pincers in one hand and bandages in the other and the inside of his shelter with such a green, filthy smell coming out of it that you'd think the roof would burst! I filled seven of my wagons, sent them back and went forward with the remaining three. We were climbing now, up through the Forest road, the shell, very close, making a terrific noise, and in between the scream of the shell the birds singing like anything!

The road turned the corner and then we were in the middle of it! Now here's the worst thing I've seen with my eyes since I came to the war—worst thing I shall ever see perhaps. One looks back, you know, to one of those old average afternoons at Polchester, my father coming back from golf, I myself going into the old red-walled garden for tea, with some novel under my arm, the cathedral bell ringing for Evensong just over the wall across the Green, then slowly dropping to its close, then the faint murmur of the organ. Some bird twittering in a tree overhead, buttered toast in a neat pile placed carefully over hot water to keep it warm; honey, heavy home-made cake, perhaps the local weekly paper with the "Do you know that ..." column demanding one's critical attention. One's annoyed because to-morrow some tiresome fellow's coming to luncheon, because one wishes to buy some china that one can't afford, because the wife of the Precentor said to the Dean's sister that young Trenchard would be an old man in a year or two.... One sips one's tea, the organ leads the chants, the sun sinks below the wall.... That! This! ... there's the Forest road hot like red-hot iron under the sun; it winds away into the Forest, but so far as the eye can see it is covered with things that have been left by flying men—such articles! Swords, daggers, rifles, cartridge-cases, of course, but also books, letters, a hair-brush, underclothes, newspapers, these tilings in thick, tangled profusion, rifles in heaps, cartridge-cases by the hundred! Under the sun up and down the road there are dead and dying, Russians and Austrians together. The Forest is both above and below the road and from out of it there comes a continual screaming. There is every note in this babel of voices, mad notes, plaintive notes, angry notes, whimpering notes. One wounded man is very slowly trying to drag himself across the road, and his foot which is nearly severed from his leg waggles behind him. One path that leads from the road to the Forest is piled with bodies and is a stream of blood. Some of the dead are lying very quietly in the ditch, their heads pillowed on their arms—every now and then something that you had thought dead stirs.... And the screaming from the Forest is incessant so that you simply don't hear the shell (now very close indeed)....

There is, you know, that world somewhere with the Rev. Someone lecturing on Fools and "the class 'Ruysdael' costing in the neighbourhood of $100." At least, it's very important if I'm to continue to keep my head steady that I should know that it is there!

It seemed that we were the first Red Cross people to arrive. Oh! what rewards would I have offered for another ten wagons! How lamentably insufficient our three carts appeared standing there in the road with this screaming Forest on every side of one! As I waited there, overwhelmed by the blind indifference of the place, listening still to the incredible birds, seeing in the businesslike attentions of my sanitars only a further incredible indifference, a great stream of soldiers came up the road, passing into the first line of trenches, only a little deeper in the Forest. They were very hot, the perspiration dripping down their faces, but they went through to the position without a glance at the dead and wounded. No concern of theirs—that. Life had changed; they had changed with it.... Meanwhile they did as they were told....

We worked there, filling our wagons. The selection was a horrible difficulty. All the wounded were Austrians and how they begged not to be left! It would be many hours, perhaps, before the next Red Cross Division would appear. An awful business! One man dying in the wood tore at his stomach with an unceasing gesture and the air came through his mouth like gas screaming through an "escape" hole. One Austrian, quite an old man, died in my arms in the middle of the road. He was not conscious, but he fumbled for his prayer-book, which he gave me, muttering something. His name "Schneidher Gyorgy Pelmonoster" was written on the first page.

We started for home at length. Our drive back was terrible. I find that I cannot linger any longer over this affair. Our carts drove over rough stones and ruts and we were four hours on the journey. Our wounded screamed all the way—one man died.... My candle is nearly out. I must find another. In one of its frantic leaps just now I fancied that I saw Marie standing near the door. She looked just as she always did, very kind though smiling.... Of course it was only the candle. I must be careful not to encourage these fancies. But God! how lonely I am to-night! I realise, I suppose, that there isn't one single living soul in the world who cares whether I die to-night or not—not one. Durward will remember me, perhaps. No one else. And Marie would have cared. Yes, even married to Semyonov she would have cared—and remembered. And I could always have cared for her, been her friend, as she asked me. I'm pretty low to-night. If I could sleep.... Boof!... There goes the candle!

Wednesday, August 4th.... I am growing accustomed, I suppose, to Semyonov's company. After all, his contempt for me is an old thing, dating from the very first moment that he ever saw me. It has become now a commonplace to both of us. He is very silent now compared with the old days. There has been much work yesterday and to-day, but still last night I could not sleep. I think that he also did not sleep and we both lay there in the dark, thinking, I suppose, of the same thing. I thought even of myself, my sense of humour has never been very strong, but I can at any rate see that I am no very fine figure in life, and that whether such a man as I live or die can be of no great importance to any one or anything, but I do most truly desire not to make more of the matter than is just. A man may have felt himself the most insignificant and useless of human creatures all his days, but face him with death and he becomes, by very force of the contrast, something of a figure.

Here am I, deprived of the only thing in life that gave me joy or pride. I should, after that deprivation, have slipped back, I suppose, to my old life of hopeless uninterest and insignificance, but now here the death of Marie Ivanovna has been no check at all. I half believe now that one can do with life or death what one will. If I had known that from the beginning what things I might have found! As it is, I must simply make the best of it. Semyonov's contempt would once have frightened the very life out of me, but after that night of his arrival here it has been nothing compared with the excitement of our relationship—the things that are keeping us together in spite of ourselves and the strange changes, I do believe, that this situation here is making in him. The loss of Marie Ivanovna would two months ago perhaps have finished me. What is it now beside the wonder as to whether I have lost her after all, the consciousness of pursuit, the longing to know?...

Durward and I have spoken sometimes of my dream of the Forest. It must seem to him now, as to myself, strangely fulfilled; but I believe that if I catch the beast it will only be to discover that there is a further quest beyond, and then another maybe beyond that....

At the same time there's the practical question of one's nerve. If this strain of work continues, if the hot weather lasts, and if I don't sleep, I shall have to take care. Three times during the last three days I have fancied that I have seen Marie Ivanovna, once in broad daylight in the Forest, once sitting on the sofa in our room, once at night near my bed. Of course this is the merest illusion, but I have hours now when I am not quite sure of things. Andrey Vassilievitch told me something of the same to-day—that he thought that he saw his wife and that Nikitin told him the same yesterday. The flies also are confusing and there's a hot dry smell that's disagreeable and prevents one from eating. I know that I must keep a clear head on these things. If only one could get away for an hour or two, right outside—but one is shut up in this Forest as though it were a green oven.... I ought to be sleeping now instead of writing all this.... I must say that I had a curious illusion ten minutes ago while I was writing this, that one of the wounded, in a bed near the door which is open, began to slip, bed and all, across the floor towards me. He did indeed come closer and closer to me, the bed moving in jerks as though it were pushed. This was, of course, simply because my eyes were tired. When I try to sleep they are hot and smarting....

I interrupt Trenchard's diary to give a very brief account of the impression that was made on me by my visit to the three of them with some wagons four days after the date of the above entry. It must be remembered that I had not, of course, at this time read any of Trenchard's diary, nor had I seen anything of him since the moment of Semyonov's arrival. My chief impression during the interval had been my memory of Trenchard as I had last seen him, miserable, white-faced, unnerved. I had thought about him a good deal. Those days at the Otriad had been for the rest of us rather pleasantly tranquil. There was no question that we were relieved by the absence of Semyonov and Trenchard. Semyonov was no easy companion at any time and we had the very natural desire to throw off from us the weight of Marie Ivanovna's unexpected death. I will not speak of myself in this matter, but for the others. She had not been very long in their company, she had been strange and unsettled in her behaviour, she had been engaged to a man, jilted him, and engaged herself to another—all within a very short period of time. I, myself, was occupied incessantly by my thoughts of her, but that was my own affair. The past week then with us had been tranquil and easy. On my arrival at the "Point" in the Forest I was met at once by a new atmosphere. For one thing the war here was on the very top of us. Only a few yards away, towards the end of the garden, they were digging trenches. Somewhere beyond the windows, in the Forest, a battery had established itself near a clearing at the edge of a hill, the guns disguised with leaves and branches. Soldiers were moving incessantly to and fro. The house seemed full of wounded, wagons coming and going. They were digging graves in the garden, and sheeted bodies were lying in the orchard.

My friends greeted me, seemed glad to see me for a moment, and then pursued their business. I was entirely outside their life. Only ten days before I had felt a closer intimacy with Trenchard, Andrey Vassilievitch and Nikitin than I had ever had with any of them. Now I simply did not exist for them. It was not the work that excluded me. The evening that passed then was an easy evening—very little to do. We spent most of the night in playing chemin-de-fer. No, it was not the work. It was quite simply that something was happening to all of them in which I had no concern. They were all changed and about them all—yes, even, I believe, about Semyonov—there was an air of suppressed excitement, rather the excitement that schoolboys have, when they have prepared some secret forbidden defiance or adventure. Trenchard, whom I had left in the depths of a lethargic depression, was most curiously preoccupied. He looked at me first as though he did not perfectly remember me. He, assuredly, was not well. His eyes were lined heavily, his white cheeks had a flush of red that burnt there feverishly, and he seemed extraordinarily thin. He was restless, his eyes were never still, and I saw him sometimes fix them, in a strange way, upon some object as though he would assure himself that it was there. He was obviously under the influence of some deep excitement. He told me that he was sleeping badly, that his head ached, and that his eyes hurt him, but he did not seem distressed by these things. He was too strongly absorbed by something to be depressed. He treated me and everything around him with impatience, as though he could not wait for something that he was expecting.

I have seen in this business of the war strange things that nerves can do with the human mind and body. I have seen many men who remain with their nerves as strong as steel from the first to the last, but this is, I should say, the exception and only to be found with men of a very unimaginative character. As regards Trenchard one must take into account his recent loss, the sudden stress of incessant exhausting work, the flaming weather and the constant companionship of the one human being of all others most calculated to disturb his tranquillity. But in varying degrees I think that every one in this place was at this time working under a strain of something abnormal and uncalculated. The very knowledge that the attack was now being pressed severely and that we had so little ammunition with which to reply, was enough to strain the nerves of every one. Trenchard told me, in the course of the conversation, that I had with him during my second day's stay, that his visit to the lines some days earlier (this is the visit of which he speaks in his diary) had greatly upset him. He had been disturbed apparently by the fact that there were not sufficient wagons. The whole sense of the Forest, he told me, was a strain to him, the feeling that he could not escape from it, the thought of its colour and heat and at the same time its ugliness and horror, the cholera scarecrow in it, and the deserted town and all the horrors of the recent attacks. The dead Austrians and Russians.... But I repeat, most emphatically, that he was not depressed by this. It was rather that he wished to keep his energies fresh and clear for some purpose of his own, and was therefore disturbed by anything that threatened his health. He was not quite well, he told me— headaches, not sleeping—but that "he had it well in control."

And here now is a strange thing. One of the chief purposes of my visit had been to persuade one of the four men to return with me to the Otriad. Molozov had asserted very emphatically that none of them should be compelled against their will to return to Mittövo, but he thought that it would be well if, considering the strain of the work and the Position, they were to take it in turns to have a day or two's rest and so relieve one another. I had had no doubt that this would be very acceptable to them, but on my proposing it, was surprised to receive from each of them individually an abrupt refusal even to consider the matter. At the same time they assured me, severally, that the one or the other of them needed, very badly, a rest. After I had spoken, Nikitin, taking me aside, told me that he thought that Andrey Vassilievitch would be better at Mittövo. "He is a little in the way here," he said. "Certainly he does his best, but this is not his place." Nikitin wore the same preoccupied air as the others.— "Whatever you do," he said, "don't let Andrey know that I spoke to you." Andrey Vassilievitch, on his side with much nervousness and self-importance, told me that he thought that Nikitin was suffering from overwork and needed a complete rest. "You know, Ivan Andreievitch, he is really not at all well; I sleep in the same room. He talks in his sleep, fancies that he sees things ... very odd—although this hot weather ... I myself for the matter of that ..." and then he nervously broke off.

But with all this they did not seem to quarrel with one another. It is true that I discovered a kind of impatience, especially between Andrey Vassilievitch and Nikitin, the kind of restlessness that you see sometimes between two horses which are harnessed together. Semyonov (he paid no attention to me at all during my visit) treated Trenchard quite decently, and I observed on several occasions his look of puzzled curiosity at the man—a look to which I have alluded before. He spoke to him always in the tone of contemptuous banter that he had from the beginning used to him: "Well, Mr., I suppose that you couldn't bring a big enough bandage however much you were asked to. But why choose the smallest possible...."

Or, "That's where Mr. writes his poetry—being a nice romantic Englishman. Isn't it, Mr.?"

But I was greatly struck by Trenchard's manner of taking these remarks. He behaved now as though he had secret reasons for knowing that he was in every way as good a man as Semyonov—a better one, maybe. He laughed, or sometimes simply looked at his companion, or he would reply in his bad halting Russian with some jest at Semyonov's expense.

Finally, to end this business, if ever a man were affected to the heart by the loss of a friend or a lover, Semyonov was that man. He was a man too strong in himself and too contemptuous of weakness to show to all the world his hurt. I myself might have seen nothing had I not always before me the memory of that vision of his face between the trees. But from that I had proceeded—

It was, I suppose, the first time in his life that the fulfilment of his desire had been denied him. Had Marie Ivanovna lived, and had he attained with her his complete satisfaction, he would have tired of her perhaps as he had tired of many others, and have remained only the stronger cynic. But she had eluded him, eluded him at the very moment of her freshness and happiness and triumph. What defeat to his proud spirit was working now in him? What longing? What fierce determination to secure even now his ends? The change that I fancied in him was perhaps no more than his bracing of his strength and courage to face new conditions. Death had robbed him of his possession—so much the worse then for Death!

Upon this day of icy cold, as I write these words, I am afraid that my account may be taken as an extravagant and unjustified conceit. But that I do most honestly believe it not to be. I myself felt, during my two days' stay in that place, the strangest contact with new experiences, new developments, new relationships. Normal life had been left utterly behind and there was nothing to remind one of it save perhaps that "Report on New Mexico" still there on the dusty table. But there was the heat; there were the wheeling, circling clouds of flies, now in lines, now in squares, now broken like smoke, now dim like vapour; there was that old familiar smell of dust and flesh, chemicals and blood; there were the men dying and broken, fighting like giants, defeating fears and terrors that hung like grey shadows about the doors and windows of the house.... Every incident and experience that we had had at the war, every incident and experience that I have related in these pages seemed to be gathered into this house.... As I look back upon it now it seems, without any extravagance at all, the very heart of the fortress of the enemy. I do not mean in the least that life was solemn or pretentious or heavy. It was careless, casual, as liable to the ridiculous intervention of unimportant things as ever it had been; but it was life pressed so close to the fine presence of Fate that you could hear the very beating of his heart. And in this Fortress it seemed to me that I, who was watching, outside the lives of these others, an observer only whom, perhaps, this same Fate despised, asked of God a sign. I saw suddenly here the connexion, for which I had been waiting, between the four men: There they were, Nikitin and Andrey, Semyonov and Trenchard—Two Wise Men and Two Fools—surely the rivalry was ludicrous in its inequality ... and yet God does not judge as men do. Nikitin and Semyonov or Andrey and Trenchard? Who would be taken and who left? I recalled Semyonov's jesting words: "Even though it's the wise men succeed in this world I don't doubt it's the fools have their way in the next."

I waited for my Sign....

Last of all I can hear it objected that every one was surely too busy to attend to relationships or shades of relationships. But it was this very thing that contributed to the situation, namely, that, in the very stress of the work, there were hours, many hours, when there was simply nothing to be done. Then if one could not sleep times were bad indeed. Moreover, even in the throng of work itself one would be conscious of that slipping off from one of all the trappings of reality. One by one they would slip away and then, bewildered, one would doubt the evidence of one's eyes, one's brain, one's ears, the fatigue hammering, hammering at one's consciousness.... I have known what that kind of strain can be.

I left on the second morning after my arrival and returned to Mittövo alone.

Trenchard's Diary. Tuesday, August 10. Durward has been here for two days. He's a good fellow but I seem rather to have lost touch with him during these last days. Then he's rather bloodless—a little more humour would cheer him up wonderfully. We've all been in mad spirits to-day as though we were drunk. The battery officers have got a gramophone that we turned on. We danced a bit although it's hot as hell.... Then in the evening my spirits suddenly went; Andrey Vassilievitch gets on one's nerves. His voice is tiresome and I'm tired of his wife. He tells me that he thinks he sees her at night. "Do I think it likely?"

Silly little ass—just the way to rot his nerves. Funny thing to-night. We were playing chemin-de-fer. Suddenly Semyonov said:

"Supposing Molozov says that only one of us is to stay on here." There was silence after that. We all four looked at one another. All I knew was nothing was going to move me away from this place if I could help it. Then Semyonov said:

"Of course I would have to stay."

We went for him then. You should have heard Nikitin! I didn't believe that he had it in him. Semyonov was quiet, of course, smiling that beastly smile of his.

Then at last he said:

"Suppose we play for it?"

We agreed. The one who turned up the Ace of Hearts was to stay. You could have heard a pin drop after that. I have never before felt what I felt then. If I had to return and leave Semyonov here! They say that the attack may develop in this direction at any moment. If Semyonov were to be here and I not.... And yet what was it that I wanted? What I want is to be close to Marie again, to be there where Semyonov cannot reach us. I believe that she might always have cared for me if he had not been there. Whatever death may be, I must know.... If there is nothing more, no matter. If there is something more—then there is something for her as well as for me and I shall find her, and I must find her alone. There's nothing left in life now to me save that. As I sat there looking at the cards I knew all this, knew quite clearly that I must escape Semyonov. There's no madness in this. Whilst he is there I'm nothing—but without him, if I were with her again—I was always beaten easily by anybody but in this at least I can be strong. I don't hate him but I know that he will always be first as long as we're together. And we seem to be tied now like dogs by their tails, tied by our thoughts of Marie....

Well, anyway I turned up the Ace. My heart seemed to jump right upside down when I saw it. The others said nothing. Only Semyonov at last:

"Well, Mr., if it comes to it we'll have to see that it's necessary for two of us to be here. It will never do for you and me to be parted—"

Meanwhile, the firing's very close to-night. They say the Austrians have taken Vulatch. Shocking, our lack of ammunition.... God! The heat!

CHAPTER V

THE DOOR CLOSES BEHIND THEM

Trenchard's Diary. Saturday, August 14th....

Captain T— died this afternoon at four-thirty. A considerable shock to me. He was so young, so strong. They all said that he had a remarkable future. He had dined with us several times at Mittövo and his vitality had always attracted me; vitality restrained and drilled towards some definite purpose. He might have been a great man.... His wound in the stomach did not hurt him, I think. He was wonderfully calm at the last. How strange it is that at home death is so horrible with its long ceremonies, its crowd of relations, its gradual decay—and here, in nine out of every ten deaths that I have seen there has been peace or even happiness. This is the merest truth and will be confirmed by any one who has worked here. Again and again I have seen that strange flash of surprised, almost startled interest, again and again I have been conscious—behind not in the eyes—of the expression of one who is startled by fresh conditions, a fine view, a sudden piece of news. This is no argument for religion, for any creed or dogma, I only say that here it is so, that Death seems to be happiness and the beginning of something new and unexpected.... I believe that even so hardy a cynic as Semyonov would support me in this. I and Semyonov were alone with young Captain T— when he died. Semyonov had liked the man and had done everything possible to save him. But he was absorbed by his death—absorbed as though he would tear the secret of it from the body that looked suddenly so empty, and so meaningless.

"Well, I'm glad he was happy," he said to me. Then he stood, looking at me curiously. I returned the look. We neither of us said anything. These are all commonplaces, I suppose, that I am discovering. The only importance is that some ten million human beings are, in this war, making these discoveries for themselves, just as I am. Who can tell what that may mean? I have seen here no visions, nor have I met any one who has seen them, but there are undoubted facts—not easy things to discount.

Sunday, August 15. Things are pretty bad here. The Austrians have taken Vulatch. Both on the right and on the left they have advanced. They may arrive here at any moment. The magnificence of the Russian soldier is surely beyond all praise. I wonder whether people in France and England realise that for the last three months here he has been fighting with one bullet as against ten. He stands in his trench practically unarmed against an enemy whose resources seem, endless—but nothing can turn him back. Whatever advances the Germans may make I see Russia returning again and again. I do from the bottom of my soul, and, what is of more importance, from the sober witness of my eyes, here believe that nothing can stop the impetus born of her new spirit. This war is the beginning of a world history for her.

Krylov this afternoon said that he thought that we should leave this place, get out our wagons and retire. But how can we? At this moment, how can we? We are just now at the most critical meeting of the ways—the extra twelve versts back to Mittövo may make the whole difference to many of the cases, and the doctors of the Division, Krylov himself admits, have got their arms full. We simply can't leave them.... There has been some confusion here. There doesn't seem any responsible person to give us orders. Colonel Maximoff has forgotten us, I believe. In any case I think that we must stay on here for another day and night. Perhaps we shall get away to-morrow....

I had a queer experience this afternoon. I don't want to make too much of it but here it is. I went up to my room this afternoon at five to get some sleep, as I'm on duty to-night. I lay down and shut my eyes and then, of course, as I always do, immediately saw Marie Ivanovna. I know quite clearly that this present relationship to her cannot continue for long or I shall be off my head. I can see myself quite clearly as though I were outside myself, and I know that I'm madder now than I was a week ago. For instance in this business of Marie Ivanovna, I knew then that my seeing her was an illusion—now I am not quite sure. I knew a week ago that I saw her because she is so much in my thoughts, because of the intolerable heat, because of the Flies and the Forest, because of Semyonov. I am not sure now whether it is not her wish that I should see her. She comes as she came on those last days before she left me—with all the kindness in her eyes that no other human being has ever given me before, nor will ever give me again. To-day I looked and was not sure whether she were gone or no. I was not sure of several things in the room and as I lay there I said to myself, "Is that really a looking-glass or no?" "If I tried could I touch it or would it fade from under my hand?" The room was intolerably close and there was a fly who persecuted me. As I lay there he came and settled on my hand. He waited, watching me with his wicked sneering eyes, then he crept forward, and waited again, rubbing his legs one against the other. Then very slyly, laughing to himself, he began to tickle me. I slashed with my hand at him, he flew into the air, sneering, then with a little "ping" settled on the back of my neck. I vowed that I would not mind him; I lay still. He began then to crawl very slowly forward towards my chin, and it was as though he were dragging spidery strands of nerves through my body, fitting them all on to stiff, tight wires. He reached my chin, and then again, sneering up into my eyes, he began to tickle. I thought once more that I had him, but once again he was in the air. Then, after waiting until I had almost sunk back into sleep, he did the worst thing that a fly can do, began, very slowly, to crawl down the inside of my pince-nez (I had been trying to read). He got between the glass and my eyelash and moved very faintly with his damnable legs. Then my patience went—I did what during these last days I have vowed not to do, lost my control, jumped from my bed, and cursed with rage....

Then with my head almost bursting with heat and my legs trembling I had an awful moment, I thought that I was really mad. I thought that I would get the looking-glass and smash it and that then I would jump from the window. In another moment I thought that something would break in my head, the something with which I kept control over myself—I seemed to hear myself praying aloud: "Oh God! let me keep my reason! Oh God! let me keep my reason!" and I could see the Forest like a great green hot wave rising beyond the window to a towering height ready to leap down upon me.

Then Semyonov came in. He stood in the doorway and looked at me. He must have thought me strange and I know that I waited, staring at him, feeling foolish as I always do with him. But he spoke to me kindly, with the sort of kindness that there is sometimes in his voice, patronising and reluctant of course.

"You can't sleep, Mr.?" he said.

"No," I answered, and said something about flies.

"What have you been doing to the looking-glass?" he asked, laughing, for there the thing was on the floor, broken into pieces. I am sure that I never touched it.

"That's unlucky," he said. "Never mind, Mr.," he said smiling at me, "twenty-two misfortunes, aren't you? Always dropping something," he added quite kindly. "More, perhaps, than the rest of us.... Wash your face in cold water. It's this infernal heat that worries us all."

I remember then that he poured the water into the blue tin basin for me and then, taking the tin mug himself, poured it in cupfuls over my hands and arms. I afterwards did the same for him. At that moment I very nearly spoke to him of Marie. I wished desperately to try; but I looked at his face, and his eyes, laughing at me as they always did, stopped me.

When I had finished he thanked me, wiped his hands, then turning round at the door he said: "Why don't you go back to Mittövo, Mr.— You're tired out."

"You know why," I answered, without looking at him He seemed then as though he would speak, but he stopped himself and went away. I lay down again and tried to sleep, but when I closed my eyes the green beyond the window burnt through my eyelids—and then the fly (I am sure it was the same fly) returned....

Monday, August 16.... Lord! but I am tired of this endless bandaging, cleaning of filthy wounds, paring away of ragged ends of flesh, smelling, breathing, drinking blood and dust and dirt. The poor fellows! Their bravery is beyond any word of mine. They have come these last few days with their eyes dazed and their ears deafened. Indeed the roaring of the cannon has been since yesterday afternoon incessant. They say that the Austrians are straining every nerve to break through to the river and cross. We are doing what we can to prevent them, but what can we do? There simply IS NOT AMMUNITION! The officers here are almost crying with despair, and the men know it and go on, with their cheerfulness, their obedience, their mild kindliness—go into that green hell to be butchered, and come out of it again, if they are lucky, with their bodies mangled and twisted, and horror in their eyes. It's nobody's fault, I suppose, this business. How easy to write in the daily papers that the Germans prepared for war and that we did not, and that after a month or two all will be well.... After a month or two! tell that to us here stuck in this Forest and hear us how we laugh!...

Meanwhile, for the good of my health, I'm figuring very clearly to myself all the physical features of this place. It's a long white house, two-storied. The front door has broken glass over it and there's a litter of tumbled bricks on the top step. After you've gone through the front door you come into the hall where the wounded are as thick as flies. You go through the hall and turn to the left. There's a pantry place on your right all full of flies and when you open the door they unsettle with a great buzz and shift into all sorts of shapes and patterns. Next to them is our sitting-room, the horrid place always dirty and stifling. Then there's the operating-room, then another room for beds, then the kitchen. Outside to the right there's the garden, dry now with the heat, and the orchard smells of the men they've buried in it. To the left, after a little clearing, there's the forest always green and glittering. The men are in the trenches now, the new ones that were made last week, so I suppose that we shall be in the thick of it very shortly. That battery at the edge of the hill has been banging away all the morning. What else is there? There's an old pump just outside the sitting-room window. There's a litter of dirty paper and refuse there, too, that the flies gather round. There's an old barn away to the right where some horses are and two cows. I have to keep my mind on these things because I know they're real. You can touch them with your hands and they'll still be there even if you go away—they won't walk with you as you move. So I must fasten on to these things about which there can't be any doubt. In the same way I like to remember that book in the sitting-room—Mr. Glass who lectured on "Fools," the Ruysdael, and the Normal Pupils who acted Othello. They're real enough and are probably somewhere now quietly studying, or teaching, or sleeping—I envy them....

A thing that happened this morning disturbed us all. Four soldiers came out of the Forest quite mad. They seemed rational enough at first and said that they'd been sent out of the first line trenches with contusion—one of them had a bleeding finger, but the others were untouched. Then one of them, a middle-aged man with a black beard, began quite gravely to tell us that the Forest was moving. They had seen it with their own eyes. They had watched all the trees march slowly forward like columns of soldiers and soon the whole Forest would move and would crush every one in it. It was all very well fighting Austrians, but whole forests was more than any one could expect of them. Then suddenly one of them cried out, pointing with his finger: "See, Your Honour—there it comes!... Ah! let us run! let us run!" One of them began to cry. It was very disagreeable. I saw Andrey Vassilievitch who was present glance anxiously through the window at the Forest and then gravely check himself and look at me nervously to see whether I had noticed. The men afterwards fell into a strange kind of apathy. We sent them off to Mittövo in the afternoon.

I want now to remember as exactly as possible a strange conversation I had this evening with Semyonov. I came up when it was getting dusk to the bedroom. One of the Austrian batteries was spitting away over the hill but we were not replying. Everything this afternoon has looked as though they were preparing for a heavy attack. Our little window was open and the sky beyond was a sort of very pale green, and against this you could see a flush of colour rising and falling like the opening and shutting of a door. Everything quite silent except the Austrian cannon and a soldier, delirious, downstairs, singing.

The Forest was deep black, but you could see the soldiers' fires gleaming here and there like beasts' eyes. Our room was almost dark and I was very startled to find Semyonov sitting on his bed and staring in front of him. He looked like a wooden figure sitting there, and he didn't move as I came in. I'm glad that although I'm still awkward and clumsy with him (as I am, and always will be, I suppose, with every one) I'm not afraid of him any more. The room was so dark that he looked like a shadow. I had intended to fetch something and go away, but instead of that I sat down on my bed, feeling suddenly very tired and lethargic.

"Well, Mr.," he said in the ironical voice he always uses to me.

(I would wish now to repeat if I can every word of our conversation.)

"Krylov has been again," I said. "He told Nikitin that we ought to go to-night. Nikitin asked him whether the Division had plenty of wagons and Krylov admitted that there weren't nearly enough. He agreed that it would make a lot of difference if we could keep this place going until to-morrow night—all the same he advised us to leave."

"We'll stay until some one orders us to go," said Semyonov. "It will make a difference to a hundred men or more probably. If they do start firing on to this place we can get the men off in the wagons in time."

"And what if the wagons have left for Mittövo?"

"We'll have to wait until they come back," he answered.

We sat there listening to the cannon. Then Semyonov said very quietly and not at all ironically, "I wish to ask you—I have wished before—tell me. You blame me for her death?"

I thought for a moment, then I replied:

"I did so at first. Now I do not think that it had anything to do with you or with me or with any one— except herself."

"Except herself?" he said. "What do you mean?"

"She wished it, I think."

His irony returned. "You believe in the power of others, Mr., too much. You should believe more in your own."

"I believe in her power. She was stronger than you," I answered.

"I'm sure that you like to think so," he said laughing.

"She is still stronger than you...."

"So you are a mystic, Mr.," he said. "Of course, with your romantic mind that is only natural. You believe, I suppose, that she is with us here in the room?"

"It cannot be of interest to you," I answered quietly, "what I believe."

"Yes, it is of interest," he replied in a voice that was friendly and humorously indulgent, as though he spoke to a child. "I find it strange—I have found it strange for many weeks now—that I should think so frequently of you. You are not a man who would naturally be interesting to me. You are an Englishman and I am not interested in Englishmen. You are sentimental, you have no idea of life as it is, you like dull things, dull safe things, you believe always in what you are told. You have no sense of humour.... You should be of no interest to me, and yet during these last weeks I have not been able to get rid of you."

"That is not my fault," I said. "I have not been so anxious for your company."

"No," he said, speaking rather thoughtfully, as though he were seriously thinking something out, "you regard me, of course, as a very bad character. I have no desire to defend myself to you. But the point is that I have found myself often thinking of you, that I have even taken trouble sometimes to be with you."

He waited as though he expected me to say something, but I was silent.

"It was perhaps that I saw that Marie Ivanovna cared for you. She gave you up to the end something that she never gave to me. That I suppose was tiresome to me."

"You thought you knew her," I said, hoping to hurt him. "You did not know her at all."

"That may be," he answered. "I certainly did not understand her, but that was attractive to me. And so, Mr., you thought that you understood her?"

But I did not answer him. My head ached frantically, I was wretchedly in want of sleep. I jumped to my feet, standing in front of him:

"Leave me alone! Leave me alone!" I cried. "Let us part. I am nothing to you—you despise me and laugh at me—you have from the first done so. It was because you laughed at me that she began to laugh. If you had not been there she might have continued to love me—she was very inexperienced. And now that she is gone I am of no more importance to you—let me be! For God's sake, let me be!"

"You are free," he said. "You can return to Mittövo in an hour's time when the wagons go."

I did not speak.

"No, you will not go," he went on, "because you think that she is here. She died here—and you believe that she is not dead. I also will not go—for my own reasons."

Then he jumped off his bed, stood upright against me, his clothes touching mine. He put his hand on my shoulder.

"No, Mr., we will remain together. I find you really rather charming. And you are changed, you know. You are not the silly fool you were when you first came to us!"

I moved away from him. I could not bear the touch of his hand on my shoulder. I had, I repeat, no fear of him. He might laugh at me or no as he pleased, but I did not want his kindness.

"My beliefs seem to you the beliefs of a child," I said, trying to speak more calmly. "Well, then, leave me to them. They at least do you no harm. I love her now as I loved her when I first saw her. I cannot believe that I shall never be with her again. But that is my own affair and matters to no one but myself!"

He answered me: "You have a simple fashion of looking at things which I envy you. I assure you that I am not laughing at you. You believe, if I understand you, that after your death you will meet her again. You are afraid that if I die before you she will belong to me, but that if you die first you will be with her again as you were 'at the beginning'?... Is not that so?"

I did not answer him.

"I swear to you," he continued, "that I am not mocking you. What my own thoughts may be does not interest you, but I have not, in my life, found many things or persons that are worth one's devotion, and she was worthy of being loved as you love her. Such days as these in such a place as this must bring strange thoughts to any man. When we return to Mittövo to-morrow night I assure you that you will see everything differently."

He felt, I suppose, that he had been speaking too seriously because the ironic humour with which he always treated me returned.

"Here, Mr., at any rate we are. I'm sorry for you—tiresome to be tied to some one as uncongenial as myself—but be a little sorry for me, too. You're not, you know, the ideal companion I would have chosen."

"Why did you come?" I asked him. "Durward was here—we were doing very well—"

"Without me"—he caught me up. "Yes, I suppose so. But your fascination is so strong that—" He broke off laughing, then continued almost sharply: "Here we are anyway. To-night and to-morrow we are going to be lively enough if I know anything about it. I'll do you the justice, Mr., of saying you've worked admirably here. I wouldn't have believed it of you. Let us both of us drop our romantic fancies. We've no time to spare." Then, turning at the door, he ended: "And you needn't hate me so badly, you know. She cared for you in a way that she never gave me. Perhaps, after all, in the end, you will win—"

He gave me one last word:

"All the same I don't give her up to you," he said.

When I came downstairs again it was to find confusion and noise. In the first place little Andrey Vassilievitch was quarrelling loudly with Nikitin. He was speaking Russian very fast and I did not discover his complaint. There was something comic in the sight of his small body towering to a perfect tempest of rage, his plump hands gesticulating and always his eyes, anxious and self-important, doing their best to look after his dignity. Nikitin explained to me that he had been urging Andrey Vassilievitch to return to Mittövo with the wagons. "There's no need," he said, "for us all to stay. It's only taking unnecessary risks—and somebody should take charge of the wagons."

"There's Feodor Constantinovitch," said Andrey, naming a feldscher and stammering in his rage. "He's re-responsible enough." Then, seeing that he was creating something of a scene, he relapsed into a would-be dignified sulkiness, finally said he would not go, and strutted away.

There were many other disturbances, men coming and going, one of the battery officers appearing for a moment dirty and dishevelled, and always the wounded drowsy or in delirium, watching with dull eyes the evening shadows, talking excitedly in their sleep. Semyonov called me to help in the operating room. Within the next two hours he had carried out two amputations with admirable cool composure. During the second one, when the man's arm tumbled off into the basin and lay there amongst the filthy rags with the dirty white fingers curved, their nails dead and grey, I suddenly felt violently sick.

A sanitar took my place and I went out into the cool of the forest, where a silver pattern of stars swung now above the branches and a full moon, red and cold, was rising beyond the hill. After a time I felt better and, finding that I was not needed for a time, I wrote this diary.

Tuesday, August 17th. It is just six o'clock—a most lovely evening. Strangely enough everything is utterly quiet—not a sound anywhere. You might fancy yourself in the depths of England somewhere. However, considering what has happened to-day and what they expect will happen now at any moment, the strain on our nerves is pretty severe, and as usual at such times I will fill in my diary. This is probably the last time that I write it here as we move as soon as the wagons return, which should be in about two hours from now.

All our things are packed and I shall slip this book into my bag as soon as I have written this entry; but I have probably two or three hours clear for writing, as everything is ready for departure. Meanwhile I am wonderfully tranquil and at peace, able, too, to think clearly and rationally for the first time since Marie's death. I want to give an account of the events since my last entry minutely and as truthfully as my memory allows me.

At about half-past eleven last night Semyonov and I went up to our bedroom to sleep, Nikitin being on duty. There was not much noise, the cannon sounding a considerable distance away, but the flashlights and rockets against the night-sky were wonderful, and when we had blown out the candle our dark little room leapt up and down or turned round and round, the window flashing into vision and out again. Semyonov was almost immediately asleep, but I lay on my back and, of course, as usual, thought of Marie. My headache of the evening still raged furiously and I was in desperately low spirits. I had been able to eat nothing during the preceding day. I lay there half asleep, half awake, for, I suppose, a long time, hearing the window rattle sometimes when the cannon was noisy and feeling under the jerky reflections on the wall as though I were in an old shambling cab driving along a dark road, I thought a good deal about that talk with Semyonov that I had. What a strange man! But then I do not understand him at all. I don't think I understand any Russian, such a mixture of hardness and softness as they are, kind and then indifferent, cruel and then sentimental. But I understand people very little, and in all my years at Polchester there was never one single person whom I knew. Semyonov is perfectly right, I suppose, from his point of view to think me a fool. I lay there thinking of Semyonov. He was sleeping on his back, looking very big under the clothes, his beard square and stiff, lit up by the flashing light and then sinking into darkness again. I thought of him and of myself and of the strange contrast that we were, and how queer it was that the same woman should have cared for both of us. And I know that, although I did not hate him at all, I would give almost anything for him not to have been there, never to have been there. Whilst he was there I knew that I had no chance. Marie had not laughed at me during those days at Petrograd; she had believed in me then and I had been worth believing in. If people had believed in me more I might be a very different man now.

I was almost asleep, scarcely conscious of the room, when suddenly I heard a voice cry, "Marie! Marie! Marie!" three times. It was a voice that I had never heard before, strong but also tender, full of pain, with a note in it too of a struggling self-control that would break in a moment and overwhelm its possessor. As I look back at it I remember that I felt the passion and strength in it so violently that I seemed to shrink into myself, as though I were witnessing something that no man should see, and as though also I were conscious of my own weakness and insignificance.

It was Semyonov. The flashlight flashed into the room, shining for an instant upon him. He was sitting up in bed, his shirt open and his chest bare. His eyes were fixed upon the window, but he was fast asleep. He seemed to me a new man. I had grown so accustomed to his sarcasm, his irony, that I had almost persuaded myself that he had never truly loved Marie, but had felt some sensual attraction for her that would, by realisation, have been at once satisfied. This was another man. Here was a struggle, an agony that was not for such men as I.

He cried again, "Marie! Marie!" then got up out of bed, walked on his naked feet in his shirt to the window, stood there and waited. The moonlight had, by this, struck our room and flooded it. He turned suddenly and faced me. I could not believe that he did not see me, but I could not endure the unhappiness in his eyes and I turned, looking down. I did not look at him again but I heard his feet patter back to the bed; then he stood there, his whole body strung to meet some overmastering crisis. He whispered her name as though she had come to him since his first call. "Ah, Marie, my darling," he whispered.

I could not bear that. I crept from my bed, slipped away, closed the door softly behind me and stole downstairs.

I cannot write at length of what followed. It was the crisis of everything that has happened to me since I left Petrograd. Every experience that I had had was suddenly flung into this moment. I was in our sitting-room now, pitch dark because shutters had been placed outside the windows to guard against bullets. I stood there in my shirt and drawers: shuddering, shivering with hatred of myself, shivering with fear of Semyonov, shivering above all, with a desperate, agonising, torturing hunger for Marie. Semyonov's voice had appalled me. I hadn't realised before how strongly I had relied on his not truly caring for her. Everything in the man had seemed to persuade me of this, and I had even flattered myself on my miserable superiority to him, that I was the true faithful lover and he the vulgar sensualist. How small now I seemed beside him!—and how I feared him! Then I was at sudden fierce grip with the beast!... At grips at last!

I had once before, on another night, been tempted to kill myself, but that had been nothing to this. Now sick and ill, faint for food, I swayed there on the floor, hearing always in my ear—"Give way! Give way!...

You'll be in front of him, you'll have left him behind you, he can do nothing ... a moment more and you can be with her—and he cannot reach you!"

I do not know how long I fought there. I was not fighting with an evil devil, a fearful beast as in my dreams I had always imagined it—I was fighting myself: every weakness in the past to which I had ever surrendered, every little scrap of personal history, every slackness and cowardice and lethargy was there on the floor against me.

I don't know what it was that prevented me stealing back to my room, fetching my revolver and so ending it. I could see Marie close to me, to be reached by the stretching of a finger. I could see myself living on, always conscious of Semyonov, his thick beastly confident body always there between myself and her.

I sank into the last depths of self-despair and degradation. No fine thing saved me, no help from noble principles, nothing fine. The whole was as sordid as possible. I knew, even as I struggled, that I was a silly figure there, with my bony ugliness, in my shirt and drawers, my hair on end and my teeth chattering. But I responded, I suppose, to some little pulse of manly obstinacy that beat somewhere in me. I would not be beaten by the Creature. Even in the middle of it I realised that this was the hardest tussle of my life and worth fighting. I know too that some thought of Nikitin came to me as though, in some way, my failure would damage him. I remembered that night of the Retreat when he had helped me and, as though he were appealing visibly to me there in the room, I responded; I seemed to feel that he was fighting some battle of his own and that my victory would fortify him. I stood with him beside me. So I fought it, fought it with the sweat dripping down my nose and my tongue dry. "No!" something suddenly cried in me. "If she's his, she's his—I will not take her this way!"—then in a snivelling, miserable fashion I began to cry, simply from exhaustion and nerves and headache. I slipped down into a chair. I sat there feeling utterly beaten and yet in some dim way, as one hears a trumpet sounding behind a range of hills, I was triumphant. There with my head on the table and my nose, I believe, in a plate left from some one's last night's supper, I slept a heavy, dreamless sleep.

I woke and heard a clock in the room strike three. I got up, stretched my arms, yawned and knew that my head was clear and my brain at peace. I can't describe my feelings better than by saying that it was as though I had put my brain and my heart and all my fears and terrors under a good stiff pump of cold water. I felt a different man from four hours before, although still desperately tired and physically weak.

I went softly upstairs. The light of a most lovely summer morning flooded the room. Semyonov was lying, sleeping like a child, his head pillowed on his arm. Very cautiously I dressed, then went downstairs again. I did not understand now—the peace and happiness in my heart. All the time I was saying to myself: "Why am I so happy? Why am I so happy?"...

The world was marvellously fresh, with little white glittering clouds above the trees, the grass wet and shining, and the sky a high dome of blue light, like the inside of a glass bell that has the sun behind it. Here and there on the outskirts of the Forest fires were still dimly burning, pale and dim yellow shadows beneath the sun. Men wrapped in their coats were sleeping in little groups under the trees. Horses cropped at the grass; soldiers were moving with buckets of water. Two men, at the very edge of the Forest, stripped to the waist, were washing in a pool that was like a blue handkerchief in the great forest of green. I found a little glade, very bright and fresh, under a group of silver birch, and there I lay down on my back, my hands behind my head, looking up into the little dancing atoms of blue between the trees and the golden stars of sunlight that flashed and sparkled there.

Happiness and peace wrapped me round. I cannot pretend to disentangle and produce in proper sequence all the thoughts and memories that floated into my vision and away again, but I know that whereas before thoughts had attacked me as though they were foul animals biting at my brain, now I seemed myself gently to invite my memories.

Many scenes from my Polchester days that I had long forgotten came back to me. I was indeed startled by the clearness with which I saw that earlier figure—the very awkward, careless, ugly boy, listening lazily to other people's plans, taking shelter from life under a vague love of beauty and an idle imagination; the man, awkward and ugly, sensitive because of his own self-consciousness, wasting his hours through his own self-contempt which paralysed all effort, still trusting to his idle love of beauty to pull him through to some superior standard, complaining of life, but never trying to get the better of it; then the man who came to Russia at the beginning of the war, still self-centred, always given up to timid self-analysis, but responding now a little to the new scenes, the new temperament, the new chances. Then this man, feeling that at last he was rid of all the tiresome encumbrances of the earlier years, lets himself go, falls in love, worships, dreams for a few days a wonderful dream—then for the first time in his life, begins to fight.

I saw all the steps so clearly and I saw every little thought, every little action, every little opportunity missed or taken, accumulating until the moment of climax four hours before. I seemed to have brought Polchester on my back to the war, and I could see quite clearly how each of us—Marie, Semyonov, Nikitin, Durward, every one of us—had brought their private histories and scenes with them. War is made up, I believe, not of shells and bullets, not of German defeats and victories, Russian triumphs or surrenders, English and French battles by sea and land, not of smoke and wounds and blood, but of a million million past thoughts, past scenes, streets of little country towns, lonely hills, dark sheltered valleys, the wide space of the sea, the crowded traffic of New York, London, Berlin, yes, and of smaller things than that, of little quarrels, of dances at Christmas time, of walks at night, of dressing for dinner, of waking in the morning, of meeting old friends, of sicknesses, theatres, church services, prostitutes, slums, cricket-matches, children, rides on a tram, baths on a hot morning, sudden unpleasant truth from a friend, momentary consciousness of God....

Death too.... How clear now it was to me! During these weeks I had wondered, pursued the thought of Death. Was it this? Was it that? Was it pain? Was it terror? I had feared it, as for instance when I had seen the dead bodies in the Forest, or stood under the rain at Nijnieff. I had laughed at it as when I had gone with the sanitars. I had cursed it as when Marie Ivanovna had died. I had sought it as I had done last night—and always, as I drew closer and closer to it, fancied it some fine allegorical figure, something terrible, appalling, devastating.... How, when I was, as I believed, at last face to face with it, I saw that one was simply face to face with oneself.

Four hours I have been writing, and no sign of the wagons.... I am writing everything down as I remember it, because these things are so clear to me now and yet I know that afterwards they will be changed, twisted.

I was drowsy. I saw Polchester High Street, Garth in Roselands, Clinton, Truxe, best of all Rafiel. I went down the high white hill, deep into the valley, then along the road beside the stream where the houses begin, the hideous Wesleyan Chapel on my right, "Ebenezer Villa" on my left, then the cottages with the gardens, then the little street, the post-office, the butcher's, the turn of the road and, suddenly, the bay with the fishing boats riding at anchor and beyond the sea.... England and Russia! to their strong and confident union I thought that I would give every drop of my blood, every beat of my heart, and as I lay there I seemed to see on one side the deep green lanes at Rafiel and on the other the shining canals, the little wooden houses, the cobbler and the tufted trees of Petrograd, the sea coast beyond Truxe and the wide snow-covered plains beyond Moscow, the cathedral at Polchester and the Kremlin, breeding their children, to the hundredth generation, for the same hopes, the same beliefs, the same desires.

I slept in the sun and had happy dreams.

I have re-read these last pages and I find some very fine stuff about—"giving every drop of blood," etc., etc. Of course I am not that kind of man. Men, like Durward and myself—he resembles me in many ways, although he is stronger than I am, and doesn't care what people think of him—are too analytical and self-critical to give much of their blood to anybody or to make their blood of very much value if they did.

I only meant that I would do my best.

Later in the morning the firing began again pretty close. Andrey Vassilievitch came to me and wanted to talk to me. I was rather short with him because I was busy. He wanted to tell me that he hoped I hadn't misunderstood his quarrel with Nikitin last night. It had been nothing at all. His nerves had been rather out of order. He was very much better to-day, felt quite another man. He looked another man and I said so. He said that I did.... Strange, but I felt as I looked at him that he was sickening for some bad illness. One feels that sometimes about people without being able to name a cause.

I have an affection for the little man—but he's an awful fool. Well, so am I. But fools never respect fools.... Strange to see Semyonov. I had expected him for some reason to be different to-day. Just the same, of course, very sarcastic to me. I had a hole in one of my pockets and was always forgetting and putting money and things into it. This seemed to annoy him. But to-day nothing matters. Even the flies do not worry me. All the morning Marie has seemed so close to me. I have a strange excitement, the feeling that one has when one is in a train that approaches the place where some one whom one loves is waiting.... I feel exactly as though I were going on a journey....

Since three o'clock we've had a lively time. The attack began about five minutes to three, by a shell splashing into the Forest near our battery. No one killed, fortunately. They've simply stormed away since then. I don't seem to be able to realise it and have been sitting in my room writing as though they were a hundred miles away. One so used to the noise. Everything is ready. We've got all the wounded prepared. If only the wagons would come.... Hallo! a shell in the garden—cracked one of these windows. I must go down to see whether any one's touched.... I put this in my bag. To-morrow ... and I am so happy that...

The end of Trenchard's diary.

These are the last words in Trenchard's journal. It fills about half the second exercise book. The last pages are written in a hand very much clearer and steadier than the earlier ones.

I would like now to make my account as brief as possible.

Upon the afternoon of August 16 we were all at Mittövo, extremely anxious about our friends. Molozov was in a great state of alarm. The sanitars with the wagons that arrived at about four o'clock in the afternoon told us that a violent attack in the intermediate neighbourhood of our white house was expected at any moment. The wagons were to return as quickly as possible, and bring every one away. They left about five o'clock in charge of Molozov and Goga, who were bursting with excitement. I knew that they could not be with us again until at any rate nine o'clock, but I was so nervous that at about seven I walked out to the cross and watched.

It was a very dark night, but the sky was simply on fire with searchlights and rockets, very fine behind the Forest and reflected in the river. The cannonade was incessant but one could not tell how close it was. At last, at about half-past eight, I could endure my ignorance no longer and I went down the hill towards the bridge. I had not been there more than ten minutes and had just seen a shell burst with a magnificent spurt of fire high in the wood opposite, when our wagons suddenly clattered up out of the darkness. I saw at once that something was wrong. The horses were being driven furiously although there was now no need, as I thought, for haste. I could just see Semyonov in the half light and he shouted something to me. I caught one of the wagons as it passed and nearly crushed Goga.

We were making so much noise that I had to shout to him.

"Well?" I cried.

Then I saw that he was crying, his arms folded about his face, sobbing like a little boy.

"What is it?" I shouted.

"Mr...." he said, "Andrey Vassilievitch...." I looked round. One of the sanitars nodded.

Then there followed a nightmare of which I can remember very little. It seems that at about four in the afternoon the Austrians made a furious attack. At about seven our men retreated and broke. They were gradually beaten back towards the river. Then, out of Mittövo, the "Moskovsky Polk" made a magnificent counter-attack, rallied the other Division and finally drove the Austrians right back to their original trenches. From nine o'clock until twelve we were in the thick of it. After midnight all was quiet again. I will not give you details of our experiences as they are not all to my present purpose.

At about half-past one in the morning I found Nikitin standing in the garden, looking in front of him across the river, over which a very faint light was beginning to break....

I touched him on the arm and he started, as though he had been very far away.

"How did Trenchard die?"

He answered at once, very readily: "About three o'clock the shells were close. The wagons arrived a little before seven so we had fully four anxious hours. We had had everything ready all the afternoon and, of course, just then we couldn't go out to fetch the wounded and I think that the army sanitars were working in another direction, so that we had nothing to do—which was pretty trying. I didn't see Mr. until just before seven. He had been busy upstairs about something and then at the sound of the wagons he came out. I had noticed that all day he had seemed very much quieter and more cheerful. He had been in a wretched condition on the earlier days, nervous and over-strained, and I was very glad to see him so much better. We were all working then, moving the wounded from the house to the wagons. We couldn't hear one another speak, the noise was so terrific. Andrey and Mr. were directing the sanitars near the house. Semyonov and I were near the wagons. I had looked up and shouted something to Andrey when suddenly I heard a shell that seemed as though it would break right over me. I braced myself, as one does, to meet it. For a moment I heard nothing but the noise; my nostrils were choked with the smell and my eyes blinded with dust. But I knew that I had not been hit, and I stood there, rather stupidly, wondering. Then cleared. I saw that all the right corner of the house was gone, and that Semyonov had run forward and was kneeling on the ground. With all the shouting and firing it was very difficult to realise anything. I ran to Semyonov. Andrey ... but I won't ... I can't ... he must have been right under the thing and was blown to pieces. Mr., strangely enough, lying there with his arms spread out, seemed to have been scarcely touched. But I saw at once when I came to him that he had only a few moments to live, He had a terrible stomach wound but was suffering no pain, I think. Semyonov was kneeling, with his arm behind his head, looking straight into his eyes.

"'Mr., Mr.,' he said several times, as though he wanted to rouse him to consciousness. Then, quite suddenly, Mr. seemed to realise. He looked at Semyonov and smiled, one of those rather timid, shy smiles that were so customary with him. His eyes though were not timid. They were filled with the strangest look of triumph and expectation.

"The two men looked at one another and I, seeing that nothing was to be done, waited. Semyonov then, speaking as though he and Mr. were alone in all this world of noise and confusion, said:

"'You've won, Mr.... You've won!' He repeated this several times as though it was of the utmost importance that Mr. should realise his words.

"Mr., smiling, looked at Semyonov, gave a little sigh, and died.

"I can hear now the tones of Semyonov's voice. There was something so strange in its mixture of irony, bitterness and kindness—just that rather contemptible, patronising kindness that is so especially his.

"We had no time to wait after that. We got the wagons out by a miracle without losing a man. Semyonov was marvellous in his self-control and coolness...."

We were both silent for a long time. Nikitin only once again. "Andrey!... My God, how I will miss him!" he said—and I, who knew how often he had cursed the little man and been impatient with his importunities, understood. "I have lost more—far more—than Andrey," he said. "I talked to you once, Ivan Andreievitch. You will understand that I have no one now who can bring her to me. I think that she will never come to me alone. I never needed her as he did, No more dreams...."

We were interrupted by Semyonov, who, carrying a lantern, passed us. He saw us and turned back.

"We must be ready by seven," he said sharply. "A general retirement. Ivan Andreievitch, do you know whether Mr. had friends or relations to whom we can write?"

"I heard of nobody," I answered.

"Nobody?"

"Nobody."

Just before he turned my eyes met his. He appeared to me as a man who, with all his self-control, was compelling himself to meet the onset of an immeasurable devastating loss.

He gave us a careless nod and vanished into the darkness.

Sir Hugh Seymour Walpole, CBE was born in Auckland, New Zealand, on March 13th, 1884.

His parents had moved to New Zealand in 1877, but his mother, Mildred, unable to settle there, eventually persuaded, in 1889, her husband, Somerset, an Anglican clergyman, to accept another post, this time in New York.

Walpole's early years involved being educated by a Governess until, in 1893, his parents decided he needed an English education and the young Walpole was sent to England.

He first attended a preparatory school in Truro. He naturally missed his family but was reasonably happy. A move to Sir William Borlase's Grammar School in Marlow in 1895, found him bullied, frightened and miserable. He later said, "The food was inadequate, the morality was 'twisted', and Terror–sheer, stark unblinking Terror–stared down every one of its passages ... The excessive desire to be loved that has always played so enormous a part in my life was bred largely, I think, from the neglect I suffered there".

In 1896 Somerset Walpole, hearing of his son's unhappiness, moved him to the King's School, Canterbury. For two years he settled but was undistinguished as a pupil. The following year, 1897, Walpole senior was appointed principal of Bede College, Durham, and his son was moved again; to be a day boy for four years at Durham School. Day boys were regarded as the underclass by boarders, and Bede College was the subject of snobbery within the university. His sense of isolation increased. He continually took refuge in the local library, where he read all the novels of Austen, Fielding, Scott and Dickens and many others. He was voracious in reading.

Walpole wrote in 1924: "I grew up ... discontented, ugly, abnormally sensitive, and excessively conceited. No one liked me—not masters, boys, friends of the family, nor relations who came to stay; and I do not in the least wonder at it. I was untidy, uncleanly, excessively gauche. I believed that I was profoundly misunderstood, that people took my pale and pimpled countenance for the mirror of my soul, that I had marvellous things of interest in me that would one day be discovered".

From 1903 to 1906 Walpole studied history at Emmanuel College, Cambridge and there, in 1905, had his first work published, the critical essay "Two Meredithian Heroes". Here he met and fell under the spell of A C Benson. Walpole's religious beliefs, previously sacrosanct, were fading, and Benson helped him through that personal crisis. Walpole was also attempting to cope with his homosexual feelings, which, for a while, focused on Benson.

Benson gently declined Walpole's advances. They remained friends, but Walpole, feeling rebuffed, gradually downgraded the relationship. Two years later Benson's diary entry on Walpole's subsequent social career reveals his thoughts on his protégé's progress: "He seems to have conquered Gosse completely. He spends his Sundays in long walks with H G Wells. He dines every week with Max Beerbohm and R Ross ... and this has befallen a not very clever young man of 23. Am I a little jealous?— no, I don't think so. But I am a little bewildered ... I do not see any sign of intellectual power or perception or grasp or subtlety in his work or himself. ... I should call him curiously unperceptive. He does not, for instance, see what may vex or hurt or annoy people. I think he is rather tactless–though he is himself very sensitive. The strong points about him are his curiosity, his vitality, his eagerness, and the emotional fervour of his affections. But he seems to me in no way likely to be great as an artist.

Somerset Walpole, himself the son of an Anglican priest, hoped that his eldest son would follow him into the ministry. Walpole was concerned for his father's feelings. So much so that on graduation from Cambridge in 1906 he took a post as a lay missioner at the Mersey Mission to Seamen in Liverpool. He described that as one of the "greatest failures of my life". Walpole resigned after six months.

From April to July 1907 Walpole was in Germany, privately tutoring children before returning, in 1908, to teach French at Epsom College.

Walpole now found the desire to fully immerse himself in the literary world. He moved to London to become a book reviewer for The Standard and to write fiction in his spare time. He had by this time come to terms with his homosexuality. His encounters were discreet, as they were illegal in Britain. He was constantly searching for "the perfect friend".

In 1909, Walpole published his first novel, The Wooden Horse, the story of a staid, snobbish English family shaken by the return of one of their own from a more out-going New Zealand. The book received good reviews but sold little.

Better was to come in 1911 when he published Mr Perrin and Mr Traill. The Guardian observed that "the setting of Mr Perrin and Mr Traill was clearly drawn from life". The boys of Epsom College were delighted with the thinly disguised version of their school, but the authorities were not, and Walpole was persona non grata there for many years. It was an early illustration of his capacity, noted by Benson, for unthinkingly giving offence, though being hypersensitive to criticism himself.

In early 1914 Henry James wrote an article for The Times Literary Supplement surveying the younger generation of British novelists and comparing them with their eminent elders. In the latter category James put Bennett, Conrad, Galsworthy, Hewlett and H G Wells. The four new authors were Walpole, Gilbert Cannan, Compton Mackenzie and D H Lawrence. From Walpole's point of view one of the greatest living authors had publicly ranked him among the finest young British novelists.

As war approached, Walpole realised that his poor eyesight would disqualify him from serving in the armed forces. He volunteered for the police, but was turned down. He then accepted an appointment, based in Moscow, reporting for The Saturday Review and The Daily Mail. Although he was allowed to visit the front in Poland, these dispatches were not enough to stop hostile comments at home that he was not doing his bit for the war effort.

Walpole was ready with a counter; an appointment as a Russian officer, in the Sanitar. He explained they were "part of the Red Cross that does the rough work at the front, carrying men out of the trenches, helping at the base hospitals in every sort of way, doing every kind of rough job. They are an absolutely official body and I shall be one of the few Englishmen in the world wearing Russian uniform".

While training Walpole spent many hours gaining fluency in Russian, and writing a literary biography of Joseph Conrad.

In the summer of 1915 he worked on the Austrian-Russian front, assisting at operations in field hospitals and retrieving the dead and wounded from the battlefield. Writing home to Arnold Bennett he said "A battle is an amazing mixture of hell and a family picnic—not as frightening as the dentist, but absorbing, sometimes thrilling like football, sometimes dull like church, and sometimes simply physically sickening like bad fish. Burying the dead afterwards is worst of all."

During a skirmish in June 1915 Walpole rescued a wounded soldier; his Russian comrades refused to help and this meant Walpole had to carry one end of a stretcher, dragging the man to safety. He was awarded the Cross of Saint George.

In October 1915 he returned to England to visit family and friends and to stay at a cottage he had purchased in Cornwall. In January 1916 he was asked by the Foreign Office to return to Petrograd.

Before going his novel, The Dark Forest, was published. It drew on his experiences in Russia, and was more sombre than much of his earlier fiction. Reviews were highly favourable; The Daily Telegraph commented on "a high level of imaginative vision ... reveals capacity and powers in the author which we had hardly suspected before."

Back in Petrograd his diary entry for March 13th records "Thirty two today! Should have been a happy day but was completely clouded for me by reading in the papers of Henry James' death. This was a terrible shock to me."

By late 1917 it was clear to Walpole and the authorities that his work was at an end. On November 7th he left, missing the Bolshevik Revolution, which began that very day.

In London Walpole was appointed to a post at the Foreign Office and remained there until resigning in February 1919. For his wartime work he was awarded the CBE in 1918.

Walpole continued to write and publish and now also began a career on the highly lucrative lecture tour in the United States.

He made his first lecture tour in 1919, receiving an enthusiastic welcome wherever he went. It was noted that Walpole's "genial and attractive appearance, his complete lack of aloofness, his exciting fluency as a speaker and his obvious and genuine liking for his hosts" combined to win him a large American following. The success of his talks led to an increase in lecturing fees, greater sales of his books, and large sums from American publishers keen to print his latest fiction.

A keen music lover, Walpole, in 1920, heard a new tenor at the Proms, impressed he sought him out. Lauritz Melchior became one of the most important friendships of his life, and Walpole did much to foster the singer's budding career. Wagner's son Siegfried engaged Melchior for the Bayreuth Festival in 1924 and succeeding years. Walpole attended, and met Adolf Hitler, then recently released from prison after an attempted putsch.

In 1924 Walpole moved to a house, Brackenburn, near Keswick in the Lake District. His large income enabled him to maintain his London flat in Piccadilly, but Brackenburn was his main home for the rest of his life.

At the end of 1924 Walpole met Harold Cheevers, who soon became his friend and companion and remained so for the rest of his life. Cheevers, a policeman, with a wife and two children, left the police force and entered Walpole's service as his chauffeur. Walpole trusted him completely, and gave him extensive control over his affairs. Whether Walpole was at Brackenburn or Piccadilly, Cheevers was almost always with him, and often accompanied him on overseas trips. Walpole provided a house in Hampstead for Cheevers and his family.

During the mid-twenties Walpole produced two of his best-known novels in the macabre vein that he drew on from time to time, exploring the fascination of fear and cruelty. The Old Ladies (1924) is a study of a timid elderly spinster exploited and eventually frightened to death by a predatory widow. Portrait of a Man with Red Hair (1925) depicts the malign influence of a manipulative, insane father on his family and others.

Walpole continued a series of stories for children, begun in 1919 with Jeremy, taking the young hero's story forward with Jeremy and Hamlet (the boy's dog) in 1923, and Jeremy at Crale in 1927.

In 1930 Walpole wrote possibly his best-known work, Rogue Herries, a historical novel set in the Lake District. The Daily Mail considered it "not only a profound study of human character, but a subtle and intimate biography of a place." He followed it with four sequels and an almost finished fifth.

Hollywood, in the shape of MGM, invited him in 1934 to write the script for a film of David Copperfield. Walpole enjoyed life in Hollywood, but as one who rarely revised any of his work he found it a bore to produce sixth and seventh drafts at the behest of the studio. He also had a small acting role in the film; he played the Vicar of Blunderstone delivering a boring sermon that sends David to sleep.

Walpole's performance was a success. The sermon was improvised and the producer, David O Selznick, had mischievously called for retake after retake to try to make him dry up, but Walpole fluently delivered a different extempore address each time.

The critical and commercial success of the film led to a return in 1936. Arriving, he found the studio had no idea which films they wanted him to work on, and he had eight weeks of highly paid leisure, during which he wrote a short story and worked on a novel. He was eventually asked to write the script for Little Lord Fauntleroy. He spent most of his fees on paintings; he was an avid collector and left many to the Tate in London on his death. His last lecture tour, also in 1936, was primarily to raise funds to pay US taxes which he had neglected to pay earlier.

In 1937 Walpole was offered a knighthood. He accepted although Kipling, Hardy, Galsworthy had all refused. "I'm not of their class... Besides I shall like being a knight," he said.

Walpole's taste for adventure did not diminish in his last years. In 1939 he was commissioned to report for William Randolph Hearst's newspapers on the funeral in Rome of Pope Pius XI, the conclave to elect his successor, and the subsequent coronation. In the weeks between the funeral and Pius XII's election Walpole, with his customary fluency, wrote much of Roman Fountain, a mixture of fact and fiction about the city. It was his last overseas visit.

After the outbreak of the Second World War Walpole remained in England, dividing his time between London and Keswick, where he continued to write with his usual speed. He completed a fifth novel in the Herries series and began work on a sixth.

Unfortunately his health was undermined by diabetes. He overexerted himself at the opening of Keswick's fund-raising "War Weapons Week" in May 1941, making a speech after taking part in a lengthy march.

Sir Hugh Seymour Walpole, CBE died of a heart attack at Brackenburn, aged 57 on June 1st, 1941. He was buried in St John's churchyard in Keswick.

Hugh Walpole – A Concise Bibliography

Books
The Wooden Horse (1909)
Maradick at Forty: A Transition (1910)
Mr Perrin and Mr Traill (1911) (Revised for the US version as The Gods and Mr Perrin)
The Prelude to Adventure (1912)
Fortitude (1913)
The Duchess of Wrexe, Her Decline and Death (1914)
The Golden Scarecrow (Short Stories) (1915)
Prologue
Hugh Seymour
Henry Fitzgeorge Strether
Ernest Henry
Angelina
Bim Rochester
Nancy Ross
'Enery
Barbara Flint
Sarah Trefusis
Young John Scarlet
Epilogue
The Dark Forest (1916)
Joseph Conrad (1916)
The Green Mirror (1918)
The Secret City (1919)
Jeremy (1919)
The Art of James Branch Cabell (1920)
The Captives (1920)
The Thirteen Travellers (Short Stories) (1920)
Absalom Jay
Fanny Close
The Hon Clive Torby
Miss Morganhurst

Peter Westcott
Lucy Moon
Mrs Porter and Miss Allen
Lois Drake
Mr Nix
Lizzie Rand
Nobody
Bombastes Furioso
The Young Enchanted (1921)
The Cathedral (1922)
Jeremy and Hamlet (1923)
The Crystal Box (1924) Privately published by Walpole – limited edition of 150 copies
The Old Ladies (1924)
The English Novel: Some Notes on its Evolution (1924)
Portrait of a Man with Red Hair (1925)
Harmer John (1926)
Reading: An Essay (1926)
Jeremy at Crale (1927)
Anthony Trollope (1928)
My Religious Experience (1928)
The Silver Thorn (Short Stories) (1928)
The Little Donkeys with the Crimson Saddles
The Tiger
No Unkindness Intended
Ecstasy
A Picture
Old Elizabeth (A Portrait)
The Etching
Chinese Horses
The Tarn
Major Wilbraham
A Silly Old Fool
The Enemy
The Enemy in Ambush
The Dove
Bachelors
Wintersmoon (1928)
Farthing Hall (1929) With J B Priestley
Hans Frost (1929)
Rogue Herries (1930)
Above the Dark Circus (1931) Published in the US as Above the Dark Tumult
Judith Paris (1931)
The Apple Trees: Four Reminiscences (1932) Limited edition of 500 copies
The Fortress (1932)
A Letter to a Modern Novelist (1932)
All Souls' Night (Short Stories) 1933
The Whistle
The Silver Mask

The Staircase
A Carnation for an Old Man
Tarnhelm – or The Death of my Uncle Robert
Mr Oddy
Seashore Macabre – A Moment's Experience
Lilac
The Oldest Talland
The Little Ghost
Mrs Lunt
Sentimental but True
Portrait in Shadow
The Snow
The Ruby Glass
Spanish Dusk
Vanessa (1933)
Extracts from a Diary (1934) Privately published by Walpole
Captain Nicholas (1934)
Cathedral Carol Service (1934) An episode from "The Inquisitor"
The Inquisitor (1935)
Claude Houghton: Appreciations (1935) With Clemence Dane
A Prayer for My Son (1936)
John Cornelius: His Life and Adventures (1937)
Head in Green Bronze and Other Stories (1938)
Head in Green Bronze
The German
The Exile
The Train
The Haircut
Let The Bores Tremble
The Honey-Box
The Fear of Death
The Field with Five Trees
Having No Hearts
The Conjurer
The Joyful Delaneys (1938)
The Sea Tower (1939)
Roman Fountain (1940)
The Bright Pavilions (1940)
The Blind Man's House (1941)
Open Letter of an Optimist (1941)
The Killer and the Slain (1942)
Katherine Christian (1943)
Mr Huffam and Other Stories (1948)
The White Cat
The Train to the Sea
The Perfect Close
Service for the Blind
The Faithful Servant

Miss Thom
Women are Motherly
The Beard
The Last Trump
Green Tie
The Church in the Snow
Mr Huffam – A Christmas Story

Short Stories
The following stories appeared in the Windsor Magazine

The Dog and the Dragon In Reminiscence (October 1923)
Red Amber (December 1923)
The Garrulous Diplomatist (December 1924)
The Adventure of Mrs Farbman (January 1925)
The Adventure of the Imaginative Child (February 1925)
The Happy Optimist (March 1925)
The Dyspeptic Critic (April 1925)
The Man Who Lost His Identity (May 1925)
The Adventure of the Beautiful Things (June 1925)
The War Babies are Growing Up! (November 1934)

Plays
The Young Huntress (1933)
The Cathedral (adaptation of his 1922 novel) (1936)
The Haxtons (1939)

Editor
In 1932 Walpole edited The Waverley Pageant: Best Passages from the Novels of Sir Walter Scott. In 1937 he edited a compilation of short stories, A Second Century of Creepy Stories (Hutchinson, 1937), by a range of writers including Guy de Maupassant, M. R. James, Henry James, Walter de la Mare, Oliver Onions, Walpole himself ("Tarnhelm") and twenty-one others.

www.ingramcontent.com/pod-product-compliance
Lightning Source LLC
Chambersburg PA
CBHW051244170626
46809CB00004B/1485